These Obstrep
A History of

To Yvo[nne]
on your 3[?]
something th Birthday
Lots of love
with Michelles
from Oisín
Angie + Andrew

MARY JONES

These Obstreperous Lassies

A HISTORY OF THE IWWU

GILL AND MACMILLAN

Published in Ireland by
Gill and Macmillan Ltd
Goldenbridge
Dublin 8
with associated companies in
Auckland, Delhi, Gaborone, Hamburg, Harare,
Hong Kong, Johannesburg, Kuala Lumpur, Lagos, London,
Manzini, Melbourne, Mexico City, Nairobi,
New York, Singapore, Tokyo
© Breslin Benevolent Fund, 1988
0 7171 1629 8
Index compiled by Helen Litton

Print origination in Ireland by
The Type Bureau, Dublin
Printed in Ireland by Criterion Press,
Dublin

All rights reserved. No part of this publication
may be copied, reproduced or transmitted in any
form or by any means, without permission of the
publishers.

Contents

Acknowledgements
1. 'And thus make men of you all' — 1
2. Of barricades, and ballrooms … — 21
3. Mr Quill and colleagues — 32
4. 'Denmark House Desperadoes' — 44
5. Matters Political — 54
6. An Bhean Oibre — 70
7. Paradise of Dissent — 88
8. 'These obstreperous lassies' — 100
9. Queen of our home — 113
10. The resistance — 134
11. Beyond factory gates — 150
12. The Roaring Forties — 166
13. Modern Times — 188
14. The Feast of Bealtaine — 208
15. 'It's over to you now, ladies' — 231
16. Old disputes, new terrain — 252
17. Under siege — 273
18. Labouring women — 293
19. Parity begins at home — 313
20. The future of work — 337
21. Postscript — 359

Notes — 371
Abbreviations — 398
Select Bibliography — 400
Index — 405

Acknowledgements

In the course of completion of this work both it and the author have benefited from criticism and support from many quarters. A preliminary manuscript provided the focus for battles, but not blows, and the final text stands as testimony to the many struggles of the working women of Ireland. Special thanks are due to the Breslin Benevolent Fund and to its chairperson, Padraigín Ní Mhurchú, whose own commitment to the recognition of the history of working people made her an admirable peacemaker when the implications of that recognition became disconcertingly contemporary. The author is also particularly grateful to Hugh O'Connor, whose quiet dedication in compiling his own labour history collection, most particularly in relation to Helena Molony, has been remarkable. Other acknowledgements are due to the hidden labour of Éilis Brennan, the copyeditor, whose patience in the face of the thankless task of coping with the minutiae of the text was exemplary, and to Deirdre Rennison, of Gill and Macmillan, whose diplomacy in the face of the author and other authorities qualifies as high art. Two personal acknowledgements are also appropriate: to my companion and critic, John Horgan, a debt of honour has been incurred for support above and beyond; and, finally, to Brian Condon, historian and teacher, and doyen of those who aspire to be counted as such.

CHAPTER 1

'And thus make men of you all'

By 8 p.m. the hall and balcony were full. A reporter for *The Irish Worker* noted that 'women workers in their thousands, all classes, all sections, were there. It was an impressive sight that will not soon be forgotten.'

On Tuesday, 5 September 1911, in the Antient Concert Rooms at Pearse Street, Mr Murphy, President of Dublin Trades' Council [DTC], called the meeting to order. The speakers — Countess Markievicz, Jim Larkin, James Nolan and Hannah Sheehy-Skeffington — were centre stage. Prominent among the supporting cast were Delia Larkin and P. T. Daly. Markievicz rose to speak.

> Without organisation you can do nothing and the purpose of this meeting is to form you into an army of fighters. . . . As you are all aware women have at present no vote, but a union such as has now been formed will not alone help you to obtain better wages, but will also be a great means of helping you to get votes . . . and thus make men of you all.

To a chorus of cheers and laughter, the meeting proceeded. James Nolan, Dublin Trades' Council, pointed to women in England, organised workers who could claim 'eleven shillings and twelve shillings for doing the same work that the unorganised Irish girls only get half a crown or three shillings for'.

While Mrs Sheehy-Skeffington, feminist and sufragette, felt it was 'desirable that we should work together for the welfare of both sexes,' Mr Larkin, founder, in 1909, of the Irish Transport and General Workers' Union [ITGWU], charged the newest recruits to the trade union ranks with responsibility for maintaining the virtue of the race.

> Women are the basis of a nation's wealth. On them practically depends the efficiency and welfare of the race. Good or bad, the men are what the women made them.

The following Saturday *The Irish Worker*, edited by Larkin and published weekly, saluted the women who had flocked to the meeting in defiance of those who had claimed it was 'utterly impossible to get a number of women to come together for any demonstration.' It reported Dublin agog with gossip and comment.

On 19 August *The Irish Worker* called for the formal recruitment of women into a women workers' union. The militancy of such women in Dublin was already evident and gained impetus with the action, on 22 August, of 3,000 women at Jacob's factory withdrawing their labour in pursuit of a pay claim. The claim was conceded, and in its wake Delia Larkin made a passionate appeal to women of the working-class to organise and consolidate their gains. She appealed to

> Sisters . . . whether you work in the mill, the factory, biscuit or jam, sack or packing — whether you are a weaver, spinner, washer, ironer, labeller, box-maker, sack-mender, jam-packer, biscuit-maker — whatever you are or wherever you work . . . to enrol in the new Irish Women Workers' Trade Union.

Such women had for long graced the factory floors and sweatshops of Ireland. Before the turn of the century, beginners at shirt, collar and handkerchief manufacture were, when convenient, paid two shillings a week for their labours; pickers, weavers, burlers and twisters were fined for damage to their cloth; in the paper mills, finishers were locked out for lateness, and parents charged dressmakers that 'during apprenticeship girls are kept running messages, holding pins and irons.' In the shops, assistants were charged 3*d.* for lateness and 'for failing to sell an article they say the fine is

2s. 6d.' Hours were long, holidays few, and working conditions a breeding ground for disease.

In 1894, in the context of the establishing of rural industry under the auspices of the Congested Districts Board,[1] and the reorganisation of urban industry in areas as diverse as linen and whiskey, beer and biscuits,[2] a major investigation into the Conditions of Women's Work in Ireland was undertaken on behalf of the Royal Commission on Labour.[3] The Misses Orme and Abraham, Assistant Commissioners, recorded conditions so diverse that while some young girls developed consumption and rheumatism — the legacy of moist heat in gas-filled rooms — others enjoyed workroom accommodation deemed by Miss Abraham to be 'excellent'.

> The largest workroom is a hall, lofty and well ventilated. There is absolutely no smell, as the cloth worked here is all of good quality. In this room are five long tables at which the workers are almost entirely women.

In the same year the Irish Trades Union Congress was formed. While this was acknowledged as a significant step for labour overall, of the thousands of workers represented in its ranks, none represented women or the unskilled. For the Irish woman worker, the mark of the advance of labouring man would be the retreat of women into a well-kept home — an end to the toil and exploitation which was the hall-mark of factory life. One letter to *The Irish Worker* noted: 'Some people tell us that woman's place is in the home; that she should devote all her energies towards making it bright and cheerful. But it is very little of the home working women see'.

By 1910, the linen industry in Belfast 'employed twice or three times as many female workers as males',[4] and although overall employment in this industry declined in the twentieth century, other areas, including agriculture and domestic service, were notable for the employment of women. Jim Larkin cursed the conditions endured by the biscuit makers at Jacob's, '. . . conditions that were sending them from this earth twenty years before their time'. Historical accounts, where the establishing of an all-women's union is considered at all, differ as to the basis for the decision to found an autonomous organisation. While some have suggested that the decision reduced to questions of Larkin's 'personal conservatism',[5] others have acknowledged the existence of other complexities. Larkin's Union was acknowledged as 'the first Irish union to adopt a socialist programme, and the first union to advocate the organisation of all workers, skilled and unskilled, in industry'.[6] Such a programme hardly suggests a deliberate intent to exclude women, but amongst organised workers demarcation lines ensured that incursions would not be wholeheartedly welcomed.

When William O'Brien later claimed that Larkin had interpreted Rule 5 of the ITGWU to the effect that 'persons' referred to a male only membership,[7] this must be seen in the context of craft traditions where the exclusion of women was commonplace, and in combination with a legacy of unresolved political differences between O'Brien and Larkin. The question of structural ambiguities does not, however, of itself explain Larkin's decision.

The years up to and including 1911 were marked by a wave of strikes and 'unprecedented' industrial unrest, both in Dublin and beyond.[8] Having had, by 1911, extensive practice in the difficulty of reconciling the interests of skilled and unskilled in the organisation of male labour, Jim Larkin could not have been indifferent to the potential for resistance amongst his own ranks should women be invited to join their numbers. As Keogh and others have noted, women by this stage were also more prominent in public life. However, in the absence of more detailed documentation on the views of women workers themselves, it is impossible to gauge the extent to which the impetus for a separate union came from the grass roots.

Craft-based unions had long controlled entry to their trades as a means of protecting their skills — a legacy for sons, rather than daughters, sisters or wives.[9] Despite support and sympathy from individual men, little institutional protection was offered to women — a vulnerability copper-fastened by the terms of indentures under which apprentices were often forbidden to join trade unions without the express consent of their employers.[10] Many women, while lacking formal training, were nonetheless experienced workers and found a ready market, with the attractions of cheap labour not lost on their employers.

> Where men and women are engaged, where they both work the same number of hours, and produce the same amount of work . . . the women for no other reason than that they are women, are paid considerably less than men.[11]

In November 1910 at Abbey Street, *The Irish Independent,* the 'oldest established newspaper in Ireland', was accused of sweating: 'of bringing in women to learn the work and thus dispose of men. . . . This bringing in of women to do the men's work must be stopped'.[12]

To organise and to protect was clearly not universally popular. 'Looking glass', in writing to *The Irish Worker* in 1910, echoed a sentiment already expressed in the columns of the daily press:

'Have they not plenty of work in their own sphere of life without encroaching on the men?'

The movement of women in the factories and workshops of Ireland had begun long before the meeting at the Antient Concert Rooms in 1911, but on that evening the meeting in question bore witness to a new conjunction of interests: of women workers, diverse in claims and skills; and of men of the trade union movement, representing members equally diverse, with skills developed and trades organised. Despite differences in terms of both priorities and territorial claims, all shared one commitment — to place the needs of working people on the agenda of Irish public life.

Three weeks later, Delia Larkin spoke on behalf of those who paid sixpence to join the Irish Women Workers' Union [IWWU] and promised a contribution of 'tuppence' a week to the new union, and of those who did not. She served notice that woman's place must change.

> The women of Ireland are as awake as the men, they are weary of being white slaves who pass their lives away

toiling to fill the pockets of the unscrupulous employers, receiving for their labours not sufficient to enable them to exist. The wages and conditions of the working women in the city of Dublin are a rebuke to any country.[13]

Rejecting outright the ambition of advancement for a selected minority, Delia Larkin, first General Secretary of the IWWU, stated the terms under which change would be negotiated:
'We do not want a certain few to be doing well, we want all women workers to at least be in a position to procure the ordinary necessaries of life.'[14]

For the first months of its existence, the IWWU sought its recruits under the guidance and financial wing of the ITGWU.[15] Jim Larkin formalised the link by assuming the office of President, and rent-free rooms were provided at Liberty Hall. Delia Larkin, as editor of the 'Women Workers' Column' of *The Irish Worker*, had already indicated her priorities for those whom she sought to lead. The 'Column' would, she suggested, be devoted to the interests of women both in the home and at work, and in calling for contributions from her readers, Miss Larkin offered guidelines — relating to the house: 'hints on how to keep it clean and lessen labour'; on cooking: 'recipes must not take the form of elaborate dishes . . . and if possible let us dispense with that too widely used utensil, the frying pan'. In the area of dress reform, frills were to be dispensed with and, although guidelines for future directions were unclear, a call for the revival of the language and of national dress suggested both an eye for the traditional and the General Secretary's own nationalist disposition. Miss Larkin felt the national costume to be 'healthy, picturesque and those who have seen it worn must agree it is particularly becoming to the Irish *cailín*'. In celebrating the red flannel petticoat the new Secretary was adamant that 'the contaminating influence of other countries' was to be dismissed.

Regardless of style, readers of the column were left with few illusions about the necessity for women workers to relieve themselves of the burden of housework. Walls were to be covered with paint, not paper; floors to be stripped and left bare, and household linen reduced to essentials. Detailed instructions on how to achieve such interiors were given and the lives of women would be transformed with a flourish .

> With all this brokerage cast away, most of the curtains disposed of, and the brass and steel ornaments sold to the antique man, we lighten the household work.

With the domestic arena thus laid bare, Delia Larkin welcomed women to the workplace. She urged them to recognise their own value and to refrain from underselling their labour: 'remember although you cannot very well do without working, neither can the employers do without your labour.' In the familiar Larkin style she then proceeded to upbraid them for 'whining and lamenting your wretched condition when deliberately and with your eyes open you place yourselves in the position of slaves.' Yet the slaves could dance and on All Hallow's Eve the members held a social. Dancing commenced at 8 p.m. sharp. Members were 'at home' to friends and sympathisers at the Antient Concert Rooms, and Professor Morrison's string band played until dawn.

At a local level the Union confronted major problems of status between women workers. Typists stood aloof from girls in trade, 'they in their turn looked down haughtily on the factory hand, and again you do not find the factory girls associating with the girls who hawk their goods in the streets'.[16]

At the national level the position of many low-paid workers, notably women, was to be formalised under the terms of the Trades' Board Act, due to come into force in Britain in 1912. Delia Larkin was unanimously elected to serve as a delegate representing the women workers of Dublin on the Irish Trades' Board [ITB]. On 7 January the first meeting was held in Belfast, prior to the formal signing of the Act, and the lines of battle were rapidly drawn.

> At the opening of the meeting the representatives of the Dublin employers (mark this well) moved that they did not consider that cardboard boxmaking was a sweated industry, and it should never have come under this Act. I

wonder how two shillings and sixpence a week for twelve months for a girl of eighteen appeals to honest-minded people as a non-sweated industry; we evidently have many things to learn.[17]

Back in Dublin letters to the Union from domestic servants in Limerick made clear the need to organise beyond the factory gates.[18] Early efforts, however, revealed only difficulties: the isolation of such women and the fact that so few of them were concerned with matters of a union. With some exasperation *The Irish Worker* asked, 'when are the domestic servant class going to wake up?'

In the factories, meanwhile, women found new support for their grievances. Sackmakers at Keogh's with over twelve years service were paid 6s. a week for heavy labour. On seeking improvement from Mr and Mrs Keogh the workers were informed that, but for the goodness of their employers, they and their families would be despatched to the Dublin Union. Their own Union responded: 'If being an inmate of the Union is any worse than being employed in Messrs Keogh's sweating den, then God help the inmates of the various Unions.' On 13 May a strike was called, and by 1 June the 'Women Workers' Column' had declared a victory.

The women of Keogh's were not alone in seeking to redress the balance. The majority of women workers received from 2s. 6d. to 6s. for a full week's labour. A few received between 7s. and 9s. After a year of existence the Union claimed that its members now received a measure of compensation for injuries at the workplace, that conditions in factories had improved, that either money or one week's notice of dismissal had been secured, and that in some areas increases in wages were evident. During strikes, scabs were named, addresses given, and, should any confusion as to their identity persist, a rogues' gallery of dishonour was given pride of place in *The Irish Worker*. The 'Women Workers' Column' continued to denounce starvation wages for waitresses and domestic servants and the twin evils of poverty and drink amongst the women of Ireland were highlighted with informed compassion.

For working girls, many of them recent migrants from rural

Ireland, an IWWU social club was formed. Liberty Hall became its focus.

> Here they meet every evening in the week and amuse themselves as they desire. They have a choir and a dramatic class. The Irish language is taught, as well as Irish dancing.

The women formed part of the Irish Workers' Choir[19] and defied their conditions of labour by welcoming 1913 with a dance at 91 Harcourt Street. With great, and acknowledged, style, they entertained their friends, and as *The Irish Worker* graciously observed, 'quite a large amount of talent was discovered among the white slaves of Dublin.'

Early in the year the girls of the Savoy Café refused to accept wage cuts of 50%. They were locked out and *The Irish Worker* published a picture gallery of 'The Savoy Scab Octet'. A strike at Pembroke Laundry, involving fourteen girls and two vanmen, provoked a plea from the 'Women Workers' Column': 'Girls, don't scab on your sisters — keep away from Pembroke Laundry', and when Maguire and Paterson's tried to reduce wages, the Column threatened:

'Patersons and their friendly match will receive short shrift if they persist in their present campaign against Irish girls.'

The tactics reflected the times. By 1913 the move to reduce the wages of the working class had gained momentum. The Union claimed that there was 'no class of work where women are employed which is not sweated'. All disputes arose from poor conditions and calls for 'a reduction in their already miserable wages' and to join a union, for both men and women, became a costly act of defiance. Employers warned their female employees not to do so, and required them to sign a commitment to stay away from Liberty Hall and the IWWU or to face dismissal.[20]

Since 1912 the IWWU had conducted its business from temporary premises in Great Brunswick Street. No documentation or official records of the Union remain for this period and it is unclear whether the strained relations — later evident between Delia Larkin and Liberty Hall — were the basis for the move, or if the move signalled the establishment of greater autonomy for the Women's Union. Every night the women workers were urged, through the medium of prominently displayed posters, to climb the stairs to a small lecture room, to ask for the secretary, and to 'join your own Union, organised by Irish Women Workers, controlled by Irish Women Workers in the interest of Irish Women Workers'.

On Mayday 1913 the 'small but representative' ranks of the IWWU marched in Dublin for the first time. Factory workers, shop assistants, tailors, dressmakers and typists stood together. The boost to morale was to prove essential. Four months later, hardship, riots and demonstrations had become the hallmark of Dublin working-class life. By August the strike of tramway workers had led to the mobilisation of police and on 31 August Larkin addressed the crowds assembled in O'Connell Street from the balcony of the Imperial Hotel (now Clery's). His immediate arrest provoked bitter disturbances. In September, Larkin was remanded in custody and the ITGWU and Liberty Hall became the focus of a major struggle. The tramway strike and the battle against the leading employer William Martin Murphy challenged the right of employers to refuse recognition to trade unions. At Jacob's, members of the IWWU came into direct conflict with their employer as women workers joined battle to defend the right of working people to combine in their own interests.

On 6 September 1913, under the banner of 'Tyranny in Dublin', *The Irish Worker* gave a graphic account:

> On Monday morning three girls wearing their union badges were approached by Jacob's tool, Miss Luke, and told to remove their badges. They refused to do so and were dismissed.

They were joined by others: two hundred and fifty women, to the surprise of onlookers, also refused and were instantly dismissed. By the end of the day, with ports around the country alerted to black Jacob's goods, three hundred and ten members of the IWWU had lost their jobs. Scabs were named, but Jacob's marked only a beginning. Throughout the city, one thousand one hundred members were locked out for refusing to give up their right to organise.

With no immediate prospect of a return to work, a new phase of organisation to resist employer intimidation began. The Transport Union planned to use its mansion at Croydon Park to develop employment for the women who had been locked out. The 'Women Workers' Column' outlined a proposal to

> set a number of women and girls to work making shirts, dresses, underlinen etc., particularly for the use of their own class. . . . It is intended to employ all the women and girls . . . in the particular branches they understand, such as biscuit making and bread making.

The Lock-Out lasted for seven long months. Throughout, the IWWU provided breakfast every morning for three thousand, and hot dinners to expectant mothers; it paid its members victimisation pay, and supported without reserve the right to join a union. By May, however, the end of the Lock-Out was marked by over half of the members of the IWWU failing in their claim to be re-employed. With depleted ranks and scarce resources, the IWWU was in considerable disarray.

In a valiant attempt to revive the Union and its membership, Delia Larkin took the by now well established IWWU Dramatic Society on tour to England.

> I have about four hundred or five hundred on my hands, and I hope that by giving these stage performances to be able to start cooperative industries for them. We are asking for nothing.

The intention was to raise funds and to start industries for women — to build on their skills by following specific lines of development:

> It would be quite impossible to start anything like a factory. But I am going to begin this constructive policy by starting workers' restaurants throughout Dublin.[21]

Advertisements were placed in *The Irish Worker* for the Irish Women Workers' Co-operative Society [IWWCS] to be based at Liberty Hall, for 'the women's own industry, owned and controlled by women workers'. Recruitment began again, with the scale of contributions reflecting the differing clientele. The entrance fee was now either sixpence or threepence, subscriptions either 'tuppence' or a penny.

The 1913 Lock-Out had, however, left other scars. The absence of IWWU documentation for this period and the lack of detail in the relevant ITGWU records mean that any interpretation of the events following Delia Larkin's return from England has to rely on conjecture rather than other, more reliable, foundations. On returning to Ireland with her troupe, Delia Larkin became the focus of 'a very delicate question'. As is documented elsewhere,[22] tactical differences arising towards the end of the Lock-Out did not leave Liberty Hall untouched. Whether the effect of such tensions, particularly in relation to Larkin, extended to his sister Delia, is unclear, but the tenor and focus of complaint which became evident in 1914 suggests that the *modus operandi* employed by the increasingly militant Miss Larkin did not find favour with the ITGWU executive. The ITGWU minute-book records that on Saturday night, 5 September 1914, the question of 'Miss Larkin and the large front room' was placed on the agenda. Mr Foran, in the chair, explained that Miss Larkin had broken the lock of the piano, refused to acknowledge any damage, and was 'out to cause disruption among members of the Union'. It was resolved, unanimously,

> that the Branch Secretary be, and is, hereby instructed to notify Miss Larkin that this Committee consider it desirable in the interests of the Union that she . . . should look for some other premises to carry on the work of the Women Workers' Union.

By Tuesday the committee were in receipt of a letter from Jim Larkin informing them that a general meeting would be held the following Sunday to discuss the action taken in regard to the Secretary of the IWWU. While welcoming the letter from their General Secretary, the committee threw down the gauntlet and resigned *en masse*.[23] No further reference is made in these minutes to the context whereby the piano incident provoked such a drastic response.

The ITGWU was, in the wake of resumption of work following the Lock-Out, forced to reassess and to reorganise. Members had lapsed, and organisation had 'collapsed in many areas'. The difficulties of financing and assisting may have prompted moves to further distance the IWWU from Liberty Hall, but such a lack of solidarity was not evident in the championing of women workers in the pages of *The Irish Worker*, now under the editorship of James Connolly. What is more likely, given the context of activities after the Lock-Out relating to the founding of the Irish Citizen Army [ICA] by Larkin, Connolly and Captain Jack White in 1913, was that Delia Larkin, her own nationalism well established, became a focus for the early tensions evident from the end of 1914 onwards, on the part of those who feared that further organised militancy from within Liberty Hall would invite the suppression of the Union.[24]

The minutes of the ITGWU suggest only that a crisis had passed. Prior to the October meeting a new committee had been elected, comprising a majority of those who had earlier tendered their resignations. Larkin prepared to leave for America, intending to raise funds and moral support for his beleaguered union, and he bequeathed control of both the ITGWU and the ICA to James Connolly. By December Connolly's further ambitions in both arenas were thwarted by the suppression of *The Irish Worker* under the Defence of the Realm Act.

By 1915 the ITGWU was under severe financial and organisational strain. The stress of 1913, the departure of Jim Larkin, and the tensions endemic to the reorganisation of the labour movement in a hostile climate prompted Delia Larkin to reassess her own position. She sought to establish herself politically, and ran as Labour Party candidate for North Dock Ward in the Poor Law elections. She polled badly, and in the aftermath her retreat from active involvement in the Irish labour movement was marked by speculation couched in innuendo relating to her personal disposition. A clearly hostile climate was, to some extent, offset by the public support she continued to command from the depleted ranks of women workers. Such support, however, having found no avenue for its expression within Ireland, dissipated, and in 1915 she made common cause with other workers and joined the ranks who were forced by circumstances to take the boat from the North Wall to Liverpool.

While Madame Markievicz had urged women workers to make ready for battle, the streets of Dublin had formed the backdrop for other activities. James Connolly, organiser for the Transport Union, had in 1911 saluted Walter Carpenter, Amalgamated Society of Woodworkers [ASW] and, in later years, OC of the Boys' Corps of the ICA. Carpenter had been imprisoned for acts of subversion during the visit of King George and Queen Mary to Ireland. At a meeting promoted under the auspices of Inghinidhe na hÉireann[25] and the Socialist Party, he had shared the platform with two fellow-subversives, Miss Molony and Mr McArdle, who had been detained in Mountjoy Jail for similar involvement in disturbances surrounding the king's visit. With a flair for the dramatic, Connolly greeted Carpenter, but added that 'perhaps higher in the degree of criminality, they had Miss Molony'.

Helena Molony, by profession a member of the Abbey Theatre since 1909, mounted the platform, acknowledged her public and, having again endorsed the sentiment of Walter Carpenter that 'King George was the descendant of the worst scoundrel in Europe', was promptly re-arrested in the middle of her speech and returned to Mountjoy to await the king's pleasure.

Miss Molony had, in 1910, become one of the first political prisoners of the era. A member of Inghinidhe na hÉireann, founded by Maud Gonne in 1900, she had been involved in the instruction of young children in the Irish language, Irish history, dancing, singing and cultural subjects, and had started the campaign in Dublin for school meals: 'our aim was to have a school refectory where a child could eat a full meal in a civilised fashion'. Her enthusiasm for more covert activities was, however, clear. The organisation was also involved in widespread anti-recruiting campaigns and appeals to young girls not to associate with 'the red-coated soldiery' then a regular feature of the city streets. As editor of *Bean na hÉireann (Woman of Ireland)*,[26] the monthly paper of Inghinidhe na hÉireann since 1908, Helena Molony had been credited with influencing Countess Markievicz to support the nationalist cause. The paper left few in doubt regarding Miss Molony's own political disposition — 'complete separatism; the rising cause of feminism, and the interests of Irishwomen generally'. Although of no political affiliation, it included labour notes and the editor corresponded with Connolly during his period in America.

Following the visit of King George V, Miss Molony had been jailed for echoing Carpenter and for throwing a stone (which missed) at a shop window containing effigies of the visitors. Originally charged with 'high treason', the charge was later reduced to 'using language derogatory to His Majesty'. Of the lower status of her crime she confessed: 'in my heart of hearts, I felt degraded by such a miserable accusation'.[27] Following her arrest in 1911 she was sentenced to a short term of imprisonment or the payment of a fine. She chose jail, but her fine was paid by Anna Parnell, and for a brief period she left Ireland. By 1912 she had returned and during the Lock-Out she played in *The Mineral Workers* at the Abbey Theatre. Between scenes, she addressed the workers from the steps of Liberty Hall, urging them to unite, to organise, and to fight.

In the aftermath of the Lock-Out, with Jim Larkin in America and Delia forced to concede a tactical retreat, James Connolly had taken responsibility for the remnants of both the ITGWU and the IWWU, and for the Workers' Co-op begun by Delia Larkin in defiance of those employers who had discarded women workers in their hundreds. Connolly asked Helena Molony to join him in the task of reorganisation. Writing of the years that followed, Miss Molony spoke of her inheritance:

> If the simile 'a wolf in sheep's clothing' be used, the Worker's Co-op might be descibed as 'a tigress in kitten's fur' being carried on as it apparently was by a group of working women for whom I acted as secretary.[28]

Following 1913 the IWWU had faced severe problems. No agreement to prevent victimisation had been secured and in *The Irish Worker* Connolly claimed that in this regard the employers of women's labour were the worst offenders.

Now, faced with the continued unemployment of women, who had paid so dearly for their loyalty to Liberty Hall and the IWWU, Connolly and Molony revived plans for the Workers' Co-op and began moves to develop skills and markets for the women workers. The Workers' Co-op was based in a shop at 29 Eden Quay, in premises attached to Liberty Hall. 'It specialised in a man's working shirt called "The Red Hand", priced at 2s. 6d., which immediately found a ready market'. A friend of Connolly's trained the women as cutters, an area previously the preserve of men, and the members of the Transport Union were urged by the women to put 'The Red Hand' on their backs as a fitting partner to the badge on their lapels.

In recruiting women workers from further afield, Helena Molony conceded her own limitations.

> I had no experience or idea of any kind of organising and it was really he [Connolly] who did the work, coming with me to the various factory gates to try to enlist girls into the Union.[29]

Under the banner of the Textiles Section of the IWWU, Connolly and Winifred Carney of the ITGWU had earlier appealed to 'Linen Slaves of Belfast' to fight capitalism and to join the cause.[30] Now back in Dublin, in the wake of 1913, Helena Molony claimed it was 'uphill work' to pull the Union together and to continue such organising. In November 1915 she read a paper on 'Women's Wages and Trade Unions' at a Women's Industrial Conference held at the Mansion House. Although it received scant attention in the daily press, a report of the Conference appeared in *The Irish Citizen*. The Conference consisted 'mainly of women workers with practical expert knowledge of Irish conditions and interested in women's industrial advance'.[31] Helena Molony informed those present

> that trade unionism barely exists in Dublin. Women workers are still suffering great hardships, still earning the same wage as four years ago. Some grown women could only earn 3s. a week.[32]

Where wages were higher, as in the confectionery trade

which offered a minimum wage of 10s. for adult women workers, the women remained vulnerable: 'they were often dismissed and their place filled by young girls at 5s.'

While Helena Molony and Connolly continued their attempts to organise women workers, other interests in this terrain were noted. An Irish branch of the British-based National Union of Women Workers [NUWW] was formed in Dublin. On Wednesday, 10 November, a representative of the NUWW spoke of the need for 'further cooperation among all women workers of every shade of opinion'. The Vice Presidents nominated at this meeting were Lady Fingall, Lady Arnott, Lady Wright, Lady Holmpatrick, Mrs Haslam, and Miss White, LL.D. As *The Irish Citizen* wryly remarked on its front page:

> It does not look as if the aims of the new body to unite 'women of every shade of opinion in Ireland' are likely to be accomplished, the Vice President and Committee chosen apparently being restricted practically to women of precisely the same shade of opinion.[33]

Despite the threat from such incursions the IWWU claimed that some limited progress had been made in wage standards as a result of their campaigns. To join any union, however, was still to court dismissal. Although recruitment continued throughout these years, as tension increased in Dublin the focus of the IWWU became that of the Co-op, of the national cause, and of active support for the Irish Citizen Army, formed in 1913 in response to industrial oppression and now the vanguard for the Rising of 1916.

In a small room at the back of the Co-op at Eden Quay, some months after the suppression of *The Irish Worker* in 1914, *The Workers' Republic* was printed and published. Connolly served as editor and asked Helena Molony to act as registered proprietor. Under the terms of the Defence of the Realm Act in so doing she became personally responsible for 'any treasonable matter' published. Her commitment to the cause was shared by her fellow workers. All the women connected with the Co-op were members of the IWWU and bore arms for the Irish Citizen Army.[34] The daily round of business for the Co-op, in effect, provided a shop front for industry of a quite different order.

By 1915, members of the Citizen Army were under orders to resist both arrest and any attempted seizure of documents or property. As Helena Molony recalled, the early struggle for an Irish Workers' Republic — the major demand of the ICA — prompted a ready response to demands for action outside the industrial sphere. The women workers of 1915 were, therefore, 'ready for the party of police which arrived at our shop to seize *The Workers' Republic* and other "seditious" literature'.

On this occasion Connolly was informed of their presence and quietly appeared at the door in the back of the shop which connected it to Liberty Hall.

> He asked the police for their warrant and was told they had none. Then, as they had piles of our publications in their arms, he drew his revolver and said, 'you drop those papers or I'll drop you'.[35]

In the face of such a challenge, the police retreated, and the members of the Co-op present — Jennie Shanahan, Rosie Hackett and Helena Molony — hid the papers in the back room. Countess Markievicz who, in calling to the Co-op, had stumbled on the first raid, made ready with the women for the return bout. Later that day, when the police returned with both an inspector and a warrant, Connolly conceded an inch:

'Very well, you can search the shop — but behind the counter is Liberty Hall and warrant or no warrant you won't search that'.

Behind the counter Connolly stood with drawn revolver. His comrades in arms stood their ground, and 'we were all armed, which fact helped to make up the inspector's mind as to the undesirability of raiding Liberty Hall'.

Between skirmishes, business continued: the Co-op had expanded and now the shop on Eden Quay boasted 'the manufacture of men's shirts and children's pinafores, the sale of ladies' shoes and stockings . . . and the sale and distribution of *The Workers' Republic*'. Less publicly, however, flags, armlets and badges were produced and a private post office flourished 'as a receiving depot for small parcels of arms and ammunition'.

While members of the Co-op were engaged in such labours, their Secretary divided her time between the Abbey, recruitment for the IWWU, and Cumann na mBan.[36] By this stage Cumann na mBan was widespread; the commander of the British Forces in Ireland deemed it 'a very dangerous body', and a resumé at the Chief Secretary's Office in Dublin Castle referred to its activities as

> First Aid, Nursing, Drill and Signalling, Rifle Practice, organising the National Boy Scouts, collecting money for the purchase of rifles. . . . There can be no doubt that as in the days of the Land League, the Ladies' League took up work when the original organisation was suppressed, so now there is reason to believe that the Cumann na mBan will use every effort to carry on the treasonable work of the Irish Volunteers.[37]

In January 1916, Helena Molony and James Connolly were house guests of Countess Markievicz at Surrey House.[38] At *The Workers' Republic*, despite increasing tension within Liberty Hall regarding the close association of the ICA with the Transport Union, Connolly had urged immediate action in the bid for an Irish Workers' Republic. England at war, he argued, should present Ireland's opportunity. The anti-conscription struggle, born of the British intent to recruit in Ireland for its armies, had drawn organised workers further into the ranks of the Citizen Army and of the Irish Volunteers. In October 1915 the Dublin Trades' Council passed a resolution suggesting that such a tactic would best serve the move to resist the conscription of Irishmen to the English cause. Tensions were, however, evident both between the ICA and the Volunteers over questions of timing and tactics, and between the ranks of organised Labour regarding Connolly's activities and his position as General Secretary of the Transport Union.

By Sunday 16 April the momentum for the Rising dominated Liberty Hall. All ranks of the Citizen Army, men and women, and the Fianna, organised by Cumann na mBan, assembled in the square outside. Under Citizen Army orders, a large green flag, heralding the gold harp 'without a crown', was hoisted above the parapet by Molly O'Reilly. The flag had been made by Mary Shannon, machinist at the Worker's Co-op, and, like the colour-bearer, a member of the IWWU.

Between shifts preparing moulds and lead slugs for cartridges, the Workers' Co-op members readied themselves for battle. Rosie Hackett was directed to join the garrison at St Stephen's Green; Helena Molony and Jennie Shanahan joined the comrades at City Hall. On Easter Monday morning, the flag that flew over the General Post Office [GPO] bore witness to the part played by the Irish Women Workers whose labour had put it there.

By the end of Easter Week, the front of Liberty Hall lay in ruins. On 11 May, all books and records from the building were seized by the British military.[39] On 12 May James Connolly was executed. Countess Markievicz, earlier sentenced to death, was condemned to penal servitude for life. Helena Molony, acting Secretary of the IWWU, having been marched from Ship Street Barracks to Kilmainham Jail, was among five women interned in England.

CHAPTER 2

Of barricades, and ballrooms . . .

Within a few months of the Rising most of those interned in Britain had been released. Two women, however, were detained at His Majesty's pleasure. Helena Molony and Winifred Carney, both Citizen Army, both trade union officials, refused to organise any defence or pleading of their cause other than that which came from the Dublin Trades' Council [DTC]. In acknowledgment of this, the meeting of the DTC on 6 November 1916 suggested that their detention was related to their activities in the labour movement and that the women 'looked to their own class to secure their freedom'. A resolution, passed unanimously, called for their immediate trial by a civil tribunal or their release from Aylesbury Prison. In Dublin, meanwhile, the Irish Women Workers' Union survived in little other than name and somewhat dented spirit. With her own capacity to organise women workers constrained by circumstance, Helena Molony sought assistance on their behalf from outside her class — and looked to the quiet suburb of Killiney and to an uneasy alliance rekindled in the uncertainty of the times.

Louie Bennett was the eldest daughter of Mr James Cavendish Bennett, an auctioneer shunned by his own family for the social disgrace of being 'in trade'. Miss Bennett had been educated in London at an Academy for young ladies, where she and her sister alarmed the genteel by forming a defiantly 'Irish League'. On completion of her schooling she travelled extensively, penned the first of two romantic novels, and returned to Ireland in search of a crusade. In 1910 she became actively involved in the Irish Women's Suffrage Federation [IWSF], formed the Irish Women's Reform League [IWRL], and through her association with the Irish

Women's International League [IWIL] became a staunch advocate of passive resistance, and of militancy without violence. In 1913, distressed by the Lock-Out, she crossed the river to Liberty Hall and shared duties with Hannah Sheehy-Skeffington, Countess Markievicz and other women whose class loyalty had been shaken by the tactics employed against the working people of Dublin. In the aftermath she maintained her links with the labour movement but resisted the momentum for more militant organisation, generated by Connolly and supported by Helena Molony, urging instead passive resistance and a place for compromise in a society moving headlong into conflict. Shortly after the Rising she was employed correcting proofs on *The Irish Citizen,* official organ of the suffragist movement and by tradition supportive of organised labour.

Although voicing grave reservations about the wisdom of linking the cause of nationalism to that of the trade union movement, by the end of 1916 Louie Bennett had responded to overtures from Helena Molony at Aylesbury Prison that she undertake responsibility for the reorganisation of the Irish Women Worker's Union. In heeding the call, Louie Bennett sought the assistance of her lifelong friend and neighbour Helen Chenevix, graduate of Alexandra School and Trinity College, daughter of a bishop of the Church of Ireland, suffragette and pacifist. Miss Chenevix had earlier been involved with Louie Bennett in the establishment of the Irish Women's Suffrage Federation, and later in the formation of the Irish Women's Reform League.

To what extent the Irish Trades Union Congress influenced their decision to revive the IWWU is unclear. While R.M. Fox, in his biography of Louie Bennett, points to the persuasive impact of Miss Molony's pleading, other sources suggest a more structured response to the plight of working women. The sequence of events following the Rising were suggested in a series of newspaper articles dealing with the life of Louie Bennett, and suggested that 'although she had been thinking hard about the formation of a union for women workers, it was this Congress that gave Louie Bennett the impetus which she needed'. Both this and other sources[1] suggest that two women were invited to attend Congress in Sligo in 1916 and were directed by the Executive Committee to take responsibility for organising women in the trade union movement.[2]

However, the Report of the 22nd Annual Irish Trades Union Congress and Labour Party, held in Sligo in 1916, contains no record of such a directive. Further, Marie Perolz, later Acting President of the IWWU, attended Congress as a delegate for the Women Workers' Union. Throughout the Congress Miss Perolz was an active participant, notably in relation to the amending of resolutions to include a recognition of women workers. This was particularly relevant in a resolution relating to amendments to the Trades' Board Acts, which referred to the 'low rate of wages' prevailing in the distributive trade. Miss Perolz succeeded in having this resolution amended by the addition of the words 'and among women workers in the printing and sorting trades'.[3] A further amendment occurred in a resolution condemning sectional unions, and making reference to 'men employed in any one industry': Miss Perolz called for the words 'and women' to be added. More importantly, perhaps, the delegate for the Women Workers' Union contributed to the formulation of the National Labour Programme, which considered 'the future needs of Irish Labour'. On Miss Perolz's suggestion, to 'Irish Labour' was added:

> such a programme to include (a) schemes for medical inspection for schoolchildren, maternity centres and similar reforms, to promote physical welfare of children of the working classes, and (b) for the adequate participation of men and women workers in the administration of justice.[4]

The claim that two women were specifically directed by Congress to organise women workers was refuted by William O'Brien, who gave his account of the circumstances leading to the reorganisation of the IWWU following his return from internment in the summer of 1916.[5] In the last month of that year he stated that Misses Bennett and Chenevix had presented for appointment at Liberty Hall with himself and Thomas Foran, President of the Irish Transport Union. Miss Bennett, offering both credentials and a willingness to undertake the task of reorganisation, suggested 'that it would not be possible to get new members to come to Liberty Hall, and that it would be better to have a room elsewhere'.[6] By the end of the meeting, agreement had been reached that the IWWU would move from Liberty Hall and assume its independence as a prelude to securing membership; that organisation would begin with women in printing and that the good ladies would neither seek nor receive any payment for their labours.

Before the end of the year the IWWU had secured a room, courtesy of the Dublin Typographical Provident Society [DTPS], at 35 Lower Gardiner Street. Louie Bennett recalled times both exhilarating and exhausting, as she and Helen Chenevix organised meetings with the able assistance of 'a friendly priest, Fr Flanagan', who was to be a staunch supporter of the Union throughout his life. No records remain of these times, and personal accounts in the daily press invariably conflict. By Christmas, however, the internal organisation of the revived Union became a subject for discussion with the return of Helena Molony to Ireland.

At the beginning of 1917 the IWWU claimed membership from printing and boxmaking, from laundries and textiles — 2,300 women on the move.[7] By February the internal structure designed to serve such women was agreed, and on 3 February 1917 *The Saturday Post* published the details:

> The following officers have been elected for the Irish Women Workers' Union:
>
> *Hon. President*: Madame Markievicz.
> *Acting President*: Miss Perolz.
> *Vice-Presidents*: Dr. K. Lynn, Mrs Ginnell and the Misses Chenevix BA, L. Bennett, Maud Eden, Madeline ffrench-Mullen, and Harrison.
> *Executive*: The Misses Bird, Caffrey, Davis, Hunt-Hackett, Murtagh and Ryan.
> *Hon. Treasurers*: Miss J. Shanahan, Miss M. Geraghty.
> *General Secretary*: Miss H. Molony.
> *Clerk*: Miss R. Hackett.

All the women involved as officers of the Union had demonstrated a commitment to the cause of labour and to the cause of women. Some came from the barricades, some from the ballroom. While many were destined to serve primarily as moral support, others would undertake the daily grind. All however, claimed the territory and promised their allegiance:

Each For All: All For Each.

Through force of circumstance an agenda was set. In 1917 Brigid Bryan was appointed an official of the Printers' Section, and a campaign to organise women in print began. Such women worked a 52-hour week, and were earning between 7s. and 10s. for their labours. The refusal of the Dublin Master Printers' Association [DMPA] to recognise the IWWU led directly to confrontation, and the involvement of the Union in a six-week strike and lock-out. With resources strained, the women looked for financial and moral support from other quarters. The DTC offered both, and the victory eventually claimed laid the basis for the organisation of women in the trade. Throughout, the women were given strike pay — an assurance, in effect, that membership of a union would offer both a platform from which to assert their rights as workers and a means whereby the income upon which they depended would not be the first casualty of their struggles. The six-week strike cost the Union £507.16s.

With organisation in Printing and Kindred Trades [PKT] under way, the Union looked further afield; in the textile industry it sought, for the first time, the cooperation of employers in favouring union labour. The move signalled a tension within the Union itself, with the legacy of 1913 and 1916 overruled by the art of compromise. In writing to Messrs Hill and Sons, Lucan Woollen Mills, in December 1917, Louie Bennett offered her terms to the masters of industry.

> We would assure you, in return, both for our part and on behalf of your women workers, that we should make every reasonable effort to cooperate with you in securing good work from your employees. We desire to have it understood that it is not our wish or purpose as a trade union to set ourselves in opposition to the employers.

Differences were to be seen as those of opinion, not class,

and by 28 March 1918, when the IWWU was first registered as a trade union, the Misses Bennett and Chenevix had assumed the positions of Honorary Secretaries. The change spoke less of internal conspiracy and power struggles than of rising discontent throughout the country. In 1918 Madame Markievicz was arrested and imprisoned in Holloway. Helena Molony, Kathleen Lynn, Marie Perolz, Madeleine ffrench-Mullen, Rosie Hackett, Jennie Shanahan and others, all members of the ICA, were on full alert. In the general exodus from the shop floor to the armed struggle, the internal organisation of the IWWU was massively depleted. Those who remained, by default, established the priorities for the organisation of women workers.

Although the tone now became conciliatory rather than confrontationist, the Union as an organisation did not stand apart from the times. In April 1918 the British government extended conscription to Ireland and, in the outcry that followed, the IWWU supported the one-day general stoppage of industries on 23 May. The Union entered wholeheartedly into its first public campaign. The Anti-Conscription Campaign included a 'solemn pledge for the women of Ireland', signed by the IWWU and, on Louie Bennett's estimate, two-thirds of Irish women.

> Because the enforcement of conscription on any people without their consent is tyranny, we are resolved to resist the conscription of Irishmen. We will not fill the places of men deprived of their work through refusing enforced military service. We will do all in our power to help the families of men who suffer through refusing enforced military service.

On Sunday 9 June, they marched and the changing priorities of the IWWU were underlined. Louie Bennett, in reporting to the International Congress of Women [ICW] in Zurich in 1919, claimed that the Pledge 'bound us to support the men in their opposition by every means in our power, <u>without resort to violence</u>'.[8]

The effects of the war on the Irish industrial front were particularly apparent in relation to the employment of a predominantly young female workforce. In 1918 a memorandum by Sir Thomas Stafford and Mr Frank Brook of the Committee on Reconstruction of the Viceroy's Executive Council made reference to the fact that:

> the women of every class, apart from munitions workers, who will find their occupations gone when the soldiers return to resume their old duties in shops and public offices and when the munition works close down . . . will be very large. . . . Mostly, the women are young and have homes and parents to whom they can, temporarily, return, and they have proved their value and efficiency in so many new paths of industry.[9]

In the areas where such women were employed, the IWWU began to explore the possibilities of militancy without recourse to violence. In Waterford, the Union came into direct conflict with Irish employers who had contracted to manufacture munitions for the British government. T. Thompson and Son Ltd., general engineers,

> . . . took on the making of 18 Pdr. shells and installed machinery purchased from the Lee Arrow Company, Cork, all of which was new. Shortly afterwards difficulties arose with the women's labour union. The firm cancelled the contract and shut down the factory and the plant is standing idle.[10]

In Victorian tones, but with unmistakable resolve, the Union served notice on other employers that despite the unsettled times it would not accept any diminution of its claims on behalf of the working women of Ireland. Writing to Wm. & M. Taylor, Tobacco, Cigarette and Snuff Manufacturers, on 2 April 1918 in reference to workers enjoying a weekly wage of 8s., few concessions were apparent.

> We beg to remind you of the great hardships endured by the working classes at the present time owing to the high prices of all the necessaries of life, and of the urgent need for a higher level of wages for women workers. In consideration of all the facts we wish to claim on behalf of your women employees a minimum

wage of 15s. per week for all workers of a year or more service.[11]

While the question of wages was paramount, the conditions of labour for working women were deemed no less critical. Miss Chenevix, consistently to the forefront of such campaigns, made the first claim to the Leinster Laundries' Association [LLA] for a reduction of the standard working week from fifty to forty-five hours. In so doing she served notice of the Union priorities for all its members: '. . . an eight-hour day and one half-holiday is a fair standard for all workers'. While Miss Chenevix doubted 'if employers always realised what an asset to them the good health of the employees is', those same employers were seen to be diligent in catering for their own needs. In response to the claim, the Union was informed that 'As the military authorities have commandeered the Standard Hotel, and Mr Foster is going away on a well-earned few days' holiday, the matter must lie over for a few days'.[12]

Membership increased — some actively recruited by the Union, others calling to 'Head Office' at the new premises of the IWWU at Denmark House. From Messrs McMaster Hodgins, Castleknock, came twenty-five girls from the Blacking House; from Lamb Bros. jam factory sixty-four women applied to join. The benefits of organisation appeared boundless, with employers attributing all ills to the onslaught of the IWWU. Edward Hely & Co., Envelope Manufacturers, wrote that

> After 40 years I and my father before me had never sent off any employee but on account of your society's action we have lost already half our English trade and it seems as if we will probably lose the whole lot of it.

From within the trade union movement itself support was forthcoming. The Transport Union, Inchicore Branch, claimed solidarity with the now fully independent Union, and suggested, 'anything that is in our power to help you in the interest of trade unionism and the social and domestic development of our sisters we, the committee, will do our best to strengthen your cause'. The capacity of some members of the movement to harbour a blind spot in relation to their sisters was, however, noteworthy. When Dublin Trades' Council discussed the successful termination of the hotel workers' dispute Mr Foran waxed eloquent on their achievement.

> These men were, he said, of great value to the Labour Movement, and during their strike they had behaved in a splendid fashion. The great majority were women, and they walked out leaving everything behind them.[13]

And thus make men of us all!

By 1918 the Union claimed 5,300 members: printers, laundresses, and general workers. It had affiliated with Dublin Trades' Council and with the Irish Trades Union Congress and the development of its policy reflected the priorities of those who set its agenda. Louie Bennett and Helen Chenevix were most in evidence; Helena Molony had retreated to the position of official with responsibility for the organisation of domestic workers. Documentation for the period is almost non-existent, and that which remains is controversial but offers little conclusive evidence. It is clear from these sources, however, that there were political differences within the Executive of the IWWU. In August 1918, Delia Larkin returned to Ireland. She applied to rejoin the IWWU, and was refused. On 13 August 1918 P.T. Daly, President and Secretary to Congress and a long-time political associate of Jim Larkin, complained to Dublin Trades' Council on her behalf. A letter was sent to Miss Bennett requesting a deputation from the Union to explain this turn of events. In replying, she indicated a measure of tension in the camp.

> I am sorry we cannot manage to send a deputation to meet Miss Larkin on Thursday, August 29, as I wish to be on that deputation myself and I have an important engagement. We shall be happy to go on Thursday, September 5, if equally convenient. Will you kindly arrange with Miss Molony yourself.[14]

Miss Larkin expressly requested both a formal deputation

and the presence of Miss Molony. As a body, the IWWU had expressed no hostility to Larkin and played no apparent role in the wave of anti-Larkinism directed against 'Big Jim'. In 1924 the Union would support the affiliation of the Workers' Union of Ireland [WUI] to Congress. Some years later, however, Helena Molony, while President of Congress, resigned from all committees on the Dublin Trades' Council rather than support the affiliation of the Workers' Union of Ireland to that body. Her opposition to the affiliation, which was contrary to the instructions of the IWWU Executive, was, she said, based 'on strong convictions personally that it would not be in the best interests of the Labour Movement'.[15]

At this distance in time, it is not possible to identify the basis for these 'strong personal convictions'. Clearly, however, both Miss Molony and one, unspecified, section of the Union were against Miss Larkin's re-admission. That section alleged that such a position would 'cause serious trouble in the Union'.[16]

In what became a campaign of no great honour to any of the parties concerned, letters were sent, allegedly from the women workers. Apart from what can be assumed from later evidence in relation to Miss Molony's sentiments, no Executive resistance was evident, but their silence was eloquent, and equally effective. Arrangements to attend at Dublin Trades' Council proceeded with no great haste. Using the excuse that Miss Larkin was currently employed as a clerk, the Executive directed her to apply to the Irish Clerical Workers' Union [ICWU]. They also, however, refused to admit her, and from these sources it appears that Delia Larkin found herself alienated from a variety of sections within the trade union movement.

The minutes of the Dublin Trades' Council for 23 September bristled with innuendo but shed little light on the context in which Delia Larkin, first General Secretary of the IWWU, and one of the earliest champions of working women in Ireland, found herself so unceremoniously discarded. In those minutes Mr Foran claimed

> The whole thing about Miss Larkin was camouflage . . . certain persons had been seduced and were being used

to vilify the Transport Union. They had gone behind Miss Larkin.

> Scandalous attack! *(A voice)*
> Hear, Hear! (*Voices)*
> Shut up! (*Another voice)*

In the face of such a confusion of purpose, the Dublin Trades' Council claimed it had no authority to deal with the matter, and 'the whole matter would have to be settled by the women workers themselves'. The DTC executive, however, approved a resolution that 'Miss Larkin be recommended not to press for application for membership to the IWWU'.[17]

The women workers were deafening in their silence. The lack of ready documentation points long-term to a need for further enquiry. In the short term, however, what was evident was that the IWWU could and would engage in political disputes, both publicly and privately. In an institutional sense, and given the temper of the times, this was hardly remarkable. The women workers, in short, were novices no longer.

CHAPTER 3

Mr Quill and colleagues

Despite the completion of its novitiate, as an organisation the Union had in fact laid few foundations in terms of either policy or structure. The first official minutes of the Executive in 1919 refer to neglect both of the audit and of general records, and in spite of increasing membership the Union faced considerable financial difficulties. As an essential preliminary to the organisation of women workers, and despite their involvement and that of their officials in the events in Dublin surrounding the constituting of the first Irish parliament — the Dáil — the IWWU, to survive, had to put its own house in order. While the Dáil ratified the Declaration of the Irish Republic, more mundane matters became the daily fare of the Union.

A finance committee was appointed and procedures for the collection and invoicing of contributions were established. Staff members and officials were required to attend the office to cover a six-day working week, with the 'office door to be closed to all newcomers after 9.30 p.m.' Miss Bryan, Printers' Official, was joined by Miss Behan, 'recognised organiser for the Laundresses and to take charge of their Registers and Pay sheets'. For General Workers Miss Cullen was to assume full responsibility. Miss Molony proposed that the Union appoint an organising committee, and a Miss Magee, currently of London, but clearly of Irish origin, was proposed by the Misses Bennett and Chenevix as National Organiser for the IWWU. The appointment was never made, although the precise reasons are unclear.

Although representing only a passing discord within the Union, the necessity to formalise internal organisation and procedure became apparent in the period of disquiet following Miss Bennett's attempt to place an 'outsider' in the position of forewoman at Taylor's Tobacco Company. Personal interventions of this order were not new — the absence of procedure in fact facilitated the initiative necessary for survival in the early years. It became, however, a point of some contention, as the Union sought to organise itself on more professional lines.When challenged on her attempt to facilitate the appointment of 'a Miss Shanagan from outside Taylor's Tobacco Company', Miss Bennett claimed the right to act in a personal capacity despite her official position as General Secretary to the Union. How widespread such interventions were in similar organisations is difficult to gauge, but quite clearly the IWWU was not unique in this regard. The capacity of the IWWU to survive the early years had, as in other unions, depended heavily on the political will of many of its leaders; now to call these leaders themselves to order demanded a measure of political will, *par excellence.*

Such internal disputes were no less political in their origins than were disputes throughout the trade union movement. Questions of procedure demanded resolution; would those in executive positions exercise collective or individual power? Would the political aspirations of nationalists, in such times, be eventually constrained by the advocates of conciliation? In other institutions of the labour movement the legacy of 1913, 1916 and the challenge that the Dáil now represented to the Westminster government provoked a period of tension which served to exacerbate difficulties and to promote splits that only time would reconcile. Although later affiliating with the breakaway group, in one such split — in the skirmish relating ostensibly to testimonials — the IWWU gave little evidence of its appreciation of the internal politics of the Dublin Trades' Council. Tommy Lawlor, a tailor by trade, and a full-time organiser of the ITGWU since 1917, was charged by the Executive of the Council with having contravened Council policy by being in receipt of a 'testimonial' from the employees of the Poor Law Union. Lawlor denied knowledge of the circular seeking funds on his behalf and, while the complexities bear some consideration,[1] the episode clearly served as a focus for the resolution of other tensions relating primarily to strategy.

When the Executive report on the question of testimonials was rejected by the Council on 16 June, the Executive resigned. In 'the Parliament of Labour', the full implications of this rejection are discussed, and the suggestion made that this 'was eventually to lead to a split in the Council and the formation of a rival Dublin Workers' Council [DWC] in 1921'.[2]

From the IWWU, Louie Bennett despatched a letter of condemnation which showed little awareness or political will to engage in the developments considered internal to the DTC. The IWWU's tendency on this occasion to reduce such struggles to the realm of the personal was made explicit when, on a proposal from Miss Molony, IWWU delegates to the Council were withdrawn for six months, 'or until such time as the Council takes to realise that it is there to advance the cause of Labour and not to further petty personal quarrels'.[3]

Such reluctance may have been in response to the high price paid for earlier incursions into the political arena, on a Union rather than merely on an individual basis, in both the Lock-Out and the Rising. The institutional focus of the IWWU, while 'guerilla warfare'[4] rumbled throughout Ireland, became increasingly focused on what were perceived to be the needs of Labour rather than on the demands of the national struggle. The context in which such decisions were taken, however, cannot be discounted. The IWWU was, in effect, in its infancy as a Union, the lack of internal accountability, for example, reflecting in large part the teething troubles of an essentially new organisation, albeit one with a 'history'.

While proposing 'revolutionary' changes in education schemes 'to meet the real needs of the rising generation', and making preliminary moves to secure the services of a woman doctor to be available for consultation by its members, the still relatively inexperienced Executive were required to make decisions and state union policy that had been seen on no agenda. Policy of sorts, however, was slowly formulated. In the short term, although the Union was undoubtedly preoccupied by the daily round, it also directed its energies to specific campaigns. In 1919 it asserted fundamental opposition to Trade Boards as wage-fixing machinery, protesting that employers were given licence to elevate to the status of wage the lowest rate agreed by the Boards. A leaflet opposing their establishment 'with a caricature designed by Mrs Plunkett' was printed — the first of many, as the pamphlet and the poster became major forms of recruiting members and enlisting public sympathy. Against unscrupulous employers they directed such publications where consumption was greatest. At Mitchell's Bead Factory, where homeworkers were paid by the 'decade', Mr Mitchell pleaded unfair competition and sought protection from the importers of foreign rosary beads. The Union charged him with exploitation and, with missionary zeal and considerable effect, took their pamphlets and their cause to the church gates.

On the shopfloor fundamental disputes were coming to the surface. At Williams & Woods girls had been asked to pack cases, an area considered to be 'men's work'. Although instructed by the Union not to do so, 'there are six girls at present employed at it and feared loss of their jobs if they refused to oblige'. At Goodbody's, Cigarette and Snuff Manufacturers, the Union was informed that 'if we are to employ girls they must do the work they are told to do'. At Messrs Thom, lines of demarcation established by male workers were considered by employers to be movable feasts in relation to the employment of women, who were changed from one class of work to another with few concessions to Union protest.

By 1919 it had become clear that if women were to organise and to move beyond the level of general and unskilled workers they would have to adopt procedures and structures to establish, protect and develop their trades. The early skirmishes to claim territory for women workers were civil, but concessions were few. On 4 June 1919, the Union called a special meeting to consider measures to be taken in response to the 'Transport Union taking over IWWU members'. An attempt was to be made at 'friendly understanding' and a joint committee of both unions to discuss mutual needs of members was proposed, but failed to materialise. From the craft-based unions, more specific grievances were directed against the IWWU itself. On 23 October 1919, the Executive received a deputation from the Bookbinders' Society which gave detailed complaints regarding the encroachment of areas deemed the preserve of men.

> Mr Quill explained that Messrs Caldwells, Mitchells, O'Loughlin Murphy's and Powell Press were not all Society shops and these firms employed girls on men's work. He reported that three girls in Caldwell's were employed on book-binding although an agreement had been made with this firm some time ago, by which they promised not to employ any more girl apprentices on this work.

Mr Quill and his colleagues suggested that the girls at Caldwell's leave, and that the Bookbinders' Society would finance them at the current rate of pay 'until they found suitable employment'. The finding of employment deemed 'suitable' would, however, be their own responsibility and the concession to furnish them with funds would not become standard procedure should women workers attempt to make further incursions into men's territory. The Union undertook to speak to the girls in question, but the objective to exclude women was foiled with consummate skill.

By 1919 the Union could claim all women in printing as its members. In addressing the difficulties raised by the Bookbinders' Society, Louie Bennett couched her proposals for their future workplace conduct in impeccable trade union terms.

> Now that the organisation of the Printing and Kindred Trades is complete, and feeling that the time has come to make an effort to strengthen our position and remove causes of irritation that exist, it is hereby resolved that the undertaking given to the Dublin Branch of Bookbinders' and Machine Rulers' Society be immediately put into operation.

The proposals, however, were founded on a resolution of a different order.

> That where vacancies occur at processes of book-binding for which men are paid a higher fixed scale of wages, such vacancies shall not again be filled by female

apprentices or learners on any terms other than the scale of wages paid to the men on similar work.[5]

In Denmark Street, meanwhile, the business of the Union continued apace. In October the IWWU held its first Convention of members and at a general meeting held soon afterwards, 'for advertisement purposes', a programme was launched for a 30s. minimum wage and a 44-hour week for women workers. The press were invited to attend, and were 'instructed on points for publication'.

Over the previous two-year period, however, the finances of the Union had suffered greatly and the expense of maintaining benefits involving strike and victimisation pay made its position extremely vulnerable. The Executive reported in July 1919 that it had only £68 to cover expenses, and no capital assets that could be realised to defray costs. Despite earlier assistance from the Dublin Trades' Council during the printers' lock-out, since 1918 the Union had also been involved in strikes at Irwin's and at Hely's, and the prolonged lock-out of tobacco workers had forced the Union to plead inability to pay strike monies.

Although benefits had been curtailed and a levy imposed on all members for an 'indefinite period', the rank and file indicated their willingness to suspend immediate need in return for long-term gains. At Hely's of Denmark Street, a proposal to close the printing works by the men withdrawing their labour made it evident to all that, should the women support the strike, they would not find strike pay forthcoming from their own union. Welcoming their offer of solidarity and acknowledging their difficulties, the men raised a levy to partially compensate the women, but clearly losses were felt by the members of the union. When the strike went ahead, the women came out.

At Irwin's, the dispositions of a number of working women towards more militant action caused the Executive to raise its collective eyebrows and urge restraint in regard to the unspecified tactics adopted by 'the girls'. While Miss Chenevix proposed that 'this Union policy should not allow any destructive action', 'Miss Bennett . . . suggested that if the girls were found guilty of any further rough conduct they would be fined 1s. for each offence to be deducted from strike pay.'[6]

In trade union circles the financial embarrassment of the IWWU prompted both suggestions for resolution and other proposals of a more long-term nature. Towards the end of 1919 the IWWU received a letter from the Transport Union asking the women to, in effect, re-join the larger union as a section. The IWWU did not in principle oppose the combining of effort to secure improved conditions for its members — in September it had begun actively negotiating with the Transport Union to arrange the payment of affiliation fees to cover industries where men and women worked together. This move, which eventually failed, was considered a purely tactical decision by the IWWU; where men dominated in a particular industry, women could be dramatically affected by decisions they had no part in making. The affiliation fees were an attempt to ensure that some benefits negotiated within industries would extend to women, and also that women who were drawn to the Transport Union as a more powerful body would retain their membership of the IWWU.

The loss of members evident in these years now presented a major problem for the Union, and the Executive minutes of 11 September record disquiet at Transport Union methods in swelling their own ranks at the expense of others. It was recorded that a meeting had been called by that union for all laundresses at Thomas Street. The IWWU Shop Steward, Mrs Turney, reported that 'a number of women went over and joined the Transport. She says that something must be done at once to prevent any other laundry workers falling away'. However widespread such undermining was, the overall loss of members from the IWWU between 1918 and 1919[7] could not, however, be explained solely by reference to the use of such methods.

The war in Europe had ended and many of the men who had fought in the British Army had returned to reclaim their jobs. In addition, many of the early members of the Women Workers' Union owed, and gave, their allegiance primarily to Liberty Hall,[8] and undoubtedly where men and women worked together as semi-skilled or unskilled workers, more effective negotiating positions were possible if all belonged to the same union. Much of the drift expressed enlightened self-interest on the part of working women rather than a specific lack of loyalty to a Union as yet in its infancy. Others, however, were clearly unwilling to suspend their immediate demands for the assumption of long-term gains; they joined the IWWU in expectation of collective advance in terms of their conditions of labour, and retained their right to withdraw should the Union fail to significantly improve the quality of their working lives. From Blackrock Hosiery the Union received a rather terse missive:

> Dear Madam,
> I want to tell you we are not having any more to do with the Union as the girls have refused to pay any more money until you do something for us. . . . We are tired hearing we are getting our back money. . . . I expect they [the officials] quite forgot there is such a place as the Blackrock Hosiery.

When the Transport Union showed a willingness to capitalise on the drift, however, they were given short shrift by the IWWU which 'would not entertain the idea of the IWWU becoming a section of the Transport Union as we do not approve of their policy or methods'. This was, indeed, the least of their criticisms. In rejecting such overtures, the Executive reaffirmed its own commitment to a separate women's union.

> We consider it necessary for women to have a special organisation of their own at the present time as men are not likely to look after the women's interests.[9]

The move to recruit members outside Dublin came, in part, from this steady loss of membership. Since 1918, the Union had moved to organise women in the provincial houses of the printing trade, and from Waterford it was reported that 'Miss McCarthy has organised fowl pluckers in Waterford district'. Miss Bennett visited Belfast to discuss conditions in textiles and other trades, and later spoke at a public meeting at Edenderry in response to a request from Edenderry and District Trades' and Labour Council for the Union to organise the women of the area. In Dublin, efforts to extend the area of recruitment led to the courting of nurses. Acknowledging the change in terms of status that such expansion suggested, Miss Bennett, in a note scribbled between meetings, informed Miss Malone, clerical officer, that 'the maternity nurses are to meet in Denmark House on Wednesday afternoon next. Will you see that the big drawing room is cleared up to give an air of high respectability for that occasion?'

After what was reported to be an impressive campaign by Miss Bennett, the secretary of the Irish Nurses' Union [INU] was co-opted by the Executive. Under a negotiated agreement, the Irish Nurses' Union retained its status as an independent organisation in relation to the administration of all affairs, other than finance, which became henceforth the responsibility of the IWWU. Structural support from the Union, however, was recognised as being invaluable. On 13 November 1919 the Executive endorsed the nurses' decision to send a delegate to Dublin Corporation to protest at a particular sanatorium being 'taken over by the nuns'. It charged that such a move was 'neither good business nor patriotism', and Mrs Mortished was authorised by the Union to act as their secretary at a rate of 30s. a week.

The Union also attracted interest from other quarters. Mrs Buckley, secretary of the Irish Branch of the Women's Federation (a British organisation) and a strong opponent of OBU ['One Big Union'][10] on the basis that such large institutions would tend to absorb women's interests into those of the labour movement as a whole, sought talks with the Executive with a view to forging a link between the Federation and the Union. On 4 December Miss Bennett reported to the Executive the extent of Mrs Buckley's ambitions for a more widely-based Federation: 'she proposes that we should take in all classes of women workers — and get the other women's organisations to join us to form the Irish Women Workers' Federation' [IWWF].

The Irish Branch of the Women's Federation was linked both structurally and financially to Britain. Branches retained one-sixth of all funds, and returned five-sixths to head office in London. A staunch nationalist, Mrs Buckley indicated that her members were now in favour of forming a purely Irish organisation, with the focus on women along lines of gender rather than as members of particular industrial groupings. The proposals to form a federation included allocating Mrs Buckley a position as an official of the IWWU with responsibility for the organisation of domestic workers. Such internal reorganisation would necessitate the moving of the current official for such workers, Miss Molony, from this area and, it was suggested, into the position of deputy or 'lieutenant' to Miss Bennett. Despite some strong and vocal opposition from members of the Executive regarding the practice of recruiting officials of the Union from outside their own ranks, the proposed reorganisation took place and Mrs Buckley became an official for the domestic workers. This group within the Union, potentially bigger than other sections should organisation be successful, became, like the Nurses' Union, a separate organisation, retaining autonomy in all matters other than finance.[11] When the terms of amalgamation were agreed, enthusiasm for the project ran high. Mrs Mortished immediately proposed 'that we should send a memo to the Transport Union asking them to hand over all their women members'. With surprising optimism, given their recent very public rejection by the IWWU, Miss Molony ventured that 'under these circumstances, we would have no difficulty in getting the women from the Transport Union'.[12]

Louie Bennett had consistently fostered hopes for a federation of women, but the previous experience of the Union's difficulty in uniting women across class lines and on the basis of their gender was not hopeful. In 1919 the resistance Delia Larkin had earlier confronted in regard to women workers and status reasserted itself. At Waterford, Luke Larkin, President of Waterford Trades' Council and a major supporter of the Union outside Dublin, sought the assistance of the IWWU in bringing women into the labour movement. Earlier attempts to do so had been made by the Trades Council and had patently failed and Mr Larkin

> could not for the life of him understand the meaning of the class distinctions existing, particularly among female workers. . . . It was time these foolish ideas vanished

from their midst because they were all brothers and sisters in one great army. Had it ever occurred to them that the girl workers were one of the chief obstacles in the path of progress of the Labour Movement?[13]

Miss Bennett, speaking later at the meeting organised by the Council, expressed disappointment that Mr Larkin had felt obliged to speak as he had done. The benefits of organisation were, she claimed, abundantly clear to all. The IWWU, she argued, had 'reduced the hours of the laundry workers by five and doubled their wages'. She urged the women of Waterford to re-assess their position and, challenging what she perceived as Mr Larkin's litany of woes, she asked:

> Was there any woman in Waterford, however well off she might be, who did not want to join a trades union because there were some poor people in it she did not want to mix with? Equality was the first word they had to get into their minds because all had the same battle to fight, and after that they must have solidarity.[14]

If such women were not courted and organised, the regulation of their wages would come automatically under the machinery of the Trades Boards, a move that both the IWWU and the labour movement overall believed to be against the interests of working people. The Trades Boards Act 1909 had set up a number of Boards in England and provisional orders confirmed by Parliament had extended these to a number of industries in Ireland. The Trades Boards Act 1918 sought to further consolidate the machinery to regulate wages and to provide for minimum rates to be paid in specific trades. At the Irish Labour Party and Trades Union Congress in 1919 the Executive of the IWWU urged Congress to respond to such developments and to set up its own machinery, suggesting the establishment of an Industrial Board to provide for conciliatory intervention if necessary and to promote industrial reforms, 'an Industrial Board purely Irish in composition, purely Irish in its interests, and so constituted as to minimise any designs to undermine Labour's power'. When such a suggestion was met by little enthusiasm, concern was voiced by the Union that the movement was more and more accepting the conciliatory intervention of the Government through the Ministry of Labour, and that the system of Trades' Boards, in effect, 'marks another step towards compulsory arbitration'.

Dealings of the IWWU with an earlier Minister of Labour had been both dramatic and, in retrospect, efficient. In the brief period marking the life of the first Dáil, dealings with Madame Markievicz, Minister of Labour of Dáil Éireann, were remembered with some nostalgia by Louie Bennett, who recalled Madame Markievicz walking into an early version of the employer-labour conference, gun in hand.

> The conference had droned on for hours. Miss Bennett was eloquent, the employer was adamant, and no appreciable advance had been made. Then Madame Markievicz strode in, pulled out her gun, pointed it at the terrified employer — 'ten minutes to settle, after that I shoot!' The employer settled after seven minutes.[15]

By the end of 1919 such anecdotes had been consigned to history. The first Irish parliament had been suppressed and, under authority from Britain, armed Auxiliaries, the Black and Tans, were introduced to Ireland. When Louie Bennett declared women workers 'altogether against having anything to do with the Ministry of Labour',[16] the IWWU was declaring itself against the representatives of forces it had long associated with moves to undermine the rights of working people in Ireland.

> The Women Workers object to truck of any sort with a Government which insults and coerces Labour Representatives, denies the workers the right of free speech and demonstration, and organises a band of spies to keep watch of every movement against trade unionists. In Ireland especially we need to beware of such a Government.[17]

By the end of 1920 Ireland was under arms, and within the IWWU revolutionaries and pacifists had found common cause.

CHAPTER 4

'Denmark House Desperadoes'

In a period when Ireland was riven by conflicting political loyalties, the aspiration to transcend any such differences on the Union front was undermined on industrial realities. In the face of fluctuating membership and conflicting loyalties amongst women workers, the 1920s were marked by the harsh reality confronting one shop steward:
'I am killed from asking them to pay'.[1]
The IWWU now offered members a range of benefits. For specific contributions different levels of payment would be made for strike, lock-out or victimisation. On completion of five years' membership, women workers 'shall be entitled to a sum of £5 on marriage', and the payment of 3*d.* for fifty-two consecutive weeks would ensure a contribution of £3 towards the costs of one's own funeral. Such provisions did not, however, conceal the distance between aspiration and reality. The Rules of the IWWU stated that the object of the Union was to 'improve the pay and conditions of Irish women workers', such improvement to be seen as part of an ambitious programme to alter radically Irish society. The focus of policy was for the right of the Irish people to form their own government; for equality of opportunity for all men and women; for control of industries by the workers engaged in them and for a change from 'the competitive system of production for private profit to a cooperative system of production for human use and happiness'.[2]
Sponsorship of the cooperative movement had been signalled by Union provision of accommodation for the Irish Nurses' Co-operative Hostel; a commitment to equality of opportunity had been implicit in the agreement reached within the Bookbinders' and Kindred Trades; the call for an

independent Industrial Board had established the Union's reluctance to accept structures imposed on the Irish workforce by the British Government. While some progress had undoubtedly been made, the IWWU was not, however, immune to dissent from within its own ranks.

The leadership of the IWWU had been formed, and forged, in hard times. Women from diverse backgrounds, with priorities and politics often in conflict, were drawn to the labour movement. Few other institutions in Ireland offered women access to political power and the umbrella cause of working women sheltered a wide range of intent; as had been evident since 1916 the Union did not speak with one voice, and it was neither necessary nor prudent for it to do so. Regardless of their own personal and political priorities, however, the leadership of the IWWU could not postpone indefinitely an assessment of its own agenda.

Women workers, the habits of collective action competing with the more ingrained response of self-interest, persisted in dealing directly with their employers. Work was priced, scales negotiated and shifts altered with no reference to the IWWU. Time served was of little consequence: when Frances Brown, litho feeder, began work in 1908, she served for two years as 'taker off' at Messrs Leckie & Co. Between 1911 and 1914 she was employed by C.E. Litho Printing & Co. Ltd. In 1919, after a break in her working life, she returned to Messrs Alex Thom & Co. Ltd. as 'learner to the feeding'. The IWWU protested. Alex Thom and Co. responded, 'seeing that you claim that she is entitled to be considered a journeywoman, we propose giving her notice next weekend to discontinue her employment with us'. The Union demurred, and Mrs Brown retreated to the ranks of the learners.

Between shifts, May Bannon, box-maker, gave birth to seven children. In the early 1920s, for a penny a day for each child, Mrs Moore's crèche at Richmond Hill, Rathmines, assumed responsibility for three of her offspring. While the Dublin Box Company welcomed her labour, May's capacity to reproduce provoked managerial comment. Following pregnancies spent nursing a 'banger' — a mechanical stitching machine in widespread use in the trade — May's children came forth, 'black and blue'.[3]

Throughout industry, abuse of the Truck Act[4] was widespread and, in a series of letters relating to the practice of deducting fines for spoiled work, the Union protested at the deductions made from the wages of some of its women members.[5]

After a decade of political upheaval and the demands of the national struggle, officials of the Union were forced to confront the reality of such lives. Many of the women elected in 1917 to serve the IWWU had lent considerable moral support but remained, by and large, committed to other areas of work. In 1919 Dr Kathleen Lynn, Chief Medical Officer of the Citizen Army, Vice-President of the IWWU, had founded St Ultan's Hospital for Infants. Among her 'committee of devoted women' was Madeline ffrench-Mullen, sergeant of the Citizen Army, Vice-President of the IWWU, secretary to the hospital from its foundation and imprisoned in 1920 for subversive activities. More prominent members of the Union found their commitment to other causes compelling. In Dublin, the ICA was on full alert, and in the years between 1916 and 1923 Helena Molony 'was one of the old group of Irish women who were always to be acquired for special service during the years of active service'.[6]

In 1920 Louie Bennett travelled to America to plead Ireland's cause and to protest at the licensed brutality of the Black and Tans. Her experience there was to be fundamental to the growth of her conviction that reason, with a dash of diplomacy, would triumph over vested interests — a conviction that would prompt both admiration and discord in the years to come. In an interview in *Reynold's News* many years later Miss Bennett referred to this American experience and the purchase of a hat, symbol of her belief that the affairs of state were largely dependent on questions of style. On arriving in New York she had been persuaded to abandon her somewhat dowdy cloche and to sport 'a pink feathered creation'. The effect convinced her that 'a woman in public life could afford to be neither dowdy nor eccentric, so I took the hat home with me to Ireland'.[7] With the confidence born of her class and her conviction, Louie Bennett left the business of the Union in the hands of Helena Molony and Helen Chenevix and travelled to England to see Lloyd George — by appointment — and to 'persuade him to take the Black and Tans out of Ireland'. She was given five minutes to state her case. While the power of her argument and the theatrical effect of the 'pink creation' undoubtedly made her a formidable advocate, the Black and Tans, nonetheless, remained.

The divided attentions of the leadership were accompanied by decisions taken with good intent, but with little regard for their implications or for consultation with those most immediately affected. When agreement was reached regarding the combining of the interests of the IWWU and the Federation of Women Workers [FWW], Miss Byrne, Printers' Official, had protested both at the appointment of Mrs Buckley as an official and at the ignoring of specific requests from the women workers. She argued that the printers had asked 'for an organiser chosen from their own ranks', one familiar with the trade and the employers. This had been refused on the grounds of economy, yet since then, she argued, two other officials had been appointed without reference to the rank and file. Although Mrs Buckley would later make a considerable impact as an official, she also voiced reservations at the assumption that the legacy of the Federation could be assumed 'by agreement'. Seventy members from the Federation in Derry ought, she argued, to be actively recruited to the IWWU. Miss Chenevix was directed by the Executive to deal with the matter, but her time was constrained by the laundry claims already in progress and she was unable to do so. By March the women workers of Derry had joined another union.

Such episodes, conducted within the context of political unrest and the daily demands of a Union servicing the individual needs of its members, suggested carelessness rather than abuse of power. The Union was an institution in transition — caught between the charms of the family business and the ambitions of the entrepreneur. Unlike many other institutions of the labour movement, it was subject to tensions which were essentially class-based. Inevitably, political differences were articulated through the *personae* of those who occupied centre stage. The process of transition placed greater structural constraints on the ambitions and aspirations of individual members — but criticism was rarely oblique and generally proved creative.

In 1920 Miss Cross, Treasurer, announced to the Executive that she considered it 'unfair' that some people should be given 'soft jobs' and 'big wages' while the Misses Behan, Cullen and Bryan, 'had the hard work to do'. The reference to 'soft jobs' suggested the perception of a certain glamour attendant upon the activities of more prominent and more powerful members. The 'big wages' were largely mythical, although by this stage all officials were paid, and Miss Bennett received a salary deemed appropriate to the General Secretary of a trade union. Miss Chenevix, the conciliator, argued that parity of wages would be inappropriate and beyond the capacity of the Union coffers to bear; such a suggestion was, in short, 'quite impossible'. Miss Bennett, acknowledging some justice in the grievance, announced both a readiness and a desire to be paid as a piece-worker, available on a consistent basis but retaining the right to pursue other interests in the general cause of women and workers. Such an arrangement would, she suggested, allow her to continue to 'feel free to take a month's leave without pay if she wished'.[8] In the case of Miss Molony, an increase in salary was unanimously agreed, 'as her present wage was quite inadequate remuneration for the excellent work she is doing for the Union'.

As a matter of course, ground was conceded and settlements made. Before any other business, a truce was declared and Denmark House left in some degree of order.

The continuing and inevitable involvement of the leadership and the rank and file in other causes undoubtedly impinged on decisions made at Executive level. Towards the end of 1919 a series of letters in the *Voice of Labour* had been interpreted by the suffragist movement as 'anti-feminist' propaganda, and in the suffragists' paper, *The Irish Citizen*, the *Voice* was criticised for undermining the activities of feminists. In a move of solidarity, discreetly expressed as 'a cost-cutting exercise', the IWWU ended its subscription to the labour paper and reviewed a long-felt need for an organ of propaganda for women workers.

Some commitment to greater participation by members in the affairs of the Union had been suggested by discussions arising out of the first Convention of the IWWU in 1920.

> The Irish Women Workers' Union inaugurated on St. Brigid's day what they hope may be the beginning of a Parliament of working women in Ireland. They held a convention of delegates from all their branches and industrial sections and discussed alterations and improvements in the Constitution and aims of the IWWU.[9]

The need to publicise and to organise was now seen as pressing. Branches were being established and some means of communicating with members outside Dublin was considered essential to progress.

In March 1920 the Executive, with the consent of the members, committed £3 a month from Union funds to *The Irish Citizen* in return for the use of that paper as the official organ of women workers. This paper had, since its foundation in 1912, periodically voiced its concern about the sweatshops of Dublin and Limerick and the exploitation of the women of the working class. By 1914, however, it had demonstrated a remarkable absence of knowledge of any attempt to organise such women. Its class bias was evident both in its editorial content and in the range of advertisements from the purveyors of fine food and goods which sought the custom of a financially secure sector via its pages. In 1917, however, in a concession to self-criticism and undoubtedly influenced by Louie Bennett and Helen Chenevix, it had indicated through its editorials that theoretical concerns with the industrial workforce would be more appropriately given a lower priority. In welcoming a series of lectures on trade unions it had, indeed, roundly upbraided some of its readers for tendencies towards the luxury of armchair philosophy.

> We welcome evidence that the leisured class begin to appreciate the value of the movement. But surely the time is past for merely sitting listening to lectures on the subject — let the educated and leisured women of Dublin come right down among the workers and learn

by practical experience the meanings and purposes of trades unions.[10]

The Irish Citizen continued as the voice of the suffragist movement. The change was, however, self-evident, and the ironically captioned 'Denmark House Gossip' issued monthly briefs on the actions and aims of the IWWU.

The resolution to advance the cause of women workers extended beyond the noble aim of propaganda. In response to the very clear vulnerability of working women with no benefit for sickness or pension rights, the Union revived an old ambition to promote a Pensions and Benevolent Scheme and Loan Fund. The Loan Fund would be directed at the more pressing needs of the members — of those women on half-time at the woollen mills in Co. Waterford and the many others in 'distress or old age'. While acknowledging the need for such immediate reforms, long term a larger vision was undoubtedly evident.

> We want to make it a big and important scheme extending to women workers of all classes, and becoming gradually a sort of Bank to provide help of many various sorts to young and old.[11]

To establish such schemes women workers were daily urged to support the Union in all its battles and to secure their rights as working people. No area was left to chance. In prolonged conference with the Master Printers, officials sought improvements on the 3s. 6d. increase offered to women. While the Masters were condemned for seeking 'to buy women's labour at the lowest price', women themselves were criticised for their lack of pride: 'they are skilled workers and they should demand and secure the position and pay of skilled workers'. From references in the minutes it is evident that questions of hours of work, of the right to work and 'of work before and after childbirth', were regularly debated amongst the leaders of the Union. The imperative to unionise, to persuade all women to combine and to articulate their needs, was made more stark by the appraisal by the leadership of the problem of the continuing 'apathy of women workers' and the evident need 'to educate them in trade unions'.[12] An agenda to establish rights for women workers was set.

By June, the 'Denmark House Desperadoes'[13] were reporting from the front line:

> We have never alarmed employers so much as by asking them to establish an apprentice system for girls. We have done this in the cases of the laundry and the printing workers, and were met at first by blank refusals —
> 'What you propose is revolutionary', said one employer.

Miss Bennett, far removed from the Academy for Young Ladies, retorted:

'I suppose they think only Bolshevists would ask employers to give women a proper industrial training. But, truly, Dublin employers are enough to drive all of us to Bolshevism.'[14]

Miss Bennett's own views on appropriate training were, however, constrained by her assumptions about a woman's place. Such assumptions were of critical importance, given her position of power within the only trade union catering for women workers. In a series of articles debating the continuing need for an Irish women's trade union, published in *The Irish Citizen* at the beginning of the year, she argued that although much could be done to raise the status of working women, 'I do not think that the time has come for women to break in on the men's industrial preserve'.[15] She suggested, instead, cooperation with men of the working class, and a move to improve the status of women workers through the medium of a Women Workers' Federation — combining the interests of all women in industry rather than restricting the focus to those in particular sectors.[16]

A number of the difficulties encountered in the move to organise such women were those common to the labour movement overall. The attractions of England and Scotland as workplaces for the Irish working class were compounded by widespread unemployment at home. While for the entire trade union movement, priorities of necessity focused on the level of wages, for the IWWU, in addition, the question of conditions of labour became inextricably linked with moves to improve the general lot of the working woman.

In 1922 the Union welcomed the announcement that 'one woman factory inspector had been appointed, which is not enough of course, but a good beginning'. Louie Bennett outlined for Miss Stafford the problems relating to the irregularity, and hence instability, of women's employment, and in particular to the widespread use of homeworkers. The factory inspectors, by definition, had little effect in the implementation of legislation when work was done in private homes and, despite some attention, the problem persisted. In 1924, members of the Paper Bag Manufacturers and Printers' Association approached the Union expressing concern that the practice of bag-making in private homes was increasing. Miss Bennett wrote to the Town Clerk detailing the protest of the IWWU.

> Our primary objection to the practice arose owing to the fact that it leads to sweated work and undercutting an agreed standard of wages. But information we have received makes us realise how dangerous it is from the point of view of public health that some paper bags, often used afterwards for articles of food, are made in such houses as the workers of Dublin are condemned to inhabit.[17]

Two weeks later Helena Molony led a Union delegation to Dublin Corporation to register the 'Dublin Workers' Grievance'.[18] The problem was, however, perceived by the Corporation as one requiring the attention of the Public Health Committee, and the industrial questions relating to undercutting of women's wage standards could not therefore be addressed. The Union responded by taking the initiative and, issuing a circular to all employers outlining its objection to such work, informed them that the practice 'has been forbidden under the rules of the IWWU, consequently women who accept this work in future will not be trade unionists'. The threat, however couched, was destined to be ineffective; where poorly paid or underemployed women workers were offered such work, trade unions were unable to extend either their brief or their solidarity from the shop floor to workers' homes, and the practice persisted in the areas of bag-making, rosary bead assembly, textiles and other industries.

The problems for women workers were not confined to the home front. Where women were employed within factories many were paid on the basis of piece rates. Employers argued that the adjustment of rates for such work was not a matter for negotiation with a trade union. The IWWU, however, disagreed. 'This is not a matter of asking for a favour, but for an adjustment of the method of payment which will secure to your employees the same average wage as in other shops.'[19] Members of Messrs Thom's workforce urged the Union to strike a rate based on time; particular classes of piece-work, faulty machinery and the preferential distribution of 'good work' left women with wage levels which rarely reached the average and bore no relation to their labour time. Messrs Thom, with other women consistently available to fill their ranks, responded in time-honoured fashion. Twenty piece-workers were served notice of one week, and a letter was despatched to the Union:

> We do not give up or relinquish in any way the rights and customs of our trade to employ piece-workers as heretofore, if we do think fit to do so at any time.[20]

In the face of such intransigence, the 'Denmark House Desperadoes' retreated to consider their case.

CHAPTER 5

Matters Political

Much support for women workers was forthcoming from the trade union movement as a whole. Specific unions, however, continued to undermine the IWWU. The Rulers' and Bookbinders' Union [RBU] had been noted in 1920 as 'casting wistful eyes upon the printers' section of the IWWU', but greatest hostility was reserved for what was perceived as the imperialism of the Transport Union. In *The Irish Citizen*, comment from Denmark House was barbed.

> There's a wily bird that saves itself by grabbing the nests of other birds. . . . I think the Transport Union imitates the habits of the cuckoo, flitting cheerfully from place to place, chanting its monotonous 'OBU, OBU', whilst the humble sparrow of Denmark House rears a clamorous family for it.[1]

Despite resistance from employers and the threat of erosion from within the labour movement the Union retained its own commitment to the national organisation of women workers. In 1918 Mrs Callender, from Dublin, had become organiser for Waterford and had opened a branch of the Union in that city.

The Domestic Workers' Union [DWU], under the authority of Mrs Buckley, had moved in 1920 to 42 North Great George's Street, and 'owing to the many enquiries for maids received from ladies in all parts of the country', had opened a Registry Office and campaigned for 'good wages, fair conditions, to secure good service'. In Freshford, Co. Kilkenny, shop assistants worked twelve and fourteen hours a day with no half-holidays. At the request of sixteen of these assistants, the Union opened a further branch in Kilkenny and reported in the *Citizen* that 'we have secured for all except those in one firm a 25% increase in wages and a reduction in hours; and we are out on a campaign for the weekly half-holiday'.[2] Recruits were drawn from the Kilkenny Woollen Mills and with enthusiasm revived the Union's extra-curricular activities by the formation of the IWWU camogie team. Other women from the laundries, however, having been active in the General Strike of April 1922,[3] were dismissed from the convent laundry in Kilkenny and it was reported that 'orphans are doing the work in their places'. The Union response was swift; letters were despatched to the parish priest and to the bishop and Kilkenny Corporation was presented with proposals to lease the Bath premises to the Union for development as a cooperative laundry. The outcome, unfortunately, was not recorded, but registering such intent undoubtedly impinged upon the deliberations of the City Fathers.

In Cork the mill girls at Douglas called a strike to compel 'blacklegs to join the Union'. Miss McCarthy was sent to direct operations and the services of a full-time organiser for the city were sought. In this and other centres, however, the impact of the Civil War on the activities of the IWWU was pronounced. The effect of unemployment in Cork was dramatic, business in the mills slack and the 'generally unsettled nature of things' led to postponement of further activity in the south until the Dáil decision on the Treaty became known. Elsewhere, on a campaign of organisation throughout the country, Miss Chenevix travelled to Galway seeking an increase on the 23*s.* per week being offered to the women at the woollen mills. Returning to Dublin via Co. Mayo, she was detained 'owing to military operations', and the organising campaign came to an abrupt halt.

Back in Dublin the city was awash with IWWU red 'No' posters, rejecting out of hand the latest moves by employers to resolve their own difficulties by a reduction in the wages of women employees. When Leinster Laundries' Association [LLA] wrote to the IWWU urging a conference to discuss proposed reductions, the IWWU refused to attend and announced instead its ambition to establish cooperative laundries and to seek parity of wages with women workers in

Manchester and Liverpool. Already beset by problems from institutional laundries, the Association retreated from the prospect of further competition. While few details of pay bargaining procedures at this time are extant, the IWWU was in regular correspondence with the London-based Labour Research Department and the International Labour Organisation [ILO] in Geneva, and undoubtedly used figures drawn from these sources to some effect in negotiating on behalf of Irish women workers. Such triumphs as those recorded with the Association were, however, offset by concessions made in other sectors; in printing, a cut of 2*s.* a week was agreed between employers and officials, to the general dissatisfaction of members who felt that both Miss Bennett and other delegates had overstepped their Executive powers in agreeing to such a settlement.[4]

In Sligo, Drogheda and Donegal working women indicated a willingness to organise. The Union responded, but learned also the limitations of its own structures when these were faced with a transient workforce: the annual migration of the fisher girls of Donegal to Scotland effectively curtailed Union action on their behalf. In Dublin, other difficulties became apparent. An agreement was reached with the Clerical Workers' Union to 'organise women clerks and secretaries who do not wish to join a mixed Union'. At Messrs Marks of Henry St, the Union found a sympathetic employer but a most reluctant workforce. It mounted an offensive, picketed and issued handbills at the end of the working day. In this instance the reluctant were wooed, and won. Elsewhere, however, women's work was again under threat. The Irish Binders' Union [IBU] entered into a secret agreement with their employers regarding the taking over of work 'hitherto done by women', and the substitution of Union members by men on the glueing machine posed 'a threat of a long-term nature' in Messrs Eason.[5] The girls came out but agreed to return pending a conference with the alliance of unions in the print and paper industry. A general meeting of the printers' section of the Union condemned the action of the binders and calls were made for a major conference to discuss the question of women's work. Response from the print and paper industry was, however, muted.

Overall, the organising campaign bore fruit. By 1922 new areas offered great potential for recruitment and the Union welcomed box-makers, clerks, knitters and cleaners.[6] To cater for new members and to secure their loyalty, 2% of Union income was allocated for educational purposes. A history class was started and the library, which had been part of the Union since the move to Denmark House, was expanded. New and larger premises were established at Eden Quay, and the recruitment of officials became formalised: 'a preliminary examination in essentials' would ensure that women workers were well served. Progress and disputes continued within a context of Civil War where the Union spent its days on 'efforts to secure shelter and food for the poor people during the disturbances in Dublin', and many of its members spent their nights debating the virtues or otherwise of the Treaty to establish Partition. As an institution the IWWU conscientiously avoided the articulation of policy of a partisan nature; members, including officials such as Helena Molony, were active in their protests against the Treaty, but the politics of others can only be assumed. The IWWU, instead, focused on the material effect of the War on the lives of its members. A solicitor was appointed to file compensation claims for loss of wages by members due to the fighting, and the President of the Provisional Government was informed by the Union of 'the very serious amount of unemployment existing among women'.[7]

At a meeting on unemployment held in the Mansion House on 22 November 1922,

> Speakers made special reference to the fact that government departments place contracts for uniforms, hosiery goods, mattresses, boots, leggings and custard powder abroad, whilst Irish factories capable of supplying such goods are at least partially idle.

Charging the Provisional Government with the responsibility of pursuing a means to alleviate the hardship endured by working people, the IWWU submitted a memorandum on the employment of women,[8] detailing the cost of unemployment, the stagnation of Irish industry, and the huge outlays on imported goods. The home government was urged, in effect, to develop home industries. 'If work is not provided relief must be given, since no government may allow its citizens to perish for want of the ordinary necessities of life'. Certain industries were indicated as potential employers of women, such as sugar confectionery, which if developed would provide employment both in itself and in 'box-making, cardboard and tin'. In Wexford the memorandum pointed out that 'two well-equipped knitting factories are almost idle, employing a dozen women instead of 80 or 100'. The Government was urged to place contracts with such industries, any costs which might be incurred being seen as more than compensated for by increased employment.

Employers were also urged to join forces with the Womens' Union and the memorandum gave detailed proposals for specific developments.

> The Blackrock Hosiery Company are prepared to open a workshop for making woollen underwear in Dublin, if they are secured government contracts and if the government would arrange to pay the wages of learners for a short period. Such learners could be drawn from the ranks of those now drawing the unemployment benefit.[9]

Knitting, weaving and production of religious books were considered for development, and market gardens 'for the production of onions and early spring vegetables might advantageously be started on tracts of vacant land in the vicinity of Dublin'. To facilitate such growth, it was announced that 'there are already a number of fully qualified women gardeners who could be employed as instructors'.

A deputation from the Union was invited to attend the Trade Branch of the Ministry on 11 January 1923 to discuss the proposals. The Minister of Finance was invited by the Ministry of Industry and Commerce to attend.[10] On 9 January, however, the Department of Finance indicated in a departmental minute that it was not deemed advisable that 'M/F shd be represented at a conference on these highly controversial subjects'.[11] Predictably, more formal tones were adopted in the letter the following day, indicating the reluctance of the Minister to be represented when the deputation from the IWWU entered the fray.[12]

Such action undertaken by the Union clearly had political implications. Matters political, however, were considered by members to be no part of its brief, and overt political gestures were not encouraged. When the Women's International League wrote asking for cooperation from the Union in seeking a reprieve for the man accused of killing Sir Henry Wilson, 'the matter was deemed political and ruled out of order'. This stance was not new. In 1919 when Maud Gonne established a committee to enquire into the treatment of Irish political prisoners, 'Miss Bennett explained that this enquiry should be made from purely humanitarian, not political reasons'. Politics, however, were precisely if quietly defined. In the same year four members of the Union had been proposed for the Municipal Elections, and later for the election of Poor Law Guardians. Quite clearly the definition of what was deemed 'political' was dependent on an Executive interpretation of the intent and aspiration of what was proposed. Political actions such as the raising of a levy to assist railwaymen refusing to handle munitions in 1920, the urging of a truce in hostilities between Britain and Ireland in 1921, and attendance at conferences to discuss developments of 'Military Policy by which civilian work is to an increasing extent being brought under control of the army', were often initiated and consistently supported by an articulate Union leadership. Official comments on the Civil War, however, created tensions within the Union as in the country as a whole. At the end of 1922 a resolution from the Union calling for an end 'to the disastrous Civil War which is ruining the economic life of the country', cautioned that 'the subject should be regarded rather from an economic than a political standpoint'.[13]

The rules of the IWWU did not by definition preclude alliances with political parties which accepted its policies and its programme, and a number of overtures were made by the Executive in the direction of the Labour Party. In early 1923 Miss Bennett attended a meeting organised by that party in the Mansion House and entered an arena where articulate women trade unionists found only a measured welcome. It was proposed at that meeting that only those women should be admitted to membership who were relatives of trade unionists, and although 'after great discussion' it was agreed to 'admit them on the same terms as men', no formal agreement was proposed. In the absence of such an agreement, the Union took its own initiatives. In a discussion on 'General Policy and Plans for the Future' at the Annual Convention in February 1923, Miss Bennett proposed that a sub-committee, composed of Executive and non-Executive members of the Union, be elected 'to deal with social, civic and educational matters'. The committee would be directed to act in unison with, but remain independent of, the Women's Labour Council.[14]

Such deliberations remained on the internal agenda of the Union, but with requests from the Cork women to resume activities in the IWWU branch there, and from Limerick Trades' Council to revive and extend the organisation that had been underway prior to the lock-out, matters political retreated. Miss Buckley caught the steamer to Cork and Miss McCarthy was despatched from Waterford to Limerick for a six-week campaign. Slackness was everywhere apparent and members at the Annual Convention resolved to resist wage reductions proposed by employees. Yet, despite such resolve, reductions had become acceptable in the effort to stem rising unemployment. In May 1923, they were accepted in bagmakers' rates, and at Lucan Woollen Mills reduced rates were proposed to offset the increasing tendency of employers to use juvenile labour. In direct response to this trend, and indeed threat, the Union began a campaign to urge the raising of the school leaving age to sixteen years.

Throughout the country, the economy faltered. In Drogheda, Cahill's closed, leaving fifty printers idle, and in Waterford bacon factories closed without explanation or notice the day after issuing a threat to reduce wages. The women received no unemployment benefit, as their loss of work was judged by the County Referees to be related to the dockers' strike, by now at its height. After five weeks, and following an appeal by the Union, the court agreed to the women bacon curers receiving unemployment benefit. The success of the appeal was far-reaching. It set a precedent for the payment of benefits to women affected by lock-outs, and led directly to the establishment of a Joint Industrial Council for the industry — the second such council in Ireland and the first with IWWU representation.

Following five weeks of financial stress, however, the members were deeply critical of what was perceived to be Union inaction in relation to their by now urgent need to be recompensed for their loss of wages. With some reluctance, but acknowledging the grievance, a grant was given, stretching already depleted Union finances even further. The levels of unemployment profoundly affected Union income; arrears, always a difficulty, led to radical action and to the expulsion of members, and at Eden Quay officials and staff were asked to accept reductions in pay. Increased organisation, in tandem with the shedding of members in arrears, resulted in the maintenance of income levels, but expenditure was heavy, and aggravated by the legal costs incurred in supporting the fight of the Waterford case. By 1923, the salary bill for permanent staff of the IWWU was £26 3s. 0d. a week, plus £7 for organisers.

In an attempt to rationalise internal procedures and cut costs, Miss Kay McDowell had been appointed in the same year to take charge of all clerical work, to card index the membership, and to do a yearly audit for the Union. A member of a family originally from the North of Ireland, Miss McDowell's grandfather had been editor of *The Morning News*, and then of *The Freeman's Journal*. He had been sacked from the latter, having taken Parnell's side, had sued the owners for wrongful dismissal, and had won — the first such case to succeed in Ireland. He had taken responsibility for Kay McDowell and her brother when they had been orphaned at an early age, and she had been intended, along with her brother, for a career in law in her uncle's office. The death of her brother in France as a volunteer in 1916 led her, however, to abandon law and to travel to London. The McDowells, fearful that she might make 'an unsuitable match', urged her to return to Dublin. In 1922 she was introduced by her uncle, later the Union's solicitor, to Miss Bennett, and secured employment in the Union.

While this appointment was seen as an attempt to rationalise resources, other cost-cutting exercises could no longer be avoided. Miss Bennett and Miss Molony accepted reductions in salary of 10s. per week, and the Nurses' Union was informed that the IWWU could no longer afford to pay any surplus expenditure incurred. Organisation in both Limerick and Cork was effectively curtailed by the simple lack of resources.

Few unions at this time were immune to such problems and 'poaching' was rife. While the IWWU charged a 'cross-Channel union' with endeavouring to organise at Clarke's Tobacco Factory, where the majority of workers were its members, the ITGWU protested against similar activities when the women workers took over 'their' shop assistants at Watson's. Few were totally innocent of such charges, but inter-union cooperation was also evident. To protect home industries, and reduce unemployment, Miss Bennett urged her members to: 'Smoke Irish', and, with the Guild of Church Industries,[15] joined in efforts by other unions to promote the sale of Irish prayer books, holy pictures and rosary beads.

By 1924, although moves to reduce wages continued, the finances of the Union were reported to be 'fair', and the Union well pleased with its own position in the trade union movement: 'We are now recognised as the representative society of women workers in Ireland'. The Annual Report, in keeping with the function of such documents, criticised and praised in turn. Arbitration, to which the Union had had to submit in the printers' dispute involving the proposed reduction by the Dublin Masters in apprentice numbers, was seen to operate against the interests of working people:

> Our experience in this case has taught us finally that the workers can never with safety leave their interests in the hands of an arbitrator not belonging to the working class — no more arbitration for women workers![16]

The Civic Committee, chaired by Miss Chenevix, was applauded for its coverage of matters relating to factory inspection, the opening of public squares for use as playgrounds for children, and a campaign against the threatened reduction in old age pensions. Special commendation was also extended to the members of the Apprentices' League which, under the auspices of the Union, had organised classes in 'singing, cooking, home nursing and gymnasium'. The question of political action was also raised by members at the Annual Convention of 1924 when some delegates indicated a desire to see a woman representative in the Dáil. The discussion is not recorded, and the matter was closed with a note that 'it was finally agreed that for the present it is wiser for the IWWU to devote themselves to industrial action'. By July, however, with the preparation for the 1924 Congress of a statement from the Union relating to the split in the ranks of the Transport Union, the political approach of the IWWU became somewhat clearer.

Five delegates from the IWWU attended the Irish Labour Party and Trades Union Congress of 1924. The Misses Brennan, Gloucester, Kelly, Molony and O'Connor were the bearers of a statement to the Congress relating to the question of official recognition by affiliated unions of the Workers' Union of Ireland [WUI]. The dispute between Jim Larkin and the ITGWU was considered by the Union to demand both 'a settlement of the sharpest points of difference',[17] and the necessity for Congress itself to resolve any ambiguities as a means of re-establishing its authority as the central body of the labour movement. Miss Bennett, acting for the Executive of the IWWU, wrote to Mr Johnson of the Irish Labour Party and Trades Union Congress, urging that the afternoon and evening of the first day of the 1924 Congress be devoted to a consideration of means of resolving the differences between the ITGWU and James Larkin. Johnson cited procedural difficulties and refused to change the agenda, despite the fact that the IWWU was supported both by Trades' Councils and by other unions.

The position of the IWWU in relation to this split in the trade union ranks was coloured by its own history of hostilities in relation to the ITGWU and by its loyalty to Larkin as a major instigator of the moves in 1911 to authorise the founding of the IWWU. Urging that the Marino dispute be used as a test case the IWWU, however, characteristically refrained from an overt taking of sides and, while supporting the affiliation of the Workers' Union of Ireland to Congress, reserved its most grave criticism for the Congress itself. The affiliation was supported in specific terms.

> The IWWU suggests that if the union [Workers' Union of Ireland] will conform to Trade Union principles, especially those relating to transfer from one union to another, and the cooperation essential to safeguard the interests of all and any group of workers, then the affiliated Unions follow the ordinary Trade Union code in relation to the Workers' Union.[18]

The detailed statement from the Executive of the IWWU castigated Congress for its failure to deal with the split, and echoed the sentiment expressed in other quarters that Congress was dominated by the ITGWU. While James Larkin was, the statement held, 'officially and actually associated with the Moscow Communist International', such an association, the Union felt, called for a sympathetic but critical response from the Irish trade union movement. A grave crisis was in the offing.

> If the movement does not meet it with sympathetic understanding and support it where its ideals seem to lead to the uplifting of the workers, and equally criticise and condemn its methods where they violate human rights and liberty.

The crisis between the two unions was seen to be the concern of all, and had to be resolved, but more critical for the IWWU was the state of Congress itself, which 'stands in most immediate peril'. Referring to the agenda which had been held sacrosanct by Johnson, the Executive statement pointed to 'its appalling vacuity' as evidence of a loss of confidence by the trade union movement in its central organisation.

> They feel it is futile to send in resolutions which are rarely allowed time for consideration. . . . There has not been sufficient personal contact with the rank and file all over the country. There has been no educational campaign, no propaganda. . . . The rank and file remain in ignorance of whatever activities there may be at the Headquarters. . . . We claim that they [Congress] have failed to assume all the responsibilities or to use the powers of initiative their office gives them.[19]

The IWWU urged Congress to recognise the spirit of such criticism and 'to accept it as the outcome of a sincere desire to restore unity and enthusiasm to the movement'. Reform was necessary, and the IWWU urged that the Executive of Congress be divided into Industrial and Political Committees, with a committee representative of trade unions and a clear brief to 'avoid the impression of localism'. The Assistant Secretary of Congress, they proposed, should deal with the industrial side of the labour movement, and the Leader of the Labour Party with the political side. To promote democratic participation, an educational campaign and a weekly or monthly journal were suggested. More contentiously, and in a move seen by the Union as fundamental to the progress of women in the industrial workforce, the IWWU indicated a willingness to cooperate in its own demise by urging inducements for existing craft workers to open their doors to the unskilled.

The five delegates from the Union articulated their concerns throughout the four days of Congress: the statement from the IWWU did not, however, reach the floor. A motion, proposed by Miss Molony, moved

> That it be the first business of the Trades Congress to give its attention to ending the internal disputes at present disrupting the Labour Movement which are the cause of great scandal, growing weakness, and a loss of confidence among the rank and file.[20]

Speaking to the motion, she reiterated the Union's regret that time would not be made available for discussion at greater length. It was conceded from the platform that there was general agreement on the spirit of the resolution and, on the advice of the Chairman, it was withdrawn. An assumed willingness in spirit to resolve the dispute did not, however, translate into effective action. Although registered as a union in July 1924, the Workers' Union of Ireland remained excluded from Congress until the 1940s, its affiliation then being established in the wake of the split of the Congress itself.

The statement from the IWWU, although read from no platform, remained on record. It established the commitment of the women's union to extensive democracy within its own structures and represented a conviction that democratic organisation, and an informed working class, were fundamental to the realisation of trade union ideals.

From its earliest days the IWWU had sought to change the position of working women by a combined assault on three levels — the social, the political and the industrial. Its concern for the well-being of its members extended to the provision of dramatic clubs, dancing classes, and the establishment of a holiday home at Larch Hill, rented by the Union since 1920. The social aspect of the Union was a major attraction: Larch Hill played host throughout the summer months to printers and maids, to box-makers and clerks, and picnics and excursions became as important a foundation for loyalty to the Union as did matters industrial. The success of this venture prompted more speculative moves. The Annual Report for 1924 recorded that the Union had 'acquired a field at Killiney, close to the station and the sea, for a summer recreation club. A tennis ground has been made there which will be fit for use in the coming summer'.[21] Social concerns undoubtedly moved beyond the immediate, and the formation of the Civic Committee formalised the procedure for implementing IWWU proposals for change at the social level. From the mid-1920s onwards, its brief extended to discussion of the question of raising a fund for the building of working-class houses, and circulars giving details of the scheme were issued from the IWWU, 'it being felt that the demand would come most effectively from women'.[22]

By this time unemployment among women, already widespread, was aggravated by the displacement of workers following the introduction of new machinery. Such change was accompanied by employer moves to link rules governing the employment of women in printing to the agreed introduction of time dockets, the speeding up of machinery and the use of work measurement schemes. The early warnings of such change in the work process prompted the Executive to again urge members to consider extending industrial concerns to the formal political arena.

At a special convention in October 1924, the Executive

sought a mandate to promote a political fund to be directed towards the election of women to local government and public boards. The Union's rules as presently construed, they argued, gave it no power either to nominate its own, or to support candidates nominated by other Labour bodies. The mandate was not forthcoming. From Messrs Dollards in particular the women in printing indicated that they were emphatically opposed to the raising of monies for such a fund, and delegates from Browne and Nolan voiced the concerns of their members by pointing to the more pressing needs of the unemployed. Instructing delegates to the convention to return to their members and discuss the matter, Miss Bennett proposed that the general meeting to be called to discuss the formation of a political fund would now also formulate a Union response to unemployment.

The anxieties of the women in the workplace were not without foundation. At H. M. Woods, Boxmakers, a machine had been installed which displaced ten women and employed 'two girls who were underpaid,'[23] and the introduction of pressing machines into the laundries had dramatically reduced the wages of the ironers.[24] In March 1924 the IWWU rejected the Dublin Master Printers' Association's [DMPA] insistence that new rules governing the employment of women in the printing trade[25] should include the use of time dockets. Having secured by this stage only tentative agreement on spoiled work and on the ratio of apprentices to journeywomen, discussion on the rules ended dramatically following the DMPA demand. The IWWU outlined its opposition to the dockets and to the working methods intrinsic to their introduction:

> Under a daily time docket system the employer would lose the advantages he now gains from quick and willing workers, and the officials of the Union would be driven into the position of advising women to make out for themselves a standard of output which would not penalise the slower workers. . . . This would be more essential because the women have not won the security the men have, in a rule limiting the number of apprentices in proportion to journey women.[26]

The continuing lack of specific rules governing ratios of journeywomen to apprentices would now, however, assist the employers who 'can always draw on a large reserve of unemployed girls and the temptation to weed out all but the most efficient women becomes irresistible'.[27] At Goodbody's, the move had already begun, but when time dockets were proposed by management they were roundly rejected by the women workers. Moves to mechanise the work process were combined with proposals from employers that women accept piece rates rather than time rates for machine folding,[28] and at Messrs Thom it was 'proposed to put feeders on folding work when not busy on machines'. In the absence of any more persuasive means to hand, women workers were instructed by their Executive to combine their resources and to resist.

The widespread impact of unemployment in undermining the demands of those at work effectively cleared the industrial agenda of other concerns. Following the organisation of a public meeting in October 1925 to discuss a response on behalf of the unemployed, the IWWU authorised a propaganda poster and began to campaign in earnest. The Union proposed reforms in the Unemployment Insurance Act to extend the rights of widows with one child and of single women with no dependants, and sent an open letter to all members of the Dáil and Seanad urging them to 'secure relief for the unemployed by extending the payment of Unemployment Benefit to all disemployed men and women'.[29] It protested further that special relief was being given through the machinery of the Poor Law rather than through employment exchanges, thus suggesting charity rather than entitlement. At the opening of the Dáil session in November, Miss Molony and Miss O'Connor organised a poster campaign, 'which attracted much interest'. The campaign, organised in cooperation with the Council of the Unemployed, involved weekly meetings of the unemployed where speakers from the Union were prominent, and culminated in a deputation to the Civic Commissioners and the Poor Law Commission. The results were claimed to be dramatic:

> A procession of men and women marched first to the

> City Hall and set their demands before Commissioner Murphy; we then marched to the Dublin Union where, being obliged to wait for two and a half hours to see the Commissioners, we were allowed to share the paupers' dinner. We claimed, among other things, the immediate starting of relief works, the opening of a Coal Fund, and provision of meals for women and children. Within a week all these claims were fulfilled in part .[30]

This campaign served to redefine priorities in relation to political allegiances. When the Labour Party wrote in March appealing for help and support in their political organisation, the tempering effect of the politics of the workplace was made clear: 'it was agreed that in reply the IWWU should express its regret that the Party was not equally concerned about industrial matters'.[31] Other institutions of the labour movement were similarly admonished. On 10 December, following a letter from the Dublin Workers' Council [DWC] 'intimating they could do nothing more in furtherance of the unemployment campaign', the IWWU representatives resigned from the Council. The move represented the culmination of IWWU disaffection over a long period; the Annual Report for 1926, in announcing withdrawal from the Council, gave the basis for Union criticism.

> Your Committee have felt for a long time that the Workers' Council was not sufficiently active in the interests of Dublin trade unionists, and we especially disapproved of their failure to carry out any strong agitation on behalf of the unemployed.

This largely tactical withdrawal was not without political purpose, and served as a prelude to later moves made by the IWWU, and particularly by Helena Molony, to organise a conference of those unions affiliated neither to the Workers' Council nor the Trades' Council, with a view to forming proposals for healing the breach between the two bodies that had occurred in 1921.

CHAPTER 6

An Bhean Oibre

When women workers had initially resisted granting a mandate to establish a political fund, the grounds advanced were that more pressing matters warranted attention. The unemployment campaign itself, and the housing campaign inaugurated by the Union and now supported by 'a group of concerned persons', had, however, received prominent and pleasing coverage in the national press, while the increased use of propaganda posters marked the development of an awareness by the Executive of the need to publicise widely the impact of the Union and all its works. This consciousness of the need for further organisation and for propaganda was not confined to the leadership. At the Annual Convention Miss Molony thought 'more extensive effort should be made to organise honorary or associate members, women of all classes who take an interest in women's work',[1] and from the floor of the Convention 'some of the delegates expressed the wish that a monthly propaganda paper or sheet be run by the IWWU, and promised help in distribution'. The question of a journal was raised again at the Organising Committee and on 10 March 1926, 'it was decided to have it an eight-page paper and to print 2,000 copies at first'. In May 1926 Volume 1, No. 1, of *An Bhean Oibre* [The Woman Worker], was published, price 1*d*. (one penny).

An Bhean Oibre served a number of functions. In 'Workshop Talk' members were urged to reflect upon major questions confronting the Union and to propose resolutions for Convention:

'Is the IWWU to take any part in the forthcoming elections?

'Are we to nominate candidates for the Labour Party Panel?'[2]

'What are we to do to press forward the campaign for shorter working hours?'[3]

'How are we to end the system which is making Dublin a centre of industrial employment for little girls?'[4]

It served to alert members to moves by employers to speed up machinery and to 'institute a system of shorter hours and reduced wages'. Such moves were widely resisted in the laundries, where the idea 'was to secure the same output of work in a shorter period of hours', a move considered 'particularly pernicious' in an industry 'where the hot, moist atmosphere already tends to weary and debilitate the workers'.[5] Similar tactics were evident in the tobacco industry, and notice was served on its managers

> that we, Irishwomen, mean to uphold human life and health as more valuable than big dividends.[6]

The pages of the monthly paper were also used to articulate the basis for policy decisions and to seek a mandate for any changes proposed. The IWWU's reasons for advancing protectionist trade policies as a safeguard for Irish industry — a policy upon which the labour movement as a whole was divided — were given in great detail. Further information, couched in colourful and provocative terms, was provided in relation to working conditions. In the case of the nurses and other workers in charitable institutions:

> They wear out their health in long hours, hard work and hard conditions, for a miserable salary, and they are expected to do it quite happily because it is so nice to be helping the sick poor! But if it's so nice to be doing these good works, why should only poor people be asked to sacrifice health and the ordinary comforts of life?
>
> Why not get the women who play bridge and golf and spend hours with their dressmakers, to do their share of these good works without any pay at all?[7]

An Bhean Oibre, in common with the membership, also had a lighter side which was well catered for in the pages of the journal. Short stories and hints on cooking and cleaning competed for space with 'Replies from Salome' — a column in which moral certitude was the order of the day. To 'No Longer Worried', Salome replied:

'I am glad that you took my advice. Never forget that your Maker loves you'.

'Davis', from Terenure, however, was upbraided for the audacious tone of her letter, which

'. . . suggests you contemplate proposing to him? You are an exceedingly foolish girl. You will lose him absolutely if you attempt such a thing'.[8]

Once the married state had been achieved, however, Salome dispelled any lingering confusion. To 'Married' she issued this warning:

'You say you don't love your husband. Well, you had better make up your mind to try and love him. Remember you have only been married three weeks'.

For those more securely wed, few confusions were evident regarding woman's place, and Salome served notice on her readers that the IWWU would not support unconditionally the right of married women to work. 'Worker' was clearly instructed on correct procedure:

'You say your husband objects to your going back to work. Well, considering he is earning £4 a week, don't you realise he is right? I think you are exceedingly selfish to want to take up a job which you don't need when there is so much unemployment'.[9]

The effect of the paper either as propaganda or as an information sheet is difficult to gauge. By 1927 the Executive was raising questions about its financial viability, and although it continued into 1928 it was distributed free of charge and was used primarily as a means of internal education and propaganda.[10] This marked a further development in the function of the Union, as it widened its brief to include the education of its own membership. As an institution for working women, it protested at threats from whatever quarter to the rights of working people; it was, in fact, the first Union to recognise that the wage of 32s. offered to men working a 50-hour week on the Shannon Electrification Scheme 'was a direct threat to the women workers' standard of wages'. The move was presented as an attempt to 'drag Irish workers

Lambkin's tobacco factory, Fishers Street, Merchant's Quay, Cork, pre-1920

Raspberry picking on Jennings' farm, Victoria Cross, Cork, pre-1920. Our Lady's Mental Hospital in the background

Women workers at Cleeve's toffee factory in Limerick during the 1920s

The folding room at the printing works of M.H. Gill and Son, Dublin about 1930

Contrasting poses of Countess Markievicz, President of the Irish Women Workers' Union in 1918

Members of the Irish Women Workers' Union outside Liberty Hall, Dublin in 1913

A group of workers at the Dublin Labour Conference on the steps of Liberty Hall in 1921

back to the sweated level by exploiting the miseries of the unemployed'.[11]

By now such miseries were close to home and there were a considerable number of women on the Union's own unemployment register. In the printing industry, slump was widespread and the industry itself faced structural change with new machinery and competition from imported printed matter. Skilled labour, male and female, was leaving Ireland and many journeywomen were unemployed. Between 1924 and 1925, 230 women from Printing and the Kindred Trades had become unemployed, and any work in binding, stationery and paper bags was under continual threat. While the Union submitted a memorandum to the Minister of Industry and Commerce in support of protection for the printing industry, a series of letters which followed in *The Irish Times* in November debated the virtues or otherwise of such a move. In December, the IWWU participated in the printers' demonstration — a demonstration which was pronounced by all to be 'a huge success', and all printers, including the printers' section of the Union, were levied for the 'Protection Penny' to finance the campaign.

The situation became critical in Waterford. Wages for women were now 'so low as to be a danger to the Printing Trade', and in Dublin, moves to increase the use of juvenile labour threatened to undermine all gains made for women in the trade since 1917. Protectionist instincts, already signalled in *An Bhean Oibre*, and undoubtedly finding echoes within the membership, led to moves from the printers' section of the Union to exclude married women (other than widows) from work in the industry. How much support such sentiments had was unclear: Soon after this the section found a new focus for grievances, this time outside the ranks of their own union, with the first signs of a major threat to the IWWU itself.

In February 1926 the Executive, alerting members to indications that the Amalgamated Society of Bookbinders [ASB] 'are about to try to enlist our members into their union', issued a directive to eight IWWU members at Browne and Nolan who had already succumbed to the promises of the Bookbinders:

> Your decision and that of a few others to join a Trade Union with headquarters in, and governed from, a foreign country has raised an issue which the Union takes a very serious view of. . . . We therefore warn you that membership of the IWWU is an essential qualification if you wish to continue working in the Printing Trade in Dublin. . . . In the event of your ignoring this notice you will be liable to penalties under Rule 25, Paragraph 2, which will be vigorously enforced.[12]

With the threat of further defections close on her heels, Miss Bennett approached the Dublin branch of the Binders' Union, but received scant welcome. She proceeded to register the basis for Union disquiet in a letter to Mr Harroway, General President of the Amalgamated Binders, who, after proposing that he would deal with the matter on a visit to Dublin in March, expressed the hope 'that a way may be found out of this very awkward position'. Meanwhile he wrote to his Dublin branch to enquire about the basis for the complaint, and to question the claim of the branch secretary, Mr Burke, that Head Office in England had sanctioned the move to recruit members of the women workers.

'I should be pleased if you inform me who gave these instructions', he wrote. 'Poaching upon the membership of another recognised trade union is not the right way of obtaining peace and concord.'[13]

Despite a clear lack of official approval, the Dublin section continued its recruitment campaign. Members at Browne and Nolan who had joined their numbers had provoked great indignation among members loyal to the IWWU and 'it has been extremely difficult to prevent an instant and unofficial strike with the firm concerned'. With suspicion rife, many IWWU members felt constrained to reassert their loyalty:

> It is rumoured through Browne and Nolan's firm that I am a member of the Amalgamated Binder's Union. I hereby denigh this as it is not true. I am a member of the IWWU since I started my apprenticeship in Messrs Browne and Nolan and intend to continue my membership during the period I shall have to continue working in the trade.[14]

The Printers' Section, resisting any moves to deplete its ranks, was adamant; if the girls did not return to the fold 'our members would not work with them'. The Binders, however, had also reviewed their position. Changing tactics, Mr Harraway wrote asking if, indeed, the IWWU was in a position to secure the best terms for its members in the printing industry. Although, as a trade unionist, against the concept of 'poaching' on principle, Mr Harroway would, he suggested, now concede the IWWU right to continue organising those women who had been its members since 1917 only 'if you were in the position of rendering the best services to these women'. If, in effect, the Amalgamated Binders believed they could render better service to women in printing, they would respect no boundaries in regard to efforts to recruit, or poach, from the IWWU. The IWWU pointed to a membership in the trade of 1,600. The Amalgamated, they suggested, could boast but eight, all poached, and of these 'two are now disemployed, and one under notice owing to slackness'. Mr Harroway was warned not to assume that attempts to deplete the Printers' Section of the IWWU would enhance the ranks of the Binders by default.

> . . . if a breakdown in our organisation occurs, some discontents would go to your union, some to the Irish Binders, some to the Transport Union and some to Larkin's union. We believe we would still hold the majority, but real bargaining power on behalf of women would be lost.[15]

What was not added, but what had become a matter of the gravest concern, was that the break-up of the Printers' Section, the strongest section in the Union, could spell the demise of the IWWU.

The Dublin Section of the Amalgamated Binders' Union [ABU] agreed to meet the IWWU. They argued that to discontinue their campaign of recruitment from among the ranks of the IWWU would require sanction from their headquarters. The IWWU, on the other hand, looked to the reinstatement of 'our seceded members in this Union' for a satisfactory settlement to the dispute. The Amalgamated Binders' Union refused to give any such assurance that they recognised the

IWWU as the legitimate union for women in Printing and Kindred Trades [PKT] and final settlement was not forthcoming. Mr Harroway demanded, from the women, protection 'of the legitimate work of male binders' and an agreement on demarcation. The IWWU, for its part, argued that the code of honour regarding demarcation was already observed by its membership, but inter-union relationships deteriorated further when the interpretation of the agreement to settle the dispute was contested by both sides.

On 9 April the IWWU formulated a resolution for the attention of Mr Harroway:

> Unless we receive in this office not later than 14th proximate, a written agreement to the effect that the eight girls employed in the printing trades in Dublin now enrolled in the Amalgamated Binders' Union shall be re-transferred to the Irish Women Workers' Union, strike notice will be handed in to Messrs Browne and Nolan on the 15th April prox.[16]

Messrs Browne and Nolan were informed, and warned that, failing settlement, IWWU members would refuse to work with members of the Amalgamated Binders' Union. The Union sought a clear lead on the matter from Congress: 'The whole conduct of the Binders' Union in this case is a very ugly demonstration of the evil forces which are undermining the Trade Union Movement in Dublin'.[17]

Other unions were requested to voice their support by recognition of the IWWU as the 'only legitimate Trade Union for women in the Printing Trades'. The Transport Union demurred, having been involved in such organisation as long as the IWWU, but others responded positively. From Britain, Mr Harroway washed his hands of further implications and the question would now have to be resolved at local level. Pending discussion, further moves were postponed, but members were eager for action and they were 'furiously indignant because we had postponed the strike'. The Dublin Masters were warned that members straying from the 'legitimate union' had been suspended 'as they have been guilty of actions antagonistic to the interests of the IWWU', and were told that any employment of those out of work would lead to further trouble.

By the end of April the IWWU had deepened its resolve and now refused any settlement other than that 'every woman in the Printing Trade in Dublin shall hold a card of the Irish Women Workers' Union'. Such a move was seen as critical. Should the IWWU concede that the Amalgamated Binders had a right to organise among already organised women workers, several other unions would undoubtedly advance similar claims.

On 3 May 1926, such resolve reaped dividends. At a joint meeting of unions involved in the trade, a resolution recognising the IWWU as the legitimate union for women in the trade was accepted and the dispute came to an end. Miss Bennett offered her congratulations to her members. 'We are very proud of the fidelity to the IWWU shown by our members. So long as we all hold solidly together as we have done over this dispute, we can never be defeated.'[18]

Although such disputes threatened to undermine gains made by the Union, the resolution of specific questions, such as the right to organise women in Printing and Kindred Trades, represented a development for women in the labour movement. By the mid 1920s, however, the range of problems confronting organised female labour presented few such avenues for negotiation and, for a period at least, the demands of employers dominated the industrial scene.

The Union considered the problem of unemployment to be directly linked to control of imports and the increased use of juvenile and sweated labour, to the erosion of skills and to the introduction of new machinery. Few difficulties could be effectively confronted without concessions being made when a cheaper, more vulnerable workforce was readily available, where non-union printing houses accepted methods deemed to be contrary to the interests of the trade unions, and where institutional laundries submitted the lowest tenders for work which was to be done at cost by a somewhat captive workforce.[19] Other employers, such as the ever inventive Mr Mitchell, proposed that the salvation of his bead factory lay in government agreement to the use of cheaper labour — the employment of 'girls in the West of Ireland on "decade work" in their own homes'. In 1926 the Dublin Printers' Protection Campaign resumed, to confront anticipated struggles over work measurement: 'It is thought that the question of time dockets is very serious'. Meanwhile, the IWWU raised questions on the effect of extensive use of the new Roneo machines.

For the IWWU, related problems loomed large. In its Annual Report in 1926 members were alerted to the most serious problem it now confronted — the introduction of ironing machines and the consequent displacement of skilled laundry workers. In the summer of 1925 the management at E.G. Dunlop Laundry had arranged for the Calender and Collar Rooms to work a short time system on a temporary basis — groups of workers would remain out, in turn, on Mondays, and would lose their wages and bonuses for that day. When the summer was over, however, and extra work from the colleges resumed, the system of short time became permanent. Claiming increased problems related to the coal shortage, management deprived ironers of a day's work but, as trade continued at the same level, demanded a 'speeding up' on other days of the week. Already angered by the loss of the Monday bonus, the ironers now confronted their gradual displacement by the introduction of presser machines.

Women laundry workers were paid under the terms of the Piece-Work Schedule. Commercial laundries, extensively used, offered a range of services covering both personal and domestic linen. For 'dress shirts, hand ironed throughout, but not polished', women were paid 2s. 4d. per dozen, and for pleated dress shirts, subject to the same attentions, '2s. 9d. a dozen'. By 1925 an experienced piece worker who had 'been in the habit of earning upwards of £2 per week' was required instead to work a presser machine at the minimum time rate of 30s. per week. To fulfil their own promise of a cheaper service, Phoenix 'Snowhite' Laundry offered 'the Family Wash for 2s. 6d.' and refused, together with other employers, to contemplate negotiating with the IWWU on a fixed claim for 37s. 6d. a week for all ironers. In March 1926, Louie Bennett wrote to the Leinster Laundries' Association [LLA]:

> I am instructed to remind you that our Annual Convention gave very serious consideration to the position of the workers where new machinery is introduced which displaces hand workers, and we were also instructed to use all the resources of the Irish Women Workers' Union in order to safeguard the interests of our members subjected to such conditions.[20]

The LLA, having recently conceded, after a struggle lasting three years, the Union's claim for one week's holiday for laundresses, refused to enter into further discussions. In the face of the increased use of juvenile labour, the Union now moved to negotiate a reduction in overtime rates and the drawing up of a new schedule for junior workers in return for a reduction in the working week throughout the industry from forty-seven to forty-four hours. The introduction of a wage schedule for juniors conceded ground but, in doing so, the Union was endeavouring to impose some control on the movement of young girls into laundries to operate machinery and to displace experienced, and more expensive, older workers.

> We are willing to make this concession to offset the proposal re the 44 hour week, because we are anxious to substitute payment on the basis of experience for the basis of age, as we are of the opinion that 14 and 15 years is too early an age for a girl to leave school to take up industrial work.[21]

The LLA again refused, claiming that the forty-seven hours then worked was a shorter working week than that which obtained in the industry outside Dublin. In the prevailing industrial climate, threatened stoppages had little impact in the face of employer resistance and stalemate was conceded. The failure of the Union to achieve any major advance either in relation to shorter hours or to the presser machines prompted some members at the Metropolitan Laundry to refuse to pay further membership dues. In a spirited response, the Union suggested that there was a distinct lack of solidarity on this front, as 'the workers involved would not co-operate in any action we might have taken'.[22]

In the absence of any significant progress in the commercial field, the IWWU gave free rein to its opposition to the Institution Laundries. In 1928 it urged the Contracts Officer, Office of National Education, to consider carefully institutional tenders for the laundry work for preparatory colleges. While charitable institutions could present lower tenders, the Union politely argued that greater concerns should weigh in the balance, and that a gain to the state in the short term would inevitably lead to the disemployment of wage earners. 'May we venture to urge you, in the interests of women wage-earners, to make it a stipulation that these contracts shall be given to commercial laundries only?'[23]

IWWU members at Sir Patrick Dun's Hospital had been subjected to 'every form of intimidation to make them give up their trade union'. In a tirade against all such institutions, *An Bhean Oibre* challenged hospital laundries run on the lines of charitable institutions.

> It is a strange fact that charitable institutions are often most uncharitable towards their employees. We are always coming up against the notion that it is the duty of women to toil and slave for a starvation wage if they are working for a charitable organisation.[24]

Threatening to use all their wiles in defence of the 'staunch little band of members there', the Executive promised to 'make things hot for the Board of Sir Patrick Dun's'.

Despite the ability of the Hospital Board to be 'as slippery as an eel', the Union served notice that conditions must, and would, change, by whatever method was necessary to move a Board whose meetings 'are so few and far between and are kept so secret that a trade union official can only get into them by fraud or force'.[25]

The IWWU had secured its right, within the trade union movement, to organise women in Printing and Kindred Trades. Its widespread recognition by employers as the negotiating body for women workers was not, however, conceded without a struggle, or without major concessions being made.

The position of many women in industry was governed by

decisions of the Trades' Boards. For those industries considered sweated and non-organised, the machinery of the Boards had been established to fix a minimum rate to be agreed by the representatives of government, employers and trade unions on the Board. The IWWU, regarding this machinery as something which undermined the function of a trade union, had begun to campaign in 1924 for a Joint Industrial Council to replace the Cardboard Boxmakers' Trade Board, arguing that the increased prosperity of the trade and the more highly skilled work of handmade boxmaking made this industry a major potential employer for women. As such, it maintained, a Trade Board was inappropriate, particularly a Trade Board which consistently justified a minimum wage for Saorstát Éireann which was lower than that existing in England, a point of great contention 'especially when it is recalled that the cost of living is 8 points higher here than in England'.[26]

Since 1920 boxmakers, predominantly members of the IWWU and the ITGWU, had been paid the same as other women in Printing and Kindred Trades, and agreements negotiated by the unions covered all women. In 1922 a specific agreement between the IWWU and the Dublin Master Printers' Association settled wages for women in boxmaking at 33*s.* per week for those women with four years' experience. While no standard scale of piece work was negotiated, the rate for journeywomen was established. In 1928 three firms broke this wage agreement: Messrs Cherry and Smalldridge, O'Reilly's of Poolbeg Street, and the Dublin Box Company began to adopt various methods of undermining the negotiated agreement and compelled girls they employed to accept a reduction in wages. In March a meeting of employers in the Cardboard Box Trade was held and a proposal to reduce the minimum wage of time workers by 2*s.* was carried by a majority vote. The IWWU was not informed. When notices were posted on the factory floors in April, the Executive notified the three main firms concerned that the IWWU members would refuse to accept the reduction.

The Union argued — and this was supported throughout the trade union movement — that the dispute was 'a fight for general principles which are essential to Trade Unionism'.

The battles that followed, while their immediate objective was the maintenance of a fair wage standard for skilled women workers, were waged over the non-recognition of worker organisations and, by implication, the part played by the Trade Board structure in assisting employers eager to establish minimum rates as the prevailing standards.

The existence of Trade Boards in a non-sweated and organised industry was a major point of dispute. The Union argued that in such conditions the Board 'simply serves as a medium to help the employers to reduce wages'. The employers' response was that the Trade Board governed the wage standard 'and that they will not recognise the right of any other organisation to negotiate with them in regard to wages, nor will they agree to enter into any conference with the trade union on that subject'. In appealing to the Minister of Industry and Commerce, Miss Bennett protested that such an attitude was contrary to the principle underlying the Trade Board system, that the right of trade unions to negotiate a higher scale was not questioned by the Trade Board Office, and 'we know of no precedent for the attempt now being made by the Cardboard Boxmakers, that is to oust completely the Trade Union where the Trade Board operates'.[27] By lodging a formal objection to the proposals the Union secured a delay of two months. Miss Bennett reassured the members and urged stronger support for the Union.

> I am glad to inform you that the proposed reduction is not to come into operation this week and no date has been fixed for it. So our fight is postponed for the present. But I hope all our members will realise that this victory is due to the activities of the IWWU and that all the workers will in future be staunch members of the Society.[28]

A large group of boxmakers joined the Union and promised resistance to the cuts. Despite the continuing threat, however, it proved impossible to organise the Dublin Box Company, and only ten members remained loyal to the Union when that company resumed battle three weeks later. At the end of June a further notice was posted on the shop floor, stating that the reduction would come into operation in a week's time. The Union sought ministerial intervention, and a settlement. Neither was forthcoming. With the approval of the Executive, 128 Boxmakers refused their wages and ceased work. In the majority of cases, to do otherwise would have been to accept a weekly reduction of 5s.

By July, Dublin streets were covered with posters: Government Boards were condemned for setting a standard of 'starvation wages'. Leaflets castigated 'scabs' and members of the public were urged to support the battle 'to maintain a bare living wage for women'. At Burgh Quay, the first of two open-air meetings were held, and attended by large summer crowds. The speakers included Senator Seán Campbell, Mr R. M. Fox, and Thomas Johnson. Mr Johnson, Leader of the Labour Party, spoke about Trade Boards and the tactics of employers:

> I want to make it clear that when a Trade Board fixes a rate, it is a minimum rate, not a standard rate: that is to say the least efficient, the most incompetent, the meanest, the greediest and most tyrannical employer is not allowed by law to fall below that rate when paying his workers.[29]

This minimum, he argued, was now proposed by employers as the prevailing rate for women in the trade.

Other unions offered moral and financial support. The ITGWU, the earliest organiser in the trade, now conceded that the IWWU represented the majority of workers. It agreed to transfer its workers, and to support the IWWU should it seek a position on the Trade Board.

Within other unions, however, 'scabbing' was evident. The Engineering Union was informed that the daughters of one of its members, 'two girls called Smith, are working as "scabs" in Messrs O'Reilly's Cardboard Box Factory'.[30] Labels for the Dublin Box Company were being printed in private houses, and a member of the Society of Lithographic Printers [SLP][31] was accused of 'working with "scab" labour and he is actually allowing a "scab" to do the work of a girl whose legitimate job it is to feed for him and who is now on strike'. Many women who had joined the Union in the first days of battle lapsed, and returned to work, but 126 stood firm — 'picketing, parading and distributing leaflets'. The Dublin Typographical Provident Society [DTPS] gave every assistance and all the trade unions 'who were in any way likely to come into contact with cardboard boxes' refused to handle the goods.

An Bhean Oibre prepared the troops for battle.

> We know that we are in for a tough fight. But we are not afraid! We're out to win. Success lies with the workers. Let them prove now their staying power as well as their talent for smart action. . . . Our women must prove themselves as invincible as any who have yet come out on strike in this city.[32]

Seven weeks into the strike, the employers resisted any proposal for a conference because they refused 'to recognise the right of the trade union to negotiate regarding wages'. While employers resisted, members on the picket line were charged in civil proceedings.

In August Sarah Melia, Boxmaker of Townsend Street, was brought to the District Court and found guilty of 'the use of language towards Bridgit Hanraty, one of the workers, calculated to cause a breach of the peace'. The defendant was fined 40s. The use of the courts in such matters, however, prompted a strong protest by the Union.

> If justice is administered to the workers in this way they will be left open to very serious tyranny by the police, and it is for this reason that we raise this protest and urge you to take steps to ensure that social prejudice shall not influence the decisions of the judges of Saorstát Éireann.[33]

Such incidents, provoked by widespread scabbing, were not isolated.

In September Miss K. O'Connor was arrested for having thrown a scab's bicycle into the Liffey. The Executive reported: 'We have engaged a solicitor and he recommends her to plead guilty as being the best method of dealing with the case'. Miss O'Connor declared 'that she would not pay fines or compensation and objected to the Union paying either'. It was finally decided that the Union would intervene only if Miss O'Connor were to face the prospect of imprisonment. In the absence of any further reference to the case, it must be assumed that Miss O'Connor did not meet such an undignified fate.[34]

On 21 September, Mr Smalldridge discussed with his employees the question of a resumption of work. The women refused to countenance any resumption other than by arrangement with their Union. Mr Smalldridge then handed the boxmakers an agreement, 'to be submitted to us', and suggested that Miss Bennett phone Cherry and Smalldridge if the agreement were accepted.[35] In doing so, Mr Smalldridge commenced negotiations with the IWWU. At 6.30 the same evening, members of the Union in the company met at Eden Quay. The Executive put the agreement to a vote: it accepted Trade Board rates as a minimum, not as a rate, and agreed reinstatement procedures. It was accepted unanimously, sanctioned by the Committee, and on Monday the women went back to work.

Messrs O'Reilly accepted mediation by Mr Ferguson of the Trade and Industry Branch of the Department of Industry and Commerce. He agreed that the Trade Board minimum wages were to be accepted as such, that at least thirty-five 'old workers' were to be reinstated immediately, and that no new hands would be employed until all on strike had been re-employed. When an exchange of lists of the thirty-five workers began, however, Mr O'Reilly proposed that 'old workers' be interpreted as workers who 'though they had not been employed at the date of the commencement of the strike had been employed by his firm during some of the weeks immediately preceding the strike'. Mr Ferguson, for the Department, and Miss Bennett, for the Union, protested. The conference was reconvened to reinterpret this dangerously ambiguous phrase. Towards the end of the month Messrs O'Reilly submitted a new list. 'Before the vote was taken Miss Bennett explained that neither she nor the Executive recommended the acceptance of the list, which excluded some of the oldest workers'.[36]

The officials agreed with Miss Bennett, and urged the women to 'hold out' until the older workers were accepted back. Members disagreed. The matter was put to a vote, and passed unanimously. The list was accepted, and work at

Messrs O'Reilly's resumed. On foot of this settlement, the Dublin Box Company was approached by Miss Chenevix and Miss O'Connor. Having previously agreed to accept whatever terms Cherry and Smalldridge and Messrs O'Reilly agreed, Mr Woakes of Dublin Box now 'intimated that he had workers enough'. He agreed to see six girls, with no Union officials present. Three were re-employed, and the remainder would also be taken back when the need arose.

The outcome of the strike was difficult to assess. The trade union movement was united in supporting the women. Scabbing, however, undermined their case and the extent of non-union labour within the industry made any trade union vulnerable. With the cooperation of the ITGWU, the IWWU now applied for representation on the Cardboard Boxmakers' Trade Board [CBTB]. Settlement of the strike had included acceptance of the Trade Board rates as a minimum: representation on the Board itself would ensure long battles to increase the 28s. a week deemed appropriate for boxmakers. The settlement had also obliged employers to negotiate with their employees' representatives, and Trade Board decisions could not preclude further union/employer negotiations above the minimum. A battle of sorts had been won, but the losses were plain to be seen; there was bitterness towards workers who had stayed in and towards members of the Union who had scabbed, and other workers were never reinstated. For the Union, there was a recognition that structures, such as Trades' Boards, once erected, were notoriously difficult to change. For Miss Bennett, adamant in her refusal to accept a position on such Boards herself,[37] there was the acknowledgment that, in industries where women were employed, representation on the structures involved in establishing minimum rates was essential. In 1927 she had proposed, and the Executive had accepted, that the IWWU take part in Trade Boards for a year at least. The name of Miss McKnight, boxmaker, was forwarded to the Minister for Industry and Commerce and in December 1928 she became the first member of the IWWU to accept a position on a Trade Board.

Such major disputes occurred against a background of more general moves to erode women's wages — moves that received scant attention from political bodies. Towards the end of 1927, President Cosgrave had refused to appoint a woman to the Relief of Unemployment Committee [RUC]. When its report was released in February 1928 it contained no reference to women. Although all political parties had been represented on the Committee, the Union directed its criticisms at the Labour Party, 'pointing out that this ignoring of women workers had taken place in spite of the fact that there were Labour members on the Unemployment Committee.'[38]

The Executive sanctioned, too late, the issuing of leaflets and posters to formalise the protest. Members of the Senate and Dáil were circularised, and interviews were given to the press. The exclusion had been as unexpected as it was unwarranted; quite clearly, the question of the employment of women had no place on the political agenda. Its absence reflected, in part, the context of the times. In the 1920s women at work were deemed a transient, often awkward, and minority group; to be employed was considered for them, by definition, to be a less desirable status than marriage and motherhood. It reflected also the absence of women from the mainstream political movements, and the continuing refusal by the IWWU rank and file to give the Union's allegiance to a political party, or to allow the Executive to develop its own political wing.

CHAPTER 7

Paradise of Dissent

While *An Bhean Oibre,* in keeping with its function as an organ of propaganda, celebrated 'progress' and 'the steady growth of numbers', the finer detail of industrial life was somewhat blurred. The 'latest addition to our ranks is the firm of Watson & Warnock: Shirtmakers'; shirtmakers in another place[1] protested at the dismissal of 'old workers . . . to make room for younger workers', and the proposal from the Shirtmaking Industry Trade Board that rates be reduced by a halfpenny an hour.[2] With some pride, the women in the finishing trade were cheered for resistance to cuts, and were claimed to be 'organised 99% and a minimum standard of wages now established all round'.[3] Others, however, fared less well.

Armstrong's threatened either the closure of their factory or a reduction of the wages paid to women workers to 28s. a week. They suggested also that the introduction of time dockets would restore prosperity, and hence security, to the trade. Although 'feeling was against same', the Printers' Committee decided that the proposal 'was not a time docket in the objectionable sense', and accepted the terms on a temporary basis.[4] The Dublin Master Printers' Association, citing Armstrong's as a precedent, offered to resume the abandoned talks on rules to govern the employment of women in the printing trade.

Meanwhile, at Portrane Mental Hospital, the Union endorsed the initiative taken by nurses to institute legal proceedings against their employers. Wage reductions had been proposed and, although advised that the agreement which the nurses had already signed accepting 'dismissal without notice' as a condition of employment had weakened their case, the Union allocated finance to allow proceedings to continue 'in order to show up the conditions under which nurses are employed'.[5] Pursuing legal procedure for the first time, the members and Executive awaited judgment on the endeavour to improve the lot of the nursing profession.

At Eden Quay, however, all was not well. On 27 February 1929, Louie Bennett, General Secretary of the IWWU, resigned. An unspecified malaise and the added burden of an invalid mother were in part responsible: the proposed move had been tentatively placed on the Union's internal agenda since Christmas. On the settlement of the boxmakers' strike, Miss Bennett had taken leave of absence. By February, the combined effect of ill health, and a disposition directed more towards political rather than industrial matters, had prompted her to propose a major reorganisation of the IWWU. Henceforth the position of General Secretary would be held in tandem by the Misses Bennett and Chenevix, with the duties and salary appropriately divided. At the meeting called — in Miss Bennett's continuing absence — to discuss the alternatives of either restructuring the Union or of accepting Miss Bennett's resignation, the Executive was in disarray.

The implications of restructuring were both political and financial. Miss Molony argued against any arrangement which would result in Miss Bennett, after her resignation, continuing as 'a minor official'. This, she suggested, might be publicly misconstrued as demotion, and would also either create a new post, which the Union could not afford, or would displace some other official. Miss Byrne confirmed such reservations: Miss Molony was 'voicing the feelings of the members in this matter, as this extra expense was not to their liking'. Miss Chenevix, whose own brief would greatly expand if the restructuring occurred, outlined her position. Although originally salaried on a part-time basis, she had voluntarily relinquished any payment and had accepted only £2 per month on the basis of expenses incurred in the course of her union activities. In effect, she had served as assistant to Miss Bennett for some time. The arrangement in regard to expenses had lasted until Christmas when, in Miss Bennett's absence, Miss Chenevix had undertaken 'to do her work' and

Miss Bennett had insisted that she share her salary while such an arrangement continued. In the light of such revelations, the Executive now proposed that Miss Chenevix receive a full salary, pending settlement. Miss Chenevix, however, refused, and the meeting was adjourned.

On 5 March Miss Bennett returned, and enlarged upon the terms on which she would be prepared to continue her official association with the Union. She was, she suggested, prepared to continue dealing with 'Printers, Trade Boards, Factory Legislation, etc.', and would oversee office procedure, while Miss Chenevix would take responsibility for major negotiations with the employers. She would require, in addition, a further two months' leave and would propose that Miss Chenevix would assume her office as General Secretary in the interim. Despite misgivings, this proposal was accepted by the Executive for recommendation to the Convention in May.

Contributions from other speakers on this occasion suggested general dissatisfaction with the internal structures of the Union. Miss McDowell, whose position in the Union had never been made permanent, had already applied for a position outside the Union offering '£3 a week, and stood a good chance of getting it'. The possibility of losing Miss McDowell prompted Miss Chenevix to speak on her behalf. She stressed the value of Miss McDowell's services to the IWWU (in part administrative and in part official), and 'then intimated that she would be very willing to give 10s. per week off her salary in order to keep Miss McDowell'. Such characteristic generosity on the part of Miss Chenevix did not resolve the difficulties, but as all salaries and duties were subject to review at the Annual Convention a decision was taken that 'this matter could stand over'.

At Convention, on 1 May 1929, the rooms at Eden Quay boasted a 'full attendance of delegates' representing 2,553 working women: Printers (1,232), Laundresses (741), General Workers (498) and Mental Nurses (82). Miss Bennett, recently returned from leave, read the Annual Report, and recorded a difficult year. In the wake of the boxmakers' strike came calls for solidarity within the trade union movement and a ringing indictment of the machinery of the Trade Boards.

> Whereas, the exploitation of the cheap labour of women and girls is one of the causes of unemployment and poverty amongst men as well as women, this Convention protests strongly against the tendency of Trade Boards to lower the wage standard of women and girls and calls upon all workers to join in a united effort to secure for women a fair living wage and equal pay with men for equal work.[6]

From the floor the Misses Coady, Connolly and O'Kelly, of Falconer's, Kilmainham, expressed a sentiment borne of the difficulties of the times. In a motion which provoked long discussion, they urged the Convention to agree

> That no married woman (whose husband is in work) be allowed to work, there being too many single girls unemployed.[7]

Delegates voiced 'mixed opinions on the matter'. No proposal for a resolution of this undoubted conflict of interests, however, was forthcoming. The matter was deferred and the motion directed to the Printers' Section for their consideration.

From the Joint Meeting of the Executive and Finance Committees came a report that the Union faced 'the apparent necessity to reduce expenditure'. With an income of just over £60 per week, expenditure on salaries was reputed to be exceeding one third of that amount. Consultation with the staff had taken place, but it was not considered feasible either to reduce staff numbers or to ask officials to take further cuts in their rates of pay. While current expenditure was approved, there were notable casualties. There would be no increase for Miss McDowell and, for Miss Chenevix, a remuneration hardly commensurate with the work ahead of her. For Miss Bennett, there was a short term resolution of her dilemma and an indefinite postponement of an Executive decision; it was agreed that 'for the coming year the General Secretary may share her duties and her salary with the Assistant Secretary'.

On instructions from the Convention, and in recognition of the need to expand in terms of membership and resources, the Executive reviewed organisation procedure. Suggestions ranged from the orthodox to the exotic, with matters of finance and the need for supervision from Eden Quay the only constraints in evidence. Despite hard times, enthusiasm from the membership was unstinted. On May Day, a 'tableau' from the IWWU featured prominently in the daily press. Civic Week, June 1929, was utilised 'for propaganda purposes. A boat on the river as a suggestion met with general approval. And the singing therein of Labour songs'.[8]

Miss Molony, as Chairman of the Organising Committee, reported on plans to organise by industry. Outside Dublin non-union shops, particularly in printing, were 'having a negative effect on the position of the Dublin workers', and among clerks it was noted with some concern that 'unorganised men clerks are a danger in these industries'.[9] Plans were laid to organise in shirtmaking and textiles, and in cooperation with the now re-united Dublin Trades' Council, the Executive of which included Miss Molony, to run public meetings and to further promote the 'Back to the Unions Campaign' sponsored by Waterford Trades' Council. In recognition of the tools to hand, it was also thought 'that some publicity propaganda might be done through the medium of the cinema if it can be done at a reasonable price'.

Throughout industry, changes in ownership and work practices demanded from officials and members alike vigilance and expertise beyond that required in the early years. Officials were urged to acquaint themselves with literature on trade unions, cooperatives, and social policy. Recognition of the complexity of the new terrain prompted the formation of union study groups and the inclusion in the library of books by Webb on *Industrial Democracy*, and by Rowntree and Lasker on *Unemployment: A Social Study*. In addition the Union supported the move by the Dublin Trades' Council to set up a Political and Industrial Committee, 'an explanation having been given that the aim of the political arm of the Council was not parliamentary honours, but an effort to educate workers on political outlook as it affects Labour.'

Education for both members and officials, however, continued to come primarily from the confronting of problems at source. When Messrs Goodbody's closed, the firm's failure was attributed to 'undue competition from foreign countries', and many old workers were among the IWWU members given one month's notice after thirty years' service. A deputation from the Union to the Minister of Industry and Commerce protested at the effect of combines undercutting home industry, 'the crushing out of Irish concerns by Imperial competition'. Mr Dolan, acting for the Minister, 'expressed himself as being sensible to the menace of control by foreign capital, and the suggestion of licences was discussed'.[10] The Union, confident that appeals on a personal level would not be ignored, requested a meeting with shareholders; this was refused. In turn, the Government was roundly criticised for refusing to protect native industry, workers castigated for preferring Imperial tobacco to their own, and the 'Smoke Irish' campaign deemed a resounding failure. Members meanwhile were urged to be vigilant in noting any increase in English workers in the new factories. Messrs Carrolls (which had, the Executive noted, received concessions including remission of rates, relief of income tax, etc.), offered Goodbody's 'girls' employment at rates lower than those enjoyed outside Dublin. In the absence of any other option, many accepted.

In July the verdict on the Union's first incursion into the legal machinery of the State was delivered, and the Portrane nurses won their case for a restitution of arrears of salary. They promised loyalty to the Union and gave thanks for financial assistance rendered. By August, however, an appeal against the judgment had been lodged, and the case began its long journey through the machinery of the legal system.[11] The Union, buoyant nonetheless from its success in using this machinery for the benefit of working women, now turned its attention to the legal status of laundry workers. These workers, despite their employment under factory conditions, as in Command Laundry, remained classified as workers 'in domestic service'. As such, they had no entitlements under the Unemployment Acts. The workers at Command, the Union argued, were industrial workers, and proceedings began to seek an interpretation of the status of these 'domestic workers' by the Irish courts. The Command

Laundry Insurance Case was heard at Dublin Castle on 29 November. On 16 January 1930 the case went to the High Court. Mrs Buckley and a laundress from Command attended all proceedings, a full account of which appeared in *The Irishman* the following week when judgment was given in favour of the workers.[12]

The Laundresses were more than any other group in the Union at this time, affected by changing industrial methods, and by the use of juvenile male labour on pressing machines and on processes, such as starching, an area 'always women's work'.[13] A number of reforms had by now been implemented in the control of working hours, but the demand for starched collars and fancy ironing throughout the year laid the foundation for major grievances related to the length of the working day and the need for paid holidays. Following a decision by Leinster Laundries' Association to introduce staggered holidays (in preference to block holidays), and to employ a temporary workforce throughout the summer, the Laundry Council of the IWWU detailed safeguards to ensure that the permanent workforce would suffer no disadvantage. Wider questions concerning machinery and shorter hours were placed on the agenda for the Laundry AGM, but as members had already indicated their reluctance to fight the introduction of the new methods in any concerted way, little discussion was evident. The move threatening immediate erosion of handwork, both washing and ironing, and the use of young boys in the laundries, did, however, encourage new recruits. In 1930 Milltown, Kelso and Terenure Laundries were welcomed to the Union ranks and the Executive promoted the formalisation of set rules to govern the laundry trade.

The continuing absence of such rules in the printing industry led to much abuse, and in the face of widespread unemployment demarcation problems became the focus of disputes between unions. At Cahills, an urgent report to the Union gave an account of the firm 'cultivating a growing habit of employing boy feeders'. The rate for women feeders was 10s. more than that given to such juveniles, and 'today a boy was put on a feeding machine though there were three girl machine feeders on the premises, and are unemployed'.

Cahills, in their defence, reported that women were now doing work on the folding machines which had previously been done by boys.

The Annual Convention of 1929 had reiterated, despite the concession at Armstrongs, the Union's opposition to the introduction of time dockets, but differences were evident between houses and between officials and the question eventually prompted a ballot of all members in printing. There were 506 votes against, 58 for, and 11 spoiled ballot papers. As part of an attempt to circumvent the 'stubborn attitude' of the Master Printers in refusing to continue negotiations unless the dockets were accepted, an attempt was made to negotiate agreements in relation to the employment of apprentices and to adopt general rules of procedure with individual employers. The Executive sponsored the drafting of rules, despite the Masters' refusal to recognise them. Their major function would be to instruct the women workers themselves and thus dissuade them from their tendency to 'feign ignorance of what work they may or may not handle'. The matter, long-term, demanded resolution, and the Annual Report in 1930 echoed feeling throughout the industry when it noted: 'the time is coming throughout the industry when the Printer must take strong action to secure such an agreement'. The moment, however, was not yet considered opportune.

The IWWU Social Club, revived in the mid-1920s, organised drama and swimming, gymnasium on Friday nights, and regular day trips to Wicklow, the Giant's Causeway, and other spots of scenic wonder. Whist drives and musical evenings drew enthusiastic crowds, and the drawing room at Eden Quay sported great style with the presence, among the potted plants, of a grand piano. The 'offspring' of the Social Committee, 'The Dramatic and Concert Troupe', were applauded for their ability to 'give an annual entertainment which is really a remarkable exhibition of talent'. On 2 May 1930 their first public performance was given at St Theresa's Hall, Clarendon Street. The Executive promoted the campaign for 'A Woman Worker's House' which would 'provide a centre for many trade union and labour activities, offer possibilities for cultural classes and increased social entertainments, and enable our very popular library to be supplemented by a Reading Room supplied with papers and magazines'.[14]

To the dismay of an increasingly politicised leadership, however, matters beyond the shop or dancing floor were approached with somewhat less enthusiasm. Following a lamentable attendance by working women at the May Day celebrations, the Executive upbraided its tardy membership.

> Your Committee regret that comparatively few of our members show active interest in the Trade Union and Labour Movement. So far as women are concerned, the May Day demonstration organised by the Dublin Trade Union Council last year demonstrated only that Dublin women are too shy, too proud, too indolent or too stupid to support the men trade unionists in a triumphant display of solidarity.[15]

Within the Executive itself, matters political now provoked further dissent.

Formal affiliation to the Labour Party and support for a political fund had again been proposed and defeated. Although it had been previously firmly established that individual members were at liberty to pursue their own politics, a visit by Miss Molony to Russia as part of a Dublin Trades' Council delegation prompted internal rumblings about 'Communist infiltration' — rumblings echoed in the trade union movement and political life generally at the time. On her return to Ireland Miss Molony, seconded by Mrs Dowling, who before her marriage had also visited the Soviet Union, proposed that the Union purchase 100 copies of the report of the visit by the Irish delegation. At the Executive meeting on 24 April, however, Miss Byrne proposed, and Mrs Kennedy seconded, 'that we take no copies of this report'. On a show of hands the latter motion was carried. With evident surprise, and considerable vigour, Miss Molony now expressed her wish that it be recorded that

> she thought it a disgraceful thing that the Irish Women

Workers' Union should refuse to take cognizance of the report of her own fellow workers in preference to the reports of the capitalist press.

Differences were not merely those of opinion, and for the first time competing political ideologies were discussed in a public forum. At the Annual Convention heated discussion followed the proposal of a motion by Miss Bennett which, while supporting the achievements of Soviet Russia in equality, and seeking the same everywhere, 'deeply regrets that certain principles of religion or liberty which are held by the Irish people as fundamentals of a good life, are not upheld by Soviet Russia'. Having achieved a measure of concurrence from delegates in support of such principles, Miss Bennett now declared that:

'Communist affiliations are undesirable'.

In this she was supported by Miss Chenevix, who referred to the 'Marxian code', and expressed a belief that this code 'takes account only of the things we hear and feel, and heeds not the unseen things of the soul'. Miss Molony called for both the motion and the tenor of such declarations to be ruled out of order 'as it has nothing to do with trade union business which was what we came to discuss'. From the Chair Mrs Dowling suggested that the motion was indeed inappropriate, but nonetheless allowed discussion to proceed. The seconder of the motion, Miss Byrne, claimed that it had been put on the agenda 'by the express wish of members of the Union who had taken exception to Miss Molony's public connection with Communists'. The number of such members was neither asked nor ventured. The Chair ruled that neither these members nor the Union as a whole had the right to criticise what Miss Molony or any other member chose to do in private. Miss Bennett, while expressing her regret at the personal turn the discussion had taken, moved that nonetheless the resolution be put.

The resolution was carried by 40 votes to 15 and, in part, represented a vote of confidence in Miss Bennett's leadership. The consistent ideological differences between members represented by Helena Molony and Sighle Dowling, and those represented by Louie Bennett and Helen Chenevix, had, by tradition, long been accommodated by both parties and their colleagues among the rank and file. In the hostile terrain of unemployment, however, with the rising power of fundamentalisms throughout Europe, and in the increasingly intolerant temper of the times, such an accommodation could not be readily sustained.

While the political climate throughout Ireland and its institutions echoed the vulnerability of the Left, other business of the Union, of necessity, continued. While the Executive protested that the Committee formed to discuss the implications of the Legitimacy Bill of 1929 included no woman member, representatives from all sections attended a conference to discuss improved legislation for women and girls, especially relating to night work, and arranged a further meeting of 'persons and societies interested' in the same, to be held at Eden Quay. Lucan Woollen Mills were organised, and Thomson's Shirt Factory was 'to be visited'. Two hundred posters, urging support for the Union, were displayed in industrial centres throughout the city. Resolutions to Congress included one urging a fortnight's holiday pay for all workers, and Miss Bennett was nominated, in a gesture of public and private confidence, for the position of Congress Vice President. On 12 June 1930 however, Miss Bennett resigned.

'The Chairman and members of the Executive said this came as a bombshell to them'. Miss Bennett explained that 'for some time she has not been feeling equal to the job; it is difficult and trying and she is not able for it'. On a proposal from Miss Molony, she was asked to defer her letter of resignation for six months, to allow formulation of a response, and this was agreed. Two weeks later, however, the question was raised again, when Miss Bennett proposed Miss Chenevix as General Secretary, with full responsibility for all office business, 'leaving Miss Bennett free to attend to such things as juvenile employment, new machinery, etc'.[16] That Miss Bennett was amply qualified to prepare material on such developments was never in question. Her increasing ambivalence about the daily round of negotiations and office administration, however, raised major problems for a small union, financially pressed and confronted by an industrial climate which demanded its full attention if the needs of its members were to be met.

In August, in a recognition of her undoubted capacity to lead, Louie Bennett was elected unanimously as Vice-President of Congress. Yet, despite such public elevation, back in Eden Quay discussion of her status within the Union now dominated the agenda. Her proposed change of brief had been 'not favourably received'. By September, a further leave of absence was sought 'to consider whether she will reconsider her decision to resign'.[17] Talks with members of the staff ensued, and the beginnings of a dependency upon the leadership became apparent. Miss Fegan 'gave it as her opinion that the Union would collapse if Miss Bennett resigned'. Both the Chair and Mrs Kennedy protested at 'a statement like that which reflected on the capabilities of the other members of staff and the Executive and Officers of the Union'. Such sentiment, however, had echoes throughout the Union. Miss Bennett, urged to stay, revealed her hand. Although 'her health was the primary cause of her wishing to resign . . . there was no denying that friction with the staff was a factor in it'. Such friction, be it political or otherwise, now had to be be seen to end, if the talents of Louie Bennett were to be retained.

In the quiet that followed at Eden Quay, permission was given to the Anti-Imperialist League to display an 'India at War with England' poster. On 6 November Miss Bennett's proposed re-organisation of the Union was agreed. The Chair reminded members that 'it was the duty of the Secretary to organise her staff, her authority must be upheld, and any arrangements she makes, go'. Under 'Any Other Business', the Union offer of £1,250 for the purchase of Nos 7 and 8, Eden Quay was agreed, as was the purchase of a coal scuttle for the convenience of the residents of the house.

CHAPTER 8

'These obstreperous lassies'

The meeting held at Eden Quay in late 1929 to discuss protective legislation was prompted by movements, both trade unionist and feminist, in a number of countries, aimed at securing modification of the ban on nightwork for women. The ban had been imposed by an International Convention through the agency of the International Labour Organisation [ILO] in Geneva and during the 1920s the question had arisen throughout the ranks of women workers 'in an acute form'. In 1930 the Annual Report had pointed to 'the danger to the position of women workers of the existing prohibition on nightwork'. The prohibition extended from 11 p.m. to 5 a.m.

In a widespread debate amongst members, a number of options were discussed. Removal of all legal strictures, although potentially open to abuse, was considered, and it was suggested that three eight-hour shifts which were organised irrespective of gender might lay the foundations for useful development of women's position in a number of industries. At the Annual Convention in 1931, the Executive proposed that while all night work was socially undesirable, protective legislation, if it were applied, should extend to all working people. To impose protection by statute on particular groups was, in effect, restrictive, and as currently framed the International Convention served as an excluding mechanism, enshrining trade union custom as law, and affecting women's employment in areas, such as newspaper printing, bakeries, and a range of manufacturing industries. Such sentiments expressed by working women, however, found few echoes in the institutions of the working class.

On 20 May Helen Chenevix wrote to Eamonn Lynch, Secretary of the Trades Union Congress, expressing indignation at the decision of the National Executive, taken without consultation with those most immediately affected, to propose no change in the ban on night work.

> Several unions in Saorstát Éireann have women members and these, together with the IWWU, constitute a large body of organised working women. . . . We consider that their advice should have been sought as a necessary preliminary to forming any decision on the matter.[1]

Mr Lynch replied. It was, he suggested, felt by the National Executive to be in the interests of the 'vast majority of the workers of the country . . . not to entertain any alteration in the existing Convention'.[2] At Congress in August the Union resolution on the restrictions received no support and 'we withdrew in the face of opposition'. The failure even to succeed in raising the question within the forum of Congress boded ill for future developments.

In some areas women's position had, by 1930, improved dramatically. The Furnishing Trade Group had claimed, on the initiative of woodworkers, equal pay for men and women employed on spraying machines. Negotiations with the Mattress Makers' Union [MMU] had resulted in women being taken off 'dangerous machines', and men put on, but this had set a precedent of sorts in the agreement that 'a wage equal to that paid to a man had been secured for a woman employee in Phelan's who had been put on a machine usually worked by a man'.[3] Although prompted in part by the fear that the semi-skilled labour of women would undermine the certified skills of men, the adoption of the procedure of promoting equal pay as a deterrent to undercutting rates was a major development.

At Bolton Street Technical School the first craft classes for women were started. Classes for Meihle feeders attracted eighteen students and 'by arrangement' most were from the ranks of the IWWU. A class in binding was to follow, and at Parnell Square Technical School Miss O'Sullivan signalled her readiness to train girls on power machines. Such developments, however, were not reflected at the level of legislation.

The Apprenticeship Bill, seen as progress overall, did not,

as published, define 'apprentice' in such a way as to include women. Miss Bennett was directed to draft amendments to the Bill and to channel these through the Labour Party for discussion when the Bill came before the Dáil. From the shop floor came increasing resistance to moves by employers to erode customary ratios between journeywomen and learners: while managements protested that 'the exigencies of their business require these young hands', the Union refused to countenance ratios of three learners to five journeywomen.

The Union now saw the need to educate women for a working life as paramount and the Executive were urged to 'secure a speedy establishment in Dublin of classes suitable for girl learners'. Miss Molony, a member of the Vocational Education Commitee [VEC], advocated physical drill and domestic economy for all students, and Miss Chenevix and the Civic Committee campaigned vigorously for the raising of the school leaving age to sixteen, and for the provision by the government of maintenance grants to facilitate such an extension and to compensate families for the potential loss of their offsprings' earnings.

The raising of questions in other areas was considered essential. In May the Union nominated Louie Bennett for Presidency of the Trades Union Congress, with a brief to place the question of women firmly on the agenda. In August 1932 she became the first woman to hold the office of President of Congress. Her nomination and election were not, however, greeted with universal acclaim; *The Irish Worker*, having resumed publication as the official organ of the Workers' Union of Ireland, felt 'the degradation of the labour movement was completed when it elected as President a person from outside the ranks of the working class'.[4]

There were undoubtedly class tensions within the leadership, and conflicting priorities affected decision-making by the Executive. Louie Bennett's commitment to placing the needs of working women on the agenda was, however, beyond dispute. Under her tutelage a recommendation from the Union called on the International Labour Office to set up a special advisory committee to investigate the condition of women's work in all countries. In 1932, together with Miss

Stafford, Chief Inspector at the Department of Industry and Commerce, Miss Bennett was despatched to Geneva to present, on behalf of the Irish government, the case for the Irish woman worker.

It was a case prefaced by a litany of complaints — low pay, irregular hours, and the increasing use of cheap and inexperienced labour. Difficulties were seen to be compounded by the era of protectionism ushered in by Mr de Valera after he had taken office in 1932. (Eamon de Valera held the office of Taoiseach for all but six years between 1932 and 1959, and from 1959 to 1973 served as President of Ireland; in a number of areas, specifically the framing of the 1937 Constitution, his perception of a woman's place would present fundamental difficulties for organisations such as the IWWU.) At this stage, in the early 1930s, the question of protectionism was contentious. Although Union energies had been notably deployed in calls for protective tariffs in printing and in miscellaneous industries, such as rosary bead assembly, the development of governmental initiatives to promote some industries and put others under embargo was seen as problematic. In her presidential address Miss Bennett spoke about changing economic structures and the growing need for trade unions to change direction and to develop policies of workers' control, particularly in relation to increased mechanisation and its effects on employment. She also spoke about the use of differential tariffs — Dictatorship.[5]

Within those industries protected by tariffs women workers were notoriously low-paid, and in 1932 the Union backed a Dáil resolution by the Labour Party leader, William Norton, on the need for fair wages, seeking in addition an administrative framework within which the resolution would be binding on all employers. Where the needs of the 'vast majority' of the labour movement and those of women workers coincided, the Union anticipated that both the Labour Party and the Congress would negotiate on behalf of women with the same degree of commitment they displayed in their negotiations on behalf of men. Given the evidence of the division of opinion on night work, such optimism may have been somewhat misplaced. On the question of industries protected by tariff the IWWU was 'confident' that Congress would serve its needs. In other areas, it seemed, conflicting interests would be resolved on the basis of the interests of the 'vast majority'.

Throughout the 1930s the Union was confronted by the problems caused by a declining membership among women over eighteen — women who had been displaced by younger workers and who now graced the unemployment lists at Eden Quay. Under the terms of the Trade Board Act, the learner's wage scale was based on age rather than on experience. Thus, when girls over fourteen were employed in a Trade Board industry they became entitled to an increasingly higher wage, dependent on how old they had been at entry. With some predictability, the Union pointed out that 'Trade Board industries are practically closed to all applicants above the fourteen years limit'. In response, the IWWU sought Congress backing for moves to eliminate the age basis of the Learners' Wage Schedule, and to introduce in its place a schedule based on experience. The Congress, however, refused, arguing with some justice that if the age basis were abolished the distinction between learners and adults might disappear. Such reservations, in the absence of a readiness to pursue alternative considerations, did little to improve the lot of working women.

Outside Trade Board industries neither age nor experience guaranteed specific rates of pay. Rita Hanley and Essie Shepherd, fourteen years old, started work in June 1931. After three years' experience a comparative scale entitled them to 22s. 6d. for their labours. They received 18s. per week. Margaret Kavanagh, a learner at Messrs Thoms in 1931 and entitled to 19s. 7d., was paid 18s. Unemployment everywhere prompted different tactics. At Horn and Metal Industries, Manufacturers of Devotional Goods, operatives were approached by women workers from 'another firm in the same trade and rather threatening remarks were made'. Management complained to the Union that intimidation by members from Mitchell's was rife and that:

'These obstreperous lassies appear to have got the idea into their heads that we shall do harm to our competition and cause unemployment'.[6]

Helena Molony with Maude Gonne

Hugh O'Connor Collection

IWWU Archive

Helen Chenevix as a graduate of Trinity College Dublin

EXTRACT
FROM
IRISH NATIONAL ANTHEM—
"Some Have Gone to a Land Beyond the Wave"

They go to Lands where a decent standard of life obtains.

The Irish Nation asks for Athletes!
The Government asks for a Healthy and Srong Population—BUT

GOVERNMENT BOARDS
SET A STANDARD OF
STARVATION WAGES

The 126 Paper Boxmakers now on STRIKE
ARE FIGHTING TO MAINTAIN

A BARE LIVING WAGE
FOR WOMEN

The Government that Forces Down Wages is Ruining the Nation

IRISH WOMEN WORKERS' UNION
7 & 8 EDEN QUAY

IWWU Archive

A union propaganda poster for the box makers' strike in 1928

The Executive and some members about 1930

The union Concert Troupe in 1931

A union poster campaign at the opening of a Dáil session in the early 1930s

THE FORTNIGHT'S HOLIDAY AS A SYMBOL.

No doubt many people are asking themselves to-day: " Why all this fuss about a fortnight's holiday ?. Of course it is very pleasant, and no one wants to come back to work after a single week of leisure. But why do workers want to undergo the hardship and loss of a strike to secure this amenity ? Surely they have no sense of proportion ? They are sending out a salmon to catch a sprat."

Actually this is one of the situations in which the refusal of a demand is of greater significance than the demand itself. It is reminiscent of Catholic Emancipation and Women's Suffrage. The marking of a ballot paper is a small thing ; but the vote is a symbol of citizenship and the denial of the vote to any section of the community is to mark that section with a brand of inferiority. The fortnight's holiday is important ; the refusal of it to manual workers is of infinitely greater importance because of its significance. The professional or administrative worker, the clerical or distributive worker, the shareholder who does no work at all in return for his dividend, is not asked to content himself with a bare week's holiday. But the manual worker carries the brand of a " hand " and " operative," a cog in the wheel of production. The present issue between the united employers and the united workers is a phase of the age long conflict between vested interests and human life.

But surely there must be a way other than the bitter way of conflict to solve the problems of industry ? Therefore, we appeal to men and women of goodwill to approach the workers' position in industry without prejudice, but rather with an honest desire to find a way of life for the Irish people which will foster the spirit of co-operation and the principle of justice to all.

IRISH WOMEN WORKERS' UNION,
48 FLEET STREET.

July, 1945.

A propaganda sheet for the laundry strike in 1945

Under the threat of unemployment, such antagonisms were no longer novel and within the Union, an old song re-sung placed the employment of married women in jeopardy. In 1931 a valiant attempt had been made to still any murmurs of discontent and at Annual Convention, Resolution No. 3 had indicated

> That as the first guiding principle of our Union is Equality of Opportunity for all men and women, the continual objections to married women working which are raised from time to time in the Union are inconsistent and regrettable and should finally cease.

Many, however, disagreed. The Printers' Committee had been approached by women who had been members of the section 'but had left industry on marriage and now wanted to re-enter the trade'. They decided, in the interests of the vast majority, that such women could take application forms if desired, but would be called only if others failed to fill any vacancies. Within the Union itself, a particular anomaly relating to the status of women workers after marriage came to light in somewhat contentious circumstances.

In 1932 Miss Bennett sought a legal re-interpretation of the rules on the receipt of marriage benefit and on 3 March questioned the eligibility of Mrs Dowling (*née* Bowen) to hold office either as Trustee or as President of the Union. Her position in industry was deemed 'irregular' and as such she no longer operated as an 'industrial unit'. Legally, receipt of marriage benefit was defined as having terminated membership. Although entitled to re-join, and to recommence meeting the conditions for the awarding of benefits or the holding of office, the status of marriage was deemed, in effect, to mark the end of the working life of a woman.

Mrs Dowling, long active both as a trade unionist and as a socialist, protested. She had not, she argued, been informed of the implications of accepting the benefit, and the Union had shown little reluctance in accepting her continuing contributions in full. On behalf of married women employed in laundries, printing houses and every section of the Union, she pointed to a context where she was in the same position as any other working man's wife — not knowing when unemployment will overtake her — when she must add to the family income, 'we have never had enough money to keep the kind of home both myself and my husband would like to have and my having to help with the family income was always a probability'.[7]

Miss Bennett, as official adviser to the Executive in such matters, was criticised by Mrs Dowling and others for having allowed what was now seen to be an irregularity to persist for so long. Her timing in seeking a re-interpretation of the rule was, in addition, considered suspect by Mrs Dowling. Miss Bennett was, it seems, anxious to finalise arrangements to purchase a new home for the Union, a move that did not have the unanimous backing of the Executive. Mrs Dowling, as Trustee and President of the Union, was undoubtedly a dissenting, or at least cautious, voice in the proposed undertaking. The affair ended on a decidedly unsavoury note, with latent class hostilities now to the fore.

> I want to say plainly that your complete disregard of both my feelings and my reputation . . . is in strong contrast to your extreme regard for the feelings of people who are neither members of the Union nor the working class.[8]

Miss Bennett was not alone in provoking antagonisms. While the Dowling affair remained largely internal, despite its implications, others became embroiled in more public dispute.

Helena Molony was a person held in high regard throughout the trade union movement and, indeed, by de Valera himself. To an extent, however, and as a direct implication of her commitment to a socialist future, she was viewed with some disquiet within the IWWU. Having spoken at an after-Mass meeting in Cathal Brugha Street in July, Miss Molony became the focus of attention in the press, attention considered to be so unpalatable to the Union that it was considered appropriate at the level of the Executive to put an official distance between the organisation and her remarks. The meeting in question, on 17 July 1932, was chaired by Maud Gonne

MacBride and was one of a series organised by the Irish Women Prisoners' Defence League. Ireland was in the midst of the Economic War with Britain and from British political circles had come a suggestion that the Pope be asked to intervene in Anglo-Irish relations. Miss Molony commented that any such move would represent an offence to 'the high office of His Holiness'. The next day, *The Irish Independent* construed her speech as 'an attack on the Pope'. Miss Molony conceded that in addition to commenting on the 'harebrained schemes' of 'tricky English politicians' she had noted, in passing, that 'if Ireland learned anything from her unhappy history she had no reason to look with confidence for Papal intervention in Irish secular or political affairs'.[9] The passions of Catholic Ireland flared. Louis A. Tierney wrote to the newspaper editor and urged that sodalities should ensure that 'meetings by Communists, either male or female, should be attended, and hymns such as Faith of Our Fathers sung'. Amongst claims and counter claims, men and women, boys and girls were urged to form 'a Catholic Defence League . . . in every town and village'.[10]

The Union, with unseemly haste, distanced itself from its beleaguered official. The virulence of the attack spoke less of Miss Molony's dramatic talent and more of the rapidly changing political climate in Ireland. Across Europe there was widespread unemployment, economic decline and depression; Ireland was not immune to the growth of its own fundamentalisms. The success of the Eucharistic Congress, held in the same summer in Dublin, provided evidence enough of a return to moral certitudes. Louie Bennett, noting that both socialism and fascism were 'on trial', looked — with a trepidation echoed throughout the trade union movement — to the prospect of 'rapid revolutionary changes in the economic structure of many countries, our own included, in the course of the next few years'.[11]

In her capacity as Organising Secretary, Miss Molony pointed to the effect of such a climate on the workplace. Depressed trade made workers fearful of losing their jobs if they organised. This, together with 'the general apathy towards trade unions', made recruitment difficult. The difficulties experienced by all trade unions in regard to declining membership were not, however, immediately evident for women workers. In 1932 the IWWU had more than 3,300 members, but the maintenance, and even growth in numbers did not conceal the increasingly irregular forms of employment offered, the absence of a guaranteed working week and the tendency towards payment by the hour rather than on the basis of a specific weekly wage. The problem surfaced within the laundry sector.

At White Swan, where labour from Scotland had provoked great antagonism from IWWU members, and at Milltown, workers were treated as casual labour. They were placed on short time, paid by the hour, and sent home or recalled at the whim of the employer. Their position was undermined both by the introduction of machinery and by the decreased use of laundry services in a harsh economic climate. The use of inmates of 'penitentiaries' (as Helena Molony described them) as a supply of cheap labour was a further major difficulty. The total number of such workers, estimated at 600, was, it was argued, a captive workforce,[12] used to undercut organised labour by making possible the submission of cheaper tenders for any work available. The Union resolved to fight to retain the rights of its members, arguing that the inmates of such institutions should be directed to rural occupations which were of their nature non-competitive and, at most, enabled institutions to operate on a self-sufficient basis. In the short term, specific clients were approached with a view to diverting custom from institutions which used such cheap labour and towards organised houses. Among those who responded sympathetically, it is interesting to note, were the Gardaí, whose uniforms had up to then — with some irony — been carefully maintained by the inmates of institutions of the State.

The solid position of the Union in the early 1930s was undoubtedly due in part to development in industries protected by tariffs. In the area of Printing and Kindred Trades, the imposition of tariffs on stationery, paper boxes and bags increased employment. The effect of a punitive tariff in other industries involving women's employment, however, presented hitherto unforeseen problems. In 1933 the closure of Gallaher's threatened 300 members of the General Section with unemployment. Following an approach from the Union the company agreed to postpone the dismantling of machinery while moves were made on the women's behalf by Louie Bennett and a deputation of workers affected by the threatened closure. The Minister for Industry and Commerce, Seán Lemass, agreed to a temporary remission of the tax on tobacco to allow Gallaher's extra time to raise the 51% of Free State capital now required by government statute. The remission, however, came 'too late'.

Congress accepted that closure was inevitable, but voiced no objection when Miss Bennett and the workers, with more to lose, persisted in the battle. Gallaher's suggested that business might resume if the preferential tariffs were to be removed. The Union again sought the advice of Mr Norton, as, according to Gallaher's, hundreds of women workers' jobs were not yet irretrievably lost. Having dallied for years over the question of political allegiance, however, the IWWU now found doors slowly closing. With the interests of his own constituents to consider, Mr Norton refused to meet a deputation from a non-affiliated union. Mr Lemass, in his turn, refused even to consider the proposal. The tariff remained. Gallaher's factory was emptied of all its equipment, and the premises were under threat of being sold to another company. Displaced women workers from Gallaher's were experiencing great difficulty in finding work, and experienced women were being rejected in favour of younger workers. The Union proposed a compromise: should any new company claim the premises, experienced workers from Gallaher's would have to be entitled to first consideration. Mr Lemass, although sympathetic, declared any such move 'quite impossible', and reluctantly conceded to the deputation from the IWWU that 'the firms wanted young workers, never employed before'.[13]

To offset such losses in membership, organisation in industries affected positively by the tariffs had accelerated since 1932. At Mitchell's, currently prospering under a protective tariff and eager to consolidate gains, the Union agreed to back Mr Mitchell's move to have the Merchandise Marks Act applied to his trade. In return, however, the Union now demanded a fair wage, an end to home working, and a guarantee of fifty-two weeks' work a year. In the 'promising' waterproof industry, where organisation was under way, the Union came under pressure from a number of employers to challenge low labour costs, which had prompted the charge that another firm, Automac, was guilty of unfair competition. After a short and effective strike, and a further meeting with Mr Lemass, a temporary agreement offered the Union members employed in that firm a 50% increase. The application of the agreement was, however, desultory, and the manager promptly sent the workers out for 'slackness'. The workers were, the Union claimed, 'very young and he puts them in and out as he pleases'. With the prospect of a 50% increase in the rate of pay, however, the Union found immediate favour among workers throughout the industry. When Automac women came out on strike, they were unorganised; by and large, when they returned to the shop floor it was as trade unionists. Others followed, and at Casey's a meeting organised by the general workers' section established a precedent: male employees formed part of an enthusiastic audience and later expressed their interest in affiliating to the IWWU.

The waterproof trade had become a breeding ground for discontent: at Mandleberg, with no prior consultation with unions, management offered apprentices indentures which contained no reference to the customary 'guaranteed employment' clause. Already disgruntled members of the Tailor and Garment Workers' Union [NUTGW], predominantly male, approached the IWWU with a view to affiliating and negotiating together from a position of considerable strength. Within the Executive, most considered the proposal with some favour: in other unions the assistance of the IWWU, in a formal sense, in organising in small shops, was seen to be invaluable. The Rules of the IWWU did not explicitly preclude such a possibility, although quite clearly the original conventions of Union procedure did not extend to membership, irrespective of gender, across industries. The mechanism which had facilitated the entry of non-industrial groups, such as the nurses and domestic workers, under which such groups became autonomous branches under the organisation of the IWWU, was considered by the Executive to be the most appropriate means of accommodating this and future affiliations, and men who had expressed an interest in joining were asked to clear their cards with their current unions and to apply formally to join the ranks of the IWWU.

On 17 August the matter was placed on the agenda for the Executive meeting. Grave misgivings were voiced at the proposed affiliation. Mrs Buckley considered the move a 'menace' to the women workers' organisation, and Miss O'Connor claimed that they would witness the 'downfall of the Union'. Although some absences from the Executive attendance were noted, the resolution to admit the men was passed, with a concession to quieten fears of a fifth column rising, and of erosion from within of the women workers' control of their own union. 'It is to be understood that the group shall have an independent Committee and Executive and shall not in any sense control the policy of the IWWU'.[14] Financial arrangements were agreed on a temporary basis: the new branch would retain 25% of monies taken in, and the remainder would be directed to the new Union premises at 48 Fleet Street.

The move to Fleet Street was celebrated on 29 October 1933 with a housewarming. While the women's house was warmly welcomed, however, the new direction of the Union was not. By November, rumblings were evident within both the Executive and the membership. Miss Gannon, a Trustee, argued that the Executive of a Union formed and maintained by women had acted illegally in admitting men. The move had changed the Union irrevocably — it was, no longer, the Women Workers' Union, but a general union changed without reference to the consent of its members. While Miss Bennett accepted the thrust of this argument, the need to organise throughout the industry was, she argued, paramount and, as Miss Chenevix noted, having assumed such powers the Executive had gone too far to draw back. On 9 November a formal proposal was put, and passed. If this was not rescinded by Convention in 1934, the IWWU could recruit members as a general rather than as a specifically women's union.

As President of the Trades Union Congress Louie Bennett had argued trenchantly against encroachment by the State in the affairs of trade unions. Centralised decision-making was, by definition, seen as corrosive of democratic rights and a dangerous prelude to dictatorship. In principle, Convention was the ruling body of the IWWU. In practice, between Conventions those who set the agenda retained control. The situation was undoubtedly complex. The political and economic climate left working women vulnerable, particularly in areas affected by discriminatory tariffs favouring home industry. Clearly, one union negotiating for all workers within a particular industry faced an employer on more equal terms. While some movement between male and female workers was already evident in specific industries, despite the rhetoric, the resolutions, and the results of the campaign to raise the standards for women workers to those obtaining for men, undoubtedly, more concessions were made than were won. When Nellie Farrell, a casemaker for fourteen years at Cauldwell's, persisted in her right to continue her labours, the male workers at the firm walked out. Resolution of the conflict settled the case for Miss Farrell — but not for future women who might seek to enter the trade. In mattress-making, when women currently employed 'fell out', jobs would, by agreement, revert to men. At Armstrong's, 'it was agreed that the women who are now binding should be allowed to continue, but no apprentices will be allowed to learn the work'.[15]

Those concessions which were made in favour of the women threatened few existing demarcations, and although new industries — electrical appliances, metal polishers, and readymade clothing — offered potential for women's employment, the customs of the 'vast majority' would evidently be challenged by the Union only with the greatest discretion. Given the still recent experience of the Union in relation to the prohibition of women from night work, the exercise of such discretion was misplaced. Although the reluctance to challenge the movement of which it was part was a response to the uncertainty of the times, an Executive prepared to argue now with greater vigour for a complete review of demarcation in industry, and to go on the offensive, might have prepared firmer foundations on which to withstand the moves antagonistic to the employment of women which were to gather momentum over the next few years.

CHAPTER 9

Queen of our home

Calls for the restriction of work for women gained currency as unemployment rose, the loss of jobs being equated, in part, to the incursions made by women into the industrial ranks. In Ireland any effects of the Great Depression had been partially offset by Government intervention to protect home industries, but in the early 1930s the stage of industrial development and the reliance on home markets left the Irish economy less immediately vulnerable to the crash than was its immediate neighbour. The economic war with Britain did affect many industries, but in this period also those industries in which women were increasingly employed, progressed. Apart from industries protected by tariffs, the employment of women, at rates of pay in no sense commensurate with those of men, had already become a feature of new industries — in packaging, electrical appliances, readymade clothing and chemicals. By 1934, in the context of rising unemployment, hostilities were evident between workers and across sexes.

Throughout the trade union movement concern was being voiced at the potential for Fascism in a context in which government, through measures such as the tariffs and the taxation of imports, had sought to establish centralised control over economic, industrial and social development. Although such control was, potentially, the goal of both Left and Right, the context of widespread unemployment and disturbing trends in Europe prompted major misgivings at any such moves within the country. From the Congress, affiliated bodies were addressed through a circular adverting to 'The Fascist Menace to Democracy'. Public meetings were arranged, and on 6 July Miss Molony spoke at an Anti-Fascist

Meeting in College Green organised by the Trades Union Congress [TUC]. Despite its reservations regarding matters political, the Union claimed that the 'women aspect of it must be dealt with by us in a special way'.[1] They published a pamphlet, *A Wooden Horse*, and although unfortunately no copy remains in the Union archives, the title suggests the employment of specific tactics: a wooden horse, with reference to the downfall of Troy, is presented as a gift, but contains the means whereby prevailing structures could be undermined. In 1934 Mr Lemass, despite such opposition, clearly signalled his intention to move the legislative process further into the workplace by framing legislation to cover conditions of labour.

Of itself, the trade union movement was not opposed to planning for industrial and social growth. In 1932, Louie Bennett had gained the support of Congress for a proposed National Economic Council. As Charles McCarthy points out in *Trade Unions in Ireland,* the body as envisaged in 1932 would be advisory, with trade unions having considerable influence in regard to intervention in the 'industrial, economic, social and financial organisations of the Nation'.[2] But by 1934 the climate did not bode well for either consultative or advisory bodies. Previously, disquiet at the rise of Fascism had focussed on Germany, Italy and Spain; in 1934, however, the articulation of Fine Gael policy in regard to the corporate state, and the support of the Catholic Church for the form of vocational organisation outlined in Pope Pius XI's encyclical *Quadragesimo Anno,* clearly signalled that Ireland might well see the growth of a home-grown variety. What Lemass proposed in legislative provision for conditions of employment found much support within the trade union movement. From its inception, however, the IWWU had grave misgivings at developments which treated women, along with children, as the beneficiaries of 'protective' legislation which, for whatever noble or ignoble cause, restricted the right of the women of Ireland to work in industry.

By 1934 the position of the IWWU was sound. It had more than 4,000 members, drawn from twenty different industries. Although the employment of printers and laundresses had been affected by the introduction of new machinery, the

Union had maintained a united front in fighting unemployment; even within the offices of the IWWU the Printers' Section had opposed, successfully, the use of duplicating machines to produce annual reports and general documentation. Despite problems in particular sections, the development of a number of industries protected by tariffs,[3] and the extension of organisation outside Dublin ensured that numbers would increase dramatically. Citing 1933 as a 'record year', the Union claimed that 'the increase in membership has been greater than any year since 1917'.[4] Organisation in Bray resulted in the Dargle laundresses applying for membership, and prospects for further recruitment in Bray were evident from the responses to overtures from the Union in the polish and ink industries. Following a major recruitment campaign, with leaflets and posters throughout Dublin and the provinces, women in the clothing trade were eager to join the ranks. At Dundalk more than a hundred women, and seventeen men, attended a Union meeting at Taylor's Handkerchief Factory, and in 1935 a branch of the Union was established under the guidance of Mrs Fitzsimons. As with the waterproof industry, the position of unionised women was undermined if men were not also unionised. With the agreement of management, a 'cross-channel union' was already poised to recruit men. Miss Chenevix travelled by train to assess the situation and on her return she argued convincingly that the recruitment of men in this industry should take place under the aegis of the IWWU. As a result, thirteen men were given IWWU cards.

A combination of circumstances, however, began to erode the Executive's confidence in seeking to uphold its decision to admit men. In January Mr Lemass had made his first public statement regarding women's place in industry, and a deputation from the Union was despatched to the Department of Industry and Commerce. Its members urged Mr Lemass to consider a wider brief: a reduction in the working week; the application of the Apprenticeship Act controlling ratios in all new industries; and an increase in Trade Board minimum rates, for all women under the Boards' authority, to 30s. a week. The deputation was 'sympathetically received', and left the department with Mr Lemass' assurance that should legislation be forthcoming the IWWU would be further consulted.

Within a number of industries, tensions among workers became evident. At Hilton's Mattress Manufacturers, a dispute raged over demarcation, focussing on the use of the Roll Edge machine. When it had been introduced in 1925 the men had refused to operate the machine, although, quite inexplicably, they had been 'strongly urged by Miss Bennett to claim it'. By default the work had gone to women. In 1934 a dispute involving the tufting machines gave rise to a claim by the men to review their option on operating the Roll Edge machine. The IWWU fought back. A member who had operated the machine for nine years had been told by a male colleague that she could do alternative work, valued at 12s. a week. Mr Hilton entered the fray, warning that 'if he must pay men's rates then he will dismiss the women and employ men'. When agreement was finally reached the terms reflected the unevenness of negotiating power.

> The girl on the special machine is to have her wages increased; as girls leave machines, they will be replaced by men. The girl on the Roll Edge machine is to be treated as a Third Year Apprentice and wages paid accordingly.'[5]

It was peculiar to the status of women workers that, having had nine years' experience on a machine, the 'girl' in question would be recognised as a Third Year Apprentice. Hilton's, however, was merely a prelude.

In February the Bookbinder's Union called a conference involving their own members and other unions in the trade, where discussion 'hinged around the point at which men's work ended and women's began'. Again nothing was resolved, but a sub-committee, with three members from each union, was directed 'to consider the question of women's work in the binding trade'.[6] Within the Union, murmurs of discontent regarding the organisation of men became less restrained. When John Ireland & Co., Tailors, asked the Union to organise their shop, the Executive decided to refuse the offer, pending the decision of Convention. Early misgivings had some foundation. The undoubted advantages of organising along lines of industry rather than just along lines of sex were less evident in a workplace dominated by demarcations and differentials, with all tensions amplified by the spectre of unemployment. The logic of organising by industry was so closely aligned to equality of remuneration that it became self-evident folly to attempt one while the other was so clearly absent from the agenda of the trade union movement.

At Messrs Taylor's in Dundalk, the conundrum provoked by the Executive decision to admit men ended the illusion that expansion as a general union, in such a climate, could be anything other than contentious. Throughout the clothing trade women were employed on presses. In Dundalk, prior to reorganisation by the IWWU, Taylor's had placed men on such work. In 1934 Taylor's sought to replace the men by using the cheaper labour of girls and the Union, as representative of the men, was forced to support protection of the men's jobs as pressers — jobs which, in Dublin, the Union had claimed to be women's work by definition. As a short-term compromise it was agreed that the men would, on rota, return to hand pressing, and that women would resume the work of pressers. The move was unsatisfactory on all counts, and the resolution on the admission of men to the Union put by the Executive to the 1934 Convention made it clear that, by now, most members of the Executive had their reservations.

On May Day 1934, delegates filed into the hall at 48 Fleet Street. The agenda was diverse, but all delegates shared a major preoccupation: would men, in future, vote on resolutions and govern policy in the Women's Union? Miss Bennett proposed, with specific safeguards, the admission of men into the Union from those industries where women formed the majority of the workers and where the work between women and men was 'closely allied'. The intent of the resolution was to safeguard and develop those industries considered to be, by and large, the preserve of women. The resolution was lost. Another followed. The Waterproof Workers' Committee pleaded their cause: the industry must be organised, many of the men refused to join any union other than the IWWU and hence, potentially, could undermine the position of women trade unionists if they remained outside the ranks. The membership, again, refused to endorse the Executive decision, and the morning of May Day was dominated by heated debate from all quarters. Before lunch, a resolution was put: 'That the IWWU be for women only, no men being admitted as members'. It was carried, 78 to 18. Men who were members would be allowed a period of twelve months' grace in which to arrange a transfer of cards, but the unambiguous result of the ballot-box left the Executive somewhat abashed. Arising from the decision, Miss Molony drafted a further resolution urging Congress to support moves to foster the development of industrial unionism. With agreement reached, the brief tale of the IWWU, General Union, was over.

Within the year the men had transferred to the ITGWU and latent hostilities between the two unions flared. The ITGWU rejected overtures from the women workers suggesting a united front against employers. Accusing the IWWU of earlier poaching offences within the industry, the men's union now proceeded to court the women at Casey's. In August, and quite clearly with some exasperation, Miss Chenevix claimed it would be 'no loss if they seceded'. Explaining her position further, she suggested that politically it was to the workers' advantage to be organised by one union and, she added more quietly, they had always been recognised as 'bad payers' and the Union should now let them go. Despite her own advocacy of one union for the industry, Miss Bennett was less enamoured of the notion if that union was not to be the IWWU. If the ITGWU were poaching her members, then a battle would be fought. By September, however, the battle had been fought and lost, and the women at Casey's had joined the ITGWU.

Relations between the two unions did not improve. In 1934 members of the ITGWU were in dispute with the Dublin Master Printers' Association, and the prospect of a strike by the men left the IWWU in the invidious position of either being locked out or declared scabs. On 26 July, following the calling of a strike, 1,200 women declared their support for the men and were locked out. Once out, the IWWU, however, decided to advance its own claims: for wage rates commensurate with their labour, for rules to govern women in the industry, and for regulation of the ratio between apprentices and journeywomen.

'Rank opportunism', said the Masters.

'Pragmatism', said the Executive.

At a mass meeting in the Mansion House on 15 August the Masters refused to settle the women's claim until a Joint Industrial Council [JIC] was established for the trade. The IWWU, plagued by Trade Boards, had for a number of years advocated the setting up of such machinery to discuss and to control all matters affecting the workers in an industry. Mr Lemass lent support to the Masters by requesting that the IWWU withdraw its claims and allow the dispute with the men to be settled. He would, he claimed, ensure that the position of women would be given first place on the agenda of the proposed JIC and he would personally support moves to protect the position of women in printing.

The Union accepted the terms as offered. In September the dispute was resolved, but relations between the IWWU and the Printing Trade Group were soured. Having called out 1,200 women to support the men, the Union felt that such solidarity had not proved contagious. The Group had failed to back the women's claim, the JIC had not been established, and the lock-out had cost the IWWU £930 7s. 6d. — too high a price for too few returns.

In other areas the territorial claims of the IWWU were seldom infringed. For cleaners in government service the IWWU was the only union which could claim, since 1932,[7] to have called for a daily wage for such women. In 1934, however, the Government proposed that cleaning women at the Four Courts, the ESB [Electricity Supply Board] and government offices accept a reduction in their hourly rate. Such women, they claimed, were no longer required to light the fires in the halls of power. *Ipso facto*, a reduction was the order of the day. From the Union 'great indignation was expressed by Convention at this attitude of a government to hardworked women, and publicity was urged'. These women again became the focus of Union attention in 1935 following what was described in the Executive minutes as 'an ugly incident'. The case in question involved 'women being kept out after they had been absent through childbirth'. Following Union intervention, surprisingly given the ambivalence in relation to married women working, the women were reinstated, and joined the ranks of the women of Ireland who brought forth their children between shifts.

Throughout the sections of the Union, members prepared to settle for modest gains. In September a Government Order decreed that promotion to Head Nurse in Grangegorman and Portrane would henceforth require the candidate to hold the General Nursing Certificate. The already socially dubious status of the mental nurse was to be copper-fastened by the stipulation that no Mental Certificate was required. The move excluded, in effect, trained mental nurses with many years of service in notoriously difficult working conditions, and elevated the general nurse, regardless of experience within mental hospitals, to a position of authority in relation to her sister, the keeper. A Government Order, by definition, was not open to negotiation, but in 1935 the Union won from the Department of Local Government an agreement that facilities would be provided to enable mental nurses to qualify for the higher posts. The victory was somewhat Pyrrhic. No more than two candidates a year would be considered for such training, and the payment of £10 per annum ensured that only the most tenacious would apply, accepting a considerable reduction in pay for the privilege. Nevertheless, the nurses greeted the proposal with great enthusiasm. At Annual Convention the move was hailed with applause:

'It is a great triumph'.

Within twenty industries, on behalf of 4,000 women, such negotiations, triumphs, and defeats were the order of the day. Many within the leadership had been involved in this daily round for nearly twenty years, and brought to their task the weight of their experience. In the light of talk of protective legislation which promised only restrictions, a trade union movement dedicated to serving 'the vast majority', and the displacement of women by machines, the Union now took stock of the contested terrain.

In all industrial sectors serviced by the IWWU changes in working methods were affecting membership. While the introduction of protective tariffs for home industry had boosted membership, 'the machine' was seen as the greatest threat to further development. In printing, packaging, laundries, the tobacco industry, and furnishing trades the Union could, with some foundation, point to losses directly related to a changing work process. At Annual Convention in 1934 the fears of the Executive and of members had found voice in the resolution cautioning against the new methods being used to reduce wages.

> Further, the Convention, convinced that the machine is one of the chief causes of cheap labour as well as unemployment, declares that the IWWU must not allow the simplification of mechanical processes to involve a low wage standard, nor the introduction of machines where hard work has been in use to reduce the wage formerly paid for the process.[8]

To this threat was added that of displacement and 'dehumanisation' of the working class.

At Armstrong's, a machine was introduced to increase the rate of the production of envelopes. The machine, when installed, was capable of turning out envelopes, cut and stamped, at a rate of between 80,000 and 100,000 a day. Although cutters were to be most immediately affected, in production terms the machine was in effect equal to the labour of three women. At Faulat Shirt Factory the organisation of the women 'has revealed a very bad system of working. A chain system which is little short of slavery and is new to Dublin is in progress here, and must be fought'.[9] From its inception, however, working 'on the line' was seen as more or less inevitable, and the application of methods in industry which had quickly assumed the status of a natural development, a measure of the price of progress. The women were advised by the Union to consider methods of relief from the line, but the prospect of a change in the process itself was deemed 'unlikely'. The call for breaks was not new; the Leinster Laundries' Association had, earlier in the year, 'conveyed the good news that a tea interval of five minutes on late nights will be given to maintain the good relations with the IWWU'. The Union, however, was intent on the making of policy, not tea, and at Faulat Shirt Factory the first IWWU claims were submitted calling for pay increases and for negotiated rest periods for women on the line.

What was now evident to all was the changing nature of industry itself. What was evident to the IWWU was the need to combat the unemployment considered intrinsic to the introduction of such methods by calls for radical changes in the structure of the working week. What they demanded for all workers were shorter hours and higher wages. What they received, however, was protective legislation, and legal restrictions on women's right to work.

The steady incursion by the State into the industrial arena now prompted the Executive of the IWWU to re-launch its appeal to members to reconsider their position on the forming of a political wing. The acknowledgment that the concerns of women in industry extended to the political structures of the State involved a commitment by members to finance a Political Fund. Since 1917, attempts had been made to provide such a fund, and resistance by members had undoubtedly curtailed the effectiveness of the IWWU both in the Labour Party and in the Trades Union Congress. As a body the Union was unable, without the agreement of its members, either to affiliate to, or to support candidates of, any political party for public office, and although political representatives from the Labour Party had assisted in industrial matters they had done so, by and large, as the result of appeals from individual women workers who were members of that party. In 1933 the Gallaher's dispute had become sufficiently complex to persuade Mr Norton to remind the IWWU that they were not entitled to consume the time and energies of a party to which they refused to affiliate. In October of the same year, having persuaded its membership that political action to defend the rights of women was now unavoidable, the members finally agreed, following a ballot, to accept in principle the financing of a political wing of the IWWU.

Decisions could now be made on the setting of a levy and on affiliation, and from its inception the political wing of the IWWU was vigorously exercised. Members debated the most efficient ways of expending both finance and energy to gather support outside the Union for opposition to legislation being formulated by Mr Lemass for Mr de Valera's government. By the middle of 1934 trade unionists, and women workers in particular, were left in no doubt that legislation was brewing 'which will regulate the trades in which women may or may not work'.[10] It was proposed by the Executive to seek an interview with Mr Lemass and request consultative status for the IWWU in the framing of any such provisions. Meanwhile, the Union considered its own position. Finance was sound, membership steadily increasing. Unemployment figures were down and at the beginning of 1935 a report from the Unemployment Fund, chaired by Miss Molony, indicated that income from fund raising and members' contributions exceeded expenditure.

In February, Mr Lemass responded to the Union's request for consultations 'stating that he would receive a deputation from the IWWU when the final draft of the Factories' and Workshops' Bill was ready'.[11] The Union protested: it had 'hoped to influence the drafting of the Bill', and now felt keenly the absence of a direct input into the legislative procedure. In March it moved to formalise such an input, and a special Convention was called to consider two questions: affiliation to the Labour Party, and a submission to the League of Nations Conference called to consider the equality of women in industry and other spheres to be held in Geneva in June. The Convention failed to materialise; the tramworkers' strike prevented the attendance of a quorum and no decision could be made. With no formal allegiance at court, the Union was placed on the defensive. The Government made a move. An old Act was brought down from the shelf, enforcing throughout industry a mandatory holiday for women and juveniles when St Patrick's Day fell on a Sunday. In less anxious times a holiday for all workers would be welcomed; the special dispensation for women and juveniles, however, produced an acute sense of foreboding.

At the 1935 Annual Convention, the President, Mrs Kennedy, set the tone. Delegates were congratulated 'on the spirit of their members during the past year which increased the value of the Union as a fighting force for women workers'. In response, staff members gave special thanks —

during the year they had 'found in Mrs Kennedy a fair and wise President'. With one dissenting voice, the delegates voted in favour of affiliation to the Irish Labour Party and notice was served on both the Government and the trade union movement that every possible method would be employed to resist the displacement of women by men. Members spoke from the floor of their own experience to date. In laundries, presser machines appeared likely to be taken from women; in printing, the absence of rules for the employment of women and the training of apprentices had resulted in a dearth of machine feeders, and it was feared that 'the feeding might pass out of the hands of women altogether'.

In 1935 the Union went public in its opposition to such moves. In *The Irish Press* Miss Bennett responded with characteristic fervour to the 'superficial and antiquarian' opinions of their correspondent, Mr E. Shortt, in regard to the status of womankind. Pointing to his forthright championing of 'a man's right to be the protector and breadwinner', Miss Bennett charged him to take account of the elderly spinster, the widow, and the 'father with 50s. a week' and two or three adult daughters. If women were to claim as their birthright a life of 'protection and idleness', would the State provide their dole, and would men pay further taxes to finance the collective needs of the female of the species? Women, she argued, had responded to their times:

'Machinery has taken over into the factory the work that used to be done in the home. Women have followed their homework to the factory. And they are not superfluous workers. They are required'.

Should men be somewhat daunted by the invasion, the Secretary of the Irish Women Workers' Union offered them her own assurances that their domain would not be infringed.

> There are many industries for which women are better adapted than men. Textiles, sugar, confectionery, tobacco. . . . There are also many mechanical processes so monotonous that men find them intolerable. Women endure such monotony with less evil effect on their nervous system.[12]

Armed with such reflections on woman's place, Miss Bennett joined her colleagues in a deputation to the Minister. Discussion, over an hour and a half, focused on Section 12 of the proposed Conditions of Employment Act, which empowered the Government to prohibit or restrict the employment of women in industry. Mr Lemass assured the deputation that it was not his intention to infringe on women's current employment: his concern was directed at the new industries, and regulation of these workforces would proceed after the passage of the Act. Such reassurance regarding the status of existing women workers rang hollow, as word had already come from a number of officials of moves which threatened well-established women's industries. In February Miss Chenevix had reported that she had visited the Swastika Laundry and that 'in accordance with Government plans the Hoffman Presser machines in all factories will in future be worked by men'.[13] Mr Lemass refused to countenance the deletion of Section 12, but would consider 'a carefully worded amendment'. The deputation withdrew.

Back in Fleet Street, legal opinion was sought, and the Union's solicitor was briefed on proposals to be formulated into amendments. The Executive turned its collective attention to the Labour Party. The meeting with Mr Norton proved less than satisfactory: no amendment to Section 12 from this quarter would be forthcoming. Miss Bennett was instructed to 'express the members' indignation' at such a response, and affiliation fees were ordered to be withheld until further notice. The National Executive of Congress was approached. Pending a meeting with the ITGWU, Mr Lynch, Secretary to Congress, assured the IWWU that Congress would 'endeavour to come to a conclusion in accordance with our wishes'. Leaflets and posters, authorised by the Executive, conveyed to the public at large the specific grievance of women workers, and their general disquiet at the powers to be assumed by the Minister. Advertisements were placed by the Union in all the morning papers outlining the implications of Section 12, and seeking the active support of the men of the trade union movement. If Section 12 was to be challenged, the combined forces of the labour movement would have to be harnessed in advocacy of women's right to work. By June, however, it was evident that such support would not be forthcoming.

Helena Molony, in her capacity as a member of the National Executive of the Labour Party, was present at a conference called by the party to consider the implications of the Bill prior to the Annual Meeting of Congress in August. Mr Norton explained, by reference to a memorandum placed on his desk by the National Executive of Congress, that Congress, in fact, 'rather welcomed the clause as a safeguard against exploiting employers'.[14] Miss Molony informed the Executive which, having expected some support from this quarter, now retired to Fleet Street for a review of tactics. In May 1935 the Convention, with a measure, perhaps, of anticipation of such a development, had already registered a lack of confidence in both Government and Trades Union Congress .

> This Convention protests against the growing tendency on the part of Government and of the Trade Union Movement to restrict women's right to work, and calls upon the Government and the Trade Union Congress to uphold the principle that Industry shall be staffed by those best fitted for the jobs, whether men or women, and shall provide a wage scale based on equity rather than sex.[15]

A letter protesting at the proposed interference by government in the work of women had been despatched from that Convention.

On 16 May Mr Lemass replied: he was now prepared to receive deputations from interested parties to discuss amendments to the Conditions of Employment Bill. The IWWU campaign began in earnest, and Miss Bennett withdrew from the daily round to prepare strategy. Miss Chenevix travelled to Donegal to consolidate Union gains, and to discuss with the Donegal Trades' Council the question of organising textile workers. She found a climate hostile to trade unionism: of the forty girls who attended a meeting in the Trades Hall, twenty had been suspended from work 'the day after they made a move towards joining the Union'. In preparation for the League of Nations Conference in September Miss Lennon, on behalf of the Union, and Miss Chenevix, on behalf of a group of women's societies, were directed to attend both this conference and the mass demonstration of women organised to launch proceedings to combat moves by government and organised labour to fight the unemployment of men by encroaching on the rights of women.

As individuals, women in the labour movement continued to have a measure of access to power, and in 1935 at the Guildhall in Derry Helena Molony was elected Vice-President of Congress. Such access, however, did not guarantee progressive policies in relation to women workers. On Friday 20 August, the 41st Annual Meeting of the Irish Trades Union Congress [ITUC] resumed its deliberations on the third day with a discussion from the floor of 'Equal Rights and Equal Pay'. Miss Bennett proposed, on behalf of the IWWU,

> That this Congress reaffirms its allegiance to the fundamental principle of equal rights and equal democratic opportunities for all citizens and equal pay for equal work.[16]

Miss Bennett called on Congress to consider that the restrictive powers of the proposed Conditions of Employment Act were merely a prelude to other legislative developments seeking to impose 'a dangerous form of control'. The accredited representatives of trade unions could not guarantee that they would be acknowledged as representatives of workers in industry, and under Section 12 of the Bill the Minister had total discretion in regard to the employment of women. The question, she argued, 'was not a sex problem at all. It was a wage problem, and should be dealt with as such'. Mr William O'Brien, ITGWU, seconded the resolution, welcoming the opportunity, however rare, of agreeing with Miss Bennett. He would not, however, endorse her perceptions in regard to the state of industry, and ventured his union's support for Section 12. The tendency in industry, he argued, 'was to substitute cheap, low paid women's labour for men's'. Where women were organised such moves could, to an extent, be resisted, but 'generally it was very difficult to effectively organise them'. Section 12 had, he revealed, been framed in response to a request of the National Executive and, in doing so, the National Executive were considering the best interests of all the affiliated unions of the working class movement as a whole.[17]

Mr O'Brien now dismissed what he saw as Miss Bennett's rather alarmist portrayal of women driven out of employment *en masse*, and cited the clothing industry as indicative of a quite different trend.

> The real fact of the matter was that men were being driven out and in one industry — the clothing industry — they thought Section X11 might be of great use. Woman labour was 95% employed in that industry.[18]

An indication of the interests to be served by organised labour, in the future as in the past, came with Mr O'Brien's championing of the place of men in the industry which Miss Bennett claimed to have always been the preserve of women.

> She forgot a very important, ancient and honourable section of the community known as tailors [laughter] whose record went back a considerable time and who had played no insignificant part in the Trade Union Movement in Ireland.[19]

The Irish Women Workers, trade unionists since 1911, could, of course, make no such claim!

Support for Section 12 gained momentum as proceedings continued apace. The National Society of Brushmakers 'expressed the hope that the benefit would be given to men workers as far as possible under the Bill'. While Mr O'Gorman of the Irish Union of Distributive Workers and Clerks [IUDWC] pointed to the necessity to strengthen the trade union movement and thus ensure equal pay for women, Mr Birch of the ITGWU thought 'it was a very wrong thing that young girls should be sent in to factories and young men kept out'.[20] Mrs Purtell of the National Union of Tailors and Garment Workers [NUTGW] spoke for her trade in welcoming Section 12, and she was joined by others. The Typographical Association complained of 'too many women inside the factory', and added that 'they were a menace to the industrial classes'! With a dramatic fervour that could as well have graced the Abbey Theatre's boards as the Congress platform, their delegate, Mr Lloyd, continued with the observation that 'Man' was the breadwinner.

> Woman, he said, is the queen of our hearts and of our homes, and for God's sake let us try to keep her there.[21]

With such talk of breadwinners, equal pay was, quite simply, out of order. Miss Molony spoke on behalf of all women workers.

'It was', she said with measured calm, 'terrible to find such reactionary opinions expressed at that Congress by responsible leaders of labour in support of a capitalist Minister in setting up a barrier against one set of citizens'.[22]

In the hall, the quiet with which such a damning statement was initially greeted erupted in protest, and from delegates with political associations other tensions came to the fore. Senator Johnson (IUDWC) claimed that in the absence of a trade union movement able to regulate the proportion of women and men in industry, power had to be given to the legislature, or to the Minister, in the interests of the working class. Mr Norton of the Post Office Workers' Union [POWU] and Leader of the Labour Party, pointed to the early debates when he had met the National Executive of Congress. During one of the discussions he had asked Miss Molony 'whether she claimed that it should be within the right of women to be carpenters and blacksmiths?' She had immediately answered 'in the affirmative'. The bulk of the National Executive had, however, quietly demurred. Acknowledging the extent of the political moves at play, Mr Norton now claimed to recognise 'Miss Molony's hand behind the subtle, ingenious resolution they were discussing'. Such tactics were subsequently laid bare: Congress was, indeed, being asked to accept 'certain principles' in the abstract, and if the resolution was passed 'they would be told by the Women Workers' Union that that meant Congress was committed to opposing Section 12'.

'Was that not so?' said Mr Norton, T.D.

'Yes', said Miss Molony, V.P.

Mr Lynch, Secretary to Congress, rose to defend the

National Executive. Mr Norton had, he suggested, 'hoped to spear the National Executive on the horns of a dilemma'. The politics were neat, the problem less so. Congress had, historically, made no 'specific pronouncement' on co-equal rights for men and women in industry. Although he considered the trade union movement and the labour movement to be generally committed to equal rights for the sexes, the problem at present was exacerbated by the changing nature of industry itself. They were well aware of 'the advance of machinery in industry which was enabling women to displace men and was incidentally displacing both'.[23] He believed, along with most of his affiliated members, that the needs of the male industrial worker had to continue to be paramount, in essence 'preserving the greater good of the many'.

Relations on the floor deteriorated as tensions rose. Mr Lynch referred to the quite inappropriate perception, fostered by Mr Norton, of the Executive presenting its case in an 'obfuscated condition'. Mr Norton, in response, called for a public reading of the memorandum on the employment of women submitted by Congress to the Minister. This memorandum, he suggested, committed Congress in principle to the restriction of women in the workplace. Although the memorandum argued that 'changes to be made in future should be made by way of recruitment, and not by dismissal . . . the hand that had framed the memorandum was shown'.

Miss Bennett rose to conclude the case for the women workers. In the final analysis, she argued,

> This was a question of wages, and in a question of that kind were the delegates going to give the Government power to deal with one section of the community as they liked?[24]

In the short term, they evidently were. As a departing and futile gesture, the resolution was passed.

In the wake of the Congress of 1935, the IWWU delegates returned to Fleet Street. Although all were profoundly dispirited by the climate of hostility from within the ranks of the movement, the reports of Miss Lennon and Miss Chenevix from Geneva gave evidence of unexpected support for their cause. Mr Hearne of the Department of Industry and Commerce had been 'most helpful' in regard to Section 12. In addition, following the League of Nations Conference on the status of women, 'foreign women had interviews with Mr de Valera' on the question of the Bill, and the President had been reported by them as 'more or less sympathetic to the women's cause'. Following discussions in Dublin with Mr Hearne, Miss Bennett and Miss Molony now formulated an amendment offering as a compromise the allocation of specific work to women. Such a compromise bore fruit, and in October the Executive reported that 'Mr Lynch of the Trades Union Congress is now of our mind on Clause 12 and Congress will support our points'.[25] If Congress was to be forgiven for its failure to render effective support at an earlier date, the Labour Party was not, and bore the brunt of women workers' hostility for some time. The earlier decision to withhold affiliation fees was endorsed and the IWWU retained its political distance from the party until 1937.

Although the men of the trade union movement in this instance had proved reluctant allies, the Women's Societies of Ireland and Europe did not. Earlier in the year the Executive had convened a conference of all women's organisations in Dublin. The conference had formally protested to the minister at the proposed restrictions on women's work, and attention had been focussed specifically on the League of Nations Conference at Geneva. In November, after the conference had completed its review of women's status, Dorothy McArdle, the prominent republican historian and friend of Mr de Valera, and Mr Mortished of the Labour Party, had sent 10s. from Geneva as their contribution to a campaign designed to air the views of women on the proposed legislation.

A standing committee drawn from all women's societies was authorised to 'watch legislation affecting women', and telephone lines and postage facilities were provided by the IWWU. Protest would be directed 'in a big way' at a meeting in the Mansion House on 21 November 1935. From other quarters came words of encouragement. Canon John

Flanagan of the Pro-Cathedral, 'a friend whom we looked on as one of the founders of this Union', offered his own brand of solidarity.

> While I would prefer for women home work and family life to a factory career, I recognise that as things are your members must seek employment. Further, I recognise their right to choose for themselves their sphere of action in industry. . . . If such legislation gives unrestricted powers to Government Ministers it should be resisted in the interests of all who earn their living in industry.[26]

The Bill moved to the Senate. There Mrs Tom Clarke proposed, seconded by Mrs Wyse-Power, a motion to delete Section 12. Senators Douglas and Browne spoke in favour of the motion: all Labour senators, however, spoke against. The motion was lost by 19 votes to 14. Having failed so demonstrably in the halls of power, the Union now took to the streets. Members were armed with pamphlets and despatched to the Mansion House where the Fianna Fáil Ard-Fheis was in progress. Persistent attempts were made to lobby delegates and to direct their attention to the misdeeds of their Minister, 'but the police intervened'. Undaunted, the women turned their attentions to the general public, and Dawson Street was claimed as their platform. The leaflet outlining the women's position was published in its entirety in both *The Irish Press* and *The Irish Independent*. *The Irish Times*, more circumspect in such matters, refused to publish material 'reflecting on the Minister'.[27]

Within the Union, a measured defeat was conceded and the practical implications of the legislation were discussed. Miss Molony proposed that section meetings be held to explain to members the effects of Section 16 of the revised Bill, which would now give the Minister authority to restrict the employment of women workers. The Bill, when passed, would also have implications regarding hours of work — a development which presented immediate difficulties for cleaners and nurses. By early 1936, talks were also in progress between the Union and the Dublin Masters concerning the statutory provision, also included in the Bill, that workers under eighteen years of age were not to be allowed to work for more than forty hours a week. A number of firms indicated that they would be seeking exemptions from this provision: the IWWU, however, resolved to oppose all such moves.

At Annual Convention in May 1936 the delegates condemned the Act in principle. While acknowledging that there were some benefits in regard to the restrictions now imposed on the employment of young people and of outworkers, and in regard to the provision for paid holidays, the Minister was henceforth seen as 'a usurper of the functions of the Trade Union Movement', and the Conditions of Employment Act (1936) considered by the Irish Women Workers' Union to be the initiation of an industrial system controlled by the Minister for Industry and Commerce 'to an extent suggestive of dictatorship'.[28]

CHAPTER 10

The resistance

The most immediate effect of the new legislation was an increase in the use of shift work, as was evident from the number of applications by employers for licences to extend the use of the shift system into new areas.[1] Although legally excluded from the night shift, the IWWU opposed all shift work on the basis of its impact on the social and psychological well-being of the working class. Such shifts, the Union argued, started early or finished late, although they might be regarded as necessary in cases of continuous process or emergencies. An application by General Textiles, Athlone, for an initial licence for two eight-hour shifts, and the creation of a further shift as the workforce accommodated such changes, was seen by the Union as 'a bad precedent from every point of view'. The TUC was urged to impress upon the Government 'that the trade union movement do not desire to see industrialism in its worst forms in this country'.[2] The system, they argued, had failed in 'the great Lancashire cotton centre', and was opposed by trade unions in other countries. Mr Lemass was trenchantly informed that women would resist on all fronts.

> This shift system involves risks to the health of the workers and is not only a source of great inconvenience in the home but tends to disturb family relations.[3]

Such opposition, although often futile in any real sense, persisted as part of the IWWU objective in focussing on the changing nature of the workplace. Officials and the Executive both accepted the need to persist in their resistance to change deemed, by women workers, to be both inappropriate and inhumane, but accepted too often, by government and organised male labour, as the price of industrialisation. In regard to the shift system, 'it was obvious that the Department mean to countenance it, but we mean to keep up opposition'.[4]

Persistence was not new to the Union agenda: in the Annual Report for 1936-37, the hope was expressed that 'the ancient question of time dockets may finally be settled'. Despite refusals by the workers to cooperate, the question had persisted and spread. In the printing industry most houses were individually applying such methods, and hourly time dockets had been issued in 1936 to ironers at the White Swan Laundry. One major victory in worker resistance to new work methods had been claimed in the boxmaking industry. At Williams and Woods the Union launched a campaign against the Bedaux system, which involved 'an intricate method of speeding up and an actual mechanisation of the human being, which was rightly resisted by our members'.[5] After a two-week strike, a victory was claimed and 'another snake driven out of Ireland by trade union action'. By 1937, however, the time docket question had become 'acute and threatens to become a very serious situation'. The context in which such a dispute became a major battle bears further consideration.

While the Union vigilantly policed the application of the Conditions of Employment Act (and even went so far as to issue its own publication, *A Guide for the IWWU*) the impact of the legislation on the overall employment of women was, in fact, negligible. The 1936-37 period was one of the most successful for the recruitment of women — membership increased by 584 and finances were sound. Ironically, the campaign opposing restrictions on women in industry, although largely unsuccessful, may itself have prompted women workers to perceive a union 'run by women and for women' as most likely to protect their threatened interests. Advances were claimed on behalf of working women across industry.

In 1918 women in laundries had worked over 50 hours a week; they were paid between 7*s.* and 10*s.*, and had no paid holidays. By 1936 the 45-hour week had been won, a minimum wage of 32*s.* 6*d.* had been secured, and long before the

Conditions of Employment Act made some commitment to paid holidays for all workers obligatory, a week's paid holidays for laundresses had been wrested from the reluctant employers. The shorter working week, promoted by the Union as a means of combating unemployment, was now claimed throughout industry. In printing, the men urged caution, suggesting that the opportune moment was not yet nigh. The women prevailed, and in November 1936 put in their claim for a 40-hour week. Conciliation failed, strike notice was served, and on the eve of a threatened withdrawal of their labour by the women the Masters agreed to place the question of the reduction in working hours on the agenda.

In other industries the shorter working week was won without reduction in wages. At Ever Ready the hours were reduced from 48 to 44; at the Post Office Factory the Government conceded a 44-hour week; and for nurses a dramatic reduction from 56 to 48 hours was demanded — and won. The agreed reduction in this instance necessitated the introduction of broken shifts, but the Union was not averse to making a political point out of such gains for the benefit of those members of the profession in less enthusiastic sectors.

> It is amusing to note that the Nurses in the General Hospitals, who are too proud to be associated with the Trade Union Movement, continue to work a 56-hour week for sweated pay, whilst our group of Mental Nurses have raised themselves to a fair standard of life through the assistance of organised Labour.[6]

The matter of organised labour was now pressing on two fronts: prompting questions which involved organisation by the IWWU outside Dublin and the place of women in the trade union movement overall.

Within the Executive, the question of country-organising provoked differing responses, but the need to consolidate gains for working women throughout Ireland prompted a renewed campaign. Miss McDowell was despatched to Letterkenny to recruit mental nurses and to generally peruse the scene; Mrs Buckley to Balbriggan to assess the linen trade; Miss Chenevix to Wexford and Waterford to seek assistance from the Trades' Councils in organising women in the printing industry.

The question of organising these women had become acute, as gains for city houses were undermined by the tendency of employers to send work outside Dublin and thus undercut established city rates. Recruitment, however, demanded more than a statement of intent from Fleet Street, and in some sectors the basis for organisation was eroded by the absence of a grievance. At the Bulb Factory in Bray the Executive conceded that 'it will be difficult to get these girls to join up, as they have no grievances, good wages and a 44-hour week'.[7] Of Mrs Buckley's attempts to organise in Balbriggan the Union recorded 'no results', and a climate hostile to trade unions. 'They seemed to be rather well off and content with what they have'. In other areas old hostilities remained active. At Wexford Miss Doyle, shop steward, organised a recruitment meeting in the Union rooms in December 1936. She was informed that the male printers had met on Friday 4 December and all 'were very much against the girls joining the union . . . they fought terrible about it, and it was of no use'. From within their own ranks, the men earned the contempt of less self-interested colleagues.

> One of the printers told me to tell you that you should put a paragraph in the *Labour News* . . . and show the Wexford so-called great union people up a bit. . . . It would be near time to waken up some of these people, all they mind is their own pocket, they are not one bit worried over their women folk.[8]

The whole question of relations between working men and working women was raised by the Commission of Enquiry into the Irish trade union movement authorised by Congress in 1936.

In the terms of reference the IWWU was classified under 'General Workers'. Miss Molony, Vice-Chairman of the Commission, submitted the Union's reservations about this decision, arguing that the position of the IWWU, as a purely women's union, required further attention before the status of 'General Workers' could be assumed. Speaking with the authority both of her years as General Secretary and as an official of the IWWU, she indicated the view held by the Union in regard to its own status.

> The organisation of this Union was not a deliberate pursuit of a policy of organising women on sex lines, which would be theoretically wrong, but was, and still is, a temporary necessity owing to the fact that women are a separate economic class.[9]

However defined, 'a separate economic class' presented major problems in a context where the necessity to consolidate the power of the trade union movement, and oppose Government incursions which threatened to usurp its functions, had become a major priority. Miss Molony, suggesting that her reservations called for a review of the current situation rather than the framing of a more revolutionary agenda, pointed to the prevailing climate in regard to women at work. While 'the outlook of the labour movement at the present time is not one that could be calculated to inspire confidence in women', the provision within the movement of special safeguards and guarantees would be essential if women were to be asked to give up 'the power that separate existence gives them' and align themselves with other workers under the category of a 'general union'.

That the Union was prepared even to countenance such a development, in the light of the persistent undermining of their position by particular unions, was a measure of the commitment of the Executive to the trade union movement. The commitment was, however, long term, and the Annual Report for 1936-37 clearly indicated that the autonomy of women workers was the order of the day.

> The present conditions of industrialism and of the Trade Union Movement make it essential to the interests of women workers that a union catering for women only should maintain an independent existence.

Reservations about the prospect of surrendering this autonomy had clear foundations. In May 1936 the Clothing Trades' Group debated a motion urging 'that certain operations be reserved for men'. Attending the meeting, Miss Molony and Miss Chenevix voiced their strong opposition.[10]

In December the Union protested to Congress that the Typographical Association 'is blocking the organisation of women in the printing trade'.[11] By 1937 the legislative provision to formalise such exclusion had been activated.

The tailoring trade invoked the use of Section 16 of the Act, seeking Ministerial intervention to exclude women from employment in a number of tailoring processes. As a counter-claim the Union sought 1s. 5d. per hour for women, a rate equal to that of men, a move that had protected women in the waterproof trade where equal rates were already established. Resolutions of protest at any exclusion of women from positions long held in the industry were sent to 'the Minister for Industry and Commerce, the Trades Congress, Women's Organisations, and the Press'.[12] At the Dublin Trades' Council, the Tailoring Trade Group argued that as women left the industry they should be replaced by men. The IWWU representative reported to the Executive that 'they hope that all women will have gone by March 1938'.

The equal pay claims for all operations in the trade were to offset the 'cheaper labour plea', and Mr Lemass was belatedly reminded that 'he promised our deputation that women at present in the trade would not be disturbed'. Such promises were, however, immediately overshadowed by the contemporary climate, which was markedly hostile to any perception of the Irish colleen as a working woman. In 1936 Mr de Valera's Government authorised circulation of a draft copy of the proposed new *Bunreacht na hÉireann* [Constitution of Ireland].

On 13 May the political wing of the IWWU met to discuss the clauses in 'the proposed new Free State Constitution which endanger the position of working women'. A deputation to the President was authorised, but little support was expected from that quarter: in 1935 a similar deputation about the Conditions of Employment Bill recorded that 'though the President listened attentively, he could not see that men and women could be equal'.[13] The attention of the Trades Union Congress was drawn to Article 40, which sought to enshrine the civil rights of assembly and association, but which added in respect to trade unions that 'laws, however, may be enacted for the regulation and control in the public interest of the foregoing right'.[14] The focus of the Union campaign would be both those aspects of the proposed document which sought to constrain the economic activity of women outside the home, and those aspects which assumed an inequality of social function as between men and women. The campaign, already gaining momentum through the pages of the public press, would be conducted by the IWWU in cooperation with other women's societies in the organisation of poster material and of public meetings.

Dorothy McArdle, already vocal on behalf of women workers and a prominent and respected historian, joined forces with Louie Bennett in presenting the public argument on behalf of women workers against Articles 40, 41 and 45. Article 40, in permitting legislators to take account of 'differences of capacity, physical and moral, and of social function', was, they argued, 'an invitation to anti-feminist prejudice'. Article 41 (2), recognising the value of women's work within the home and endeavouring 'to provide that mothers shall not be forced by economic necessity to engage in labour' was, Miss Bennett stated, 'a danger to the employment of married women'. What, she argued, constituted economic necessity?[15] Miss McArdle acknowledged that Article 44 might, indeed, have been drafted 'with the Government intention of providing pensions for mothers'. Such largesse, however, could not be guaranteed, and the danger of such an Article was that 'without doubt, it would be cited by persons who wish to deny employment to married women'.[16] Article 45 was deemed manifestly opposed to the interests of women. Section 2 of this Article referred to the 'obnoxious phrase' of 'the inadequate strength of women', of which the State was to take account, and of the tender age of children, in endeavouring to ensure 'that women or children shall not be forced by economic necessity to enter avocations unsuited to their sex, age or strength'. Miss Bennett, whose own views on the particular capacities of women had been so recently aired, was prompted to ask of the legislature:

'Who is to judge what avocations are suited to women?'

Miss McArdle discreetly pointed to the political and economic implications of such a position:

'Will the State provide adequately for those for whom no suitable avocations are found?'

On 27 May Miss Bennett, Mrs Kennedy, President of the Union, and Miss O'Connor were invited to meet Mr de Valera. When they had expressed their general disquiet, the potential for the exploitation of women within a framework of good intentions was in part conceded. The words 'inadequate strength of women' would, it was agreed, be eliminated, and in Article 45 an amendment from the Union would be considered. The proposed amendment read as follows:

> The State recognises the right of all its citizens to work and to obtain work, and that in this respect the rights of men and women are equal, but the State shall endeavour to ensure that no citizen, or child of tender years, shall be forced by economic necessity to enter avocations unsuited to their sex, age or strength.[17]

All Dáil deputies were circularised seeking their support for the amendment, and were urged in addition to consider favourably the amendments proposed by Mrs Bridget Redmond, widow of Captain William Redmond and a member of the Dáil since 1933, who spoke on behalf of the IWWU in relation to Articles 9 and 16 referring to the political rights of women.

The other aspects of the Union campaign focused on the concept of social inequality implicit, indeed argued, in a number of Articles in the proposed Constitution. The phrase 'due regard to differences of social function' implied most distinctly, in the Union view, 'inequalities before the law'. In correspondence with *The Irish Press*, Miss Bennett asked:

'What are these inequalities? . . . Is it possible to imagine a Government using this clause to differentiate between the rights of the coal heaver and the rights of an Attorney-General or a financier? This addendum to the declaration of equal rights for all citizens jeopardises the citizen rights of workers generally and of women'.[18]

Three weeks later the Union issued a statement covering all aspects of the debate. If social function, and consequent inequality before the law were implicit, did the Government intend 'that certain individuals or groups are to be given political or economic privileges denied to others?[19] If not, the clause should be omitted. The 'tribute' to women in the home, enshrined in Article 41 (2), was dismissed as 'superfluous'.

> A Constitution is hardly the place for the expression of vague and chivalrous sentiments. Mothers would prefer concrete proposals, which would release them from the pressure of economic necessity to work outside the home. The clause as it now stands is objectionable, because it might be used as a pretext for undue interference with the liberty of women.[20]

The Annual Report of the Union in 1937 referred to the campaign promoting an 'uprising of feminist agitation in which women of every class joined', and in cooperation with others engaged in this 'uprising' the IWWU championed the cause of working women at public meetings at the Mansion House and at Rathmines Town Hall. Their elation at de Valera's concession on an amendment to Article 45, however, caused some disquiet in feminist circles.

The Union, after achieving the immediate goal of securing a commitment to amend the most offending Article, 'thought it wise to hold our hand. The matter is to be allowed to drop'.[21] Censure of such an action came from women graduates, and 'other women's societies were rather disappointed that we did not go on with public meetings'.[22] The basis for such a decision can best be deduced from an account of the political activities of the IWWU in its Annual Report of 1937-38.

> Your Committee were not prepared to join in a campaign of opposition to the Constitution on the grounds of sex discrimination. There are other articles in the Constitution which carry more serious menace to the interests of workers, both men and women, and your Committee preferred to take the more general standpoint of the Labour Movement as a whole in connection with this subject.[23]

However much individual sympathies may have responded to a campaign focusing on sex discrimination, the brief of the women's trade union was, by definition, considered by the leadership to be more pressing. Women workers were domestic servants, laundresses, cleaners and shop assistants. While few were as strong as the printers, many remained as vulnerable as the wardsmaids of the Dublin Union who, in 1937, worked 150 hours a fortnight, for £1 a week; or the women at Ideal Trading Co., Lower Abbey Street, who were anxious to join the Union, 'but timid', having wages of less than £1 a week and no overtime 'even if kept working late'.

The brief of the IWWU was not confined to meeting the immediate needs of members; since its inception the Union had concerned itself with the lives of women workers beyond the factory floor. In 1937 the Annual Report called again for the provision of working class houses, the Executive noting that 'we think it the duty of organisations, such as ours, to do all in their power to find better homes for those of our members who are compelled to live under slum conditions'.[24] Such commitment went beyond rhetoric. In November 1937 the Finance Committee discussed the transfer of £200 from its investment in the Dublin Commercial Public Utility Society to Associated Properties Ltd., 'who are building 900 homes in the Crumlin-Drimnagh area'. Miss Chenevix, consistently at the forefront of such campaigns, reported that several good building sites belonging to Dublin Corporation were for sale at a reasonable price. Miss Bennett was authorised to seek a site suitable for development by 'the Women's Housing Scheme', and to 'enquire also of large houses being purchased and divided into flats'.[25]

A campaign to oppose sex discrimination so soon after the expenditure of time, energy and money in opposition to Section 16 of the Conditions of Employment Act, was — by Executive decision — out of order. Other women's societies, however, were invited to participate in a Union campaign of a different order. In 1937 considerable attention had been given in the press to the situation of domestic workers. The Union had proposed that the State should finance training schools and residential hostels to ensure that the increasing numbers of young women forced to leave Ireland to seek work would be equipped with some basic skills. The proposal had been, at the beginning of the Constitution debate, 'coldly received', and the Union had somewhat coyly suggested that 'if women's place is in the home and by the cradle, had she not better learn to keep the home and mind the baby?'[26]

A Charter for Domestic Workers was formulated by the IWWU to 'lay down conditions of employment, and domestics should come under the Employment Benefit Scheme',[27] and despite a decidedly cool reception from the State, it remained 'the opinion of your Committee that such employment must be deliberately raised to the status of a skilled trade'.[28] In the skilled trades, however, other matters threatened. In the printing industry, the time docket dispute finally erupted.

Negotiations to clarify the position of women in printing had been in progress since 1923. Discussions to formulate rules to govern their employment, however, had foundered on the insistence by the Dublin Master Printers' Association [DMPA] that the introduction of rules be linked to the acceptance of time dockets by the women. Such dockets were contentious throughout the industry in Ireland and in England; they would, however, the Masters argued, greatly assist them in costing exercises and would also, they conceded, establish times for specific procedures and assist in the overall speeding up of work processes. In January 1937, with many houses already using the dockets in an informal sense and many others resisting, the Dublin Masters again raised the question of their use, and of the proposed rules to govern the trade.

The Printers' Committee of the IWWU and the DMPA met in conference. They agreed to specific terms under which the Committee would propose their introduction for a one-year period. The terms included a provision that dockets would be used only for the making up of costs and that any complaints from the women regarding the procedure itself could be referred to a Conciliation Committee appointed by the DMPA.[29]

On 15 September a special meeting of the Printers' Section of the Union was called by the Printers' Committee. Members 'listened attentively' while the agreement reached with the Dublin Masters was outlined. Despite an invitation to members to voice their views the hall remained silent. The Committee called for a vote to accept the use of time dockets in the printing trade in principle, subject to particular agreed safeguards proposed by the Executive of the Women's Union. An attempt was made to take the vote, but it was deemed 'abortive, tellers frustrated, meeting dispersed'. Silence, clearly, did not indicate consent. In the absence of a decision from the members, the Executive now voted to take the initiative and forward a statement of intent to the DMPA agreeing to the introduction of dockets throughout the industry.

Before the end of the month, however, resistance to this move became evident. From Messrs Dollard the dockets were returned to the Executive with a terse note from M. Mackey, shop steward:

'The girls in Dollard's Printing House refuse to write daily dockets and they are returning these dockets as a protest.'[30]

From Cahill's 'hurtful remarks' were made about abuse of Executive power, and resistance became widespread. In October a General Meeting of Printers was called to discuss the *impasse*. Miss Bennett reported to the Executive that 'it was a small meeting, but unruly'. In reviewing the situation, she defended both the Executive and the Printers' Committee's decision to accept the demands of the DMPA. To have done otherwise would, she argued, have been to court disaster, and to ensure that no gains could be made in the industry that could be guaranteed to establish the women involved as skilled labour. Miss Keegan, of the Printers' Committee, had articulated the widespread opposition of her members, 'but when she realised that the Masters were decided to have them, she agreed it was better to take them with safeguards inserted by the Union rather than have them enforced'.[31]

The Executive sought a resolution to a problem which by now threatened to split the ranks of the Printers' Section. The question would go to ballot, and a majority of two-thirds by the journeywomen would decide further action. In November the ballot took place and a majority voted against the introduction of the dockets. The IWWU now formally proposed an end to their use by the trade.

Throughout the industry resistance to this form of control by employers was noted. In Manchester, although a form of time docket was completed by women in binding, the men had refused to cooperate.[32] In Dublin, it was later apparent that resistance was less pronounced. The DMPA refused to withdraw the dockets, and reaffirmed their intention to persist in the embargo on Rules for women in the trade in the absence of an agreement. A stalemate, effectively, had been reached.

Within the Union, however, hostilities were evident. Members at Dollards made clear their disquiet at what was interpreted as an unwillingness, on the part of the Executive, to abide by decisions made by members. In March 1938 the Executive, clearly divided between the political and industrial relations aspect of the question, instructed members to cooperate in signing time dockets pending further discussions with the DMPA. For their part, the Masters conceded some ground. Mr Clarke, Secretary to the DMPA, wrote to the Union asking for a draft of rules to cover women in the printing industry.[33] The draft rules included working hours and a guaranteed working week: women, if the rules were agreed, would no longer be employed for periods of less than one week; rates for learners and journeywomen would be standardised; and the proportions for journeywomen and learners would be controlled. As a precondition for such change, however, time dockets would have to be introduced. At Annual Convention in May Miss Bennett read from the Annual Report.

> After a series of stormy negotiations the system, accompanied by substantial safeguards, was put into operation for a trial period of six months. . . . At the same time a Code of Rules to govern the employment of women was also put into operation.

While the Executive regretted the 'disappointment of the convinced opponents of Time Dockets', the establishment of the Rules would 'place our members in the position of craft workers', and members from the Printers' Section of the IWWU could now claim a 'front rank position in the Trade Union Movement'.[34]

Delegates were immediately divided, both on the decision

taken and on the method of its adoption. By 27 May the Executive were forced to issue an ultimatum to their members: acceptance of the terms on offer or strike action. The militancy which now came to the fore was all the more remarkable, given the context; legislation was available, and already moves had begun to exclude women from the tailoring trade; a Constitution had just been proclaimed which placed women firmly by home and hearth, those straying from the domestic arena could, quite reasonably, be expected to be circumspect in their activities. From the women in printing, no such diffidence was in evidence.

In July the ultimatum proposed by the Executive was put to a ballot. 684 women voted for strike action, 655 voted against. An emergency meeting of the Executive was called to consider 'the very serious position created by the narow majority who voted for strike action'.[35] The issuing of the ultimatum had clearly failed to achieve its objective, and the Executive reflected on 'the large volume of our members who voted deliberately against strike action'.[36] Those who voted in favour of strike action prompted no such reflections; the continued resistance to time dockets now constituted 'a very dubious fight'. The fear of the long-term effects of a dispute in which the Executive could not guarantee solidarity within the Union ranks loomed large. On the Printers' Committee, feelings were quite clearly mixed; three voted for strike action, and six against. The Executive summoned shop stewards and printers' delegates from Annual Convention to a meeting. Action, it was agreed, should be postponed until after the holiday season, and in September a general meeting would be asked to decide on a specific issue. Prior to that date, the Union would call for cessation of the use of time dockets at Browne and Nolan's and at Cahill's. The vote would then be taken either to endorse or to reject that action — and the question of strike action would, in the process, be defused.

Before September, however, the situation became ugly. On Thursday 4 August 1938 an anonymous letter appeared in the Dublin *Evening Mail*. The writer suggested that the Executive was endeavouring to 'conveniently overrule' the decision of members against the introduction of time dockets in the printing industry. The majority of women workers, 'Full Benefit' argued,

> are against this objectionable imposition and the Union Committee are fully aware of the fact. This attitude is not due to a guilty reticence in having exposed the amount of work done during a set period, but to a reasonable objection to having this autocratic rule imposed.

The agreement by the Executive to countenance the introduction of this system, 'after nearly 20 years' resistance', was, the writer suggested, indicative of a trend within the Union that was both increasingly political and increasingly coercive. Reference was made to a weakened Labour element in the Dáil, and the very clear attitude of the Minister for Industry and Commerce to the use of the strike weapon. By implication, the Executive was presented as capitulating to threats by Government dictate. The Executive were reminded of the limits to their power, and were warned of the possible effects of a plebiscite by members to determine 'whether the present officials are carrying out their duties satisfactorily'. While — despite the obvious conundrum in which the leadership found itself — the tactics adopted by the Executive were quite clearly opposed, a final rejoinder returned to the main source of contention: the change in work practice at the level of the shop floor. 'Time dockets might be a trifle disconcerting to the Union Executive if the idea was introduced into the routine of their own office'.[37]

This letter was, quite understandably, considered to be 'an unwarrantable slander on the Committee and officials who for the past 15 years have led the resistance to the Daily Time Dockets'.[38] In a statement prepared for the general meeting, the Executive made clear their continued opposition to the dockets, but conceded that lack of agreed resistance across unions, and within the IWWU, placed it in an invidious position. The statement pointed to the weakness of the Union position in regard to further action. The time dockets were 'accepted extensively by other unions in the trade, both here and in places outside Dublin; and . . . strike action . . . would commit us to going on strike against the wishes of nearly half our members.'[39] The Executive now committed itself to safeguarding the interests of members: the spirit of overall Union resistance to the method of time dockets would, however, continue. Safeguards would be formulated prior to their acceptance to protect slow workers, and vigilance would be maintained in ensuring that they would not be used 'as instruments of speeding up or of pacing'.

In its statement to the General Meeting the Executive had asked for a vote of confidence.

> We ask our members to have confidence in their chosen representatives and trust them to make the best settlement for the workers, and by their loyalty help them to secure whatever advantages they can to offset the dangers of this introduction.

On 15 September the General Meeting of the Printers gave conditional acceptance to their use. The contentious nature of the changes involved was conceded also by the DMPA, whose members were, for their part, urged to note that 'the utmost tact must be employed in introducing the system'.[40]

For many outside the Union the resistance by the Printers' Section represented 'an act of rebellion against the authority of their trade union'.[41] The action, however, was much more than such a statement could suggest. It was an act of defiance taken by women in the face of assumptions by government, by organised male labour, and by employers — assumptions that working women had no part to play in defining the terms of their own labour. The price they paid was high. In December, the DMPA abandoned 'tact' and issued a statement warning that all women refusing to sign the dockets would be given notice. The statement came into effect on 8 December. On that day, 60% of the women at Alex Thom signed the dockets. The remainder were given notice. Dollard's continued to resist. On 1 December the Executive reported that 'no more can be done about it'.[42] At the beginning of the New Year, a member of the Executive, Miss Kavanagh, resigned, although no explicit reason for her doing so was given, reference was made to the fact that 'at the recent crisis re. time dockets Miss Kavanagh acted counter to the decisions of the Executive'.[43]

CHAPTER 11

Beyond factory gates

By 1938 the IWWU was established as an institution representing almost 6,000 women. The events of the previous five years had made clear the intent of both government and opposition to seek to influence industrial matters, and to use the legislative process to control the development of the trade union movement. Although the Union's focus in that time had been, inevitably, on the effect of legislation concerning women, the move to impose conditions of employment by statute placed the movement as a whole in a difficult position. The Conditions of Employment Act introduced a number of progressive measures enjoying widespread support among working people, but legislative support for holidays and working hours could also undermine the necessity for working people to organise their own institutions on their own terms.

The political implications of such developments were not lost on the Executive of the IWWU. At the level of the membership, however, the reluctance to endorse a specific political voice persisted. The working class was notoriously diverse in its political ambitions: matters relating to the factory floor were considered by many to be, by definition, removed from wider political considerations. By 1937 the assumption that political affiliation would prompt political reaction, and that its absence would leave the IWWU untainted by larger ambitions, could no longer be sustained. The Executive took the initiative and argued strongly for affiliation to the Labour Party. There was 'still considerable opposition to this course, as it was felt that the party had not shown any sympathy with the feminist viewpoint'.[1] That viewpoint could not, however, be used as the measure of all political development. The position adopted by the IWWU in relation to the 1937 Constitution campaign had quite clearly indicated that battles for equality would be fought in context and would not necessarily appear at the top of the women workers' list of priorities. The Executive argued at the 1937 Annual Convention that

> a Trade Union is at a serious loss if it cannot make use of the political weapon. The growing strength of the IWWU and its widening circle of industrial interests made it essential for the Union to associate itself closely with the Labour Party.

On 8 July 1937 the Executive voted in favour of affiliation for a trial period of one year, and on the initiative of the Party the IWWU nominated Elizabeth O'Connor as their candidate on the Labour platform in South Dublin City. The campaign involved the labours of 'a band of splendid workers who gave many hours of their leisure time to addressing envelopes, canvassing, and many other forms of propaganda'.[2] The poor performance of the Party in the general election, however, was echoed in South Dublin City. Members were criticised for failing to give support to the Union candidate and the pages of the Annual Report echoed with the leader's lament: 'When will Dublin workers realise the necessity to give political power to their comrades?'

The ambitions implicit in the seeking of such power had, over time, been somewhat tempered by circumstances. The revolutionary aims expressed in the Rules of the IWWU, framed in 1920, now bore the mark of moderation and compromise — a development undoubtedly related to fluctuating fortunes within the Executive body. While continuing to champion the 'just distribution of wealth', the Union policy did not oppose 'property legitimately acquired'. Private profits were to be permissible, although a ceiling would be applied and the surplus distributed to the 'producers by hand and brain'. The question of the control of industry was to be reviewed, and a share in such control would be acceptable. For all endeavour 'cooperation, indeed, is our watchword.'[3]

Despite their defeat at the polls, the general fostering of the cooperative spirit extended into the social programme of the Union. In 1938 moves had begun to formalise the long-standing commitment by the Union to cater for the needs of its membership beyond the factory gate, and the housing scheme promoted by Miss Chenevix and fully supported by the Executive was formally inaugurated in February 1935. St Brigid's Housing Society proposed to build thirty-two houses at Larkhill, Drumcondra. As an aid to such ambitions, the Corporation offered either a grant of £50 to subsidise the cost of each dwelling, or a site to aid the overall development. The offer of the site was accepted, and support was forthcoming both from individuals and from societies. Gifts were 'promised', and it was noted that 'Mr Larkin is enthusiastic and anxious to give us any help he can'. The Engineer, Major Waller, offered his services without charge, should the venture proceed.

By September, a prospectus for the scheme was at the printers. Houses would be built in blocks of eight, costing about £570 each, and 'the lowest economic rent for the type of house we mean to erect will be 17s. 6d. a week'.[4] The original plans had detailed costs of five-roomed houses at a rent of 15s. a week. The steady increase in the proposed costs, however, was matched by a decrease in the Union's confidence in its ability to provide for its members' domestic needs. In a series of letters published in *The Torch* Miss Bennett detailed, with considerable courage, the extent of profiteering in the building trade. Such corruption, she argued, undermined the project to the extent that 'the lowest tender for building would work out at £600 per house, which would mean a rental of £1 or 21s. per week'. In 1939 women in printing were paid 35s. a week; in the match industry 34s. a week; in the soap industry 33s. 6d. a week; and in the mattress industry 25s.[5] The proposed rental could not be sustained on such levels of income. The decision to support the project was rescinded, as 'our committee realise that such a rent is quite beyond the income of our members'. The site was, regretfully, returned to the Corporation, and notice served on that body that the Union would be vigilant in maintaining its interest in the housing of women workers. In December the IWWU protested to the Dublin Trades' Council at the proposed Corporation system of rental — a system 'by which the poor are segregated into special areas, according to the rent they are able to pay. This savours of class distinction and the Executive felt that we could not allow it to pass without comment'.[6]

The concern for members within their domestic context became more pronounced as the effects of increased global tension were reflected in rising prices and threatened shortages. Rises in the cost of living effectively eroded gains made on the wages' front and convinced the Executive that the membership of the IWWU must 'come forward more determinedly into the political world and assert their views, especially on matters affecting the home and family'.[7] The tenor of the Executive's resolutions at Annual Convention sought a clear response from the members. Women were to enter the fray, but on terms considered quite specific to their calling. Of 'Women in Public Life', one resolution suggested that

> This Convention claims that in order to deal adequately with the social problems of Ireland, such as food prices, rural problems, child welfare, housing etc., intelligent women must be given greater responsibility.

The resolution was passed.

The rumblings of war now prompted calls from the leadership for a moral, rather than a military, crusade, to be championed by the women of Ireland. In such a cause, women were urged to move beyond the role of spectators and into the political field. The proposals for their *entrée*, however, suggested a dwindling residue of feminist fervour. Working women, so recently militant in defining the terms of their labour, were now to proceed in terms predominantly domestic.

The membership of the IWWU was at this stage, by and large, comprised of young, single women. The thrust of Union commitment to their wider participation in public life, however, quite clearly assumed a disposition towards marriage. From a leadership which had, almost in its entirety, rejected such a status for itself, the Misses Bennett, Chenevix, Molony, McDowell, Bryan *et al.* couched their demand for women's place in political life in terms which were redolent of matters domestic.

> We are often told that women's place is in the home. We agree that is her special sphere. It is in order to defend the home and the family that women must now take a larger part in public life and politics.[8]

To what extent such a restriction of territorial ambition to the home front was a legacy of Section 16 and of the 1937 Constitution is an open question, as, indeed, is the assumption by an overwhelmingly middle-aged, indeed elderly, Executive that it adequately reflected the needs of young women as members of a rapidly changing industrial workforce.

Within that leadership, too, the years had taken their toll. Helena Molony had been absent from her duties as an official on a number of occasions throughout 1937 and 1938. In 1937, because of ill-health, she had been unable to address Congress in her capacity as President. In notifying Congress of her regret on this occasion, she expressed the 'hope, which I feel, of being able to serve the Labour Movement in a humbler capacity in future years'.[9] Louie Bennett had also been subject to ill-health for a number of years. Having been absent from duty for two months at the end of 1938, she was granted further leave of absence at the beginning of the following year. Mrs Buckley proposed, and the Executive agreed unanimously, 'That Miss Bennett will be given six months leave with salary, without prejudice to her carrying on or staying out as she feels able'.[10]

Both women had rendered long and honourable service to the IWWU. Miss Molony was fifty-nine and Miss Bennett her senior by ten years. Although there was little indication that Miss Molony had ambitions beyond the trade union movement, Miss Bennett had on a number of occasions clearly signalled her desire to employ her talents in other fields. In 1938 she travelled to Holland to present a paper to the International Industrial Relations Institute on 'Industrialism in an Agrarian Country', and in that year also had been nominated by the Union for consideration as a Congress candidate for election to the Senate. So confident were her members about the outcome of the nomination process that the terms on which their General Secretary would leave the fold were, with undoubted fondness, clearly articulated. Either on completion of her tenure as a senator, or if she chose to leave that position under any circumstances, Louie Bennett, who was then nearly seventy years of age, received the Union's guarantee that her post would remain vacant until further notice.

> It is to be understood that in the event of Miss Bennett's selection and election that she is only on loan to the Senate and will retain her association with the IWWU. If for any reason she resigned or left the Senate, her work here will be waiting for her.[11]

Congress, however, withdrew its nominees for the senate panels on a point of principle, and Miss Bennett's ambitions failed, again, to materialise.

A change of leadership in the Union at this juncture might have been appropriate. The Auditors' Report had indicated that the IWWU was a financially strong institution: 'we have £8,000 invested in sound security and we own our premises. We have also a substantial deposit account'. Between 1938 and 1939, however, the Union had lost more than 400 members. Apprehension was evident in a political and economic climate that reflected the stirrings of war, the prospect of which had imposed caution both on industry and on trade unions. Within the Union itself, the unemployment register was testament to the necessity to prepare for further losses, to review organisation, and to examine priorities. Claims for pension schemes and a fortnight's holiday for industrial workers were put aside, as the soaring cost of living limited horizons to the need to increase wages to offset the costs of a world at war.

Although Louie Bennett's Senate ambitions were effectively curtailed, a recognition of her wide experience of matters in the labour movement came in 1938 with her appointment to the Commission on Vocational Organisation. While the trade union movement expressed grave misgivings about the Commission's terms of reference, and many refused to cooperate in furnishing details of labour organisation, Miss Bennett was entirely consistent in her approach. She would assess the merits of vocational organisation, acknowledge disquiet from trade union ranks, but would ultimately rely on her own judgment. The task of the Commission was 'to outline an organisation of the various economic groups in the community which would lead to greater efficiency and more solid cooperation'.[12] The General Secretary of the IWWU was not unaware of the implications of such a brief.

> It is possible to find in this proposal a suggestion of the Fascist system of Industrial Corporations. Hence Labour's anxiety. Your Secretary will give careful study to the subject and will be strengthened by the fact that she has behind her the knowledge and experience of such an organisation as the Irish Women Workers Union.[13]

At the Annual Convention in 1939 the apprehension evident throughout the movement was articulated by Miss Molony, with reference to the fears of a covert introduction of the corporate system 'of which the Commission was showing tendencies'. In the time-honoured tradition of Irish socialism, she pointed to a different vision — one implicit in the papal encyclicals, 'which could produce a new economic system which might revolutionise our civilisation'.

The combined forces of Miss Molony and the Pope now struck a sympathetic chord among the delegates, and the Executive Committee were instructed to organise a series of talks to highlight the Papal perceptions. Later, in its opposition to the Trade Union Bill and the Standstill Wages Order of 1941, the propaganda leaflet issued by the IWWU used the encyclical *Rerum Novarum* [the Workers' Charter] as the basis for its campaign. While accepting the decision of members to endorse the themes of, particularly, *Rerum Novarum,* Miss Bennett did not self-evidently have a commitment to socialism of this or any other variety. She herself saw the Commission on Vocational Organisation as one which had 'daringly set out to establish a new -ism, an ideology which would put not only Ireland but every small nation on the road to Utopia'.

In an article on cooperatives in *Farming Today* she later recalled her enthusiasm for the task.

> It was a grand experience. I remember walking up

Merrion Square with Father Hayes after an exciting morning session and we jubilantly told each other that this Commission had found the talisman to inspire a new world society, and that Vocational Organisation would queer the pitch for Communism, State Socialism and Capitalism.[14]

Competing visions prompted lively debate beyond Convention's ability to resolve them, but the problems of falling numbers in the Union generated discord in Fleet Street. Through the 1930s the Union offices had been staffed by both full and part-time officials. Their working week was established at a minimum of thirty hours, but the disruption inherent in the position of a union official was clearly defined.

> There can be no hard and fast rules as to the working hours of trade union officials . . . all the staff will be prepared to vary or prolong their hours with or without previous notice when need arises.[15]

In 1940 Miss Bennett served notice that, in her view, all was not well. Proposing that an apprentice be appointed to the staff 'to be trained in the duties of a Trade Union official', she suggested that 'certain important matters were not adequately dealt with at present'.[16]

When a similar proposal had been put to the Executive in 1938, on the basis of 'the greatly increased volume and complexity of the work in the General Workers' Section', Mrs Kennedy, President of the Union, had 'strongly objected', staff had withdrawn while the Executive discussed the matter, and the matter had, forthwith, been dropped.[17] A concession of sorts, however, had been made in 1939 when the Finance Committee had agreed to appoint a part-time official and Miss Ryan had been appointed at a salary of £100 a year. The latest proposal, however, to recruit an applicant from outside the Union ranks, was seen to reflect on the adequacy of existing officials and further appeared to flout the procedures whereby promotion to the position of official was made from within. It would, moreover, be perceived by the majority of the Executive as entirely unfair to introduce a further part-time official when three officials were currently part-time but available if extra duties were required.

Precisely what Miss Bennett envisaged is purely a matter for conjecture, but in the series of interviews published in *Reynold's News* she did indicate that her term at the IWWU would continue until younger members were ready to take their part in Union affairs.[18] If the proposal was to take on an apprentice to be tutored in the ways of the labour movement, however, Louie Bennett's own Executive thought such a procedure both unnecessary and unjust, and quite clearly had difficulties in considering the strategic importance of the training of younger members. It reflected poorly, Mrs Buckley argued, on a staff 'already working to their full capacity'. At the following meeting of the Executive, Miss Bennett suggested that the attitude thus expressed 'constitutes a very serious reflection on the judgment and experience of the General Secretary'.[19] The decline in Union membership over the previous two years, she argued, pointed to major failings in the organisation of the IWWU.

> For the past two years very little organisation had been done and very few new groups have come in. On the other hand members have slumped away and it has not seemed possible to follow them up or re-organise them.[20]

Arrears, she argued, posed further problems: 'little or no effort other than occasional letters is made to collect'. General workers in particular required continual attention, but the level of visits and meetings had not been maintained.

The decline noted over the previous two years had been 'to a considerable extent due to the lack of such fostering care'. If the Executive and staff did not agree with their General Secretary's proposal to remedy these self-evident ills, then ultimately Louie Bennett would refuse to underwrite any responsibility for such failings.

'I do not now hold myself responsible for the efficient organisation of the Union'.[21]

The gauntlet had been thrown down and, perhaps for the first time, was allowed to lie. The claim that either lack of organisation or inadequate fostering of members' needs had been responsible for the decline continued to be seen by the officials concerned as an unjust criticism. When the matter was raised again in 1941 three members of the Executive and Miss Bennett scrutinised the ledgers and found that the decline was neither consistent nor indicative of a major problem in union procedure; membership had, in fact, 'increased fourfold in recent years'.[22]

Miss Bennett's misgivings were not, however, without some foundation, and throughout the period of the war both numbers and Union priorities reflected the particular stresses of the times. Since 1939 the Union had been aware that the crisis of the European War would have grave effects on industry. In writing to the Trades Union Congress in September it gave some indication of the shortages of raw materials already affecting women in industry, and the subsequent threat of unemployment or short time. The IWWU now sought a conference to gather information from all trade unions in order to facilitate negotiations with the government.

> Such a conference would at least reassure the workers and give them confidence in the trade union movement by proving to them the preparedness of the National Executive to take whatever action may be possible to safeguard their interests.[23]

The printing trade had been hit almost immediately, and difficulties in the supply of newsprint and cardboard would affect IWWU members in printing and boxmaking. The Executive had been warned 'that Editors of periodicals are proposing to cease publication',[24] and other industries were similarily threatened. Laundry workers reported a shortage of starch, of certain chemicals, and of paper and twine; although employment was not yet affected, the persistence of such shortages would make closures inevitable.

By 1940 the situation had become acute. At Maguire and Paterson a shortage of chemicals threatened either the suspension of all workers or the introduction of a 40-hour week; in the laundries, fuel shortages had prompted the suggestion by the employers that the difficulties be offset by suspension of the guaranteed week and the introduction of work on an hourly basis. In August, Mirror Laundry became the first house to seek the endorsement of the Union for the implementation of such steps. The Union offered a concession: a reduction in the guaranteed working week from forty-five to forty-two hours for the duration of the war. The concession was, however, rejected. On 5 September Mirror adopted a three-day week. Six days later, with no further notice, the laundry closed. This threat to laundry workers, however, was specific rather than general. While some closed, citing their failure to locate either fuel or the tools of their trade, others enjoyed lucrative military contracts, and at Manor Mill the Department of Industry and Commerce gave permission for a 52-hour week to be worked until March 1942.[25] Employers throughout the trade sought, nonetheless, regardless of the circumstances in which they found themselves, the suspension of the guaranteed week for all women workers for the duration of the war. At the General Meeting of the Laundry Section held in the Mansion House in November the members made clear their intention to resist such a move. 'The members are solid on the question of maintaining the guaranteed week'.

Such problems were not confined to one sector. In 1941 the ITUC sought to establish the extent of shortages and their effect on specific industries. The IWWU informed Congress that in relation to its own members and the industries in which they were employed

> There are 700 workers idle owing to the closing down of the Greenmount and Boyne Linen Co. This is due to lack of yarn. . . . There is gradual cutting down of employment in Lever's soap works owing to shortage of certain essential materials. A similar position exists in the paper mills and in the cardboard box industry.[26]

In the printing industry the rotation of work, seen by the Union as the most desirable way of combating the hardship caused by lack of work, was by now the norm for women throughout the trade. In 1940 when the Printing Trades' Group proposed a 3s. 6d. increase for women in printing, the IWWU agreed on their behalf to accept only 2s. 6d. and to contribute, with the consent of the women concerned, the additional 1s. for a 'proposed unemployment pool to operate with the rotational system of unemployment'. In addition a number of employers, notably Bailey and Gibson and Brunswick Press, 'set a good example by giving a weekly grant to the unemployed workers'.[27] These were, however, honourable exceptions.

The hardship by now evident in the lives of both employed and unemployed members prompted a redirection of Union energies that would persist throughout the period of the Emergency (as the Second World War was referred to in Ireland). By 1940 the cost of living, the Union argued, had risen twenty-four points above the 1939 level. Wage increases, predictably, had not been commensurate, and 'the purchasing power of the £1 is said to be half its natural value'.[28] Such a decline in the real value of wages significantly affected the lives of working people and the IWWU moved to respond to the needs of its members.

At Fleet Street the reins of power were now, by default, in the hands of Helen Chenevix. Miss Bennett was absent for two months in the summer, and in September Helena Molony applied for three months' leave of absence without pay. By agreement she continued to attend the Rosary Bead Enquiry then in progress,[29] and to represent the Union at the Laundry Conference in November; from September to December, however, she was relieved of her duties as an official. In the absence of two such formidable talents, the quiet Miss Chenevix now came into her own.

More than any other member of the leadership of the IWWU, Helen Chenevix was inspired by, and impressively consistent in, the application of the Christian ideal. In reflecting on her work as a union official she later pointed, in an address to the Guild of Youth in 1958, to the terms of her own reality: 'no matter how secular my work might be, I always worked under a sense of guidance'. Since 1917 she had laboured on behalf of women workers, particularly those of the laundry section, and speaking on the same occasion, she recalled her earlier experience of the lot of such women: 'Once when I was a very young girl I went to a meeting in a Parochial Hall at which Dr. R.M. Gwynn read a paper on

"Women and Children in Industry". The conditions revealed in this paper made a painful impression on me'.

At that time, factory legislation permitted women in laundries to work a 60-hour week. Proposing a vote of thanks to Dr Gwynn on that occasion, Helen Chenevix recalled her father referring 'to the fact that women had no Trade Unions, and that also gave me food for thought'.[30] In her campaigns for housing, for playgrounds for children and for improving the lot of working people the effects of such an early acquaintance with less privileged lives marked Helen Chenevix far more dramatically than did any sense of personal ambition. Although never explicitly acknowledged, her energies were undoubtedly a major feature in the establishment by the Union, in 1941, of the Torch and Distaff Guild.[31] Although the daily round of Union activity persisted at Fleet Street under the calm hand of Miss Chenevix, the wheels of a different form of industry were now beginning to turn.

In September 1940 the Union authorised the purchase of a consignment of food for use by the Unemployment Fund.[32] A voucher system would ensure basic necessities were available, and discussion began on the possibility of establishing a workroom at Fleet Street. The project was begun before Christmas, and in early 1941 the Torch and Distaff Guild established a workroom at Fleet Street, open three afternoons a week. Miss Carroll, 'disemployed from Hospitals Sweeps', was appointed to take charge of proceedings. Four sewing machines were purchased with a £20 gift from Mr Somerville Large, and £250 was allocated from Union funds for the purchase of necessary materials. From McBirney's on the Quay, a 'pattern of shirt' was acquired for 1s. 6d. From Kellett's came cotton and calico. Tailors' scissors, 'a remnant of brown flannel' and wool from Macey's were combined with the resources of a box file, account book and tallies: the Guild was in business.

The workroom was organised along similar lines to the Mount Street Club.[33] Members could use machines for their own needs but, when goods were produced for sale, payment was by tally. These tallies could then be used to purchase goods from the Guild or food from the Mount Street Club. Between these two establishments a reciprocal arrangement was agreed: from the Guild, 'shirts, knitted goods and sacks' were bartered for 'potatoes, vegetables and shoe repairs'. A three-acre field, rented by 'three friends of the Guild' was cultivated, by agreement, by members of the Mount Street Club with the object of providing a range of vegetables for the unemployed on a year-round basis.

The Torch and Distaff Guild was established primarily to aid 'unemployed members in full benefit'. Eighty members a week received vouchers enabling them to purchase '3s. worth of groceries for 2s.' Messrs Knowles 'supplied us with a great variety of vegetables at market prices' and members in the summer months combined business with more pleasurable pursuits in well-attended blackberry-picking expeditions. Four and a half hundredweight of jam was produced as a result of such labours. Through the good graces of Archbishop McQuaid, duly acknowledged by the faithful, twenty tons of turf briquettes were suplied to be distributed by the Union in the winter months. At the National City Bank in College Green, however, the accounts of the Guild, despite Miss Chenevix's most conscientious efforts, were noted on occasion to be decidedly red. Nevertheless, with subscriptions from friends and from Union funds the workroom catered for a roll of seventy-two members, ninety members were supplied with fuel, and in every sense other than the financial one a decent account was consistently given.

Beyond the activities of the Guild, the Executive directed the energies of the Union in other no less worthy pursuits. In 1939 the IWWU had attempted to initiate a campaign for a food and fuel depot. This campaign was 'ignored by government.' The Union then called together other women's societies throughout Dublin, and as a result, in 1940 the Women's Emergency Committee was formed. A combination of resources resulted in the production of a draft of a Memorandum on Communal Dining-rooms, 1,000 copies of which were published and distributed under the auspices of the IWWU. The proposal evoked a modicum of interest from the Department of Defence, and the hope was expressed that 'the Government were about to take it up seriously and arrange for the coordination of all existing communal dining rooms'. Such an outcome, however, was not forthcoming.

Following a meeting with Mr Lemass at the Department of Industry and Commerce the Misses O'Connor and Bennett recorded with some exasperation their 'convinced opinion' about the limited capacity of the male of the species.

> This Department suffers badly from the lack of the housekeeper's knowledge and experience. The Lord ordained that the world should be run by men and women in cooperation, but government try to run it by men alone. And see the results![34]

By 1941 the trade union movement was embroiled in battles with a government seeking to impose 'Coercion Acts for Irish workers'. At Fleet Street, however, the war years bore witness to a casualty of quite a different order.

Helena Molony, who had been on leave of absence since September 1940, returned the cheque sent by the Executive to cover the costs incurred by her in her continuing attendance as a representative of the IWWU in matters relating to women workers. Such payment would, she felt, commit her energies at a time when impaired health and other priorities made a less definite arrangement preferable. When she failed to resume duties in December, she was asked if she wished to continue her role as an official on a part-time basis. The procedural formalities, however, became somewhat blurred, as Miss Molony's continued absence provoked defensive statements from within the Executive regarding her treatment by the Union. In February she wrote to the Executive and a meeting was arranged for March. Her by now uncertain status provoked a measure of speculation within the Executive.

On 3 April Miss Bennett reported to the Executive that she had been 'interviewed in her home by a police officer who asked her questions about Miss Molony's movements'. Helena Molony's public advocacy of both socialism and republicanism, and the common assumption that for people of these beliefs England's difficulty could be seen as Ireland's opportunity, were the probable causes of such a visitation. Despite an abundance of rumour the Union records, predictably, reveal no more of this matter. In regard to the Union itself, 'this matter' of Miss Molony's status now became the subject of 'long discussion'. The duties of all officials were reviewed, and Miss Molony resumed duties on a part-time basis, catering for 'the laundry section, nurses, Dublin Union, the Rosary Bead industry and cleaners'. In deference to her own request, few formal commitments were required — 'no fixed hours to be required for work, which will be carried out as necessary'.

In May this doughty fighter for the working class returned, and embarked on a campaign to organise domestic workers — a return, ironically, to her earliest concerns as General Secretary of the IWWU. By June, however, her energies had proved unequal to the task. She pointed to the futility of the exercise, given the isolation of such workers in private homes, and with the full agreement of the Executive the cause was abandoned. For Miss Molony, her period of tenure at the IWWU now came to a close, and in October she resigned, to the express regret of her colleagues of more than twenty five years. As a body, the Executive expressed its hope that Helena Molony would

> maintain contact with them and retain the bonds of friendship established with them through long association and many trials and triumphs jointly experienced.[35]

Such trials and triumphs had been distinguished by a passionate commitment to the women of the working class. They had been advanced with a conviction that conflict was intrinsic to the struggle and had, inevitably, provoked debate and dispute within the ranks. While such disputes had often been perceived as relating to differences on a purely personal level, the battles in which, in particular, Helena Molony and Louie Bennett engaged over the years were battles which found their *locus* in the realm of clear ideological differences.

The resignation of Helena Molony marked the end of an era in the IWWU and, to an extent, the end of what had been a largely creative tension between her radical politics and the policies of conciliation and reform which remained the hallmark of Louie Bennett.

CHAPTER 12

The Roaring Forties

While the day to day machinery of the Union was maintained, the early 1940s had witnessed the development of its benevolent, rather than its industrial, outreach. In 1941, however, the focus of the IWWU, in common with that of the entire trade union movement, was directed to proposals by the government, in the Trade Union Bill of that year, to reorganise the institutions of the working class.

In early discussions with the Department of Industry and Commerce Louie Bennett acknowledged that the question of trade union organisation 'bristles with difficulties'. She had, on an individual rather than on a Union basis, suggested to the 'open mind' of Mr Ferguson of that Department that such difficulties were 'both real and complex', and that 'the government's line on procedure ought to be investigation, consultation, and mediation before any compulsory methods were adopted'.[1] Sweet reason, however, did not prevail. The Executive directed Miss Bennett, in her capacity as General Secretary, to clarify the Union's objection to the legislation outlined to the IWWU and to inform Mr Ferguson that 'they would regard it as a serious menace to the workers' right to freedom of association'.[2] Most threatening of all the proposals in the Bill was the requirement that the trade unions should deposit monies in court, in return — in effect — for licences to negotiate on behalf of their workers. The Dublin Trades' Council spearheaded the campaign of resistance. At its meeting on 23 May 1941, having considered the Trade Union Bill, it 'concluded that it is the greatest menace to our Movement within living memory, and unanimously decided to demand its withdrawal'.[3]

A Council of Action was formed to coordinate opposition.

Its brief was to meet daily and 'to use every method within its power to secure our object'. From the IWWU Kay McDowell was nominated to represent the interests of the Union and of other small unions whose existence was threatened by the proposal that unions would have to 'freeze' a proportion of their assets before a negotiating licence would be granted. Such a requirement would, however, be waived in the case of company or 'house' unions under the effective control of employers, which would serve to restrict and hamper wage claims from within the trade union movement itself. While the Dublin Trades' Council, the representative body for 60,000 trade unionists, claimed that the Bill was 'a partisan attack on the working class', the IWWU detected the intent to formalise the complaint of Mr Lemass, now the Minister of Supply, that there were 'too many unions', by ensuring a reduction in their number through the mechanism of imposing financial burdens on all those representing a smaller and more vulnerable membership.

Arguing from the basis of its own vulnerability, the Union pointed to the low pay status of its membership and the implication for an institution representing workers 'some of whom pay no more than 6*d.* a week in contributions'. Capital accrued over thirty years had been invested in the Union premises at Fleet Street, but the circumstances of its membership, made infinitely more precarious with the Emergency, demanded the provision of a range of benefits beyond those required in many other unions. The provision of marriage, hospital and funeral benefits demanded, inevitably, a solvent Provident Fund. In addition, the Union financed schemes to assist its unemployed and, in common with other unions, required 'capital in hand to cover strikes, lock-outs etc.' If, as Mr MacEntee, Minister of Industry and Commerce, proposed, a significant proportion of Union funds were to be held by the High Court, working women would experience a reduction in benefits and, quite reasonably, would be less persuaded of the value of organised labour. While it was claimed that the intention of the legislation was to rationalise the trade union movement, its effect would, undoubtedly, be the undermining of working class organisation.

From the Council of Action came support and advice on

coordinating the efforts of affiliated bodies. The IWWU, however, while giving full support to public meetings and resolutions, struck its own note in a campaign of propaganda opposing 'Coercion Acts for Irish Workers'. The moves by government to 'destroy our hard-won Industrial Rights' were exposed as 'the thin end of the Fascist stick'. On May Day 1941 the IWWU leaflet issued by the Executive claimed the blessing of Pope Leo Xlll, whose encyclical *Rerum Novarum* cautioned workers to 'beware of State interference'. The IWWU urged opposition to government legislative proposals on five counts. They sought, the Union claimed,

- To Control the Trade Union Movement.
- To deprive the workers of freedom of choice as to their organisation.
- To conscript Trade Union funds.
- To restrict their power to strike.
- To supervise their domestic affairs.[4]

Such moves had to be resisted. Irish workers were exhorted to 'smash it, before it smashes you'. On 4 June 100 shop stewards endorsed their Union's stand and called for a withdrawal of the Bill as an infringement of both the right of free association and the right of small unions to survive on the basis of their ability to serve the needs of their members; the Bill made survival a matter relating primarily to questions of a union's financial clout.

The needs of such members were further threatened by the introduction, in tandem with the Trades Union Bill, of the Wage Standstill Emergency Order,

> which deprives poorly paid workers of the right to a living wage and imposes upon a large section of the community semi-starvation conditions owing to the soaring prices of essential commodities.[5]

In the interests of justice, the Executive claimed as a priority the need to adjust the purchasing power of working people. But claims for justice had been singularly unhelpful in efforts to protect women workers in 1936, and, in keeping with the legacy of that campaign, the IWWU reviewed the tactics of opposition. A consulting brief was given to Mr McDowell,

A deputation to Seán Lemass then Minister for Industry and Commerce to discuss the Conditions of Employment Bill on 22 May 1935. *From left*, Miss Bennett, Miss Molony, Miss Fegan, Miss O'Connor and Mrs Kennedy

Miss Louie Bennett speaking at a Dáil Election meeting in 1944 (*above*) and in her garden at Killiney in 1955

Louie Bennett and Mary Moran at a meeting of the Dublin Printing Trades Group in 1952. Michael McInerney of the National Union of Journalists is at head of the table.

Mai Clifford (Trustee), Rose Bracken (President) and Maura Breslin (General Secretary) at the Irish Congress of Trade Unions' Congress in Limerick, 1977

Louie Bennett and Helen Chenevix leading a delegation to visit Dr Noël Browne, Minister for Health, to discuss the Mother and Child scheme in 1951

solicitor and adviser to the Union over many years. At his initiative, Seán MacBride, son of Maud Gonne and an increasingly prominent barrister, and Luke Duffy of the Labour Party, advised on the tactics for a combined assault, referring the Bill to the Supreme Court on the basis of its unconstitutionality and lobbying members of both Dáil and Senate to gather support for the amendments proposed by the women workers.[6] Although acknowledged to be sound, such a move was deemed tactically inappropriate at this stage, and the IWWU Executive 'decided it would not be advisable to ask the Council of Action of the DTUC to swerve from their policy of "Withdraw the Bill".'

In July the Dublin Trades' Council sought the endorsement of all affiliated unions for a resolution to the Congress committing the trade union movement to collective resistance to the Bill, if passed by the legislature, by refusing to apply for negotiating licences. The IWWU acknowledged that such a move would be effective if solidarity could be ensured. P.T.Daly, Secretary of the DTUC, urged all comrades to look to the maxim, 'United we stand, divided we fall', adding, for the benefit of those who might doubt their resolve, 'we intend to stand'.

IWWU delegates to the conference were instructed to vote in favour of the resolution.

In August 1941 the Bill passed through all stages in the Dáil and Senate. The IWWU now proposed the holding of a special Congress to consider united action to test the constitutionality of the Act, to organise the trade union movement on sounder lines to enable it more effectively to combat further invasions by government, and to outline its own constitution for the trade union movement to meet the conditions arising in Ireland's industrial and rural life.[7]

Under the terms of Article 40, section 6 of the 1937 Constitution, it was laid down that 'laws regulating the manner in which the right of forming associations and unions and the right of free assembly may be exercised shall contain no political, religious or class discrimination'. In June Seán MacBride advised the IWWU that if the effect of the Act was to discriminate between poor and wealthy unions,[8] 'it would seem that it is *ultra vires* the Constitution on the score that it is a law regulating the right of forming unions which contains class discrimination'.[9] While the considered opinion of Mr MacBride was forwarded to the President, on 23 September the Union was informed that the President, 'after careful consideration', had decided not to refer the Bill to the Supreme Court to test its constitutionality. 'The Bill was signed by the President today and is now law'.[10]

By December the tenor of the IWWU approach had, imperceptibly, changed. The Executive agreed that 'further action will be taken by us if the other Trade Unions cooperate'.[11] While continuing to support the Dublin Trades' Council resolution that the negotiating licences would fail by default, circumstances might, the IWWU indicated, compel the union to register. In correspondence with Mrs Dunbar of the Textile Operatives' Society of Ireland, a dispirited Louie Bennett pointed out that

> The position has not changed at all. There is some ineffective opposition to the Act, but the other Emergency problems were so pressing that the opposition tends to fade out in talk. We are having a protest meeting here tonight but that won't take us far.[12]

On 26 March the Congress called a special Conference of the affiliated unions. Delegates were warned: 'The crisis is grave, the future menacing, the responsibility cannot be shelved'. The Dublin Trades' Council called on each trade union to resist this 'most dangerous and bitter blow to the industrial organisation of Irish labour'. By now even the most basic right of trade unions to negotiate for wage claims by their members was constrained by the Emergency Power Order No. 166, which came into operation on 5 April 1942. Mr P. T. Daly appealed to workers to 'prove true to themselves, the traditions and principles of the movement'. At the Annual Meeting of the Trades Union Congress in July 1942 it became clear that if the movement was to remain true to its traditions, then tradition itself would have to change.

On 15 July 1942, the National Executive of Congress moved a resolution condemning the provisions of the Act 'as inimical to the traditions of Trade Unions'. It called, further, for a pledge of support to the Labour Party 'in working for the repeal of the Act, and calls upon the Affiliated Unions to give effect to this pledge by action'.[13] Before the resolution was put, recrimination began. Mr R. S. Anthony of the Typographical Association in Cork had attended a protest meeting in Cork City Hall.

> There were less than 300 people present. We never felt so humiliated as we did on that occasion. There was something wrong there. If they had had 100 per cent organised sincerity [sic] behind the movement at that time they could have defeated the Act.[14]

The National Executive was accused of failing to coordinate opposition, and the solidarity which the movement had so proudly claimed had been somewhat lacking. 'While they were having the protest meeting in Cork other unions — some very prominent — had gone up the backstairs to put down their deposits'.

Dispute raged over the lack of commitment by the movement to the political ideals of the Labour Party, with the brave Mr Anthony suggesting that despite suggestions to the contrary no delegate could deliver his members in any political sense. Indeed, 'every pensioner in the country was an agent for Fianna Fail'. Seán O'Moore, of the Irish Seamen and Port Workers' Union, protested at the claim 'that every man who fought for independence could be bought by a pension'. Such calumny provoked a challenge: 'I am prepared to meet him inside or outside this hall on it'. Warming to the theme, Mr Lynch of the Amalgamated Transport and General Workers' Union [ATGWU] confessed to his status as 'an unrepentant sinner'. The government challenge should have been met, and he had urged the Congress to resist at the Annual Meeting in 1941. Now, with the Act enshrined in the statute books, the working class would have to continue to resist 'even if it meant the extinction of the movement; it was better to go out than to live on their knees'.[15] Post-mortems, however, were to little avail. Lizzie Caffrey of the IWWU called for a united stand.

> Workers were going through a terrible time and the

opportunity was being availed of in that situation to take away their rights. It is time we banded ourselves together in the fight for economic freedom.[16]

The motion was passed but the battle was undoubtedly lost. By October, thirty-nine Irish unions and twenty-three unions with headquarters outside Ireland had applied for licences. In its application in May the IWWU had claimed to represent the interests of 5,101 women workers. For the privilege of continuing to work on their behalf the Union deposited £4,200 with the High Court, and was granted a negotiating licence.[17]

The political complexities of the response of the trade union movement to both the Act and the Standstill Wages Order are documented elsewhere.[18] The concern of the IWWU was the concern of a small union and as such the effect of the demand to freeze a significant proportion of its assets was considerable. What is unclear, however, is the rationale behind the way in which ministerial discretion was exercised in relation to the deposits required from unions. Charles McCarthy in *Trade Unions* 1977, claimed that the exercise of such discretion could reduce the deposit required from small Irish unions by up to 75%.[19] Clearly no such discretion was exercised in favour of the IWWU, nor is there any suggestion that it was requested. The precise equation employed in regard to the relationship between membership and the deposit required is unclear. The ITGWU claimed 36,000 members in its application for a negotiating licence: a deposit of £10,000 was lodged. The Workers' Union of Ireland claimed 5,000 members and paid £1,000. In the case of the non-Irish based unions, the figures are quite inconsistent. The ATGWU claimed 4,120 members and paid £6,000, a sum that would suggest that ministerial discretion had been exercised in the case of Irish-based unions, as the ATGWU deposit was higher than that required from Irish unions with more members. Yet the National Union of Railwaymen, also a non-Irish based union, claiming 5,488 members, paid precisely the same as the IWWU — £4,200, for almost 300 more members. The Irish Bank Officials' Association, claiming 5,600 members, just over 100 more than the railwaymen, paid £5,489. The IWWU payment represented two-thirds of its annual income at the time.

Few, if any, male workers in other unions paid less than the 6*d.* per week contributed by the IWWU membership, so if the equation were based on members' contributions it should, if anything, have operated to the advantage of a small union representing women. Mr McCarthy suggested that a negotiating licence issued at the discretion of a government 'sounds quite intolerable in a free democratic society'. He also pointed to the very clear indications from Mr McEntee, Minister for Industry and Commerce, that the Bill 'did not come from his own initiative' and suggests that some unions and union officials were, at some level, involved in the exercise. However interpreted, the close relationship between the Government and the representatives of at least part of the trade union movement in framing legislation to control that movement is, by definition, problematic. What is abundantly clear is that the IWWU paid dearly for the privilege of continuing to represent the needs of women workers.

The terrain upon which such services were administered by now extended far beyond questions of industrial organisation. At an individual level the political ambitions of members of the Executive were clear: between 1942 and 1943, Louie Bennett ran as a candidate for Dun Laoghaire Corporation and for the Administrative Council of the Labour Party; Helen Chenevix ran as a candidate for Dublin Corporation; and Kay McDowell ran as a candidate for the Grangegorman Joint Committee. Although only Miss Chenevix was elected, the move into representative politics was indicative of an increasing commitment to placing women in public life, signalled at Annual Convention in 1939. Resistance to the Trade Union Act had also been resistance to the extension of government powers into 'the lives and homes' of members,[20] and by 1944 the concept of 'political' endorsed by the Union had extended to most activities now undertaken by the trade union movement.

> It ought to be clear now to all women that a large proportion of the reforms they desire involve political

action . . . Even the wage question is now a matter for Dáil debate, as the government have taken powers to put a ceiling on wages.[21]

While representative politics were an essential means 'to enable the workers to stand up against the powerful combined forces of government and capital', the Executive suggested that claims for holidays and improved working conditions 'also involve politics'.[22] The function of a trade union could not be seen by its members as purely industrial; matters industrial had now become matters political.

The entire question of working conditions received consistent attention from the IWWU. From the members there came a litany of complaints. At Ruddell's the heating was not turned on until 10.30 a.m., 'many canteens are unsatisfactory from every point of view'. At Temple Press, a new factory, 'the canteen is only partitioned from the factory. It serves also as a cloakroom . . . the lavatories immediately adjoin the canteen'.[23] At Messrs Davis, Wolfe Tone Street, 'this "factory" for making cycle bags and shopping bags, consists of a dirty draughty shed in the yard of a very dirty tenement house'.[24] Since 1940 the Union had endorsed the Women Workers' Charter proposed by the General Section of the IWWU. This sought 'clean, hygienic, well lighted and well ventilated premises' and, in every factory, the following amenities:

> . . . adequate heating arrangements; sufficient lavatory and basin accommodation; a canteen apart from the cloakroom large enough for the staff employed and provided with equipment for simple meals; cloakroom apart from factory, free from dust and suitably equipped; a bicycle shed.[25]

The Emergency had made immediate claims inadvisable, but by 1943 the Executive had outlined the Women Workers' Programme for Industrial Workers, being the result of the labours of the Executive, who 'have recently devoted much consideration to health problems, and especially to the problems of ill health and disease arising from industrial conditions'. Notice was served that every firm employing members of the IWWU would, ultimately, be required to fulfil specific obligations in regard to wages, holidays and working conditions. In recognition of the constraints imposed by the Emergency, proposals were to be implemented in two phases: one for immediate and the other for post-war realisation'. The claim served in 1943 on the Dublin District Laundries' Association [DDLA] was to serve as a blueprint for all women workers.[26] Item 2, for 'immediate realisation', gave notice of a claim for 'a fortnight's holiday, for all women of over a year's service, to begin in the Spring of 1944'.[27]

Between 1934 and 1945 six claims were made in application for a fortnight's holiday for women in the laundry industry. Throughout that time the women had protested about excessive overtime and irregular hours of work. In 1936 they welcomed the Conditions of Employment Act which regulated both practices, and served notice on their own employers that they would no longer accommodate 'specials', or guarantees given to customers that laundry would be returned in the same week if sent in later than Wednesday. In short, 'both the employers and the general public must cease to regard the laundresses as robots'.[28]

In 1939, with war imminent, the laundresses had signalled their intention of consolidating their position in the industry by calling for the gradual elimination of male labour in laundries. Although no specific move was made to formalise this intention, and the Leinster Laundries' Association refused to countenance such a development, they resolved that 'in future, without displacing any men now in employment, all washing machines and hyrdos shall be worked by women, at a wage not less than that paid to men'.[29]

Under cover of the Emergency, however, and of the 'inevitable rising of prices and loss of business', the employers refused to negotiate on holidays, demarcations, or wage levels, a refusal that served notice that the formal negotiating process would be abandoned for the duration of the war. As in other industries, the war bonus became established, with employers in effect freezing wage rates while giving no commitment to continue such bonus payments when hostilities ceased.

Between 1939 and 1945 the industry was marked by fluctuating fortunes. But despite the introduction of new machinery, and methods, into public laundries, the working conditions of such women were unique to the industry.

> Laundry work is performed standing in a heated atmosphere causing, in hot weather especially, great fatigue, excessive perspiration and blistered feet. For the first five years of the war, and at certain seasons in pre-war years, laundresses often worked from 8 a.m. to 9 p.m. or later in order to meet the public demand for quantities of washing speedily returned to the home'.[30]

The health aspects of the struggle to gain an additional week's paid holiday were advanced consistently. In January 1945 Helen Chenevix sought to engage the services of Dr P.C. Clancy-Gore, a regular contributor to *The Irish People* and assumed to have Labour sympathies. Seeking speakers for a meeting of laundresses at the Mansion House, Miss Chenevix had organised a series of contributions from 'our own ranks', but added 'it would help very much if we could have a short speech from a doctor purely on the health aspect of the matter'.[31]

An industrious workforce had not guaranteed security of employment. With petrol supplies under threat, during the Emergency the collection and delivery service of commercial laundries became restricted, and further competition came from institutional laundries, using cheap labour and undercutting established prices with a notable lack of regard for the rights of organised labour. In 1941 the IWWU urged the Heads of Institutions not to take work away from the public laundries. While the Reverend Mothers of Donnybrook and Stanhope Street Convents had 'friendly, but inconclusive' talks with Miss Brennan and Miss Chenevix, the Reverend Mothers of High Park and St Joseph's, Dun Laoghaire, failed even to reply to letters from the Union.[32] In April, Bloomfield Laundry lost a military contract to the Magdalen Asylum, Donnybrook, and twenty-five girls at Bloomfield were given notice.[33]

By 1945 the laundresses, 'worn out by prolonged overtime during the war Emergency', voted for strike action to secure a fortnight's holiday. Although this claim had been included, in recent years, by a range of trade unions and by all sections of the IWWU as part of their demands for improved working conditions for industrial workers, the laundries claimed special consideration in the aftermath of war in recognition of their vigilance on behalf of the community during the years of the Emergency. The Federated Union of Employers [FUE],[34] established in 1943 to represent the collective interests of the employing class, rejected the claim and, having instructed their members to abandon the practice of making individual accommodations with their employees,[35] intimated that no review of this position would be forthcoming until government declared a fortnight's holiday as a national institution.[36]

The decision by the employers to conduct all further negotiations through the medium of the FUE marked a major departure for trade union negotiation, and the first clash between the IWWU and that body. On 20 March the IWWU responded in kind: notice was sent to the five daily papers and to *The Irish People* that the laundresses would now exercise their rights under both the Factory Act and the Conditions of Employment Act by refusing to do overtime. Notice of their intention to strike, to cover all Dublin commercial laundries, was also forwarded to the FUE. While regretting the inconvenience to the public, the IWWU stated that 'the laundresses look for the support of all their fellow-citizens who know . . . the value of the services that laundry workers have rendered in the past'.[37] From a number of quarters such support was immediately forthcoming. Since January *The Irish People* had been outlining the case for holidays for industrial workers. Mrs Waters, on advice from Helen Chenevix, championed the cause of women earning 8*d*. an hour and with few opportunities — because of the introduction of new machinery — of improving their rates of pay. The same machinery effectively curtailed the efforts of piece workers to employ their skills as hand ironers in order to ensure a minimum wage.[38]

The overtime ban, however, prompted veiled threats from the FUE that the resulting contraction of work for the public laundries would have implications for the employment of laundresses 'when normal times return'.[39] In response, the IWWU agreed to review the ban in return for a continuation of the existing arrangement whereby laundresses could take an extra week's holiday at their own expense, and the granting by the employers of a summer bonus of £2 at the beginning of each summer. The employers were advised by the FUE to concede, contingent upon 'certain propositions in regard to strike notices'. The Union refused, insisting it had to 'preserve entire liberty of action' in such matters, and called instead for a Joint Industrial Council for the Laundry Industry, 'founded and carried on in a spirit of goodwill on both sides'.[40]

In July, three weeks before strike notice was due to expire, the IWWU issued a leaflet — the first of many employed to promote a public platform for their cause. In *Do Employers Want Strikes?*, they suggested that the 'supposedly enlightened' FUE was promoting bitter conflict by 'exasperating and combative tactics'. The laundresses had been presented as the vanguard of a 'vast campaign of unrest' for their 'audacity' in seeking conditions of employment long conceded to the non-industrial sector. In *The Fortnight's Holiday as a Symbol* the refusal by the employers was seen as of greater significance 'than the demand itself'.

> The Professional or administrative worker, the clerical or distributive worker, the shareholder who does no work at all . . . is not asked to content himself with a bare week's holiday. But the manual worker carries the brand of a 'hand' and 'operative', a cog in the wheel of production.[41]

The present dispute 'between the united employers and the united workers' was presented as an extension of old conflicts 'between vested interests and human life'.[42] At the beginning of July the laundresses called to Fleet Street to register their vote for or against strike action to secure the fortnight's holiday and the stabilisation of the war bonus as a wage. All women in full benefit and employed in Dublin public laundries (i.e. the commercial laundries, as contrasted with those laundries run by religious or similar institutions) cast their preferences. 779 voted to strike, 54 against. Failing agreement with individual employers, notice was served that all public laundries, hotels, and establishments employing laundry workers would be affected. At the height of the summer season the Hibernian, Shelbourne and Dolphin Hotels would lose the services of members of the IWWU.

> Our members, convinced that the time has come when our long standing claim for a fortnight's annual leave must be pressed to a conclusion, have decided that . . . they will cease work in all Dublin laundries on and from Saturday 21st inst.[43]

In response to a specific request from the Incorporated Orthopaedic Hospitals of Ireland, hospital laundries were excluded and agreement reached on the employment of additional staff to facilitate 'any reasonable amount of extra work from other hospitals'.[44] On 21 July, however, 1,500 women workers withdrew their labour from the public laundries.

Responsibility for the use of the strike weapon lay, in the view of Miss Bennett, firmly on the shoulders of the FUE — 'an implacable group', guilty of 'lining up against labour in a hostile block'. Such developments, she suggested, 'ought to be opposed by liberal individuals who realise that the amicable cooperation of employer and employed is essential to national prosperity'.[45] Mr Lemass, now returned to the Department of Industry and Commerce, claimed that 'higher production must precede concessions to the workers'.[46] Opposing this view, laundresses who met at the Metropolitan Hall in Dublin on 5 August made 'A Claim For Fair Play', and for 'The Right to Leisure'. The status of the women was 'the fundamental principle at issue' and Mr Lemass was urged, for the common good, to use his good offices to 'stem the growing demoralisation of industrial relations in this country, to encourage the methods of collaboration between employer and employed, which have emerged in recent years.'[47]

While such calls were not universally supported by the trade union movement, no dissent was evident within the IWWU. And, although the trade union movement was by now plagued by internal dissent, and in 1945 had in fact split,[48] support for holidays for industrial workers was immediately forthcoming from all quarters. The National Secretary of the United Stationary Engine Drivers indicated

> that we will support your union in every possible way; the people on strike are fighting our fight and no matter how we disagree otherwise our sympathies and our resources should be at the strike committee's disposal.[49]

The ITGWU Theatre and Cinema Branch warned that one of their members employed as a cleaner at the Theatre Royal was taking hotel washing and 'doing it at Tara Street Wash House'. More concerted efforts to undermine the strikers were indicated in information from the Dundalk Trades' and Workers' Council, indicating that institution laundries were taking contracts previously held by commercial laundries. Louie Bennett cautioned the Reverend Mother at St Joseph's Convent, Dundalk. 'Up to now our members have had great admiration for institutions such as yours and we would deeply regret any change in this attitude'. The Reverend Mother denied any such intention, but from Dundalk came confirmation that the Sisters of Mercy had indeed taken military contracts for St Joseph's.

> All workers employed are outside labour, but are not trade unionists. The scab work performed is military washing which was formerly done in Dublin. This is being conveyed from Amiens Street and consigned to Military Barracks, Dundalk, by railway lorry, and it is then delivered from military barracks to laundry by Army lorry.[50]

By 21 August, while the press speculated about threats of an epidemic, major concern was voiced at the added burden on the 'weary woman' at home who, unlike her sisters in the laundries, was seen to have endured 'five years of war' and to now be 'greatly affected by the laundry strike'.[51] The laundresses, however, were afforded a measure of satisfaction with the information that Mr Brenner of the Swastika Laundry had, on being requested by a colleague to 'pay the wretched week's wages and be done with it', confessed that the employing class had not been left unscathed. '. . . he told me that he had to wash his own underpants.'[52]

Within the Union, members from other sections were called to assist the laundresses in their battle. For the duration of the strike the Finance Committee authorised collection of a levy from all members of 6*d*. a week from adult workers, and 3*d*. from juniors. While some other unions gave contributions to offset costs, flag days at Mullingar were held on a regular basis to defray the costs of maintaining strike pay. Such solidarity owed much to the efforts of Mullingar Trades' Council, at whose behest Miss McDowell gave talks, and attended meetings 'to place before the workers the causes of the strike to offset biased press'. From within the membership some tensions were evident. A number of women continued to work and, while many advanced financial hardship as their reason for doing so, Marjorie Wilkinson represented dissent of a different order.

> When I joined the Union I did not realise all that a strike involved and I am sorry to say that it is against my principle to strike. Even though it cost me my job.[53]

For those more schooled in trade union practice, claiming strike pay entailed signing on each week at Fleet Street and being available for picket duty. Despite regular pressure from within the membership for concessions in relation to these requirements, they were consistently observed. While on such duty, depleted coffers and dented morale were replenished by a chorus of working women proclaiming their song, to the tune of 'Lilli Marlene'.

I
Outside the laundry we put up a fight
For a Fortnight's Holiday.
They said we would have to strike,
So we keep marching up and down,
As we nearly did for half a crown.
We are a fighting people,
Who can't be kept down.

II
Then they gave us one week,
But we wanted two,
And we well deserved it
For the work we had to do.

> *There for a long nine hours a day.*
> *In heat and steam we have to stay.*
> *Then they gave us one week out of fifty-two.*
>
> III
>
> *The employers put a statement in the 'Irish Press',*
> *It was all untrue. But how could people guess?*
> *So now that they have heard our story true,*
> *We leave it all to you,*
> *To help us in our battle,*
> *To gain what we are due.*

The song sheets sold for a penny a piece, and became the theme wherever one or more were gathered together.

When employed, the laundresses had been paid 38*s*. 6*d*. a week. For the same work in Britain women were paid 55*s*. In Dublin, other industries consistently paid more — printers and tailoresses earned 44*s*., and tobacco workers earned 42*s*. 6*d*. Although lacking status and financial clout, the laundresses did not want for spirit. Accusing *The Irish Times* of being 'too grand for dirty linen', and of failing to ask pertinent questions about the employers' refusal to attend a conference called by Mr Lemass, four laundresses upbraided liberal Dublin for its noted preoccupation with style, rather than substance.

> We read your paper sometimes pasted up in those Fleet Street windows and we see it full of news about foreign countries and pictures of people no-one ever saw in Dublin. And Mr Quidnunc writes about all the fun going on at the Tattoo and the food and drink at the great ball and the boxing match with Mr Lemass sitting in the £10 seat to watch it. And Myles na Gopaleen [gCopaleen] has a column all to himself. Is it really funny? If he'd write it in Irish we might understand it better than that grand English of his. And you had nearly a page of a letter from New York telling how the girls there do their hair. But with all that you have only two lines or so for 1,500 Dublin women on strike and no word at all about the sort of work they had to do.[54]

The letter was published, and drew a wide response. *Quidnunc*, suitably abashed, covered the remainder of the strike and 'dramatised the situation effectively'.[55] From Captain Robert W. Lefroy, Co. Kildare, came support for a case he believed to be 'most reasonable' and a rejection of the assumption that one week's holiday 'is sufficient or even Christian'.[56]

Through the medium of the Department of Industry and Commerce the FUE agreed to cooperate in setting up a Court of Inquiry, as requested by the Union, to establish the justice or otherwise of the laundresses' claim. Although supporting such an enquiry in principle, the Union resisted any move to persuade the women to return to work pending the results from this cumbersome form of industrial enquiry. The Department, however, supported FUE calls for a resumption of work before there was to be any further negotiation. On 5 September the Union pointed to the difficulty of persuading members to return to work without any concessions, after two months on strike. 'It would be almost impossible to gain their assent to such a proposal unless it was accompanied by a definite plan'.[57] But relations with the Department were not good and became further strained when it refused to grant striking laundresses permits to go to England to seek temporary employment. Such action on the part of the government was considered an infringement of the rights of women workers to seek employment wherever they desired to do so, but despite Union protests the ban on the issuing of the permits was maintained. From the trade union movement, however, further support was forthcoming. The ITUC requested all affiliated unions to contribute financially to ensure that lack of resources would not force the IWWU to surrender to the FUE terms. Such a move, it argued, 'would be little short of a tragedy and would constitute a standing disgrace to the Irish trade union movement'.[58]

In response to the groundswell of public opinion, Louie Bennett and Helen Chenevix circulated 'An Open Letter to the Public'. The letter served notice that the FUE call for 'unconditional surrender' by the laundresses would be met by a resolve from working women to expand the agenda. Referring to the post-war phase envisaged in the Women

Workers' Programme, they pointed to the changing industrial scene.

> It is obvious that with the ending of the war scientific invention must turn from destruction to production. In other words more and more labour saving machinery will be devised and introduced into every kind of factory. But for the workers this will only mean an increase of unemployment, poverty and doles unless it is accompanied by the curtailment of working hours.[59]

Availing of the climate of public goodwill, the IWWU moved to consolidate its gains. Writing to the Dublin Trades' Council, the Union sought support for a public meeting on 23 September. A 'big demonstration' was envisaged. 'We propose to make the platform a women's platform as this might make a novel and effective appeal to the public'.[60] On the following Sunday Councillor Eleanor Butler addressed an enthusiastic crowd in O'Connell Street and proposed a resolution endorsed by the platform, which was passed unanimously:

> That this meeting deplores the fact that An Taoiseach has not intervened to prevent the prolongation of the laundry strike through the obstructionist policy of the Federated Union of Employers.[61]

In the crowd Thomas McQuaid, an 'employer of labour', noted the presence on the platform of a dozen laundresses, 'mostly young girls, but appeared aged far beyond their years'. Writing to *The Evening Mail* he condemned the 'public shame and disgrace' associated with the government's refusal to intervene, and even to nationalise the laundries, if necessary, in order to end 'one of the blackest chapters in the lives of these poor people'.[62]

On 4 October the IWWU sought counsel from the ITUC and the DTUC to discuss the implications of failure to settle the strike. On 6 October Union representatives met those of the FUE at the Department of Industry. Under the terms of a proposal 'submitted through a friend', the IWWU considered a return to work under specific guarantees that negotiation on the fortnight's holiday would begin two weeks after work resumed; that a Joint Industrial Council for the Industry be formed; and that arrangements be made to control the extent of overtime in the industry. The FUE gave a commitment that it would, on the resumption of work, meet the ITUC to consider the fortnight's holiday. The Laundry Branch of the FUE recommended 'that granting of holidays be favourably considered'. On 9 October, however, the suggested return to work was rejected outright by the women. In an open letter to all members of the Oireachtas, the Chairman of the Strike Committee, Margaret McGrath, made clear that the laundresses were intent on continuing the struggle. Claiming the right to 'Adequate leisure, a just wage and respect for personal dignity', they served notice on public representatives that 'when our just claims are justly met we will return to work'.[63]

The employers responded in kind. The Dublin and District Laundries' Association placed a boxed advertisement in all the daily newspapers detailing their readiness to negotiate once work had been resumed. Its message, 'Do the Workers Know This?' was a clear attempt to undermine the solidarity of the IWWU. From Fleet Street, the Executive hit back. 'The workers are requested to resume work, await a decision on the claim for an indefinite period and perhaps eventually find that the claim will not be conceded'.[64] From a mass meeting of laundresses came a resounding 'No!' The employers' willingness to 'consider' was not enough. 'Laundry employers have had eleven years to consider this claim'.[65]

In the thirteenth week of the strike William Norton TD was asked by the Union to organise a deputation to Mr Lemass to 'place before him the views of the 1,500 laundresses on strike'. The Dublin Trades' Council suspended standing orders to allow a deputation from the IWWU to state their case. Mark Daly, Secretary of the DTUC, called for solidarity with the by now financially beleaguered union. The women on strike needed money.

> It is believed that they should be assured of a sum equal to their ordinary week's wages. The Federated Union of Employers have lined up their forces. Can and should not the the Unions do likewise?[66]

By now the need for such support was critical. The IWWU overdraft had been increased to £6,400, and the Executive agreed with the Finance Committee that the 'substantial investments' of the Union would have to be 'realised if necessary'.[67] The resolve of the trade unions was matched by that of many citizens of Dublin.

> It is rarely that public sympathy is solidly behind a body of strikers, especially when personal inconvenience is involved, but that it is behind the laundry workers now can hardly be doubted.[68]

By 26 October the scent of victory was in the air. The FUE had indicated a willingness to reconsider their position. The combined forces of the women workers and the general public had persuaded employers of labour that the industrial workforce, no less than its masters, required a reasonable respite from toil. From 'A Worker' came a tribute to the leadership of the IWWU — to Miss Brennan, the laundry official, Miss McGrath of the Strike Committee, and Miss McDowell. The letter expressed the writer's appreciation of

> the splendid work yous have done for us in this strike . . . Only for you the worker would be lost if we had not great women to fight for us after all yous brought the Employer to their knees and they had to submit.[69]

From the Kelso Laundry came letters of thanks to Miss Bennett and the officials. 'Never doubting we were behind you we nonetheless realise the enormous odds you had to fight'.[70] The victory was considered to be larger than the laundry workers': 'It is "women on the march". Your laundry workers have made history'.[71] Congratulations poured into Fleet Street from all quarters — unions, associations, citizens of Dublin. The Executive, in turn, applauded its own members' courage and determination.

> The Executive wish to convey to each and all of you their appreciation of the honour and encouragement your brave stand has given to the whole trade union movement.

On 30 October the agreement between the IWWU and the FUE was formally enacted. It laid down 'that all women workers employed in laundries operated by members of the Federation shall receive a fortnight's holidays, with pay, in the year 1946'. On 6 November the Laundry Committee met to consider the cost. 'The following statement of the Union's financial position in relation to the strike was given:

- £10,600 was paid out in strike pay during 14 weeks.
- Out of this total, £7,000 had been paid from Union funds.
- Donations and collections amounted, up to date, to £2,553 6s. 9d., and a little money was still coming in.

Special thanks were given by the Union to Thomas Johnson, John Swift, and Deputy Larkin 'for their loyal help'. Patrick Campbell, *Quidnunc* in *The Irish Times*, received an honourable mention, and acknowledged the letter from 'Dear Miss Bennett and Dear Miss Chenevix'.

> . . . I am keeping it as evidence of the fact that I once served some slightly useful purpose. It was easy to write about people with such immense spirit.[72]

CHAPTER 13

Modern Times

'Your Committee have maintained a constant campaign of "nagging" in regard to working conditions'.[1] The triumph of the laundry strike served to whet the appetite for more ambitious claims on behalf of working women. In pursuit of employers, where premises sported 'leaky roofs . . . dirt and dust' IWWU officials found a largely indifferent breed, whose response to the claims for 'human needs and rights throw a strange light on Ireland's Christian Civilisation'.[2] In the absence of sufficiently accommodating employers a specific campaign directed at improving the whole area of working conditions for laundresses began.

At Harold's Cross, where laundresses were required to clean the premises at the close of the working day, the Union promoted the services of a cleaner.

> We have a number of cleaners in our Union and we consider that these people have as much right to full time employment at their own jobs as laundresses, dressmakers, stationery workers or anyone else.[3]

Meanwhile, at the Joint Industrial Council for the Laundry Industry[4] Miss Chenevix pursued the matter further. The workers' side contended 'that full time cleaners should be employed in all laundries'. Complaints had been received, she said, that such institutions were 'swept once a week and washed once a month'. These conditions could not be allowed to prevail, and 'each laundry should be scrubbed at least once a month with soap and disinfectant'.[5]

The management at Swastika was persuaded of the necessity to provide a canteen and cloakroom facilities and 'a room equipped for treatment of minor accidents or indisposition'.[6] At the Laundry Council, members were vigilant in recording the habits of their masters: 'Terenure Laundry was swept only, and not washed'; 'Kelso has all cleaning done by the juniors, including the toilets'.[7] Miss Chenevix, arguing that 'girls fortunate enough to own bicycles should be able to use them for work', waxed indignant when the Harold's Cross Laundry failed to respond to Union requests for the betterment of the working class.

> We are surprised and indignant to find that you have never taken any step to provide your workers with decent accommodation for their bicycles, or with cooking facilities in the dinner hour, although it is a long time since the lack of these things was brought to your notice. Such apparent indifference to simple needs of the workers is very hard to understand.[8]

While the Managing Director at Bloomfield Laundry was called to order — 'the workers tell us that some of the windows cannot be open or shut and are therefore useless for ventilation'[9] — the Matron at St Mary's Chest Hospital was advised that the principles of hygiene in the hospital laundry were somewhat lacking. 'The workers are rather uneasy about the fact that the baskets containing soiled linen are not washed or fumigated and they think that these may be a source of infection.'[10]

The employers were by now acutely aware of the tenacity of those in their employment, and this undoubted advantage on the Union's side meant that changes in working conditions were marked throughout the Dublin laundries. The Laundry Committee did not stint in their praise. Miss Burke reported that 'conditions were good in Milltown, and that dinners were provided on four days of the week for 3s. 6d. . . . also tea for 1d. a week'.[11] Although few workers availed of the service, 'the Imco canteen gives dinner for 1s. 3d.[12] Kelso were building a mess room, and the Metropolitan 'now had a big stove, and any worker who wanted a hot lunch could have it cooked for her'.[13] Milltown was claimed as 'a model laundry — good canteen, "Music while you work", etc.', and at Swastika the ambitions of management soared to new heights.

> I received your letter of the 24th ult. and was pleased to hear that you had heard favourable reports as a result of the repainting of the interior of the Laundry. It is our aim to make the surroundings and conditions under which the girls work as pleasant as possible, and I think the new colour scheme has a very pleasing effect.[14]

Such enthusiasms were, however, hardly commonplace.

The grievances voiced by women workers extended across industries, from agricultural workers to those in domestic service, from shirtmakers to the ranks of professional women. In the early 1940s Molly Lambe was one of hundreds of women, aged between sixteen and eighty years, who were employed as fruit pickers at Scott's farm in Malahide, Co. Dublin. In a Dublin marked by high unemployment, seasonal work in agriculture served to fill pockets and feed families when little else was available. Conditions were poor. Few agricultural labourers were organised and, although officially working an eight-hour day, the women were often required to work until nightfall when the season was at its peak. They were paid for the time spent picking — rain heralded a retreat to the cowshed, the suspension of pay, and an idle day waiting for their labour to be repurchased at the discretion of Scott's. Molly Lambe is a woman of considerable spirit. She tells of the day when she and twenty others walked off the job following a long day's work and a long wet day's waiting. She recalls the farmer's response, as the women walked away from the farm:

> He got in his red car and herded us back like sheep. And, what's worse, we let him.

Next day, through no coincidence, the IWWU arrived at Malahide. The women retreated, again, to the cowshed. Louie Bennett climbed on her box, took stock of her surroundings, and asked of the women and anyone else who cared to listen:

'And where is your canteen?'

Some jeered and many laughed. But most, like Molly, were delighted. They told Miss Bennett that they were in their 'canteen' — the cowshed into which they had been herded the previous day. For 1s. 3d. a day, and 3d. a week, the fruit-pickers of Malahide now joined the ranks of the IWWU alongside the women of industry. Elsewhere, similar conditions prevailed. At an egg-packing firm in 1948 a member reported that 'work was carried on in a stable, in dirt and general discomfort'.[15] At Messrs McLaughlin's Clothing Factory, shirtmakers complained of premises that were 'cold and comfortless . . . when the girls are kept working until 8 p.m. they are given only a quarter of an hour for tea, which they take on the stairs'.[16] For wardsmaids, conditions of labour were considered by women to be so unpalatable that 'it has now become almost impossible to find anyone willing to undertake this work'.[17] At St Laurence's Hospital the Union reported 'maids still sleeping in the old basement bedrooms, with no heat in the winter'.

While all laboured under poor conditions for long hours, some individuals were also prey to the petty tyranny of their supervisors. At St Laurence's Hospital, 'Helen Thackaberry appears to her fellow workers to have too much to do'.[18] The abuse of power was not confined to the quiet corridors of institutions: at Dargle and Bray Laundry a complaint was made to the Union which gave some indication of the vulnerability of the piece workers — of the women dependent on the goodwill of charge-hands to ensure sufficient 'journey silks and 2s. work' to guarantee a living wage.

> . . . now for instance Mrs Hannan is on the giving out of work and she is one that keeps me down from earning a desant wage. She gives the paying work to her own sister and other palls and I never get a thing from her only plenty of 3d. work. She murders me with <u>them</u> alright.[19]

In the early 1940s the Union had reported the movement of the unemployed to Britain to seek war work. 'Very large numbers of women as well as men are leaving Ireland every week.'[20] While the exodus of young women from Ireland was most notable amongst the domestic servants, however, the problem of maintaining the services of professional women was also noted by the Union in its Memorandum on Emigration, submitted to the Commission on Emigration in November 1948. In Britain 'all the professions give an assured status to women' and Ireland experienced 'increasing difficulty in meeting the demand for nurses'.

At Grangegorman, the Union complained of cases where there were '33 homicidal patients with one nurse on night duty'.[21] When such nurses claimed an increase, and equal pay, in 1946, the Board had recommended increased rations and a cash payment which ensured the maintenance of differentials between the nurses and the male attendants. 'This differentiation is resented by our members who are doing the same work under the same conditions as the men'.[22] On appeal to Dr Noel Browne, Minister for Health, the women received the same increase and rations as the men, but the Union now pointed out that the status they could claim in Britain, 'where equal pay for equal work is no longer merely a slogan', was a further encouragement to professional emigration. When such women sought to redress their grievances in the time-honoured fashion by taking the boat to Liverpool, the reluctance of Irish employers and government to meet their claims earned its own reproof.

> The 'skivvy' of former days now works in England on an eight hour day basis and a wage of £2 per week with full board.

While government called for greater efficiency and higher productivity, the IWWU related widespread industrial malaise to a contempt for the needs of working people. Ireland's workplaces, the Union suggested, 'match her slums'. In a detailed Memorandum on Factory Premises the Union recorded a Dickensian landscape that provoked no outrage.

> Industries are carried on in rotten old houses, in basements, out-houses, tenements, places where it is impossible to meet the human need for sanitation, light, heat and ventilation.

Although pointing to 'extreme but not exceptional cases', the IWWU served notice that 'we could name firms of high repute where the industrial drive has led to overcrowding and workers are located in dilapidated rooms or basements no better than a cellar'.[23]

To redress such grievances, and halt 'the exodus of young women from Éire', the Union urged the government to amend the Conditions of Employment Act to cover factories and workshops: to have the Factory Inspector's Department 'constituted on modern lines': to employ more women inspectors; to take cognisance of 'Industrial Health and Industrial Psychology'; and to endow universities to research the implications in these areas. From trade unions, the Women Workers called for reform of working conditions to be made 'a primary and urgent plank of their programme'.[24] Their concern was echoed throughout the movement. The question of workers' health was discussed at Congress in 1948 and a conference on Working Conditions in Industry was convened by Congress at the beginning of the new year.

By May 1949, however, the Executive recorded 'a slow unfolding of social and political development which must cause considerable anxiety to trade unions'.[25] The disquiet was general: the ban on wage increases, the price of essential commodities, and the demand for greater production from 'American guardians of the Marshall Plan'. More ominous still was the introduction of 'new machinery and new methods of industrial organisation', methods which tended, they felt, 'to make the worker still more a cog of the machine than hitherto'.[26]

'Time and Motion' studies were being undertaken in Dublin. The system, based on principles of mechanisation devised by Frederick Winslow Taylor, an engineer, was aimed at maximising output by reducing the work process to its component parts. 'The workers are induced to speed up by a bonus on output, and the whole layout of the factory is planned to curtail inessential movements and waste of energy'.[27] The need to increase productivity was widely acknowledged and efficiency methods 'which make the factory a field of activity for the workers' were considered by the Union to be quite acceptable. The methods proposed, however, were claimed to 'make the worker the factory's tools' and as such were rejected by both Executive and members.

Since 1947 members had been reporting the increased pacing of machinery and the consequent stress experienced by workers. At Maguire and Patersons, 'machines used to do from 17 to 19 cases per day, and now do 20 which involves a strain on the girls'. The new production levels had been achieved both by speeding up and by reducing the number of machines involved in a process. A machine was standing idle, and Union suggestions of further recruitment to produce greater levels of output in fewer hours were 'not feasible under present conditions'.[28] Throughout the laundry industry the pace of calenders was agreed by all workers to be 'much too great' and, at Court Laundry, developments along 'scientific lines' were proceeding under the direction of a new breed — the Industrial Consultant.

> Every Department is organised so as to secure the utmost support from every worker. Every movement is calculated and the general layout is arranged in such a way as to require the least possible effort from the worker . . . the worker's output is calculated by a system of stop-watch timing.[29]

When average outputs were established a bonus was paid on any excess. The system, however, was complex. As piece workers and as time workers, women had become adept at assessing bonus systems — a necessary strategy for women in textiles and laundries where, as noted earlier, work was often distributed by supervisors not averse to the exercise of petty tyranny. With the introduction of 'scientific measurement', however, such safeguards were not maintained. 'The system is so complex that few, if any, of the employees understand it or are able to calculate their bonus.'

With the increased cost of living the 'lure of a bonus' undoubtedly served to persuade workers to 'accept new schemes unreservedly'. To offset the exploitation of their members' officials proposed explicit safeguards: the establishment of a Works Committee, with trade union representation, 'to study the scheme and watch its effects'; provision for workers made redundant by new techniques; information on the method of calculating the bonus, and provision for this to be paid on team or department output.[30] The extent to which such procedures were actually implemented is difficult to establish, but by 1949 members of the IWWU instructed the Executive, in direct response to the speeding up process, to claim a 40-hour week in all industries where such methods were employed.

Maguire and Paterson, previously considered by the Union to be 'a model factory', now became the focus of a dispute which found echoes in other industries as the new work process developed. On 25 May a meeting of members instructed officials to notify management that women would no longer continue working the 44-hour week.

> We have been informed by our members in your employment that machine power in your factory has been raised to a higher level and that consequently the women are speeded up to an intolerable degree.[31]

The IWWU renewed its claim for a 5-day week of forty hours. As had happened in 1947, the directors refused to negotiate and in July a mass meeting of all employees instructed the Union to appeal to the Labour Court and to claim a shorter working week with the 'objective of a progressive advance to the 40-hour week'.[32] At Annual Convention the Trade Union Congress was 'urged to launch a campaign for a shorter working week', and at Levers and at Maguire and Patersons the use of 'speed machines' was examined by Congress.

At Court Laundry, meanwhile, the bonus system provoked differing responses among the women workers. 'The senior girls do not like it, but the juniors do. Some get large bonus, others very small.'[33] Motives, however, were not universally those of a mercenary nature. Younger working women welcomed the 'neutral' rule of the machine. Where their predecessors had condemned the tyranny of overseers, the new working woman entered into direct competition with her machine and a different order of working relationships developed. Concerted opposition was difficult, due to the uneven pace of the implementation of the new methods and the introduction of new machinery. Maguire and Paterson had modern buildings and had equipped a canteen and rest room for its workers, and the new process was introduced in this particular industry long before it became widespread. The laundries were also in the vanguard of such changes. Here, notably improved conditions were evident, in terms of both the fortnight's holiday and improved conditions at the workplace. In such a climate resistance was spasmodic and the potential for opposition across any particular industry was difficult to realise in a context in which many continued to employ the old methods and to utilise old machinery.

In the trade union movement as a whole changing work processes were, to some extent, seen as inevitable. The methods of work measurement, imbued with the aura of 'science', were perceived in some sense as natural. Pockets of discontent, however, were evident. At the Court Laundry, ironers were 'very much opposed to the bonus system'. The ironers, together with colleagues from the Workers' Union of Ireland, and accompanied by Denis Larkin, attended a laundry section meeting in December 1949.

> There was a full discussion over the proposed extension of the Time and Motion Bonus system to these workers, which would mean changing them from the piecework system which they have always had to a system with bonus on output . . . . The ironers strongly resented this change and it was agreed that the unions should make a strong effort to avert it.[34]

A deputation from both unions met directors of the Court Laundry and a trial period was agreed.

In February 1950, with a new basic rate of £3 5s and bonus, the ironers decided to continue working the bonus system. At Armstrong's, a scheme was agreed for the envelope department, and at Dollard's, where women had consistently refused to sign time dockets, it became clear that the leadership of the IWWU would encourage conciliation rather than conflict.

> In Dollard's firm a scientific management plan is causing much heartburning amongst the staff, but with careful supervision from the Trade Union it may have beneficial results for the workers as well as for management.[35]

Although resistance would later be evident at General Textiles Ltd,[36] and at Urney Chocolates,[37] for the IWWU the major battle over new methods, and the principle of timing work in relation to specific processes, had been recognised, fought and lost in 1938 in the Time Docket Dispute. While Louie Bennett and others maintained an intellectual interest in the effect of such schemes, they undoubtedly resisted any moves, particularly from Dollard's, to revive an old campaign. Neither the leadership, nor the trade union movement, were unique in expressing ambivalence: both Lenin and Trotsky, while not wholly uncritical, 'saw Taylorism as "a great scientific achievement" in "elaborating the correct methods of work" and as a necessary component of modernising the Soviet Union'.[38]

The extent to which pressure of other business influenced the almost imperceptible acceptance of the individual bonus and work measurement schemes is also difficult to establish. In 1949 Union membership stood at 6,782. Of these, 1,705 were printers, 895 paper boxmakers, 1,957 laundresses, 286 nurses, and 2,139 general workers. While Miss Bennett retained her position as General Secretary, at seventy-nine years of age her contribution was principally evident in the various memoranda on emigration, factory conditions, and equal pay.[39] The main burden of running the Union fell on Miss Chenevix and Miss McDowell, and by 1949 both were actively involved in an overtly political sense. Miss McDowell was a member of the Administrative Council of the Labour Party, and was Chairperson of the DTUC Women's Council of Action, and Miss Chenevix was a Dublin City Councillor and Vice-President of the Trade Union Congress. Lizzie Caffrey, long an activist in the labour movement, had replaced Helena Molony as IWWU member on the Dublin Trades' Council Committee.

Other matters also loomed large. Towards the close of the decade a major dispute erupted in the printing section — a dispute which seriously undermined IWWU claims to be a national organisation of women in that industry. At the Monument Press in Bray three journeywomen were dismissed and three fourth-year apprentices were let go in response to slackness in the trade. The dismissals, however, followed a claim by the IWWU for the establishment of a set rate for provincial houses that would be more commensurate with the Dublin rate. As a house renowned for the excessive use of junior female — and hence cheap—labour, the loss of work for journeywomen and girls due to completion of their time represented a flouting of the ratios agreed in 1938 under the rules governing the employment of women in the printing trade. It was also perceived as deliberate provocation: while these women were out for 'slackness', skilled men were working overtime and feeding machines normally fed by girls.[40] In response, the IWWU imposed a ban on overtime for their members. Mr Flynn of the Monument Press claimed that this broke the negotiated agreement and signalled quite clearly that the position of the IWWU was under threat.

> There are other unions who have organised the women in provincial offices and it has been stated, on their behalf, that the number of their members in provincial offices far exceed those of your union.[41]

While Monument had previously employed thirty-two members of the IWWU, by late 1949 only thirteen remained. Time sheets produced by the women were now conceded by Bray Urban District Council to be a basis, if Mr Flynn chose to exercise his power, for dismissal 'as a result of unpunctuality'.[42] While the persistence of such practices undoubtedly weakened the IWWU's negotiating position, the hostility evident in the correspondence from Mr Flynn suggested that other factors were serving to undermine the authority of the Union. If the IWWU proceeded with its claim that working conditions for women in provincial houses would have to compare favourably with those in other houses, Mr Flynn warned that he would attempt to impose the ultimate sanction.

> If you persist in your present policy the Irish Master Printers' Association may be asked to approach the Minister for Industry and Commerce to consider whether or not your negotiating licence shall apply to the provincial areas . . . and the IMPA may also consider whether they will refuse to recognise your union in provincial offices.[43]

The question of organising rights was contentious. In 1945

the Irish Bookbinders' and Allied Trades' Union [IBATU] had applied for sole organising rights for bookbinding, including women. Although at that time the rules of the Bookbinders' Union precluded the admission of women as members, their right to organise the trade was conceded under the terms of the Trade Union Act 1941, which recognised their majority status within that section of the printing industry. As such a decision would clearly undermine the negotiating authority of the the IWWU in representing women in printing and allied trades, the Union contested this decision in the Supreme Court. Their claim, that the decision in favour of the IBATU was *ultra vires* the Constitution in regard to freedom of individual choice of a union, was upheld.

The decision, a victory for the IWWU, extended also to other small unions and provided a measure of protection against encroachment by larger institutions. The memorandum from the IWWU which accompanied the application to the court claimed that IBATU had further and particular ambitions in regard to territory held by the women workers, and that it was, in effect, seeking 'to ensure that in future this work will not be done by members of the IWWU and not by women'.[44]

The matter, despite the decision of the Supreme Court, was clearly not resolved. IBATU continued to recruit women in printing, and through meetings and advertisements in the daily press sought to undermine loyalty to the IWWU in the city. In 1948 IWWU members refused to work with ex-members who had joined the IBATU and strike notice was served throughout the industry that unless such practices ceased the IWWU would take the ultimate step and withdraw their labour. The case was referred to the Labour Court, and in the court's final recommendation the binders' union was rebuked for 'reprehensible poaching',[45] and forced to concede Dublin city and county to the IWWU. Provincial houses, however, would now be free to choose their own union. Subsequent to the recommendation, the IBATU changed its rules to allow women to join, and proceeded to organise outside Dublin.

When the Monument moved, in effect, to challenge the IWWU to withdraw its claim for a set rate for provincial houses or withdraw its labour, the Union chose the latter course. Thirteen women, and two boys who were members of the ITGWU, came out, and pickets were placed on the Monument Press. Inter-union relations declined quite dramatically. In August, Louie Bennett wrote to J.P. Forrestal, Secretary of the Typographical Association:

> I regret very much that the Typographical Association is not taking the matter of our dispute with the Monument Press more seriously. Your members are very sharply criticised for working with unorganised men and boys who are now employed on the women's work.[46]

The Association asked all journeymen and apprentice members to confine themselves to normal letterpress work. No reference, however, was made to working with scab labour. In October, the Monument Press officially dismissed the women on strike and advertised for

> Smart girls for the following vacancies: printing machine feeders; book folders and folding machine operators.

As stated in the advertisements for the positions, all applicants were required to be members of the Irish Bookbinders and Allied Trades' Union.

At Florence Road, Bray, a public meeting organised to rally support for the women on strike sounded a historical note in relation to the dynasties of Irish political life. Louie Bennett, having shared both battles and wit with 'Big Jim' and James Connolly, now graced the platform with their offspring — James Larkin TD, and R.J. Connolly TD. In company with Bray Trades' and Labour Council they protested at the behaviour of Monument and IBATU 'in the strongest possible way'.

On 20 October the IWWU informed the Dublin Trades' Council that a further development was now afoot, calculated both to break the strike and to undermine all negotiations to better the conditions for women in the provincial houses.

> The Irish Bookbinders' Union have signed an agreement with the Irish Master Printers' Association which en-

Louie Bennett and Helen Chenevix at Killiney in 1955

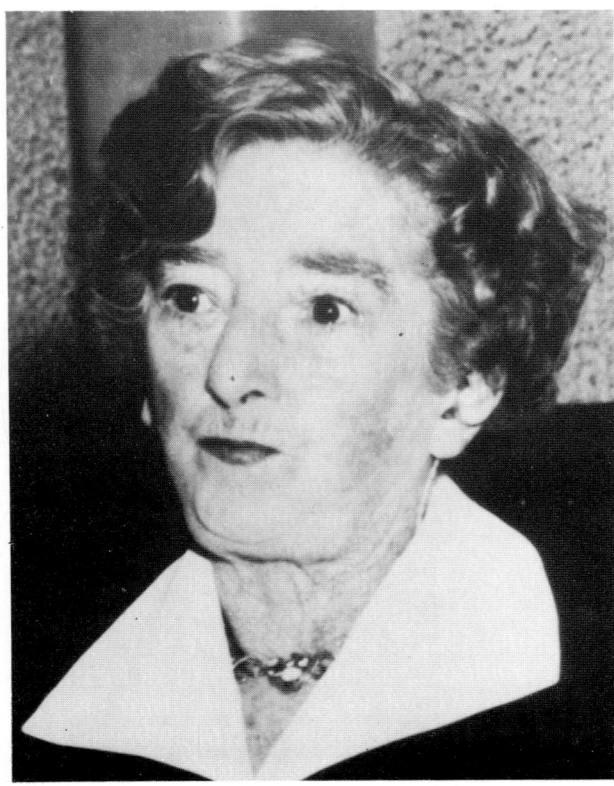

Kay McDowell, General Secretary of the Union from 1957

CARDBOARD BOX STRIKE

WHY has the Strike of Cardboard Box-makers lasted for Seven weeks?

BECAUSE the Employers concerned persistently refuse to enter into a Conference with the Trade Union.

WORKERS! Stand by the women who are making this long fight in defence of the right of the Trade Unions to negotiate for the workers on the subject of Wages and Working Conditions.

IWWU Archive

TO WOMEN WORKER[S]

DO YOU WANT a fair wage standard?

DO YOU WANT to hold your Bonus as a wage?

DO YOU WANT Security of Employment so that y[ou] cannot be dismissed without goo[d] cause?

DO YOU WANT a Fortnight's Annual Holiday with Pay?

DO YOU WANT Good Factory Conditions, Good Heat, Good Light, a Good Cloakroom, a comfortable Dining Room and a break for Tea in the forenoon?

DO YOU WANT Sickness Benefit, Hospital Benefit, Convalescent Facilities, Marriage Benefit?

YOU CAN GAIN THESE ADVANTAGES AS A MEMBER OF THE IRISH WOMEN WORKERS' UNION
48, FLEET STREET, DUBLIN

Extract from Irish National Anthem—

"Some have gone to a Land beyond the Wave"

They go to lands where a decent standard of life obtains.

The Irish Nation asks for athletes.

The Government asks for a healthy and strong population.

But Government Boards set a standard of Starvation Wages.

Extracts from propaganda posters issued by the Union

Beware

To all Workers!

All Cardboard Boxes coming from O'Reilly's, Poolbeg St.; Dublin Box Company and Cherry and Smalldridge are Scab work, done by Scab Labour.

DON'T TOUCH THEM!

LAUNDRESSES!

Come to the
MANSION HOUSE
ON
Tuesday, 30th January,
at 7.30 p.m.
TO DEMAND A

FORTNIGHT'S HOLIDAY

You first asked for this in 1934

Why not get it in this year 1945?

IWWU Archive

IRISH WOMEN WORKERS' UNION

STRIKE AT MATCH FACTORY

Our members in Maguire & Paterson's have been on Strike for three weeks in the most severe weather of the year. In order to be able to add something to the Strike Pay which they are receiving under our Rules, the Executive Committee are asking every working member of the Union to pay a levy of **2d. per week** as long as the Strike lasts. This levy, which is compulsory, will start in the week ending 11th February.

H. S. CHENEVIX
Secretary

48 Fleet Street
Dublin
3rd February, 1956.

COERCION ACTS
FOR IRISH WORKERS!

The new Trade Union Bill and Standstill Wages Order aim to destroy our hard won Industrial Rights. The Government proposes by this legislation —

To control the Trade Union Movement,
To deprive the workers of freedom of choice as to their organisation,
To conscript Trade Union Funds,
To restrict their power to strike
To supervise their domestic affairs.

This is the thin end of the Fascist stick!

Irish Women Workers' Union

ANNUAL GENERAL MEETING

at the O'CONNELL HALL,
42 Upr. O'Connell Street

On Thursday, May 4th, 1950
at 8 p.m.

ALL members must help in the plan of Campaign to be launched at this meeting. It means SEVEN THOUSAND WOMEN WORKERS organised to win A JUST WAGE; HEALTH and HAPPINESS at work and at HOME.

LOUIE BENNETT
Secretary.

48 FLEET STREET,
DUBLIN.

IWWU Archive

Irish Women Workers' Union

ANNUAL GENERAL MEETING

WILL BE HELD AT

THE MANSION HOUSE

ON

Tuesday, May 6th, 1952, at 7.45 p.m.

Following reports of Convention decisions a discussion will be opened at 9 p.m. on

THE BUDGET

HOW IT LOOKS TO THE WOMAN IN THE HOME
IN THE FACTORY
ON THE FARM

Speakers from various women's organisations have been invited to join in a united campaign for protection against high prices and unemployment.

IRISH WOMEN WORKERS' UNION
48 FLEET STREET, DUBLIN

Irish Women Workers' Union

At a Shop Stewards' Meeting, on 28th October, it was decided to form a

SOCIAL CLUB FOR I.W.W.U. MEMBERS

This Social Club will organise Outings, Theatre Parties, a Gym. Class, Whist Drives, &c.

A very small Annual Subscription is proposed.

Members wishing to join will please sign form at foot and bring it with sixpence to a **General Meeting** to be held on **Monday, November 18th,** at 9 p.m. at 7 Eden Quay.

APPLICATION FORM.

I would like to become a Member of the I.W.W.U. Social Club.

Name

Address

I enclose Sixpence.

IRISH WOMEN WORKERS' UNION

HEALTH
SAFETY
WELFARE

Workers of Dublin, men and women, join the campaign to secure good conditions for all workers in all occupations. Voice your claims at

A PUBLIC MEETING

IN THE

MANSION HOUSE

ON 1949

Tuesday, May 17th at 8·30 p.m.

Guest Speakers will include—
The Rev. Thomas Counihan, S.J.
Dr A. J. O'Sullivan, Industrial Medical Officers' Association.
Robert Morgan, President, Dublin Trade Union Council.
R. Roberts, Sec., Irish Trade Union Congress.

NOTE :
Members of the I.W.W.U are requested to attend Meeting at 7-30 p.m. to hear Report of Convention proceedings.

Bills announcing the Annual General Meeting of May 1950 and May 1952 *(top)*; advertising the formation of the IWWU Social Club *(bottom left)*; and announcing a public meeting in May 1949 *(bottom right)*

dorses a scale of wages our members have refused and which already operates in Waterford.[47]

Employing her considerable tactical skills, Louie Bennett moved rapidly onto the offensive. Writing in *The Irish Independent* she castigated the agreement negotiated by the Irish Bookbinders' Union, which established a wage of 52s. 6d. for journeywomen for a 42½-hour week in provincial printing houses. She used the occasion to announce that the agreement would apply in Waterford, where the IWWU had recently secured for its members a wage of 55s. for a 42½-hour week. The 55s. rate also applied in the Bray Printing Company and two other provincial concerns were considering a similar rate.[48]

On 21 October *The Irish Times* carried an announcement from Fleet Street: 'The Irish Women Workers' Union wish to inform the public that the strike at Monument Press, Bray, still continues', and on 22 October, under 'Situations Vacant', *The Wicklow People* included a further reference to that establishment.

> Any girls wishing to apply for work in the above are advised to communicate first with the Irish Women Workers' Union.

Girls who did so were informed that the firm had dismissed its entire staff of girls for their temerity in seeking improved working conditions. 'We believed that any girl who stood for decent conditions and wages would suffer acute discomfort should she find herself in the position of applying for a job which rightly belongs to the girls on strike'.[49]

This appeal, however, was to prove largely ineffective. By the eleventh week of the strike, six new girls had replaced the thirteen dismissed. All carried IBATU cards. In November the Executive reviewed the situation. Letters were sent to the Trades Union Congress, and the Congress of Irish Unions citing the behaviour of both the Binders' Union and the Typographical Association. Neither Congress nor the Binders' Union replied to the charge.

The Bray Council of Action interviewed Mr Flynn, who

agreed to reinstate some strikers but not those involved in the original dismissal. The Union refused to accept such terms, but on 15 December, in the fifth month of the strike, the IWWU conceded defeat. The twelve girls and two boys continued picketing. A number of them had been offered alternative employment and the Union now committed itself to finding work for the girls. 'They are to get first preference for any jobs in Dublin.'[50] On 11 February 1950 the strike ended: all members having, by then, found alternative work.

The defeat at Monument Press was reluctantly accepted, but marked a low point in terms of Union morale. In 1950 Louie Bennett sought a meeting of the Finance Committee to discuss the terms of her retirement. On 14 March she delivered a statement to the Executive conceding that, at eighty years of age, she no longer 'felt equal to the full strain of the office of General Secretary'. Although her retirement had for some time been anticipated, she offered, instead, her resignation from the post she had held since 1917. It would seem reasonable to suggest that an announcement of retirement would have been both appropriate and a means of allowing the Executive to accept and adjust to the inevitability of a change in the status quo. A resignation, particularly given Miss Bennett's use of this mechanism in the past as a means of reasserting her control, left the Executive with a dilemma: to accept could have been interpreted as a reproach to the General Secretary; a rejection of the offer merely an echo of earlier times, and a continuation of the prevailing order. The Executive refused the resignation.

In thirty three years' service to the Union Louie Bennett had endeavoured to use her skills to improve the lot of working women. Her strengths in negotiation and in the analysis of industrial development had served to ensure that the IWWU entered the era of scientific management and changing work processes with the financial and political authority to continue as a viable force in the labour movement. In her early years as General Secretary she had threatened to resign on at least five occasions. Undoubtedly, the tactic of the threat was used to some effect in establishing her authority and since 1940 little overt criticism of her form of leadership had been evident from other members of the Executive.

Throughout her period of office Louie Bennett was notable for her conviction that the personal intervention by the individual could be politically effective. With de Valera, Lemass and MacEntee she had acted in a dual capacity, as General Secretary and as informed citizen — often authorising dual communications which were not always consistent with each other, following deputations to ministers or departmental heads. On a number of occasions Miss Bennett was forced by the Executive to reiterate the Union position when it appeared likely that she was advancing, under the banner of the greater good, presumptions which were not always in the industrial interests of women, as in her correspondence with the Department of Industry and Commerce prior to the passing of the Trade Union Bill. Over such a long period as General Secretary, however, she evoked undoubted affection from most quarters of the Union, yet many spoke also of her acute awareness of her status as leader, and of the strong sense of the righteousness of her position. As she grew older, this assumed a decidedly evangelical flavour: with the zeal of a convert or, perhaps, overly sensitive to her position as the Protestant leader of a predominantly Catholic membership, she encouraged the publication by the IWWU of *Peace and Fraternity*, a pamphlet 'Addressed to Women of Every Nation', endorsing the 'Discourse of the Holy Father' to the Catholic women working for the attainment of peace.[51] Whatever their intrinsic value, the appropriateness of such publications for industrial workers facing unemployment and the harsh realities of emigration or destitution was not immediately obvious. Her growing tendency to authorise the despatch of copies of IWWU resolutions on domestic and international affairs to the Vatican was a clear indication that a review of her role in the Union might now have been appropriate.

By 1950, however, a mutual — and unproductive — dependency between the General Secretary and her Executive had become apparent. When her resignation was refused the Finance Committee proposed that she take leave of absence from her office for one year, 'while still being available for consultation and advice when necessary'. This consultative position would, at her own request, entail a reduction in salary, and Miss Chenevix and Miss McDowell would 'assume full responsibility for the work of the Union'. On 30 March the deliberations of the Executive were finalised: Miss Bennett would take leave of one year from July 1950. She would receive full pay.

It is difficult to avoid comparing this decision with the accommodation offered to Helena Molony. Miss Molony worked for the IWWU from 1911 to 1940, a period of almost thirty years marked by major trauma in the labour movement. When she left the service of the Union it was on a disability allowance of £6 a month, and over the years she was placed in the invidious position of having to seek her own increases in that allowance to meet the rise in the cost of living. Ten years after Helena Molony's departure, Louie Bennett, having served in the Union from 1917 to 1950, was granted, at eighty years of age, leave of absence for a year on full pay.

Such a disparity pointed to a structural weakness. The disposition of Union resources, however generous or niggardly, is of course an internal matter for the institution concerned. What the retention of Miss Bennett's services suggested, however, was an increasing conservatism in the development of the IWWU. The industrial terrain was changing rapidly. Within the leadership of the IWWU women younger than Miss Bennett had served apprenticeships of quite unwarranted length: Kay McDowell had been in the Union for almost thirty years and was recognised, especially by the Printers' Section, as someone who was as familiar with the industrial scene as anyone on the shop floor. In terms of the expectation of power, however, she was faced with an incumbent unwilling to relinquish the reins, and an heir apparent, Miss Chenevix, who might also be asked to serve the interests of working women into her eighties. The advanced years of Miss Bennett and a number of officials, such as Mrs Buckley, Miss Bryan, Miss Chenevix and, to an extent, Miss McDowell, gave the IWWU a public face that reflected some wisdom but had only a limited and historically specific appeal to the daily life of young industrial workers.

Louie Bennett remained a politically astute and an intellectually informed observer of a changing industrial Ireland. At a consultative level she had enormous reserves to draw on in advising on future developments. Initially, this status appeared implicit in the proposals advanced by the Executive, and on 15 August Miss Bennett officially became Consultative Secretary. Her brief, however, did not change dramatically and she retained her position in the Union for a further five years. While Miss Chenevix and Miss McDowell became joint Acting Secretaries 'responsible for the routine work of the IWWU' the Executive directed that 'all three Secretaries' would attend Executive and Finance Committee meetings.

> Miss Bennett will continue to act in major wage and dispute negotiations . . . she will be responsible for activities in connection with Factory Inspection, welfare conditions, social and health services and similar matters. She will be available to meet by appointment any member wishing to consult her personally on any Trade Union matter.[52]

Miss Chenevix would take responsibility for 'Laundresses, Cleaners and Wardsmaids, Sugar Confectionery, Clothing trades, Levers and General Workers'. Miss McDowell's members would include 'Printing and Kindred Trades, Nurses, Packers, Linen and Cotton, Maguire and Paterson, Tobacco and Mitchells'.[53]

Within the trade union movement women were, by 1950, becoming somewhat more assertive. At a special wages conference held on 18 May, the National Executive of the ITUC 'accepted a proposal by the Irish Women Workers' Union that a Women's Advisory Committee be set up'.[54] At the IWWU, notice had been served since 1948 that neither Congress nor FUE could assume indefinitely that women would accept arrangements they considered inappropriate for a permanent section of the industrial workforce. In that year, a proposed agreement between the two bodies on wage increases had been rejected by the IWWU.

> The terms of the agreement leave women in the unsatisfactory position existing under the Emergency, when it became a custom for the Tribunals to dismiss the women's case under a formula of 50% of the increase granted to the men in the industry. My Committee claim

that the women's position in industry be considered on its merits rather than in relation to the position of men.[55]

The question of equal pay for equal work received considerable attention in 1950 when the ILO requested affiliated bodies to complete a questionnaire on 'Equal Remuneration for men and women for work of equal value'. The IWWU, in its Annual Report for 1949-50, published 'Notes' on the question, which, while clearly flying the feminist standard, echoed the old refrain regarding 'jobs which are admittedly women's jobs'. Such jobs 'should carry a wage equal to the value of the job, free from sex discrimination', but other demarcations would continue to be treated as given.

> There is no marked tendency here for the displacement of men by women in industry. There is in fact in most industries a clear line of demarcation between the jobs assigned to each sex.[56]

The position of the IWWU in relation to any breach of such demarcations was well established.

While Helena Molony had claimed the right to territory 'from carpenter to blacksmith', the IWWU as a body made no such challenge to the prevailing order — perhaps influenced, in part, by the fear that this policy might become a two-edged sword, and that women might lose more than they might gain by declaring open season in the employment market. In seeking a rate for the job, however, the Union was clearly challenging the 'family factor' implicit in the male industrial wage.

> The wage structure in most industries is based fundamentally on the theory of the family wage. The evaluation of the job is not made purely on its value. The evaluation is influenced by consideration of the family factor and the consequent needs of a man with dependents to a higher wage rate than the average woman. This theory leads to many injustices.[57]

Since 1949 the Union had consistently claimed a minimum wage of £3 a week 'for all women workers, unskilled (so called! No work is unskilled!) or semi-skilled'.[58] While its first claim for equal pay had been made in 1946 it was not until the early 1950s that this claim, to the City and County Managers' Association on behalf of female psychiatric nurses, was served collectively by the IWWU, the WUI, and the ITGWU.

All three unions had a long association with the nursing profession and had fought together for many years for recognition of the status of the psychiatric nurse. While members of this section had participated in IWWU affairs since joining the Union in 1920, their impact at the level of decision-making in the IWWU was not evident until 1950 when Maura Breslin, a staff nurse at Grangegorman Mental Hospital, represented women workers as a delegate to the Dublin Trades' Council. Her increasing participation in Union matters coincided with other moves.

While Miss Bennett remained at the helm, the death of Miss Bryan, a printers' official, forced a reorganisation of the staff. In the short term Miss McDonnell, previously a part-time official, was interviewed by Miss Bennett and took the position. Her death in the middle of the year, however, was followed by the subsequent appointment of a younger woman, which marked a review of the practice of employing persons of advanced years. In January 1951 Kay McDowell was appointed by Mr Norton to the Prices Advisory Committee. The appointment to the position of 'Éire's No. 1 woman price watcher' was greeted in the daily press with a reference to 'the brown eyes of Kay McDowell'. It was, however, a personal triumph, and celebrated by the purchase of a new coat! For the period of her anticipated absence from the Union Miss McDowell was to be paid a retainer of £1 per month, and further personnel changes were authorised to take account of her absence. Jenny Murray, a laundress, and daughter of Theresa Behan, the first laundresses' official of the IWWU, took up duty on a temporary full-time basis as official for the general workers.

CHAPTER 14

The Feast of Bealtaine

In 1950 the IWWU had almost 7,000 members. Although the cost of living had eroded some of the effects of improvements in wages for industrial women workers, the Union reported that, overall, its own finances were sound and that in 1951 it had 'a substantial surplus in hand'.[1] Union officials were each given a rise of 15s. Given such a surplus, and the need to maintain the benefits of unionisation in financial terms, the Union now reconsidered the provision of a pension scheme. The Secretaries were directed to 'collect information as to the working of pension schemes in industrial concerns'. While the existing Union Pensions and Benevolent Fund was seen to be 'not sufficiently appreciated', a pension had in fact been given to a member on her retirement in 1942, and certain sectors, notably the laundresses, contributed to provision for an income after their retirement.

For specific groups within the Union, however, an industry-based scheme was essential. Mrs K. O'Brien of the Royal Hibernian Hotel laundry urged Miss Chenevix to keep the needs of such groups in mind when framing resolutions for Annual Conventions.

> . . . don't forget something about pensions of some kind as I can't see if the Minister has made any allowance for the single woman who cannot work and is not old enough for the Old Age Pension.[2]

In the years between 1950 and 1955 the Executive submitted a series of proposals for such schemes to the membership,[3] yet no mandate was forthcoming. The reluctance of women workers to consider the question of pensions related in part to their expectation of marriage and financial dependence and in part to their perception of themselves as a transitory workforce. Although many who were in receipt of Marriage Benefit terminated their employment, either through choice or because of the existence of a marriage bar,[4] others remained in the labour market as an irregular but consistent workforce. In laundries, printing houses, textiles, confectionery and nursing, Union records suggest that while marriage generally represented the end of full-time industrial employment for the majority of women, work for those who were married was both available and availed of. Despite the irregular nature of employment for many single women, and the tendency of younger girls to frequently change their employment, and their general unwillingness to provide for their retirement by way of contribution to a pension scheme, the IWWU records do not suggest that the Union membership ever passively accepted their conditions of labour as an industrial workforce. The concerns of the leadership in this area reflected both their own interests and the demands coming from the rank and file.

In 1952, however, during the course of discussions about the proposed form of the Annual Report, the Executive gave the first indication of a distinct lack of interest by members in any long-term commitment to involvement in the affairs of the IWWU as an institution.

> It was agreed that this report is very valuable, but it was felt that it failed to get into the hands of the members, who indeed do not evince much interest in it as a whole.[5]

That the report failed to reach the members pointed to organisational difficulties. That members lacked interest, however, suggested structural problems, perhaps endemic to institutions, but exacerbated by the seeming reluctance of the IWWU actively to foster the talent among its membership, for the express purposes of encouraging successors. This oversight was undoubtedly reflected in the continuing dependence upon a leadership that had changed little since the Union had re-formed in 1917. The fear of change at this level was evident in the letter from the President, Nellie O'Brien, to Annual Convention in 1951.

> Dignified leadership has led us up to the present day. We have only to look at the Trade Union world today and see what happened to others could happen to us if it were not for that leadership.[6]

The records of the Union suggest a membership distinguished by its vitality and by considerable talent.

At Grangegorman, 'Nurse Breslin and Miss McDowell attend a riotous meeting';[7] at Dublin Port Milling Company the women refused to accept an offer of 5s., 'which is half of that awarded to men'. Girls were recorded as being 'determined to fight',[8] and on an individual basis a number of members showed clear potential. At Harvey's in Waterford, Miss White progressed from evening classes, sponsored by the Union, to full-time attendance at University College, Cork. In 1950 she completed a course in worker education and while she is on record as thanking the Union 'for our generous help in financing her',[9] and may indeed have been committed in other quarters, no further reference is made to a woman whose undoubted contribution via the Union itself to the working class would have been invaluable.

At Nation Health Insurance, Kathleen Coyle, one of three typists who were members of the IWWU, was a fund of information on grading and re-grading, keeping Mrs Buckley and Miss McDowell fully informed on such matters, on the activities of other unions and on the ambitions of management. Miss Coyle served, in effect, as shop steward for the Union in her area, and in correspondence with Mrs Buckley displayed a zest which, by now, was somewhat absent from the deliberations of Fleet Street.

> Don't flatter yourself that you scared the daylights out of us about arrears — it is only our New Year's Resolution to be models of all the virtues!!! We fear the Committee of Management will suggest that virtue is its own reward — if so, the virtue won't last long.[10]

While neither Miss White nor Miss Coyle continued their careers within the IWWU, their rationale for such decisions in a personal sense is, by definition, unclear from Union records. The difficulty in holding the interest of young women workers, so evident in years to come, may have reflected some institutional shortcomings in the IWWU, but also pointed to another cause: a reluctance by women in various sections to tolerate indefinitely conditions for the Irish woman worker which compared so poorly with those 'across the Channel'.

In 1950 the WUI drew the attention of the IWWU to the Mental Health Service and to 'the general dissatisfaction that seems to exist among the female staff, and also the considerable number of female staff who are leaving the service'.[11]

The WUI reported 'continuous and bitter complaint over the system, or lack of system, in regard to days off duty'.[12] Few records were available, and, while some nurses enjoyed regular and rostered days off, others were called for duty seemingly at the whim of supervisors. 'Their time is reported in a most haphazard fashion.' From the litany of complaints presented by the nurses came evidence of an institutional disdain for professional competence both in Grangegorman and Portrane, where nurses were required to 'scrub passages, clean windows and climb ladders when cleaning fanlights and electric lampshades'.[13] The nature of the work of the mental nurse demanded service quite distinct from that associated with the higher status of the general trained nurse. At Grangegorman Mental Hospital nurses were often required to sleep in proximity to their patients. When on duty in observation rooms provided for such occasions,

> the nurses are required to enter them at 8.30 p.m. and they are not permitted to leave for any reason, unless they get another nurse to relieve her. . . . They have their last meal at 6 p.m. and do not receive their next meal until 9.30 a.m. the following morning.[14]

In 1951, and in the midst of disunity within the trade union movement as a whole,[15] the unions representing staff at Grangegorman and Portrane — the IWWU, the WUI and the ITGWU — joined forces.

At the suggestion of the IWWU, moves were begun to 'arrange a joint conference of representatives of the three unions catering for Grangegorman and Portrane Mental

Hospitals'.[16] Stating its brief as the trade union of women workers, the IWWU submitted to their solicitor a proposal for a claim for pension clauses in legislation that would allow full pension rights after twenty-five years' service.[17] In pressing their case with the WUI, the Union argued that pensions and entitlements raised questions that presented a different perspective for the men and women in the service. 'For various reasons the men would not have the same anxiety for a reduction of the pension period, but they propose that any amendment on this point would merely involve the optional right to retire after 25 years'.[18]

While the specific needs of women were persistently advanced at inter-union conferences, the rights both of female nurses and of male attendants were advanced in the appropriate quarters. In 1951 Helen Chenevix, then President of the ITUC, spoke to resolution 21 at the Annual Congress advancing the cause of the mental nurse.

> Recognising that modern developments in the treatment of mental illness demand from nurses of both sexes an increasingly high standard of efficiency and responsibility, Congress shall claim from the Government a code of status and remuneration worthy of this branch of the nursing profession.[19]

The Union sought, in effect, a 'fundamental review' of this 'prominent and vital department of the medical profession'.[20] Although mental hospitals were seen in recent years to have undergone a 'change for the better', the conditions under which the nurses worked were unduly subject to the whim of those in authority. 'At present they get one night off whenever it suits the Authorities to give it to them',[21] and had little redress when the rigours of their vocation placed them in positions demanding more than usual levels of resourcefulness.

In a letter from a member of the IWWU to Miss Sharkey, Matron of Grangegorman, the circumstances in which a nurse had refused to undertake specific duties indicated that a general review of working conditions was long overdue.

> I have been several times special nurse on this patient

> and owing to my experience with her I have real dread and fear of her as she threatened and tried to strangle me on each occasion leaving me very frightened of her.[22]

The immediate need to review such conditions — and those relating also to more basic matters of diet, late passes, and an 'obselete code of discipline' — occupied the energies of officials from all three unions.

In the long term, nurses at both institutions were urged to 'decide on salaries and emoluments to provide the basis for a claim from their Unions',[23] and to seek a conference with the Manager and the Minister for Health 'to remind the Minister of the vital importance of the functions of Mental Nurses'.[24] Such access to the Minister was already commonplace for other branches of the profession and was promoted by the Union as a means of stemming the tide of emigration. Newspaper reports from England and advertisements in the Irish papers made reference to nurses' working conditions abroad that revealed the need for national reform of the archaic practices in Ireland. For nurses already working in Ireland, English authorities now offered 'free travel, tickets and travelling allowance. . . . Training and promotion on completion. Dances and Cinema shows at Hospitals, coaches to Eastbourne without charge'. Further, and with an eye to the habits of the eagerly sought Irish personnel, advertisements for Hellingley Mental Hospital added a rider: 'Visiting priest holds special service for R.C. members of the staff at the Hospital each Sunday morning'.[25]

In stark contrast, applicants for positions within the institutions of Grangegorman and Portrane were informed, briefly, of the conditions for application to the service.

> Applicants, male and female, must be unmarried. Females must resign their post prior to marriage.

The tenor of the most pressing information indicated quite clearly that old tyrannies would prevail. 'Height to be given', applicants were warned, 'with boots off'! Nurses at both these institutions had been members of the IWWU since 1928, and by 1954 300 women were registered as nurses. In the years between, the Union claimed significant gains — the restitution of salary cuts which had been illegally made following an IWWU action in the Supreme Court; a reduction in working hours from fifty-six to forty-eight a week; and improvements in domestic accommodation, food and clothing standards.[26] By 1954, however, all three unions refused any longer 'to be saddled with responsibility' for conditions intrinsic to a hopelessly inadequate service.

The overwhelming shortcomings of this service were detailed in a joint memorandum in 1953, and later correspondence between unions and management pointed to 'overcrowding of patients in the day rooms and dormitories and in some cases beds made upon the floor'.[27] An analysis of female staff ratios had revealed inadequacy which bordered on neglect. In Division 14, 112 suicidal patients were under the care of eight staff; in Ward 25, 120 senile demented and mentally defective incontinent patients were dependent upon the attentions of five nurses. At night the situation became acute: in Division 11, ninety-three epileptic patients were in the charge of one nurse; in Division 18, ninety patients, all bedridden, battled for the attention of three; and, in Division 24, 160 women in seven wards, with 'many turbulent patients', kept two staff permanently occupied on twelve-hour shifts. Despite the length of such shifts no provision was made for meal relief for the total of thirty-three night staff at Grangegorman.[28]

While treatment administered in similar institutions outside Ireland had moved from the orthodoxies of major tranquillisers to the promised enlightenment of a range of therapeutic measures, including electro-convulsive therapy and more sophisticated chemotherapy, the function of the native institutions remained suspect and inadequately defined, being seen as largely custodial. In 1953 the IWWU registered a protest against the present tendency to consign aged poor people to a mental hospital, even temporarily.'[29] In 1956 the Joint Staffs' Committee of Grangegorman and Portrane demanded the attention of the Minister responsible.

> Despite the advances of curative treatment, conditions amenities and general environment are to a great extent

at the same level . . . as . . . when custody and observation were considered the only function of Mental Hospitals.[30]

In November 1951 the ITGWU had given a fortnight's notice of strike to all printing firms, and by early 1952, 200 women workers, although not directly involved in the dispute, were locked out. The Printers' Section notified the DMPA that as the women had been locked out they would not consider a return to work until their own wage claim, and that of the boxmakers, was settled. Although accused of opportunism by the Masters and by some trade unionists, the Executive sanctioned this move and the ITGWU indicated that it was prepared to support the women's claim.

In July, however, the Labour Court recommended that the IWWU members accept an offer of 3s. 6d. in settlement of their claim. On 8 August, in the third week of the strike, the 10.10 p.m. news on Radió Éireann reported that a majority of 333 women who would be affected by such acceptance had rejected the offer. A mass meeting of women in the trade, members of the IWWU and others, was called by the Union for Wednesday 13 August.

That evening at the Mansion House Louie Bennett gave a detailed statement of events to date,[31] and indicated that although the Printers' Committee and the Executive had actually been reluctant to recommend acceptance of the offer, 'they were careful not to recommend rejection'. Arising from this meeting the Executive were directed by the printers to clarify with the Labour Court the precise terms which would be associated with any acceptance of the 3s. 6d. settlement, and were further instructed to propose that this settlement be seen by all parties as a prelude to a more detailed claim for increases which would take account of the rising cost of living and the regulation of a 'just wage'. A general meeting was called for 25 August, and it was anticipated by all that, on that date and in the light of further information, a final decision could be taken on the recommendation from the Labour Court.

Before this meeting at the Metropolitan Hall, however, Miss Bennett called a special Executive meeting at Fleet

Street to discuss a resolution framed by herself urging her members to vote in favour of accepting the settlement, albeit 'under strong protest'. The meeting of the Executive was tense. Lizzie Caffrey, a printer by trade, and President of the Union, refused even to register her vote on such a move. When the remaining members voted, a stalemate was reached. At the suggestion of both the Printers' Committee and the Executive, Miss Bennett was now persuaded, with considerable reluctance, that if the resolution was to be put to the meeting it would carry no backing from the Executive and would have to be put as a personal recommendation from her. At the meeting the statement was read to the members by Miss Bennett and, having referred to the need to make specific provision for future claims and the setting up of a Joint Industrial Committee for the trade, members backed the personal recommendation of the General Secretary and voted 3:1 in favour of acceptance.

Although this was a personal triumph for Miss Bennett, the agreed return to work was patently against the wishes of the Printers' Committee and influential members such as Lizzie Caffrey. In the face of considerable and growing tension between the Printers' Committee and the Executive, Miss Bennett was asked to explain fully the basis for her recommendation. Having agreed originally to make the recommendation on the basis of her personal, rather than any collective, authority, Miss Bennett in response now indicated her belief that the Printers' Committee had, in effect, attempted to usurp her authority. What was notable, however, was that Miss Bennett's authority and that of 'the Union' were apparently interpreted by the General Secretary as being synonomous. A blurring of the dividing line between personal and institutional authority, and her interpretation of the challenge to such authority from a section of the Union, was clearly evident in Miss Bennett's stated rationale for proceeding in a personal capacity.

> I accepted the challenge as a moral responsibility but protested strongly against such unprecedented conduct on the part of the representatives elected by IWWU members to control the activities of the Union.[32]

On 11 September Miss Bennett presented a statement to the Printers' Committee and the Executive, defending her position and calling for acceptance by both bodies of the decision by the majority of members to accept the settlement outlined by the Labour Court. The statement outlined again her strong and consistent distaste for use of the strike weapon and her increasing tendency to argue on behalf of a perceived national good rather than for sectional interests. She had, she claimed, urged the women to accept the terms on the basis that

> I held it to be morally wrong for a group of workers to hold up a nationally valuable industry, and to convert a lock-out into a strike for a paltry increase in wages, which would involve loss and hardship for a large number of workers outside as well as inside the printing industry.[33]

Despite Miss Bennett's reservations and the Printers' Committee call for further strike action, the women in printing had, on their return to work in August, in fact gained quite a momentous increase in pay. Taking all increases for 1951-52 into account they had been given an overall increase of 8s. 6d. a week, 'the highest so far gained by women, with the exception of Jacob's firms'. Within the Union, however, the legacy of the lock-out was not to be pay, or proposals for further action, or even the setting up of the JIC which followed close upon the heels of the settlement. It was to be the first clear note, from within the ranks of the IWWU, of sectional rather than either personal or clearly political opposition to the authority of Louie Bennett — opposition which began to manifest itself in the creation of minor constraints on the General Secretary's actions.

In November Miss Bennett informed the Executive that she had heard rumours among printers that 'the financial position of the IWWU was seriously embarrassed as a result of the prolonged strike'.[34] On seeking the view of the Executive on the desirability of circulating a statement 'disproving these rumours', Nurse Breslin of Grangegorman, a recently elected Trustee of the Union, voted in favour of Miss Bennett's proposal. All the other members of the Executive, however, 'disapproved' and the matter was dropped.

Despite such minor frustrations, however, Louie Bennett's authority, and her capacity for work, continued almost unabated. Both she and Helen Chenevix publicly encouraged members of the staff of St Kevin's Institution to demonstrate outside the Dáil against the government's prolonged delay in dealing with the claim by general staff, and particularly wardsmaids, for revision of their basic wages. In a letter to *The Evening Mail* the Misses Bennett and Chenevix gave an account of their endeavours, through legitimate methods, to secure a means of redressing the grievances of such workers who were under government control but who, like some other workers in the public service, lacked the financial and political clout of civil servants. They applauded the action of the St Kevin's staff in mounting the demonstration, and upbraided the authorities.

> Much lip service is given at Leinster House and in Ministerial departments to the ideals of Christian civilisation. Our members would like more practical devotion to that ideal.[35]

Advancing the cause of other workers of similar status, Miss Bennett instigated the campaign on behalf of the IWWU to review the position of unestablished workers in the civil service.

As workers of indeterminate status, Union members in the Post Office Factory were entitled neither to pensions nor to sick pay, were bound by the Official Secrets Act, and had no access either to the arbitration machinery available to non-civil servants nor to the strike weapon as a means of redressing their grievances. Outside the ranks of her own workers she promoted — and won the support of her own Executive for so doing — the call to all trade unions and progressive organisations to resist the 'unwarranted wielding of power' by the State in its failure to honour the Civil Service Arbitration Awards. Post Office workers were urged to join civil servants, teachers, clerical and manual workers on Sunday 15 March to 'unite in a parade and demonstration to protest'.

Women workers, through the medium of a roneoed letter from their Secretary, were now enjoined to

> . . . assemble at St. Stephen's Green. . . . Don't stand on the sidewalk looking on. March proudly in a demonstration for justice and human rights.[36]

Louie Bennett's still powerful advocacy of the cause of women workers continued to be evident in despatches to, and disputes with, the holders of power.

In 1951 Miss Bennett had represented the Union on deputations to the Minister for Health, Dr Noel Browne, in support of the Mother and Child Scheme. This scheme was designed 'to ensure for all mothers the best medical care available, regardless of class distinctions'.[37] While wholeheartedly supporting the scheme itself, the Union had urged that it should be 'linked with a comprehensive plan for Health Services . . . ensuring the best possible medical care for all contributors alike . . . irrespective of their social standing, wealth or poverty'.[38] In common with both Congress and DTUC the Union pressed for a scheme without a means test, and although generally supportive of Dr Noel Browne in the ensuing battle with the bishops, conveyed to him the regret of the women workers 'that no woman doctor has been appointed to the Medical Committee appointed as Consultant Council in connection with a Mother and Child Scheme'.[39]

The question of the means test became the focus of opposition by the hierarchy and the Catholic Church, as well as from the powerful lobby of private medical practitioners. Under the general rubric of protection of family life and the 'right' of the family to care for its own without benefit of, or hindrance by, state intervention, the episode became notorious for the blatant exhibition of church power in matters political. The Union, in the face of the public battles between Dr Browne and the hierarchy, advocated the use of delaying tactics to allow time to formulate 'an alternative to the means test basis'. The delay was not secured, and the Union noted with regret that 'now we are in the hands of the Medical Association and their records of reform are not encouraging'.[40]

In other areas, Louie Bennett remained both committed

and, at eighty-one years of age, quite clearly fully conversant with the state of the nation. In challenging the Taoiseach and his ministers to note the position of people on low incomes at a time when no compensation was given for the massive rise in the cost of living recorded in 1953, she pointed to the truism that 'such employees are not capitalists. Nor have they securities to offer for bank overdrafts to meet emergencies'. While ministers demanded 'harder work, increased output, and a stay-at-home policy', Miss Bennett retorted:

> Be patient and wait — for what? The younger workers ask and leave their country to find elsewhere the incentive and rewards that are lacking at home.

Advice was regularly despatched from Killiney to the not always responsive ranks of the trade union movement. When the Irish Management Institute was established in 1952, Miss Bennett suggested to the Dublin Trades' Council that 'as one of the functions of the Institute is to secure some satisfactory labour relations as well as maximum productivity at the lowest cost', the failure to include trade union representation was 'a strange omission in this age of Joint Industrial Councils and Labour Court decisions'.[41]

By November 1952, however, Miss Bennett was also signalling that she considered her position at the Union to have remained unchanged only because of Miss McDowell's continued absence. The acknowledgement that she 'could not guarantee to act as a substitute for Miss McDowell indefinitely' had been prompted by a letter from Kay McDowell asking for a further extension of her leave of absence to continue her work at the Prices Advisory Board.[42] Although she had, throughout, continued to attend Executive meetings, and had clearly indicated on her application for an initial extension in 1951 that 'it is always possible for me to resign from the Prices Advisory Board at any time should any emergency occur',[43] such an indefinite absence was clearly deemed inappropriate. On a proposal from Nurse Breslin it was agreed that the extension of leave be continued until the Convention in May 1953, 'when it will be necessary to make a final decision as to Miss McDowell's reinstatement or replacement'. In April, prior to Convention, Miss Bennett reported that Miss McDowell had sought a further three months' grace, 'as she would then be in a position to give a final answer to the Union with regard to her present job'.[44] The Executive passed a resolution, in effect presenting Miss McDowell with an ultimatum, 'that the suspension of Miss McDowell's employment by the Union be finally terminated on October 1st, 1953, and that she be asked to inform the Executive if she is prepared to resume her former position on that date'.[45]

Kay McDowell had worked in a range of posts with the IWWU, from administrator to official, since 1922. When she had joined the Union, under Miss Bennett's wing, she had been a young woman in her early twenties who had abandoned a career in law following the death of a much loved brother in France in 1916. In terms of the potential leadership of the IWWU she was still a comparatively young woman and her position on the Prices Advisory Board, and within the Labour Party, was a public acknowledgement of her service and commitment to the trade union movement. Despite the seeming reserve of the Executive, Miss McDowell continued her work with the Board, and her official position in the Union remained ambiguous. In January 1954 she indicated that if the IWWU should so request she would resign her position at the Board, and meanwhile she would be available at any time 'in connection with Printers' and Nurses' business'.

By February, however, it was clear that if she were to return to Fleet Street her status within the Union would, in the immediate future, remain unchanged. On 4 February Miss Bennett had again offered to resign. Again, in her eighty-fourth year, Louie Bennett was asked to stay: 'It was unanimously agreed that Miss Bennett be asked to remain as General Secretary even if her attendances at the office had to be very infrequent'.[46]

Change, however, was clearly imminent. At a special meeting on 17 February Miss Bennett reiterated her intention to resign at the end of a period of three month's notice, adding that she would be glad to continue to be available in a consultative capacity. Although in her own proposals for the reorganisation of the office Miss Bennett had conceded her advanced age and 'doubtful health', and had claimed that 'it would not be wise or honest for me to hold my present position beyond the next Convention',[48] the Executive again proved reluctant to accept the inevitability of a transfer of power.

> All were anxious that she should remain to guide the destinies of the Union, but as her health will not permit this, it was proposed by Miss McDowell and unanimously approved: that Miss Bennett be given twelve months' leave of absence with full pay, as from this date ...[48]

An immediate decision was thus postponed, but claims for the leadership of the IWWU were quickly established.

In May, Kay McDowell resumed full-time duties as an official of the Union. At a meeting of the Executive on 12 May, Miss Chenevix, the equal — if less public — partner of Louie Bennett in terms of age and status within the labour movement since 1917, was urged to allow her name to go forward for a Senate nomination. If successful, this would have rendered public acknowledgement of Miss Chenevix's service to the movement; it would also have had the undoubted advantage of relieving both the Executive and the membership of the moral obligation to facilitate the passing of the mantle of power by virtue of divine right. Miss Chenevix, however, refused.

At Annual Convention, the by now ailing Miss Bennett authorised Helen Chenevix to read a letter from the General Secretary to the women workers. The letter spoke of Miss Bennett's concern at the danger posed by the hydrogen bomb and the special mission of women in opposing its destructive force. It also stated clearly the views of this leader of women on what she saw as the 'special responsibility' of the members of her own sex.

> Personally I feel that we women have a special responsibility in this matter because our primary function is motherhood carrying with it not only the serious responsibility of bringing new life into the world but also of extending to all men and women the compassion that motherhood inspires.

A further year would pass before a resolution of the question of the leadership was complete. That year was regarded as being marked by 'a lull in wage disputes' but questions of the continual setting of the value of a woman's wages in relation to those of men occupied the attention of the IWWU and, to an extent, of the trade union movement generally.

The tendency to estimate the value of a woman worker as equal to 'half a man' had been challenged, with partial success, by the early 1950s. As the Annual Report for 1950-51 ruefully noted, 'We have now at least got a larger half'! The standard, however, was still considered 'altogether unsatisfactory', and in 1954 the Union called for 'A renewed effort to secure joint action on the part of women workers for a just wage standard based on the value of their work'.[49]

In the workplace, change was widespread. At Lever's (always a model factory in IWWU terms, despite quite notoriously paternalistic industrial relations), all adult employees were given an unsought-for increase of 4s. a week, with a pro rata increase for juniors. As skilled practitioners of the art, Lever's expounded on the virtues of scientific management. The Union applauded its sound plan 'for calculating output, methods of production, etc.', and the Executive consulted Lever's Work Committee in formulating similar production proposals for adoption in all industries where appropriate and where IWWU members were employed. Any residue of resistance to the Time and Motion System was quietened by the assumption that it was inevitable and that trade unionists should now, as a priority, become informed participants in questions relating to work measurement schemes and the bonus system. When Mitchell's Bead Factory introduced a Time and Motion System, Lever's was used as a benchmark when the new methods 'continued to give trouble'.[50]

The effect of a changing workplace was echoed in Fleet Street. While the Executive purchased a pamphlet on Occupational Psychology 'for office use' and a book on Industrial Psychology was recommended as 'a useful study for our members', members were circularised with a proposal to form a Women Workers' Club to deal with educational and social activities. By November 1954 the Social Committee had convened two meetings and 'much interest' had been shown. It was established that women workers had to equip themselves with new skills.

> It was agreed that we would avail, under the Mrs Bernard Shaw bequest, of the services of a teacher of public speaking — there would be six lectures to each course, a small fee to be paid by each pupil.[51]

The tentative agenda bore not only the unmistakable stamp of the General Secretary, but pointed also to a desire on the part of the departing leadership to focus the attention of working women on active participation in the conduct of their own affairs. The proposals for a speakers' class included 'rules for chairmanship and committee procedure'; enquiries were to be made at the People's College, now meeting twice weekly at Fleet Street, for 'lectures on economics' of a 'preliminary' nature. Further, the Executive were directed to forward an appeal to the Irish Trades Union Congress [ITUC] and the Congress of Irish Unions [CIU], 'pending settlement of the unity problem', to establish a joint committee 'to deal with the problems of unemployment, Human Rights in industry, new methods of factory organisation and similar important subjects of common and urgent importance'.[52] If sugar coating was required to ensure the palatability of such educational pills, the new Women Workers' Union Club would clearly rise to the occasion. The Club would exist, the membership was advised, also 'for social and cultural activities such as musical socials, films, debate, old time dancing and so on'.[53]

While such activities gave evidence of a concern to extend the horizons for women workers, the focus of attention at Fleet Street remained the unresolved question of the transition of power. In January 1955 Louie Bennett sent a letter to the Executive 'expressing her desire to now retire on pension'. By 4 April four nominations for the position of General Secretary had been received — Lizzie Caffrey, Maura Breslin, Helen Chenevix and Kay McDowell. Almost immediately, Lizzie Caffrey withdrew, and in doing so 'expressed the hope that this would mean Miss Chenevix would become General Secretary automatically'. The basis for such a move was unclear. Kay McDowell had the support of the Printers' Section, and Lizzie Caffrey, as a leading member of the Printers' Committee, could have been assumed to share their enthusiasm for Miss McDowell as General Secretary. Miss Caffrey's own nomination, however, suggested similar ambitions on her part and, given her extensive involvement both in the trade union movement and in the Labour Party, such ambitions were neither surprising nor inappropriate. It may be reasonable to suppose that the expectation of a short period of tenure by Miss Chenevix would have suited both Lizzie Caffrey and other contenders for the leadership, providing a period of respite and the opportunity to launch a more effective campaign for long-term leadership of the IWWU. The move to elect Miss Chenevix as leader, however, evoked a strong protest from Miss McDowell, who claimed that this statement assumed that she, and others, would be actively opposing Miss Chenevix. While clearly indicating her desire to assume such office, Helen Chenevix now characteristically demurred, reminding the Committee that under Rule 21 of the IWWU 'there was no such thing as anyone becoming General Secretary of the IWWU automatically'. Rule 21 obliged the Annual Convention, 'the supreme authority of the Union', to 'during the Feast of Bealtaine'

> make and amend rules, deal with finance, criticise and direct policy of the Union, and elect officers of the Executive Committee.[54]

Nominations for the office were sent to Fleet Street four weeks before Convention. On 4 April the Executive acknowledged that 'the overwhelming majority of nominations had been for Miss McDowell'. Kay McDowell enjoyed the full confidence of the printers and was apparently acknowledged in all quarters as having the inestimable value of being prepared 'to recognise the limits of her own power at the committee table'.

Rule 21, however, was unspecific in relation to the precise machinery for succession. At Annual Convention the air, predictably, was redolent with homage to Louie Bennett, now retired after thirty-eight years of service to the IWWU. Maura Breslin, President of the Union, took the platform and announced to the assembled delegates what by now had already been printed in the Union's Annual Report:

> On Miss Bennett's retirement Helen Chenevix was appointed General Secretary with Miss Kay McDowell as Assistant.

The mantle of power had been transferred, quietly and behind closed doors.

Helen Chenevix brought to the position of General Secretary not only wide experience but also a marked change in personal and political style. She had, in the years since 1917, served both as a Union official and as a member of Bray and District Trades' Council, Dublin Corporation, and the National Executive of the Trades Union Congress. She had gained wide respect in each capacity and had served both as President of Congress (in 1951) and as acting Lord Mayor of Dublin on two occasions between 1942 and 1950. Although a prominent member of the Labour Party, her political commitment was always guided primarily by her religious convictions. As a leading member of the Fellowship of Reconciliation and the Women's International League of Peace and Freedom she became an authority on nuclear disarmament and Vice President of the Irish Pacifist Movement. Her very public opposition to war and destruction on a global scale extended to opposition to social systems based on what she perceived as rank injustice.

> For war . . . is the intensification of all the falseness and the fraud and the cruelty that we have practiced under other names in times of so-called peace. We have prayed 'Our Father' but we have not behaved as members of one family . . . in everyday life, industrial, commercial, political, we have seldom asked,
> 'Is this the will of God?'
> We have asked, 'Does it pay?'[56]

From her earliest association with working women she championed an extension of the Union's brief beyond the factory gates to include the domestic circumstances of its members. Her concern focussed on the need for decent housing. In 1955 she protested strongly when the Dun Laoghaire Borough reversed a decision to build sixty Council houses on 'Wilkie's Field' in Killiney. Although herself a resident of that suburb, together with Miss Bennett, for over forty years, she demonstrated no reluctance to upbraid her prosperous neighbours.

> The apparent reason for this decision was that certain Killiney residents who themselves enjoy large, comfortable houses, with beautiful gardens, dislike the look of council houses, and would prefer their fellow citizens who live in slums to remain where they are — out of sight.[57]

She also agitated for the provision of playgrounds for children in the inner city, and for the State to ensure, through an adequate school meals' service, that its future citizens were not marked by the legacy of malnutrition.

While considered by much of her membership to be, like Miss Bennett, a 'Victorian lady', Helen Chenevix differed substantially from Miss Bennett in her personal style. While Miss Bennett would wax indignant, generally to great effect, Helen Chenevix was noted for the 'calm logic and courage that pervades all her arguments'.[58] In the early 1950s she was appointed by the Union to propose a resolution on world peace to the annual meeting of Congress. Congress was neither uniformly pacifist nor immune to the assorted warnings of the spectre of advancing Communism. As she advanced towards the platform the Congress was in an uproar — previous calls for disarmament and world peace had been greeted as prima facie evidence of Communist incursions into the rank and file of the labour movement.

> Delegates stood and shouted angrily. . . . Miss Chenevix walked calmly on. A frail, gentle, grey-haired tiny figure, she stood on the platform and began to speak almost in a whisper. Gradually, the uproar died, and then to a wrapt audience she spoke calmly and convincingly of the need for peace. . . . Her resolution, previously attacked as Communist, was recognised for what it was and was passed unanimously.[59]

Her brief tenure of office as General Secretary was marked not only by the same absence of drama but also by a sense that the IWWU as an institution had to appear to its membership and its public as a collective rather than as a predominantly individual endeavour. In correspondence and discourse she quietly gave credit where it was due but re-affirmed the principle that action emanating from Fleet Street was representative of 'the Union' rather than its constituent parts. A concern to establish the continuity of the institution, despite changes in leadership, was a major contribution in a period marked by proposed change on the Irish industrial front.

Across industry the move to challenge the fixed wage standards for women workers was reflecting the precision of a newly regulated workforce, and was increasingly undertaken with greater attention to analysis of the causes of the problem, rather than its symptoms, than had been evident for some years. At the Linen and Cotton JIC, Kay McDowell argued that even if wage standards had moved away from the traditional assumption of 'half for women',

> it was unusual for the majority of female workers to attain even this standard because of the fact that they were engaged for a considerable part of their time on 'bad work'.[60]

Such 'bad work' was reported to be on the increase. It was a term used to describe work with bad yarns, which broke continuously, and materials which reflected either poor workmanship in the area of production or teething troubles with automatic looms. Other changes in the employment activities of women also became evident. Women were being employed in areas and at times which had previously been dominated by working men.

Mr Lynch (ATGWU) sought an assurance from the JIC for the Textile Industry that such 'replacement of male workers by females' would be controlled. This fear was prompted by the application from the Linen and Cotton Textile Manufacturers' Association [LCTMA] for an exclusion order which would enable them to employ women for all hours except the night shift. Although not dramatic on an industry-wide basis, the increase in the numbers of women employed in textiles was not insignificant. In 1956 Robert Usher and Co. of Drogheda applied for a shift work licence. Section 6 of the application referred to 'female young persons for work Monday to Friday, 8 a.m. to 3 p.m.', and 'Adult Female Workers Only' between 3 p.m. and 10 p.m. The application was the earliest evident in the Union's history of the use of this specific shift, generally associated with the employment of married women, and known throughout a number of industries as the 'twilight shift'.

The terms of labour for working women had been negotiated in a context that was now itself undergoing profound change on two fronts — in the area of production methods on the factory floor, and in the social transition which was evident in the move away from city dwellings towards the early suburban developments. In 1955 the IWWU was involved in a dispute with the Dublin District Laundries' Association [DDLA], represented by the FUE, in relation to the rate of pay for laundresses. Submitting a claim on behalf of 1,500 women and girls, the IWWU argued that the old rates no longer reflected the changing context.

> Laundry rates had been fixed at a time when the girls lived near their work; the majority now live in new housing schemes and have increased rents to pay while incurring heavy transport costs and increased expenditure on meals away from home.[61]

The argument advanced by employers in response to such claims suggested that changing social patterns were reflected in the increased use of domestic appliances which adversely affected the laundry trade. These arguments, however, were effectively rebutted by reference to other developments which implied that the Union now incorporated a level of social and economic analysis into all its negotiations.

> Though the employers refer to competition from home laundering the Union claims that this is more than offset by the increasing population of Dublin and by the large numbers of persons who are obliged to live in flats and

in lodgings where no facilities exist for home laundering.[62]

The rationale for such claims was advanced by the Union in all quarters. As a result of specific claims, the Labour Court recommended that the wages of qualified laundresses be increased by 3s., to bring their rate for a working week of forty-five hours to 76s. Notice was similarly served on other industries where the position of working women, it was argued convincingly, had been affected by the introduction of new machinery.

In 1955 the Union claimed an increase of £1 for women printers as part of a move to seek re-evaluation of women's work in printing: new machinery had changed their work, and new negotiations must challenge the notion of its value.

> Machinery which comprises several operations formerly done by individual women but now operated by one woman must necessarily increase production and reduce overheads, thus increasing the financial value of the women's work.[63]

Future claims would serve notice on employers that account would have to be taken both of the need to compensate women for the rapidly increasing cost of living, and of the fact that women, no less than men, were engaged in work that was both skilled and arduous.

While Miss Chenevix mounted an offensive at the laundry JIC, Miss McDowell took up the cudgels on behalf of women in the clothing industry. In 1957, discussions on the proposed cost of living increase at the JIC for Women's Clothing were brought to a halt when the IWWU rejected the hallowed argument that the cost of living for women could be evaluated at a lower rate than that for the male of the species.

> The wage offer in respect of women was unsatisfactory. The claim was being made on a cost of living basis and the cost of living for adult women was no less than it was for adult men.

The affairs of working women were, quite clearly, under new management.

CHAPTER 15

'It's over to you now, ladies'

At the beginning of 1956 the Executive recorded that 'unity in the Trade Union Movement has been accomplished by a 2:1 majority'. The agreement by the TUC and the CIU to suspend hostilities led to the establishment of a Provisional Trades Union Congress with eight representatives from each of the previously rival organisations. Since the early 1950s the IWWU had been represented on a group of Irish unions which had sought to 'attain a unified trade union movement for the 32 counties in Ireland'.[1] As such, and on behalf of the 7,000[2] women it now claimed to represent, the IWWU expressed regret that no women from the trade union movement had been invited to attend the Provisional Congress.

Such an omission did not, however, deter the 150 delegates to the Annual Convention in May from clearly asserting that the status of the women's union was secure, that its finances were 'very sound', and that their commitment to future development was beyond question. Maura Breslin, President of the Union, welcomed back to the fold 'one of that group of very valiant women by whose inspiration and courage many years ago the foundations of our Union were laid'.[3] Helena Molony, now seventy-six years of age, had returned to Fleet Street to present a painting of Countess Markievicz, 'her gallant comrade and friend, and the illustrious first President of our Union'.[4] The gesture reflected an increasing awareness, fostered by Maura Breslin, of the need to reaffirm, particularly for the benefit of younger members of the Union, that what had been achieved by women workers had been won as a result of struggle rather than as the consequence of employer or government largesse.

Membership figures after 1956 were recorded in the annual

returns to the Registrar of Friendly Societies but were not, for quite obviously political reasons, recorded for some time in the Annual Reports. As presented to the Registrar the figures suggest a significant, if uneven, decline from 1952 onwards.

While members voted unanimously to increase the political levy from 6*d*. to 1*s*. per year, recognition of the increasingly political implications of claims by the labour movement on behalf of its members did not tend to reflect any commitment to active participation by the bulk of the membership. The agendas for Annual Conventions rarely suggested — with the exception of resolutions proposed by the Executive — evidence of concerns beyond those of enlightened self-interest. The absence of an international perspective and interest in matters beyond the immediately industrial had been the focus of the final letter from Louie Bennett to the members of the IWWU. Miss Bennett, while applauding the evident attention to matters relating to health and social welfare, offered a final word to the 'Dear Fellow Members' who had shared her struggle on behalf of working women.

> I suggest that the women of Ireland should step forward and arouse our stay-at-homes to look out on the world and consider what they can do to help forward this great job of world co-operation.[5]

Her regret that such women were reluctant to become involved in international affairs reflected Miss Bennett's own concerns with problems of peace, poverty and underdevelopment. For those who had inherited her mantle, however, the problem of encouraging and maintaining the active participation of members in the Union, as an institution rather than merely a benevolent society, became increasingly acute. While Miss Bennett continued, as late as November 1956, to offer advice of an increasingly spiritual and global nature, changes within the leadership of the Union were laying the foundation for the priorities of subsequent agendas.

In November, Helen Chenevix intimated that she would tender her resignation to Annual Convention in 1957. Mrs Buckley, active in the Union since the 1920s, was also—with reluctance — about to retire from the fray. Kay McDowell, as

Assistant Secretary, had the confidence of the membership; Maura Breslin, as President, commanded respect, and, at the Convention in 1956 Mai Clifford, a laundress — later to achieve prominence in the Dublin Trades' Council and in the labour movement as a whole — was elected to the Executive. At the same Convention, Resolution 11 called on the Government to introduce the PAYE system — ironically, given Mrs Clifford's very public association with the huge demonstrations in favour of tax reform in the late 1970s. While the TUC was in the process of preparing a memorandum outlining its proposals for reform of the tax system, the IWWU endorsed the PAYE system as potentially more equitable than systems hitherto employed. 'The tax should be imposed on all members of the community — at present the salaried workers are bearing the brunt of income tax'.[6]

On 25 November one of the most impressive of the 'Victorian ladies' died. Louie Bennett's passing, at eighty-six years of age, was saluted in all quarters — by workers and by employers, by politicians and by their public. That evening Ronald Mortished broadcast a fitting tribute from the studios of Radió Éireann.

> She could have had a fairly comfortable, carefree life. But she had a heart and a conscience, and they made her spend her life gladly for others, working for votes for women, for social and political reform, for international peace, for her women's trade union. She was shrewd and intelligent, though like others I did not always agree with her judgment.

On 13 December the IWWU held its first meeting since Louie Bennett's death. Boxmaking was reported as being slack; Harvey's of Waterford were seeking a five-day week, and 'there was nothing special to report from the laundry section'. Little appetite for the daily round of Union life was evident, and as Fleet Street closed for Christmas the season evoked few of the traditional festivities. It was the sombre and somewhat inauspicious end of an era.

The new year of 1957, however, marked the opening of another chapter. The commitment to maintain an all women's union 'where problems peculiar to women and their work constitute the main concern' had been reaffirmed at the Annual Convention in 1956, but few were prepared to rest content with the status of women.

> We feel that even today women's work is not sufficiently recognised, and too much of the Victorian atmosphere in which man was always right on every subject and woman was not allowed to express an opinion one way or the other still remains with us.[7]

The precise role of the Union in challenging the social status of women beyond the factory floor was undefined. For forty-five years it had served in a number of guises — from dramatic troupe to Republican cadre to women's parliament. It had responded to the stated needs of its members. The 'Union was more than a union': members had come with social problems: 'married women hospitalised, care of children, First Holy Communions. . . . People looked to the Union to do everything for them'.[8] By the 1950s, however, it was perceived, both by its members and by the wider public, as primarily a benefit organisation for working women. It was known to intervene actively on behalf of its members in relation to housing allocation and the facilitating of house exchanges for tenants of Dublin Corporation, and on behalf of those seeking additional rooms in cases of overcrowding. For Helen Chenevix and Kay McDowell, such intercessions were interpreted as part of their brief, and special pleading for their members was not uncommon.

> Our member Alice Doran now living at 20 Upper Oriel Street is still very anxious for a small cottage where she could make a home with her little nephew. We hope you will remember her when you have any such vacant.[9]

The Union had also served, almost from its inception, as an employment agency, initially catering for the placement of domestic servants but later for women from all sections of the Union. Employers were 'encouraged' to seek workers through the lists of the IWWU unemployed, and with considerable success the Union was able to ensure that women in the printing industry in Dublin city and county could not move without a Union card. Unemployed members were despatched by Fleet Street, with notes and recommendations in hand, to present themselves to the market in a time-honoured tradition.

> Dear Sir,
> The bearer of this note, Miss Jennie Geraghty, is a member of this Union, who is available for work, and we hope you may find it possible to give her a trial. She has worked in more than one industry, including the Jewellery and Metal Manufacturing Co.[10]

Requests for the talents of women workers came also from some quarters which plainly envisaged more long-term engagements.

In 1956 Miss Chenevix received a letter from a farmer in Co. Limerick, 'aged 38, fair appearance, sound and healthy' who had experienced considerable difficulty, in the light of emigration and the lure of city life, in obtaining the services of a wife.

> I wonder if you could get me an introduction from among your union members to any country girl living in Dublin or district who would fancy a farmer husband. The only qualification I would ask for is that the lady should be able to milk a cow as we are all dairy farmers here in Co. Limerick.

With due regard for the proprieties in such matters, Miss Chenevix directed the good farmer to Mrs Biddie Brewster's Marriage Bureau, in Nassau Street, Dublin.

In April 1957, the Executive acknowledged that 'statistics show a decline in membership'.[12] A committee was established, comprising Trustees, officials, and 'some experienced members' to consider organisation generally and to examine the prospects amongst 'clerical workers, radiographers and other workers . . . still unorganised'. These were now seen, in the light of the changing nature of the workforce, to offer 'a wide field for new members'.

At Annual Convention in 1957 Kay McDowell was elected unopposed to the position of General Secretary. Helen

Chenevix relinquished office within the Union with her customary quiet dignity, her contribution acknowledged and respected by all. Her continuing presence was felt largely in the field of disarmament and pacifism, and in the advancement of such causes she rented a room at Fleet Street shortly after her retirement until 1960. She maintained throughout her retirement, however, a wary eye on the activities of the employing class: in 1960 she wrote to Kay McDowell on the position of women in the offices of the Irish Sweeps.

> I happened to hear yesterday that on a recent Sunday the women employed at the Sweeps office, Ballsbridge, were forced to work all day from 10 to 6, and were locked in at lunch hour so that they couldn't even get a breath of fresh air .[13]

Kay McDowell inherited power in a Union which had established itself both politically and socially in the labour movement, and which could boast a tradition of commitment to that movement the equal of any of its contemporaries. It was now, however, urgently in need of reassessment — of its focus for organisation, of its priorities in considering the social and economic climate of a changing Ireland, and of the need to encourage and direct the vitality of its membership into active participation in their own Union. Miss McDowell — the woman whom Lottie Waldron recalled as having 'put me in mind of Bette Davis' — considered, in her address to Annual Convention, the massive problems associated with rising emigration and widespread unemployment. While such problems were clearly amenable to no easy solution, others, she suggested, were. Marked retrenchment was evident in a number of sectors. Yet, while the immediate response within the Union to the decision by a significant number of mental nurses to change their allegiance was one of deep grievance, the move was neither as dramatic nor as overtly hostile to the IWWU as such grievance suggested. Undoubtedly, the loss of members from this sector was regrettable.

> Much time and work was put in by our union on behalf of nurses in Grangegorman, Portrane, St. Kevin's and

Rialto Hospitals and after many concessions were obtained for them, they went over to another trade union.

Over the years, both Kay McDowell and Mary Sugrue had served as officials for the mental nurses. In that time they and the leadership in Fleet Street had worked in close cooperation with the WUI and the ITGWU, generally to the benefit of all. Such associations, however, were not without internal rivalries — rivalries which were often exacerbated by hospital authorities which favoured one union over another. In some small institutions the IWWU was discriminated against, to the benefit of the Irish Nurses' Organisation [INO]. In 1955 the IWWU protested to the Chief Executive Officer of St Kevin's Institution that an official of the INO had been given permission to have a meeting with nurses in their canteen, whereas a similar request from the IWWU's Miss Sugrue had earlier been refused.[15]

In the larger institutions such as Grangegorman and Portrane, the IWWU in 1954 claimed 300 female nurses — numbers which had been secured as a result of major campaigns since 1928, aimed at improving the nurses' working conditions. By 1956, however, the Shop Steward Book for Grangegorman could claim only thirty-three members, and that for Portrane only twenty-five. Arrears were a perennial difficulty, and the decision in 1956 to end the membership of defaulters accounted for a significant decline in official figures. By 1956 also, however, the perceived need for a union had diminished. The establishment of An Bord Altranais [the Nursing Board] in 1953 had secured greater parity of status for mental nurses in relation to general nurses and the establishment of An Bord, although welcomed by the Union, undercut the need for the IWWU to continue its own campaign for the recognition of such status. In 1956 an agreement with the County and City Managers' Association resulted in the Union's acceptance of a national salary scale for mental nurses and the establishment of a Joint Industrial Council. The historical role of the IWWU as a negotiator on behalf of its members with individual managers was undoubtedly affected by these developments. Finally, the problem of retaining the membership of nurses once their training had been completed, persisted. This was a point the IWWU had made on numerous occasions, particularly in relation to the necessity, in the short term, of retaining pay differentials in favour of Dublin hospitals.

When the drift away from the IWWU began in the early 1950s, it was not only a response to all these developments, but also to the reality that, despite its commitment to the nurses since its earliest years, the IWWU had undoubtedly conceded ground to the WUI, and the latter union had, in effect, acted as the instigator of most of the more progressive developments in the Mental Health Service since the 1940s.

Such losses were in no sense terminal. The analysis which was a necessary prelude to stemming the decline, however, continued. The Union revived its considered opposition to the unthinking application of automated processes. This, together with the unemployment to which it gave rise, were both advanced as further causes of problems now evident to all. Long-term strategies were discussed, and Congress was urged to take note of the concerns voiced in Resolution 21 from the IWWU.

> That in view of the advance of Automation and the speeding up of all technical operations by means of new machinery, the incoming Executive shall support every forward move for a 40 hour week with full pay.[16]

In the short term, in an endeavour to promote active participation in Union affairs, Miss McDowell asked the Executive to authorise the printing and distribution of Annual Reports well in advance of Annual Convention to ensure that the contents could be 'studied in preparation for discussion at Convention'. Following Convention, and the retirement of both Miss Chenevix and Miss Buckley, the structure of the Union was reviewed and recruits were sought to fill vacancies on the staff.

Since 1954, June Aust and Jenny Murray had held the positions of 'Junior Officials' at £5 a week. Mary Sugrue now became increasingly involved in office administration. Most officials were replaced, through death or retirement, within a comparatively brief period, and for the first time since the

1920s the age profile of the institution reflected the age profile of the membership.

Evidence of a change of pace was immediate. On 23 May Miss McDowell called a Special Executive Meeting to discuss vacancies still outstanding. She had endeavoured to organise candidates into 'union members, non-union members and impossible candidates.' Declaring herself willing to train the new appointees in trade union work, special duties and organisation, she now drew a clear line indicating that certain prerequisites would be essential in future Union personnel: 'she was not prepared to teach them the elementary steps of office routine.' With such skills assumed, Miss Hayes and Miss Nolan joined the forces of the women at Fleet Street.

If the Misses Bennett and Chenevix were to be remembered as 'Victorian ladies', Miss McDowell would be recalled as a 'Blue-stocking'. Her politics and instincts, however, were democratic. More than any other General Secretary, she acknowledged that her staff were indispensable, and was prepared to delegate her responsibilities in a way that clearly acknowledged the existence of competences beyond her own. Her own expertise in the printing industry was considered by her members to be invaluable, yet in presentations, either to committees or to the Executive, her case would always rest with the memorable phrase:

'It's over to you now, ladies'.

A competent staff, to be effective in an increasingly competitive environment, would require an informed and loyal membership. Miss Brennan reported

> . . . that there is much difficulty in getting shop stewards to act as it involves time and trouble; this difficulty is experienced in all sections, and shop steward meetings are essential.[17]

On a vote from the General Workers' Section the IWWU organised shop stewards' meetings for all sections every three months. No such meetings had been held previously, and all communication had been conducted between the General Secretary and the shop stewards involved on an individual basis. While such missives made for lively reading they provided poor training: if difficulties had earlier been encountered in harnessing the goodwill of members, these had by and large been resolved by resorting to personal appeals.

The move to implement procedural reform within the IWWU began when Kay McDowell took office. Staff and membership alike were encouraged to attend courses at the People's College and the burden of office administration was reduced by the installation of house telephones. In recognition of the move by industry, and also of members, away from the city centre and towards the far-flung suburbs, the IWWU purchased a Union car. Miss McDowell's salary was raised to £12 a week and specific guidelines were given by the Executive on the precise terms of the General Secretary's brief. 'It was emphasised that the position was full time and precludes the Secretary from taking on any outside work'.[18]

Other markers were also clearly laid down. In acknowledgment of her own history as a working woman, as a shop steward, and now as Trustee and President of the IWWU, Maura Breslin placed her trade union cards on the table. The days of expenses only, and of women of independent means at the helm, were no more.

> Miss Breslin said she would like it put on record that if and when her future wage claims were being considered, the staff were entitled, in the same way as other members, to have a discussion and to ask for an increase.[19]

Such 'professionalisation' of the IWWU was long overdue. Since 1950 the Union had lost 1,500 members — through emigration, unemployment, competition and carelessness. That such losses occurred in tandem with the retreat of the Misses Bennett and Chenevix inevitably begs questions, but interpretations which focus only or primarily on the persuasive powers of individuals are not compelling in the light of the evidence in this particular case. Undoubtedly, however, the slow pace of change within the IWWU had done little to stem the erosion of support for a small union. The potential membership of the IWWU was also diminished by social and economic developments in Ireland, and by the continuation of traditional mechanisms excluding women from the workforce. In a number of areas the loss of skilled womanpower via the boat to Liverpool and America was clearly evident. The poor provision for apprenticeships had, in addition, served to exacerbate this loss.

At Messrs Hilton, Mattress Makers, management complained of a 'serious shortage of workers . . . very short of upholsteresses'. Having approached the National Union of Furniture Trade Operatives [NUFTO] to fill such vacancies they were informed that no women were available for the work. At Hilton's request, two women were sent from the IWWU, it being accepted that, in order to secure employment, these women might have to change unions. Within twenty-four hours NUFTO had supplied their own members, and the IWWU women were not appointed. Later in 1957 a similar situation arose. NUFTO claimed that no members were available, but no objection was made to taking women from the IWWU. Two girls were taken on. A few weeks later, however, NUFTO women refused to work with any women who had not served an apprenticeship in the trade, and further, to work with members of any other union. The IWWU members were subsequently dismissed.

The problem of shortages, of both journeywomen and apprentices, remained, but some attempts were made to resolve the difficulties encountered. Of a list of thirty-six apprentices in the trade in 1950, sixteen were girls, but differentials emerged as the years of apprenticeship were completed. At the starting point, boys and girls were virtually equal, but by the fourth and final apprenticeship year a differential was well established. The provision of a fifth and sixth year apprenticeship period for boys helped to ensure that on completion of their respective apprenticeships girls were on a rate of 67s. 3d. while boys could claim 120s. 10d. In 1953, in recognition of the disincentive to girls completing their apprenticeship which was implicit in such differentials, the rules relating to weekly pay rates during apprenticeship[20] were amended to establish that minimum rates as between boy and girl apprentices were to be 'no different'. In this industry another development was now evident — one which would increasingly present the IWWU with a dilemma in relation to servicing members with different needs.

The question of the employment of married women, often on a part-time basis, had already become an issue in the case of mental nurses, where the difficulties of recruiting in both Grangegorman and Portrane had resulted in the increased employment of married women. This development occurred despite the continuing existence of the marriage bar in this sector, and the clear discrepancy in the status, both financial and otherwise, of these and other recruits to the service.

In the furniture and upholstery industry women were employed predominantly as upholsterers and polishers. At a meeting of the Apprenticeship Committee for the Furniture Trade on 16 July 1957 a proposal was made to alter the ratio of one apprentice to every two skilled workers, and a specific proposal to allow two firms to be granted permission to take on two female apprentices was also discussed. At Phelan's, trained women were reported to be already threatened with unemployment, but in the case of some of these women, it was suggested that their availability for continuous employment was, to a degree, limited. 'The women were married women who had left the trade and came back. There could be no guarantee of service, owing to domestic commitments'. Employers now sought to ensure a continuing flow of apprentices who would, throughout their lives, continue to service the industry. Such women, who would previously have been assumed to be 'non industrial units' after marriage, would now be recruited as necessary, but the particular nature of their employment would be recognised as different, not solely on the basis of gender but on the basis of constraints implicit in their marital status.

The chairman of the Apprenticeship Committee argued that the irregular nature of such employment did not preclude the need for girl apprentices to secure a supply of working women in future years.

> It appeared there was a definite shortage of female workers in the trade and that this was keeping machines idle.

This threat of idle machinery served as a foundation for the final appeal to enlightened self-interest on the part of male workers which secured the apprenticeships for girls at Phelan's. Resistance by the men to such moves could, it was suggested, 'militate against further employment of male workers'.

The claimed shortage of skilled women was not confined to this industry. In 1955 the IWWU had informed the Irish Printing Federation [IPF] that

> the printing trade is no longer a trade which attracts the best type of worker, and where we formerly had a waiting list of girls wishing to enter as learners, such a thing no longer exists.[21]

Higher rates and better conditions prevailing in other industries threatened to leave the printing industry without replacement workers in an essential sector of its workforce. By 1957, a recognition of their status and of the continuing need for women in printing was given when the IPF made explicit provision for pensions for women in the trade. This scheme reflected negotiations which had been based on the particular work patterns of such women. It was to be non-contributory, and with a shorter qualifying period for those in other industries in which women were less well established. From 1957 on, women in printing were able to claim, after a minimum of thirty-five years labour, a pension of £1. 15*s.* a week; after thirty years a pension of £1. 10*s.* a week, and after twenty years, a pension of £1 a week was payable.[22]

Such improved conditions for women did not, however, always render their position more sacrosanct. The printing industry overall was subject to fluctuations and was dependent on the securing of contracts. In 1956 the Printers' Committee reported that 'there appears to be all round slackness and that some firms were on rotation'. Such developments often related to the peculiarities of the firm involved and to the needs of the specific women workers. This was evident in the failure of De La Rue, a security printing firm, to recruit fifty women workers by internal advertisement from women who were on rotation. None of those so employed were 'interested' in returning to a full working week. At the same time, however, when Messrs Jacob suggested a four-day week to offset slackness in the trade, the proposal was rejected by members, who would not agree to measures which would reduce the guaranteed week by stealth. The Printers' Committee reported, in relation to the response by the women in De La Rue, that if the women did not claim their guaranteed week 'new cards would have to be issued and we are anxious to avoid this if possible'.[23]

The fact that the Union did not respond to their stated preference for part-time work was an important manifestation of the problems inherent in facilitating two types of membership, i.e. full-time on a guaranteed week and part-time on an irregular week. These two forms of employment increasingly co-existed, and to a large extent the demand for part-time work was coming from married women workers. This revived a number of issues — those relating to the rights of married women to work, and those relating to the guaranteed week for women workers. In the short term, the potential divisiveness inherent in the competing interests involved prompted the Executive to adopt what was, in effect, a delaying tactic. It suggested to the women from De La Rue that should they fail to return to full-time employment, the Union would be forced to facilitate the company by issuing new cards to women currently outside the industry. This, it was suggested, would have the undoubted effect of creating potential over-supply in a market where demand was subject to notable fluctuations. With obvious reluctance, the women at De La Rue returned to full-time work.

By May 1958 De La Rue had dismissed thirty women, and the dependence of this industry on the availability of contracts was made abundantly clear. While no provision existed to protect such women from instant dismissal due to the vagaries of the 'free market', they became, in effect, an experienced reserve, many of whom were married, and available for further employment when business improved. With the securing of new contracts, they returned to the workforce, and by the end of 1958 Miss Moran, printers' official, was in a position to report that the trade was busy and that 'she had cleared her unemployment register to date'.[24]

While changes in specific industries were ongoing, particular problems gave rise to disquiet in Fleet Street. In the Annual Report circulated to members Kay McDowell voiced her concern that the legacy of the IWWU was being quietly rejected by young working women. Increasingly, she felt, members were prepared to leave all decisions in the hands of shop stewards and committee members.

> I find that there is an increasing lack of interest in union matters, particularly among the younger members. In fact I would go so far as to say that many of our members have never been on the union premises.[25]

The lack of nominations for committees gave strong indications that 'younger people are not prepared to play their part'. To what extent such workers were influenced by working lives increasingly focusing on individual incentive schemes and on work measurement which, by definition, reinforced a sense of distance, rather than a bond between working people, is a moot point. The Executive did, however, continue to register its concern at the impact of such changes.

> In the coming year we would have to consider very carefully and from many angles the dangers affecting our daily lives on the change over to automation, of incentive to compete against their fellow workers.[26]

At Annual Convention 1958, the Secretary reported a reduction in the income of the Union. While this was largely attributed to the 'defection' of the nurses, the figures were interpreted as being as dismal as the list of resolutions submitted by the members themselves and was dispiriting. Claiming that no organisation could survive 'if the body of the members takes no interest in it', Miss McDowell announced that

> the agenda is a disgrace. We dare not take a big hall for an AGM because the members will not turn up. The success of the union depends on the spirit of its members. Delegates must feel heartily ashamed of the agenda. She felt ashamed sending it to the printers.[27]

While upbraided for their passivity in relation to the Union, at their places of work members of the Union were resisting the pressure of an increased rate of production.

At Morco's Clothing Factory, Mrs Farrell complained that management were 'attempting to get frocks turned at 90 minutes, priced at 3s. 4d., done for less'.[28] This first note of dissent marked the stirring of resistance by women 'on the line', and the challenge to the authority of Mrs Drew, management, by her sisters on the factory floor. 'She said that if we did not do them we would be out on the labour, but everyone stood firm!' In the printing sector, Miss McDowell extended her ambitions to challenge the figures recording the employment of women in the industry. In dispute with the IPF she argued that 'the employment of women had not compared favourably with increased production' and provided figures to suport her case. The IPF replied that such figures were inappropriate. Kay McDowell had had the temerity 'to compare the women as against the men'.

Spirit was not lacking at any level within the IWWU, but the times were undoubtedly exacting a toll. The Union and its membership were now subject to pressures and changes not previously encountered by an industrial workforce in Ireland. Time and Motion Schemes were widespread, and 'efficiency experts' and consultants a regular feature of the industrial landscape. While the Union had consistently argued for team rather than individually based bonus schemes, the latter proved more attractive at the workplace and workers had registered at least limited approval of 'increased earnings and easier methods of work'.[29] Such approval was not universal.

At Annual Convention in May 1958 Maura Breslin had used the Presidential Address to challenge the assumptions implicit in calls for progress and productivity.

> Many statements have been made by management to show that automation means progress; but what is the meaning of progress? Managements mean that without automation they cannot progress in terms of dividends.[30]

A newly elected member of the Executive, however, Bridie McCormack, strongly disagreed. She spoke in favour of the use of new machinery, pointing to the clear advantage to 'workers not tired at the end of the day', and dismissed fears that increased automation would promote unemployment.

> Machinery does not do away with work, it increases work, increases output and therefore we are able to supply a bigger market.[31]

Little consensus was evident, and both aspects of change encountered by workers were acknowledged as valid.

Convention acknowledged also the perennial 'worry and uncertainty facing members' in regard to both retirement and redundancy. While Congress was urged to 'launch an intensive campaign for the establishment of Industrial Pensions', the Executive of the IWWU accepted the need to link the undoubted appetite of the employers for automation and increased productivity, to claims from working women for benefits in kind. Increased productivity prompted the advocacy of a reduction in working hours, and in industries where automation was in progress the Union sought the abolition of overtime.

In June the Executive, in response to poor attendance at the Boxmakers' Committee, dissolved the boxmakers' section and asked the printers to co-opt a boxmaker onto their own committee. The move was not inappropriate as the two sections were now increasingly facing similar pressures at their places of work. New machinery was affecting the trade of boxmaking and carton making, and under the Rules negotiated by the IWWU and the IPF in 1938, a degree of limited interchangeability between boxmakers and printers had been agreed. The limits to such agreed movement across demarcation lines, however, had been clearly set out. At the Printers' Committee in May 1958 members reported that the Ormond Press had recorded a lack of regular work for members in the carton department. Carton workers had, for a time and without any reference to the Union, been employed on printers' work, and Mr Wilkinson, the manager, now sought permission to interchange his staff on a regular basis.

Such a move threatened both trades. Each had a four-year apprenticeship period, and apprentices, on completion of their time, achieved the status and rate of journeywomen. Ratios between apprentices and journeywomen were zealously policed, but tension existed between printers and boxmakers, in large part because women in printing had consistently claimed, and won, a higher rate of remuneration than had the boxmakers. Although some commonality still existed in these kindred trades, an agreement to extend this on a more formal basis would devalue the skills implicit in both. After a lengthy discussion 'the committee decided that it was too dangerous and that the demarcation line must be adhered to'.[32]

Similar attempts at re-negotiation, particularly in areas of skill, were evident in the laundry trade, where automation was recorded as having prompted some 'upset'. The anticipated redundancies as a result of the introduction of the new machinery in printing and the laundries, however, did not materialise. The Annual Report for 1958 now cautioned against a complacency which could lead to 'a rude awakening'. 'It may well be that although no one is knocked off, the depletion in staffs through natural wastage is not being replaced'.[33] Arguing that new methods of production generated greater profits at a lower wage cost, the Union called again for an agenda headed by the claim for shorter working hours, 'so that all available work may be shared on a just basis'. But the call by the leadership for a reduced working week and a sharing of the work available did not find an echo among the rank and file. In the laundries, and despite the Union's commitment to the abolition of overtime, this practice had increased dramatically, and in 1959 the possibility of focusing on a claim for a reduction in hours worked was somewhat reduced by the impact of a successful claim for a major increase of 7s. for laundresses in the commercial sector. For 'the first time ever this section had received back money'. Although the employers had refused to negotiate on questions of pensions for women in the laundries, this claim, and the lack of any marked unemployment, prompted the registering of 'a quiet year with the exception of one or two domestic upheavals'.[34]

Greater upheavals, however, were evident elsewhere. At the end of 1958, and without any warning, 115 members at

'It's over to you now, ladies' 249

Lever's left the IWWU and joined the Marine Port and General Workers' Union. This union was affiliated to neither of the Congresses, and members, prior to completion of transfer, were asked to meet IWWU officials to air any grievances which might, arguably, have prompted such a defection. The meeting was arranged, but no member from Lever's turned up. Only seven employees, of whom six were cleaners and the seventh the shop steward, retained their IWWU cards, from a workforce of more than 120 . Yet no indication of the basis for the dramatic departure of the members at Lever's from the IWWU is evident. Such an absence of explanations, however, suggests the evident undermining of one union by another: a recurrence of the 'reprehensible poaching' that had earlier been experienced in relation to the binders. The loss was not only evident numerically, but also had a profound effect on Union morale. While celebrating the unity of the trade union movement and voting overwhelmingly to affiliate to the united trades union body — the Irish Congress of Trade Unions [ICTU] — the Executive of the IWWU reflected on the state of the Union.

The year 1958 had been marked by few disputes and no strikes, and finances showed a surplus of £2,549. The loss of members reflected in the figures between 1957 and 1958 had not been repeated. Membership stood at 5,250, drawn from Dublin city and county, from Waterford, Buncrana, Drogheda and Navan. In the face of the sudden loss of the members at Lever's and the absence of growth in other sectors, however, prospects were not good, and the continual problem of members in arrears made financial predictions both difficult and unwise. The years ahead, the General Secretary now advised, would bring 'complete change in industrial concerns'. Such change was worldwide and 'if we as a country are to survive we must move with it'. Working people would, however, have to defend their hard-won gains.

> We have only one weapon to protect ourselves — strong Trade Union organisation — and that does not mean just holding a card.[35]

The focus for strong organisation was the Congress — the

newly-formed body which had proved, despite the omission of a woman representative in the talks on unity, to be clearly committed to the recognition of the place of women in industry.

At its first Conference in October 1959 the ICTU elected Kay McDowell to the National Executive and Lizzie Caffrey to the Standing Orders Committee. Both reported that the women had received a 'good hearing and had given a good account of themselves'. In 1960, this particular 'duet' was repeated within the Labour Party. Kay McDowell was elected to the Administrative Council and Lizzie Caffrey to the important Standing Orders' Committee. When the Women's Advisory Committee was established by the Congress 'to look after the conditions of work for women in industry', Lizzie Caffrey was nominated to the Committee by the IWWU. To the general loss of both the Union and the labour movement, Lizzie Caffrey died suddenly at the end of 1960.

From a number of quarters evidence now came of a labour movement which was responding to a changed terrain. Throughout the year the IWWU had sent members to weekend schools under the auspices of the ICTU and the People's College, designed to inform working people of changes imminent in their industries. The WUI, towards the end of 1959, sponsored a summer school on 'job evaluation'. Maura Breslin, long an opponent of such developments, attended and reported with some satisfaction that speakers at the Conference had echoed her own misgivings, agreeing 'that job evaluation is against the best interests of the worker'.[36] The increased use by employers of a technical language associated with automation and scientific management schemes was, Miss McDowell asserted, now presenting trade union negotiators with new problems. Productivity deals, couched by employers in an overly technical language, had proved notoriously difficult to negotiate at Urney's Chocolates and in other industries, and now, she suggested, 'it required the services of a specially trained official'. Writing to Ruaidhrí Roberts, Secretary of the ICTU, she urged Congress to consider the question of job evaluation and work measurement.

It seems to me that we on our side are at a considerable

disadvantage, as these efficiency experts who are employed and paid by the management must . . . be somewhat biased.

The decoding necessary for terms such as 'works specifications', and Miss McDowell's own lack of experience in discussions tended, she conceded, to put her 'on the defensive' and 'I fear that without some expert advice, we in the Trade Union Movement may be rushed into accepting these changes without being fully aware of their implications'.

In September representatives from the IWWU attended a Productivity Conference[38] which drew together workers and employers to discuss the theme 'Fitting the Job to the Workers'. The representatives attended 'useful' discussions, and the conference marked, for the IWWU, the first indication that concerted resistance either to new machinery or to new methods might be inappropriate. 'It was clear that if we are to compete in the export market we will have to accept new methods in industry'. Such acceptance, if somewhat inevitable, would however be negotiated. In November the ICTU announced the convening of a '40 Hour Conference'. Donal Nevin, Research Officer of the ICTU and long honoured in despatches from Louie Bennett, Helen Chenevix and Kay McDowell, had advised the Congress that 'the time was now opportune'.[39]

CHAPTER 16

Old disputes, new terrain

The period between 1958 and 1963 is often referred to as representing a watershed in Irish social and economic life. In economic terms the period was notable for the introduction of the First Programme for Economic Expansion, based upon a government white paper, *Economic Development,* produced by T.K. Whitaker of the Department of Finance. Seán Lemass, the major architect of the Conditions of Employment Act of 1936 and no stranger to the views of the IWWU, had succeeded Eamon de Valera as Taoiseach in 1959, and in the early 1960s had promoted major State involvement in the directing of both foreign and domestic capital through the medium of significant government incentive programmes. Living standards for many improved markedly, and the social impact of the opening of Telefís Éireann in 1962 exposed a wider population to a range of social perspectives which had, via British television, been accessible to many living on the east coast for a number of years.

Widespread industrial change, accompanied by a growth of 23% in national output,[1] was also accompanied by a social revitalisation which bore the hallmark of 'modernisation'. Such 'modernising impulses' were characterised by the ideological persuasion of two dominant features of the Irish body politic. The Catholic Church entered a new area of discourse under the reign of Pope John XXIII and the Second Vatican Council, its hallmark being the democratising tendencies which were becoming apparent within an essentially hierarchical organisation, and the impact of all this on Irish social and intellectual life could not be underestimated. Such discourse was underlined, in Ireland, by a major commitment at the level of government to the modernisation of the Irish state. 'Modernisation', however, was not ideologically neutral, and in the 1960s was defined by Lemass and by his Fianna Fáil government in precise terms. Terence Brown, in reference to the analysis proferred by the historian Joseph Lee, makes explicit the vision behind this concept:

> . . . Lemass's dedication to efficiency, his desire to remould the Irish Republic into a streamlined functional corporate state which would allow decisions to be taken with a streamlined managerial despatch.[2]

The aspiration for such change would inevitably impinge upon the character and composition of the Irish industrial workforce, and the decade of the 1960s was marked by extensive renegotiation of the place of women in industry as widespread automation, both in factories and in homes, affected industries where women played a dominant part. In the face of a reduction in its numbers the IWWU had sought to consolidate its position and to organise in a range of new industries. Male trade unionists and employers, however, shared similar goals and, inevitably, competing interests were to the fore.

While the demand for a 40-hour working week would ultimately be achieved through 'long term negotiations', in the short term each section of the Union now presented its own agenda for change, for a new form of working life. Members at Maguire and Paterson gave their priority to shorter working hours, and in 1961 the directors of the company agreed to a reduced working week, from 43¾ hours to 42½ hours. Mental nurses, a small group of whom had retained membership in the IWWU, served a claim for an upward adjustment of salaries, and called on their unions to seek on their behalf a professional status more commensurate with that enjoyed by general trained nurses. Women in the provincial printing houses, for their part, claimed 'experience pay' on the same basis as that enjoyed by women in the city. In the textile industry, meanwhile, piece work and the 'continuing problems' associated with work measurement made the resolve, of both members and leadership, to establish better working conditions difficult to maintain in the daily battle to resist attempts by employers to set new rates and cut the prices for piece work.

Internally, Kay McDowell was clearly committed to greater participation by both Executive and membership in setting the overall priorities of the IWWU. When she read a rough draft of her 1961 Annual Report to members of the Executive they were encouraged to formulate further resolutions: on equal pay for equal work, on pensions, and on factory inspection. One member of the Executive, Miss Nolan, prompted by such receptiveness, offered a considered response to at least one aspect of industrial machinery, and called for 'Abolition of the Labour Court, she thought that no good had ever come of it'.[3] While the basis for her dismissal of the Labour Court was unclear, Tess Nolan had herself established a place of some esteem in Union history. When the members at Lever's had defected in 1958, Miss Nolan had been shop steward and had refused either to condone their actions or to join their numbers. She continued to serve as shop steward for the six cleaners at Lever's who remained loyal to the IWWU and for a number of years also served as representative of general workers on the IWWU Executive.

When the Annual Report, with its adjustments, was finally delivered to members at Annual Convention, the platform enabled Miss McDowell to offer to her members her considered views on the status of working women in the decade ahead. While manufacturers were exhorted to proceed in the automation of industry with the most advanced machinery available, she suggested, the new era of production methods would have to be matched by the use of more sophisticated industrial relations. Miss McDowell believed that advance in both areas could be achieved, but that the old ways would now have to be abandoned.

> I believe we can hold our own. . . . We have good and intelligent workers. We want good and intelligent overseers, men and women. The day of shouting and bullying is over, and that was a policy that never produced the best.

On her return from a visit to Sweden and Denmark Kay

Old disputes, new terrain 255

McDowell's enthusiasms for the potential for such change had been re-kindled.

As one of a three-person team appointed by the ICTU to examine the impact of a work study on the textile industry, she had been impressed by the commitment of the Swedish Garment Workers' Union to active training of their members for the role of negotiators for the working class. Over £20,000 a year was allocated by the Garment Workers for the education of officials and of factory representatives. The vitality of the trade union movement in the Scandinavian countries was evident in their ownership of five daily newspapers, and the marked absence of any similar vitality in the ranks of the IWWU was, she suggested, more pronounced by comparison: 'No interest whatever is taken in the union or its work by the rank and file of the members'. Arrears, poor attendance at meetings, failure to turn up at conferences when sent as union representatives, and a casual attitude to the whole concept of trade unionism boded ill for the long-term prospects of working women.

Arguing that an era of rapidly changing methods required constant vigilance from the Union, Miss McDowell intimated that should defaulting by members persist, the Union would in future commit itself only to those members who demonstrated collective responsibility by the payment of their union dues. Members, in short, were warned of the inevitable consequences of their abdication as members of the labour movement.

> Don't leave your affairs in the hands of a few who regularly attend meetings. . . . If you don't attend and cast your vote you have no right to quarrel with the result or to voice the opinion that the Union is no good.[5]

While the Union undoubtedly suffered as an institution from the lack of involvement of many of its younger members, the pressures encountered by working women in their daily lives were, undoubtedly, in part responsible for their lack of energies in other areas. Many had emigrated, unwilling to wait indefinitely for the gaining of working conditions in any way commensurate to those across the Channel. For those who remained, the upheaval evident across industry left working women with few illusions as to the security of their place in industry, and the ease with which employers discarded their labour prompted younger girls and women to reassess their own commitment to life as members of the industrial workforce.

Across the board employers were loud in their complaints about a shortage of skilled women in industry. In printing, they noted a lack of interest among young girls in serving their time in the trade. The shortage, if real, was aggravated by moves by industry from city centres to new suburbs — moves that, in effect, removed the available market from ready access by those who had labour to offer. Irish Carton Printers reported that it was in the process of expanding into the export market and that its plant would be moved to Finglas. It found it impossible, following the move, to secure the services of young girls of sixteen years — the starting age for learners in the trade — and in response applied for a reduction in the age of entry to fifteen and, possibly, to fourteen, to facilitate recruitment among girl school leavers. In 1960 the Printers' Committee agreed to reduce the age limit to fifteen years.[6] The complaint of Irish Carton Printers was echoed by De La Rue, who sought, through the agency of the IWWU, sixty girls aged between sixteen and eighteen. Neither management nor union were able to recruit the necessary numbers, and De La Rue offered to recruit workers who were either younger or older than this. The company gave an indication of its concern at the shortage by declaring that it was 'prepared to take persons over 20 years and to give them extensive training for any period of short duration as suggested'.[7] This was despite the fact that the use of an older workforce of necessity committed De La Rue to greater wage costs.

The shortage reflected both the practices which had discouraged women from completion of apprenticeships, and the changing social context. Where available, employment for young women in offices and in retail outlets was more appealing than employment in a trade. Commitment to a trade demanded three or four years apprenticeship at low rates of pay, and, as the experience of journeywomen so clearly indicated, resulted in no commitment on the part of employer or government to retrain women in the event of their hard-won skills being declared redundant. The shortage, prompted by a combination of wider opportunities for women, emigration, marriage, and inadequate training, was never specifically diagnosed by either Union or employers, and the employers' capacity to 'engineer' the myth of shortage to facilitate their own needs cannot be discounted. Real or otherwise, however, the rhetoric of an under-supply of women workers prompted a range of responses, all equally threatening to the security of women already established in industry.

In 1962 the Union 'reluctantly agreed that given the scarcity of girl workers' the use of male workers would be sanctioned. Browne and Nolan, among others, had over a period of six months sought recruits to their female workforce, but neither they nor the Union had been successful. By January, IWWU members at the company reported that male members of the Binders' Union were doing work normally done by women. Miss McDowell, fearing an erosion of the women's place by stealth, called for a meeting with the employers. 'At this meeting they explained that owing to the shortage of girls they were in arrears with their orders and requested that we allow men to lend a hand'.[8] Miss McDowell, however, sought an undertaking in writing which would recognise that the work in question was, and would continue to be, defined as 'women's work'. On receipt of a letter to this effect, the Union agreed to facilitate management who, for its part, reassured the Union that it was 'not anxious that the men should do it, for economical reasons'. Undoubtedly the continuing lower value placed on the labour of women ensured, somewhat negatively, security of tenure when their labour was available.

At Mount Temple Press, however, more elaborate procedures accompanied the steady erosion of the demarcation lines which served as some protection for areas of women's work. Management, pointing both to a shortage of available womanpower and to the difficulty of retraining girls trained on the numbering machine, requested that the work should be transferred to a male operator. Despite women's long service in this area, management deployed rhetoric, to some effect, to justify long-term change by arguing that the work involved in setting was 'so complicated it is beyond a girl'.[9]

In other areas the allegation that there was a shortage of women workers was used to facilitate the introduction of new machinery and, in its wake, a different form of working day. At Harold's Cross Laundry, excessive overtime — almost a condition of the trade — was attributed to 'shortage of experienced workers'.[10] The claimed shortage was now, however, related to the need to retain viability by utilising new machines to their greatest capacity. At White Swan Laundry the management proposed to deal with both problems by introducing a particular shift on the basis of 'three or four hours in the evening time on say, two, three or maybe four nights a week'.[11] In short, this form of shift would leave the sanctity of the guaranteed week unimpaired, but would provide the employer with a part-time workforce which would have no prior claim to a guaranteed week but would be recruited with an immediate expectation of fluctuating hours. For such a shift, the direction of their policy was made abundantly clear.

> This staff could be recruited from our ex-staff who are now possibly married and who would like some extra pocket-money.[12]

While such recruits were welcomed by management, other women continued to bear the brunt of criticism from such employers and their own leaders.

By the early 1960s, the Union found itself in the unenviable position of suspecting the motives underlying the employers' voiced concern about shortages of skilled labour, but lacking adequate resources of its own to present an alternative analysis. Conceding that emigration, together with a wider choice of employment possibilities, particularly in the clerical and the retail sector, had reduced their numbers, the IWWU was forced to condone practices which were in essence unpalatable to the majority of its members. From the 1960s on, under the banner of a supposed desire to encourage women's participation in the industrial workforce, many employers heralded the move away from the skilled to the general, and facilitated a new form of employment — the irregular, generally married, part-time woman worker.

In the textile industry girls on piece-work were accused by their bosses of 'irresponsibility' and at Morco were claimed to be accustomed to taking 'French leave', most notably in the summer, when absence among piece-workers was not uncommon.[13] Morco were, however, infamous for giving 'nothing without a fight'. Piece rates in the company were, by tradition, set on samples where articles were pre-cut and pre-ironed. Women workers were then forced to locate pieces, wait for irons, and complete their labours for a price set in conditions wholly advantageous to the employer. In such a context their discontent and lack of commitment, if such were evident, reflected the quality of their employment. While the employers blamed emigration, marriage, and inappropriate training, the Union blamed lack of adequate remuneration for working women. A further element, however, could not be dismissed.

In 1961, workers at Cherry and Smalldridge had called for an annual inspection each winter to be conducted by Union officials in all places of work,

> to ensure that heating and sanitary conditions are suitable for the workers and when complaints of this nature are made they be dealt with immediately by action, as we have found that words are not enough.[14]

By 1962 the Executive was referring to evidence of considerable unrest in the printing trade, and to 'members transferring from one job to another'.[15] An increase of militancy was noted in the rank and file, and in the same year, Miss McDowell was 'chastised' by members at the Meath Chronicle for making what they saw as 'too cautious a demand': with that most intimate of knowledge enjoyed by employees in relation to their masters, they announced that 'we will not get any increase on a sympathetic letter to him'.[16] Shortly afterwards, members at Harvey's in Waterford complained that the level of Union dues was not commensurate with the service provided, and a minority refused to pay.

Across a whole range of industries, the IWWU now renewed claims for a reduction in the working week, with employers in one industry being informed that the Union had acted in response to demands from its members: 'our instructions are to endeavour to get a universal five day week'.

What was apparent from the activities of the IWWU in the early 1960s was that while employers bewailed the lack of female labour, and the officials lamented the lack of interest in Union affairs, the members — working women — were serving notice on both that their conditions of labour were found to be seriously wanting. Some improvements had been achieved, and in a number of industries the shorter working week had been won. Although still far from the 40-hour week, a shorter week of forty-two hours, without loss of earnings, had been negotiated at the Joint Labour Council [JLC] of the Women's Clothing Trade in July 1961. At White Heather Laundry the claim served by the Union for a reduced working week resulted in a 42$\frac{1}{2}$-hour week for seniors and forty hours for juniors. At Our Lady's Hospital, despite protests by management, a 42$\frac{1}{2}$-hour week was established for wardsmaids by a reduction of half an hour each day. At the insistence of the women workers themselves, a momentum had been established, but the continuing lament by employers about a shortage of skilled labour did little to encourage the masters to treat their wage slaves with anything more than the customary disdain. The status of women workers, and their potential for long-term security within industry, continued to be dependent on specific circumstances.

The term 'woman worker' tended to conceal the diversity of the IWWU as a general union. While collective negotiations were still possible, if more complex, in the printing and boxmaking industry, and in the laundries, the peculiar status of groups such as the post office factory workers, mental nurses, and the range of general workers in areas such as cleaning, sugar confectionery and metal soldering, ensured that the energies of Union officials would be largely consumed in industry by industry negotiation. This factor apart, while each industry presented complexities peculiar to its own stage of development, it remained commonplace for women to be displaced almost at will. Although sectors, such as printing, recorded no unemployment among women workers, the shedding of labour in other industries made the rhetoric about 'shortages' somewhat suspect.

If shortage was evident in the textile industry, it was a shortage that was engineered. The use of new looms at Greenmount and Boyne produced 'a lot of trouble'. The increased use of such looms was being accompanied by threats by management that boys could be employed on the new machinery if girls proved disruptive. At Robert Usher and Co., Drogheda, management dispensed with labour considered surplus to their requirements with disarming ease. When fifty-five women weavers were threatened with redundancy following the installation of automatic looms, management took refuge in the terminology of 'natural wastage', and gave some indication of the attractions of married women as a small but increasing proportion of the female labour force. Such women, it was assumed, could be conveniently employed elsewhere.

> Of the 55 weavers which we have here at the moment 25 are in the age group between 19 and 25 years of age and would appear to me to be eligible for marriage. We also have in the 55 numbered, nine young married women, and they could be classed as very likely to be leaving within the next two years.[18]

Should the hapless weavers fail to find suitable accommodation in the domestic arena, however, Robert Usher was clearly disinclined to consider alternative training. By 1963 girls previously employed on check looms which had since been dismantled were given 'other non-skilled work and standing pay'. The girls made it clear to the Union that 'they would not like to be left in this job always . . . all would be willing to learn the automatics'. Although willing, the weavers were nonetheless acutely aware of rumours that men were being brought in to work the automatic terry looms.[19]

Such rumours rapidly became reality, and in 1961 the women workers confronted an old enemy — the Conditions of Employment Act — which served effectively to curtail their employment and erode their demarcation rights in areas now affected by new machinery and new work forms. The use of such new machinery, to be considered cost effective in management terms, needed to be operated 'around the clock'. At Greenmount and Boyne in 1961 the Union protested at the employment of young boys to operate the automatic looms on all shifts, and later, at a meeting of members, they advised the women to learn how to operate the new machinery. In the short term the manager, Mr Hall, agreed to cease the employment of young boys if the women were willing to learn the new process — a move that would, however, necessitate the women doing shift work. The relevant application for an exclusion order under the terms of the Conditions of Employment Act 1936 was completed, with the application taking the form of a request to the Department of Industry and Commerce giving details of the proposed shifts. Under the Act, the Department was obliged to ascertain the views of all trade unions within the industry, and, if none exercised the virtual veto available under the terms of the Act, an Exclusion Order would be granted.

The Order was not granted for the women at Greenmount and Boyne. On 29 June 1961 the Department of Industry and Commerce indicated that the basis for its refusal to grant the licence was 'as it was against the law for women to work around the clock'.[20] Alternative shifts were, however, available, and indeed operated in other textile factories, as Greenmount and Boyne were undoubtedly aware. In 1963 the shop steward at Usher's reported a row within the industry as a number of stitchers employed on a part-time basis were also working in another factory between the hours of 7 and 10.30 p.m. Such a shift, which took some account of the restrictions under the Act, was not envisaged by Greenmount and Boyne, and in seeking a night shift for women they were undoubtedly aware that such a precedent was unlikely to be established. The refusal by government at this time to extend the working hours of women ensured that for at least part of the working day a process previously dominated by women would, by default, pass to the men.

Predictably, the automatic looms were now perceived by the women as inevitably eroding the established rights of their trade. In February 1962 Miss McDowell was called to

Greenmount and Boyne. Aware that an exclusion order had been refused, the women had rejected the imperatives of the machine and now refused to cooperate with any training offered. After considerable discussion they were persuaded by Miss McDowell 'that it was in their own interest to be trained, that eventually there would be no loom of the old type in any mill'.[21] The women were, however, cautioned against assuming that they could claim a right to the particular looms they had worked on over a period of years. The negotiations between the IWWU and the management at Greenmount and Boyne on the changeover from the old looms to the new broad looms included a directive from Miss McDowell to reluctant workers — 'Again I would like to stress the point that no weaver can claim that certain looms belong to her'.

While some workers retrained when such training was offered, older workers less willing to adapt were simply told to go. In 1962, when installation of the new machinery was virtually complete, Mr Hall 'told Anne Kelly that the machine she was working was no use any more and as there was no work for her to do she would have to go'. After considerable negotiation the Union won for Anne Kelly a settlement of £36, a recognition of 36 years' service estimated at a value of £1 per year. Anne Kelly, weaver, accepted her less than honourable discharge and settlement with grateful thanks to the Union. For others, the disregard for the industrial and moral rights of women workers was profound. While such rights had been established, they lacked a statutory basis, and the absence of such protection at the level of legislation, involved the IWWU in continual renegotiation of old terrain.

As in textiles and printing, change was the keynote in the laundry sector, and in the laundries the heady days of 1945 had long since passed. Women were overworked, obliged to do excessive overtime as an unwritten rule of their trade, and harassed by the petty tyranny of supervisors. The pressure to increase the pace of work was unremitting. At Court Laundry Ltd girls complained of the manner in which 'they were spoken to by the manager'. They pointed out that 'Miss McCoy seems to have too much to do in keeping a battery of machines supplied with work'. When the manageress, eager to eliminate unnecessary steps in a process in the interests of increased productivity, deprived Miss McCoy of the use of a table on which she could stack linen, the power of the petty tyrant was abundantly clear. 'Mrs McGrane abused Miss McCoy so much about <u>this matter</u> that Miss McCoy cried and was unable to take the tea provided at the break'.[22]

The washing machine had by now become standard equipment in the homes of those accustomed to call on the services of laundries. While new domestically-based services undoubtedly affected both the internal organisation of homes, and the lives of women at home, the laundries themselves claimed that there had been few incursions into the traditional service offered by their industry. The purchase of washing machines for domestic use had, it was claimed in newspaper reports, affected the type of service offered rather than its volume. Under the heading 'Laundries Boom in Washing Machine Age', *The Irish Times* reported that the production manager of one large Dublin laundry had suggested that the growth in domestic technology had really begun with the introduction of presser machines within the laundries themselves. While the call for a personal hand service had persisted in some areas, this service was most dramatically curtailed. When asked if the increase of washing machine sales was cutting into the trade overall, however, the manager of another laundry gave an emphatic 'No'.[23] Yet the potential was undoubtedly there, and in the next few years managers and owners of laundries were accused by Miss McDowell of publicly lamenting the loss of service and employment in the laundry sector while securing for themselves ownership of the fifty launderettes which were scattered throughout Dublin by 1967.

While such developments were ongoing, in the short term laundries called for greater productivity by employees in order to defray what they referred to as their accumulated losses. At the Court Laundry, where 150 workers of all ages and both sexes were employed, the company reported to the Union that its financial advisors claimed that to remain viable it would have to 'achieve at present prices and wage rates, a certain weekly turnover . . . the only way to process this turnover is by working the existing machinery for longer hours'. The financial advisors, in the interests of achieving such objectives, recommended the employment of fifteen girls 'all over 18 years of age for a limited evening shift from 6 p.m. to 10 p.m.' The extended working day would be offered to existing staff at overtime rates and 'thereafter additional staff will be recruited for this part-time work'.[25]

This employment of women on a part-time basis was confined neither to textiles nor to the laundry industry. During the 1960s the use of a part-time shift became evident in a number of industries, with an explicit bias in favour of married women who would, it was assumed, be seeking a subsidiary income. At Maguire and Paterson's, although the stated motives for the introduction of such a shift differed, part-time work was introduced by 1966. In response to a claim from the IWWU for a 40-hour week the company proposed the introduction of a part-time shift to ensure ongoing production levels while reducing the working week to forty hours with no loss of pay. After agreeing to compensation for the full-time women workers in the form of 'a very good service pay scheme', part-time women workers were, from 1966, employed at this factory. Although both the staff and the membership of the IWWU had previously resisted the introduction of a part-time workforce, this development was eventually negotiated, rather than resisted, in a range of industries.

This change of stance indicated the IWWU's concern to ensure, in effect, further placements for women in those industries affected by automation and new working methods. In printing, although unemployment was not a problem, women were clearly being displaced. At the Mayo News in 1963 male trade unions reached an agreement with management to ease the financial difficulties of the company by the displacement of women workers and the employment of men.

Other developments, however, indicated that the securing of a future for women workers in modern Ireland would in part be determined both by organisation and by a readiness to challenge the assumed immutability of demarcation lines between men and women in the industry. The resistance to such a challenge, however, could not be underestimated. In 1962 Major T.B. McDowell, Chairman of Management Directors Ltd, and acting on behalf of Thomson International Ltd, attended at his own request a meeting of the workers' side of the JIC for the printing industry. Mr Roy Thomson had put a specific proposal to the industry on 1 October, and Major McDowell was now authorised to seek a response. Mr Thomson had proposed to print in Dublin 'educational and cultural books for the undeveloped countries'. The process he envisaged, however, would involve the print unions in quite a radical departure in production techniques. Whereas previously print had been dominated by the hot metal process — an area of skilled labour the preserve of men — the new process drew on a number of new technological developments.

The process consisted of typing copy on an ordinary IBM typewriter which, by being connected to an electronic unit produced, simultaneously, a tape punched with special characters. A proposed new organisation, Graphic Films Ltd, which would be a subsidiary of Thomson International, would specialise in translating this tape into a photographic negative, from which a positive of the original page as typed would be produced and posted overseas to printing units in the underdeveloped countries, to be finally processed into book form. Graphic Film Ltd would initially employ thirteen men and 102 women. If the proposal permitting the recruitment of women to work on a new process deriving from a previously 'male' area was accepted, however, Mr Thomson would 'deflect some traditional printing development from countries other than the United Kingdom to Ireland'. This additional 'sweetener' would, in effect, establish in Dublin 'the most modern printing plant in Europe (Europrint) employing under normal conditions 202 men and 78 women'.[27] This departure from normal practice within the industry would require, however, if the proposal to establish both Graphic Film Ltd and Europrint Ltd was to be accepted,

> no demarcation lines between operations which are really 'office' type and should be performed by women for reasons of economy and productivity.[28]

The print unions retired to consider their verdict, and on 2

November 1962 the workers' side of the JIC completed its deliberations.

Of the four trade unions representing the industry, the IWWU alone represented the interests of women. The joint position they agreed, however, indicated the acceptance by the Union of *force majeure* on this issue, lacking as it did any measure of support which would have enabled it to challenge the status quo at this time.

> The representatives of the unions rejected the proposals to employ female labour in work normally done by male labour as being contrary to national economic interests.[29]

While women could clearly anticipate no immediate acceptance of change in their status in the printing industry of the future, the workers' side of the JIC added that some accommodation to take into account the ambitions of Thomson International would be forthcoming. The terms, however, were quite specific in relation to gender. 'They wish you to understand that they are willing to cooperate in a spirit of accommodation regarding male labour.'[30]

The representatives of the Dublin Typographical Provident Society [DTPS], Society of Lithographic Artists, Designers, Engravers [SLADE], Amalgamated Society of Lithographic Printers [ASLP] and the IWWU were, however, contacted by Major McDowell to correct any impression they might have harboured that a compromise would be acceptable on the staffing of Graphic Print which did not preclude the proposed establishment of Europrint Ltd. In a letter in October 1962, the Major reiterated the terms on offer:

> As I endeavoured to make clear . . . but to prevent the possibility of any misunderstanding and before conveying your decision to Mr Thomson, I should like it to be confirmed that your members know that the formation of Europrint Ltd., was entirely conditional on the acceptance of the proposal for Graphic Film Ltd.[31]

As the formation of both companies was contingent on the proposal being accepted in its entirety, however, neither company was established. In the era of modernisation, traditional territorial claims prevailed.

While either unprepared or reluctant in this instance to challenge publicly the territory claimed by male labour, the Union, in settlements throughout industry, continued to champion the cause of the Anne Kellys and the Miss McCoys among its 5,000 members. The threatened erosion of the many gains won by previous generations of women workers was now, however, a central issue. Kay McDowell warned her members that, despite vigilance,

> unless we can show a united front we may suffer serious infringements of the rights we have gained since the first big strike which took place exactly 50 years ago.[32]

As a small general union the IWWU faced greater problems than did unions catering for specific trades.

Although few members were unemployed, the pressure on officials to protect the territory of women workers in specific industries gave rise to constant battles. In over fifty years of existence the Union, in common with the movement as a whole, now experienced the negotiating process between worker, union and employer as irrevocably changed. As Miss McDowell elaborated: 'now these three remain augmented by Efficiency Experts, Industrial Consultants, and Government Survey Teams'. Officials were required now to do more than negotiate across a table. They had to approach that table equipped with information from a daunting array of sources: surveys had to be studied, reports assessed, and methods of work updated. While membership, both actual and potential, was drawn from a contracting base, the General Secretary envisaged a future which would be notable for an increase in the demand for additional officials and supervisory staff, building up, in effect, an institution fit for combat with the employers. Employers, meanwhile, contemplated another future: while loudly championing the cause of 'efficiency' they sought, through such means, greater control of the work process.

In 1964 the Annual Report recorded 'the introduction of something unique in the Trade Union Movement'. Although at this time reported as a National Wage Agreement [NWA] by the Union, it was in fact the thirteenth Round in 1970 which marked the official beginning of such agreements. The 1964 'Agreement' was between the FUE and the ICTU, and differed substantially from the tripartite agreements inaugurated in 1970. The 1964 Agreement was to cover a period of two and a half years and would pay an agreed 12% increase across industry.

While such agreements marked the opening of a new phase in Irish political and economic life, the principle under which the IWWU would now be required to conduct its negotiations was not wholeheartedly welcomed by women workers. The 12% increase was, effectively, reduced by the 2½% Turnover Tax introduced in late 1963, and in her annual report Kay McDowell remained sceptical about the advantages or otherwise of an agreement which offered 9½% over two and a half years.

> I am not sure whether it is really of any true benefit to us. Agreed, it prevented a 'free-for-all' which might have resulted in numerous strikes, but what in point of fact have we really achieved?

The nine and a half per cent, she argued, would not 'offset the continuing rise in prices'. More pertinently, however, in the case of women the agreement had also contained a clause which excluded women workers from receiving the minimum basic increase of £1 guaranteed to men. At the Special Congress in February 1964, Miss McDowell objected strongly to this exclusion, and in a resolution to the Annual Convention of the IWWU served notice on the trade union movement that the incoming Executive would be directed by the membership 'to resist the inclusion of such a clause in any further agreements'.[33]

Such structural changes within the ranks of labour, combined with discussions on the reorganisation of the entire trade union movement, presented the IWWU with further logistical problems. Reports from the ICTU Committee on Industrial Organisation, established some years earlier to examine the structure of all affiliated unions, required detailed comment on a variety of proposals. Kay McDowell and Jenny Murray were members of this committee, and the IWWU was informed, via the Annual Report, of the outcome of some of the meetings. General workers' unions, including the IWWU, considered the questions of federation, of industry-based unions, and of mergers. On behalf of the Union, the General Secretary rejected federation as 'merely involving the Union in greater expenses while limiting its independence.' Industrial unions would, by definition, mean the elimination of the basis of the IWWU, and mergers at this time were seen as being 'beset with difficulties'.

The committee, while making little progress in terms of overall organisation, did help to bring about some rationalisation in the areas of contributions, benefits, transfers and poaching. The last-named practice had, however, already decreased noticeably in recent years. A small union, no less than a large union, was obliged to commit time to such deliberations in order to defend the interests of its members. Miss McDowell subsequently outlined the problems created by this at the level of the ICTU itself. The need to submit observations and to attend the Industrial Committee set up by Congress, she said, took up a lot of the officials' time, and the situation was proving particularly difficult in the case of a small union with a limited number of officials.[34]

These officials were by now obliged to deal with a range of problems which left even the most competent reeling. Attending committees, assimilating surveys and meeting the daily round of members' demands called for a daunting degree of mental agility and stamina. The dismissal of two members from Cahill's, for instance — though hardly commonplace — served to caution the uninitiated against too casual a reading of the life and times of the working woman, and gave some indication of the spectrum of debate and demand that constituted union life. The 'girls' were dismissed because, it was alleged, they had a fight outside the factory. In her own defence, one girl protested and 'claimed that she did not hit the other girl and there was no reason why she should be dismissed.' On the girls' behalf their shop steward (and a member of the Executive), Miss Bridie McCormack, brought their case to Fleet Street. Having pondered the problems associated with representing both the defendant and the accused, the Executive decided in its collective wisdom that in this instance 'we could do nothing because we had no proof as to which hit the other first'.[35] The girls in question both eventually returned to Cahill's, but Miss McDowell made it abundantly clear to her Executive that their brief did not extend to civil matters, and 'it is not the responsibility of the union to look into a case of assault'.

Such diversions did not, however, serve to cloud the issues of the day. The fact that an exclusion clause in the National Wage Agreement on the £1 'floor' wage increase had failed to consider the interests of women reaffirmed the view of members that any talk of a merger between unions at this stage was entirely premature and had no place on any agenda, despite the problems intrinsic to a small institution. In the wake of the 1964 Wage Agreement and the directive subsequently issued to the Executive by Annual Convention regarding future agreements, 'idle gossip' surrounding the talks which continued between the unions was rife, however, within the ranks of the IWWU. At a personal level Miss McDowell, with some justice, pointed to her own record of forty-five years in the labour movement in the service of women workers. The assumption that she might either consider — or even be able to contemplate — a merger, within the Rules of the IWWU, without reference to her members, was, she argued, both inaccurate and hurtful.

> I would not like to think that at the end of my long service to the union any doubt or suspicion should be in any member's mind to sell out the union to which I have devoted my life.[36]

While questions of the personal loyalty of Kay McDowell were undoubtedly out of order, the General Secretary did not shrink from the task of reminding members, ranging in age from sixteen to sixty years, of the fundamental changes now evident in the industrial landscape. She pointed to the reality of their own experience, and urged them not to ignore its implications.

> You are all aware that the day of a small firm in industry is drawing to a close. It either goes out of business or

becomes part of a larger grouping and although it may still continue under its own name, it is in fact not an entirely independent unit.[37]

She reminded them also that Seán Lemass had clearly signalled his intention of framing legislation to force unions to merge if they did not do so voluntarily. The changing face of industry, the questions of demarcation, of preferential treatment for tradesmen, and vulnerability to the law, made a considered approach by the unions themselves to the rationalisation of their movement essential.

It is in the interests of all trade unions to get closer together; to act as allies rather than rivals; to cease to try to score off each other; to cease to use positions as key operatives without due consideration for other workers involved . . .[38]

Having thus presented her case, Kay McDowell, as was her wont, withdrew.

CHAPTER 17

Under siege

On 2 February 1965 a meeting on Trades Union Organisation was held under the auspices of the Congress at Wynn's Hotel in Dublin. In reporting on its proceedings to the IWWU Executive, Bridie McCormack accused Kay McDowell of 'having sold out to the ITGWU'. The claim was rejected by other members who had also been present, and when Miss McCormack was asked to withdraw her remarks, she did so. She repeated the allegation, however, at an unauthorised meeting of members at her place of work, Cahill's.[1] In response, Miss McDowell attended the next meeting of the Printers' Committee, of which Miss McCormack was chairman, and prefaced her own remarks with a reference to the 'sell-out' charge. Miss McDowell 'stated that at no time had the union been sold out on amalgamation with either the ITGWU or the WUI'.[2]

Although discussions had in fact taken place between all unions affiliated to Congress within the brief of reorganising the trade union movement, no definite proposal had emerged, 'and when it did the members would be informed and given the opportunity of deciding for themselves'.[3] Following a 'lengthy discussion' of the matter, Miss McCormack was asked to resign from her position as chairman of the Printers' Committee. She did so, but a letter of protest at this action was immediately forthcoming from her colleagues at Cahill's, who sought a general meeting of all printers. The Committee refused to sanction such a meeting and the matter was deemed to be closed.

At Annual Convention in May a sense of 'restlessness and dissatisfaction' within the Union ranks was publicly acknowledged and members were urged to ventilate any grievances they had in an open fashion. Miss Breslin, in her presidential address, sought to assert the standing of the Union as an institution representing collective, rather than individual interests, but also endeavoured to 'remind us of what the union is — 6,000 members. If the union makes a decision it is not the Executive Committee or officials who do so, but the members'.[4] The Convention, as bound by the Constitution of the IWWU embodied in the Rules of the Union, remained, she continued, the ruling body of the IWWU. In acknowledgement of the continuing disquiet among both Executive and members, a vote of confidence in the General Secretary was called for and passed. A week later, however, attendance at the Annual General Meeting was larger than had been evident for some years, and in the election of officers that followed the passing of the Annual Report, Bridie McCormack was elected President of the IWWU. A battle had begun.

When Maura Breslin reiterated the primacy of the membership of the IWWU in relation to the formulation of Union policy, her claim of 6,000 members bore little relationship to actual numbers. In 1965 the annual returns to the Registrar of Friendly Societies recorded a membership of 4,753. Given the trend towards automation in a range of industries, such figures did not augur well for the long-term prospects of a Union unable to allocate staff for extensive recruiting campaigns beyond its traditional membership. Any anticipation of future losses would also be exacerbated by the increasing evidence that, as young women workers changed their place of work with greater readiness than had their predecessors,[5] the problems of persuading them of the value of organisation and of actually dealing with a highly mobile workforce made predictions for any potential growth extremely hazardous.

Despite the reassurances to its members, the IWWU was now one of the smaller unions within the Congress. As such its resources were over-stretched and its potential impact reduced. In May the Trade Union Organisation meeting voted, with the agreement of the IWWU, that the small number of miscellaneous members within all unions should, on a voluntary basis, begin to be moved into more effective groupings. While such moves were ongoing, other developments were also evident.

The nature of the working day, for an increasing number of women, was changing. Although the majority of women workers continued to work on a full-time basis, the incidence of shift work and part-time work had, since the early 1960s, increased. At Hely Thom shifts from 6 a.m. to 10 p.m., using women who lived nearby, some of whom were married, for the first shift, had been established with no prior discussion with the Union. The IWWU was eventually informed not by its members but by the Department of Industry and Commerce, after an application had been made for an exclusion order to cover the women under the terms of the Conditions of Employment Act. The move was echoed in a number of industries — Batchelor's, Usher's, Greenmount and Boyne, Urney Chocolates, and Maguire and Paterson all applied for shift licences to facilitate later working hours for women or the use of a part-time labour force.

In August 1965 the management of Maguire and Paterson sought Union agreement to the bringing in of part-time women workers between 10.30 and 4.30 to ensure full utilisation of new machinery and to facilitate ongoing production. Management argued that the introduction of a part-time ancillary workforce would facilitate the reduction of the working week to forty hours, without loss of pay for the full-time workforce. The women, then employed on a 42-hour week, refused both aspects of the negotiation on offer, rejecting the use of part-timers even if combined with the introduction of a shorter working week.[6] In December a similar offer was again placed on the negotiating table, and again refused. By early 1966, however, members at Maguire and Paterson had agreed both to the introduction of a five-day week and of a part-time workforce. Their earlier resistance had paid some dividends: the final negotiations included an agreement that Maguire and Paterson would implement 'a very good service pay scheme'.[7]

The by now almost inevitable combination — negotiations for part-time workers and the increased labour force participation of married women workers — produced an agreement finally reached in January of the New Year which involved, in effect, the formulation of IWWU policy in relation to married women workers. In return for specific improvements in conditions for the full-time workforce, members of the IWWU at Maguire and Paterson agreed to the introduction of part-time married workers, but in a temporary relief capacity only. While such an agreement protected the full-time workforce, and by extension the majority of members of the IWWU, it could offer little security to married women returning to paid part-time work. It did, however, concede the right of management to employ an irregular workforce at a time when, in the case of Maguire and Paterson, considerable change in the use of rapidly developing technology in the printing trade was evident. By mid-1966 there was some evidence of an abuse by the company of the concession they had been given in relation to this particular workforce, with a consequent erosion of full-time employment as new technology had an inevitable impact on the amount of labour employed.[8]

The year 1965 became significant for the collective Union memory because of two related events, the lock-out of the printers and the unprecedented circumstances surrounding the attempt by a group of IWWU printers to defect from the IWWU and join the Irish Graphical Society [IGS]. In February 1965 the Dublin Typographical Provident Society [DTPS] had changed its name to the Irish Graphical Society. In doing so it opened its doors to a wider range of potential members from within printing and kindred trades, including women, and moved away from the constraints of a solidly craft-based union. In May the IGS served a status claim of 33⅓% on the Irish Printing Federation [IPF] which, if successful, would dramatically increase the differentials within the industry as between IGS members and those in other unions. The IWWU promptly served notice on the IPF that a further claim from them would seek to re-establish differentials, and would also involve a notice of intent that differentials would only be maintained pending a complete reappraisal of the value of women's labour in the industry. Miss McDowell informed the IPF:

> Since negotiating our last agreement with you this union has had under constant review the various changes in

methods of work etc. within the printing industry and has come to the conclusion that the value of a woman's work is not sufficiently recognised.[9]

The nature of the work on which the women were involved was acknowledged by all in the industry to be physically arduous. As a result, the members resisted overtime, and on this platform the Union argued that existing differentials in effect already failed to represent adequately real differences in the labour of men and women. To seek now to widen that differential further would be resisted: 'we think it fair to tell you that we would not be prepared to accept such a position'.[10]

On 26 May a meeting of the Printers' Joint Industrial Council was held at the Labour Court. Nothing, however, was resolved. Other meetings followed, but the problems posed by the status claim from the IGS did not allow for immediate resolution. On 17 June the IGS announced its intention of serving strike notice in support of its claim, to come into effect on 1 July, and on that day all IWWU members employed in houses affiliated to the IPF, either as printers or as boxmakers, were locked out. The IWWU Finance Committee struck a levy of 5s. per week on all journeywomen printers and boxmakers in non-IPF houses, and a levy of 1s. a week on all other IWWU members. The lock-out would last ten weeks. Many women, although receiving lock-out pay, moved on a temporary basis to England where work was recorded as being plentiful. At Fleet Street the Executive voted in favour of a decision requiring women who obtained such work to maintain their contributions to the Union and also to contribute, in common with other working members, the 5s. levy.

Meanwhile, at a Labour Court hearing on 15 July, the IWWU accepted a proposal originally advanced by the Rev. R. Burke Savage SJ, through the Printers' JIC. This proposal was accepted on the basis that, as outlined, it would not affect existing differentials, as the IGS claim for a percentage increase would be immediately matched by an IWWU claim for an overall increase in women's rates of £1. When the Labour Court issued its recommendation in August the

IWWU accepted, with reluctance, a final settlement of 15s. The IGS was informed that 'the claim of the IGS for a status increase of 33⅓% was not soundly based'.[11] Miss McDowell thanked the Printers' Committee, 'which did everything in its power to help and sustain me during our long struggle'. The lock-out had cost the IWWU £15,000. It was declared a 'disaster' and the final settlement 'did not go near compensating for the hardship endured'.[12] This hardship, and Miss McDowell's reference to the quality of support forthcoming both from the Printers' Committee and from the bulk of the membership, highlighted tensions which had been underlying the dispute since its inception.

Morale at the IWWU was markedly low, and by December the legacy of these unresolved tensions within the Printers' Section and between individuals provoked a further crisis. A movement gained momentum among IWWU members at Cahill's to apply for membership of the IGS. The group involved included Bridie McCormack, President of the IWWU. At the meeting of the Executive on 9 December, Miss McDowell reported that an application had been received from the IGS asking them to agree to the transfer of forty members from Cahill's. Challenged, Miss McCormack announced that she had intended to resign from the IWWU and that she and other members had been accepted into membership of the IGS. Her claim was, however, somewhat premature; Miss McDowell had contacted the IGS and the application would be rejected. Miss McCormack's position as a member of the Executive and as President, however, made her failure to notify the Executive of the impending move by IWWU members an admission of rank disloyalty. Her position was declared untenable, and the following resolution was passed, with one abstention:

> The Executive feels that Miss McCormack, in her capacity as President of this union, was neglectful of her duty in not informing the union of such a movement. The Committee therefore requests that Miss McCormack vacate her position as President and that any future nomination of her for any position as officer of the union or membership of any committee be not accepted.[13]

Bridie McCormack had served as shop steward, as chairman of the Printers' Committee, as representative of the Union on the Women's Advisory Committee, as delegate to Congress and as President of the Union. At a time when the Union was under threat from all quarters — loss of members, larger unions, and redundant industries — the decision of the IWWU Executive was final.

The incident crowned a year described as 'singularly depressing'. Any improvement in the lot of members had occurred 'mostly in firms not members of the FUE'.[14] The trade union movement was itself the focus of fundamental criticism by Mr Lemass. In March, Miss McDowell had attended a meeting in the Mansion House on industrial relations. Mr Lemass had spoken of 'too many unions and they are not strong enough'. He stated unequivocally that legislation would be brought in to correct this situation, and added that, in the interests of Irish industry, workers made redundant would become entitled to statutory redundancy payments. Both collectively and individually, however, such workers were given scant praise. The trade union movement, he claimed, had done little to cooperate under the terms of adaptation grants given to companies to facilitate re-equipment and increased competitiveness in the light of the proposed entry into the Common Market, and workers had failed to deliver in terms of greater productivity.[15]

The Economic Plan, the cornerstone of government policy for the modernisation of Ireland, was now perceived to be under threat. Such a political climate was, in the opinion of the IWWU General Secretary, actively hostile to working people.

> The position of our country today seems to me to be extremely one-sided. Every facility is being granted to the employing side by way of adaptation grants . . . while we on our side are subjected to threats of legislation against our freedom of action if we dare to try to keep some part of what we have fought for in the past.[16]

Miss McDowell's increasingly detailed and overtly political reports challenged both the government disposition in favour of the employers and the support given by the trade union movement to the principle of National Wage Agreements [NWA]. The latter criticism was based upon the realities of low pay among women workers, and suggested that such agreements were intrinsically flawed. 'The calculation of increases upon a percentage basis makes sure that the lower paid worker remains the lower paid worker'.[17] She spoke forcefully on behalf of her members. In relation to male labour, all women were lowly paid: the structure of the NWA ensured that, in the absence of corrective machinery to erode differentials, these would not only remain but would actually widen. Her Annual Report ended on a depressing note. With the prospect of further strikes in Sugar Confectionery and in the Laundry Section, Miss McDowell spoke of the unenviable position of her increasingly beleaguered staff. In the face of the challenge of a rapidly changing industrial scene, good intentions and solid commitment were not enough — the IWWU was a union under siege. As Kay McDowell said:

'All of us are at our wits' end to know how to cope'.

The fears of a disruptive Sugar Confectionery Strike were to prove groundless. The strike was enormously successful, and the General Secretary congratulated her members on 'the wonderful fight put up to get 15s. for women'. The members at Urney's reciprocated: they 'thanked Miss McDowell for her great fight for sugar confectionery workers and said that only for her they would not have done so well'.[18] After the gloom of the previous year the buoyancy of the membership was contagious. At Executive level Mai Clifford called for a vote of confidence in the General Secretary: it was passed by a large majority.

The IWWU, however, continued to face all the problems of a small organisation seeking to maintain levels of benefit and service to its members in the face of increasing competition, covert and otherwise, from larger unions that offered similar benefits for lower contributions. The problem had been evident in the course of the sugar confectionery strike. Strike pay from the IWWU was 35s. a week, while that from the ITGWU to its members, for example, was £3. 7s. 6d. a week. In 1966 at Urney's Chocolates, Tallaght, the considerable negotiating powers of Jenny Murray were called into action to ensure that the 100 members of the IWWU remained loyal. Each member was entitled, after contributing for fifty-two weeks, to strike pay from the Union. The ATGWU, also representing workers at Urney's, offered members £2 a week, after contributions had been made for only one week! The IWWU served a membership in sugar confectionery that was composed predominantly of young girls, many of whom were recent recruits to the Union and hence ineligible for strike pay. A contingency fund was immediately authorised to ensure that some monies would be forthcoming for such members in what was recognised as a competing market. A revision of the Rules to ensure that such eventualities would continue to be met was proposed for Convention.[19]

As General Secretary Kay McDowell approached her members in a significantly different vein from most leaders, and certainly in a more participatory spirit than did her original mentor, Louie Bennett. While acknowledging the need for a preparedness to lead, she was reluctant to assume the role of benevolent dictator with a passive audience. A rationalist and an extremely politically active woman,[20] she sought to present as clear a perspective of their context as was practicable to working women. Complexities in a changing workforce had to be acknowledged, but the choice of direction ultimately remained that of the members. The changes in industry, in management methods and in the extent to which government was clearly prepared to intervene to control the institutions of working people, made, she suggested, some rationalisation of the trade union movement appropriate. But if mergers were to be placed on any agenda, Kay McDowell argued that the IWWU should present itself at the negotiating table as a strong and effective force with its own identity. The obvious benefits available to members of larger unions could not be ignored, but neither could the major strength of the IWWU. The confectionery strike, she argued, would not have been won if there had been no women's union. The practice of male negotiators was to seek for women, despite their obvious skills, a settlement based on a rate 50% that of the claim for male workers. Miss McDowell claimed that through its persistence at the negotiating table the IWWU had raised that figure to 75%. In retaining their autonomy, women workers in the IWWU had the inestimable advantage of having 'their own negotiators — women — who have an undivided mind and will fight for the highest possible settlement for women'.[21]

The need also to maintain a sound financial base for the Union, and to enable it to compete more effectively in terms of benefits for members, was accepted by delegates to Annual Convention. A resolution was carried increasing all contributions from January 1967. By mid-April 1967, strike pay had been increased, as had sick pay and marriage benefit, and an additional incentive to remain loyal to the Union was devised in the form of a retirement bonus.

Both the increase in the contributions and the revised benefit scheme were an attempt to stem a flow of members from the Union that threatened to become critical. Between 1966 and 1967, over 1,000 members were recorded as having left the IWWU. The records of the Union, however, give no account of a mass exodus. From the laundries, a steady trickle,[22] indicating some 'natural wastage' served as a prelude to the widespread closure of laundries evident in the early 1970s. Over 100 members became unemployed.[23] Many women continued to leave their employment on marriage, a tradition at times encouraged, and at times lamented, by employers anxious to maintain a seasonal reserve. For some members of the IWWU also, the increased contributions were simply unacceptable: at Annual Convention members from the Bloomfield Laundry argued that 2*s.* a week was beyond the capacity of many women to pay. Such dissent, however, was not sufficiently widespread to explain losses. While transfers, particularly to the ITGWU, were evident from all sections, laundries, general workers, printers and nurses, the figures, if considered alone, are misleading. Between 1967 and 1968 the Union increased its membership by 750, leaving the real loss between 1966 and 1968 at approximately 400.

The numbers evidenced in the returns to the Registrar of Friendly Societies were — in the best trade union traditions — quite out of accord with those submitted to Congress for the purpose of calculating the allocation of delegates, and with those offered to members in the interests of maintaining Union morale. For many years, however, Kay McDowell had threatened to take action against members in arrears, a problem that existed throughout the labour movement. Such members were of no value to a Union both hard-pressed and committed to a reasonable level of benefits, and it is reasonable to assume that the figure recorded for 1966-67 reflected a tactical move by the Executive to raise contributions and benefits in tandem with a shedding of members in arrears.

When figures again rose in 1968 such growth reflected no major recruitment within the Union, but, as the losses could arguably have been accounted for by the lapsing of members in arrears the gains could, with equal validity, reflect defaulting members returning to the fold. In common with all other trade unions the IWWU viewed the state of the nation as 'precarious'. Trade unions in particular were under pressure. At no level, however, did IWWU records reflect the devastation that would have been evident in any institution if 25% of its members had simply left. The difficulty of interpreting such statistics is such that caution would warn against too great a reliance on the figures.

While such manoeuvres at Fleet Street were under way, a celebration pertaining to the Union history was deemed to be in order. The IWWU, since its first registration in 1917, had been conducting business on behalf of women workers for half a century, and the occasion was to be marked in a way the Executive considered appropriate. Initial discussions among the Executive gave rise to suggestions of dinners for union leaders and employers, and social gatherings of various kinds.[24] The outcome of such deliberations, however, indicated a reluctance on the part of an over-taxed Executive to proceed with the organisation of such proceedings — the prospect, as June Winders later recalled, 'seemed monstrous'.

At a special Executive meeting shortly before Christmas 1966, the decision was in effect taken. 'After much discussion and various suggestions it was finally decided that the most suitable and most Christian way was to donate a sum of money to the old aged living in their own homes'.[25] The donation, a cheque for £1,000, was presented with due ceremony by Maura Breslin to the 'Old People's Committee'. The

Executive's disposition to make this their 'final' decision on the matter was greeted, however, with measured dissent among the membership. Though reassurance was given that aging members of the IWWU would be eligible to apply to the 'Old People's Committee', the failure to consult more widely about other possible options was considered by many to be regrettable, and obviously resented by some members of the Union who felt that a celebration might have been more in order. The spirit of 1913, of 1916 and of 1945 had not been invoked to celebrate half a century of organised women workers. At a time when the entire Union could arguably have benefited from a social where women workers would, as in 1912, have been 'at home to their friends', a moment had been allowed to pass.

The reluctance of officials to consider more ambitious celebrations was a response to the continual pressure now felt by them in their negotiations on behalf of members. Consequent on the decline in the membership, the number of officials of the IWWU had been reduced and, for the first time in fifty years, staff closed the office on Saturdays. A 5-day week was begun. Hours, however, remained true to the tradition of trade unionism: officials were on duty between 10 a.m. and 8 p.m. on Monday, Wednesday and Thursday, and between 10 a.m. and 5.30 p.m. on Tuesday and Friday. The standard working week, in addition to evening meetings, found officials fully extended in disputes on complex agreements and defence of their territory in a wide range of industries. In the laundries, claims to improve service rates led to a lifting of the overtime ban; at the Post Office Factory the hours of unestablished workers were reduced from $42\frac{1}{2}$ to $41\frac{1}{4}$, and in 1967 the Union utilised the full machinery of the Labour Court against no less an employer than the ICTU, whose female clerical staff were IWWU members. Strike notice had been served on Congress on behalf of these members, who were being paid less than the scheduled rate. By August, all other avenues of negotiation having failed, the case was submitted to arbitration and the decision of the Labour Court came down in favour of the IWWU.

Over the years the machinery of such negotiation had

become increasingly complex. Officials of all unions had to be conversant with their trade, with a range of the new methods now employed in industry, with the procedures involved in arbitration and the complexity of Labour Court hearings. Towards the end of the sixties one such major negotiation was under way in the printing industry, focusing on the contentious area of interchangeability between women in printing and those in carton making.

The concept of interchangeability in all areas of industry had considerable appeal for employers eager to erode demarcation lines and to avail of the skills of an experienced but 'flexible' workforce. Although the IWWU had faced major problems in protecting women from the erosion of their own demarcation lines through the effects of automation, the difficulties this presented were acknowledged by the employment of one IWWU official who was almost fully employed in demarcation disputes. The move to extend the use of a flexible labour force, from the early 1960s onwards, had been directed primarily at women in the printing and kindred trades. In the early part of the decade the increased use of new machines in this industry had resulted in less work for feeders. In 1962 the Irish Printing Federation had proposed a degree of interchangeability between letterpress and litho girls, and the bindery and make-up departments, a proposal accepted by the Printers' Committee on the understanding that feeders would be given only table work and not specialised machine work.[26] Since then conditions, particularly in the kindred trades of carton making and boxmaking, had changed considerably. The use of new machinery, and increased imports, made the undoubted vulnerability to threatened redundancies of grave concern to the IWWU.

In 1965 a rationalisation programme for three companies was announced. The merger proposals, agreed between the companies since early 1964, involved Bailey Gibson Ltd, Guy and Co. Ltd, and Cherry and Smalldridge Ltd. The merger resulted in the formation of a holding company, Gibson, Guy and Smalldridge.[27] As part of the envisaged programme for the new company, Cherry and Smalldridge closed its boxmaking department, employing over forty members of the IWWU, at the end of 1965. Although the holding company had received a £70,000 adaptation grant from the government, women who had been boxmakers there for between fifteen and twenty-five years were now offered only between four and eight weeks' redundancy pay. The situation and the assessment of redundancy was considered by the Union in the light of the overall prospects in the trade, and the probability that these women would have difficulty in being placed in other houses. Following discussions, the ICTU advised Kay McDowell to take her members' case to the Labour Court.[28]

Relations between the IWWU and Cherry and Smalldridge had been strained for some time. When, in July 1965, the boxmaking department had been closed as a result of the lock-out associated with the IGS status claim, Cherry and Smalldridge had blamed the IWWU for loss of business and, by implication, for the eventual closure of the department. The losses attributed to the ten-week lock-out led to a request from the employer that boxmakers' claims be kept separate from those of printers to avoid future disputes.

The IWWU had members in seventeen firms of boxmakers. In 1963 the Boxmakers' Registered Agreement had settled rates of pay and conditions for 'female workers engaged in the production of cardboard boxes and containers in the city and county of Dublin'. Although covered by their own Registered Agreement, the women remained vulnerable to slackness and to the gradual redundancy of their trade. In October 1966 the Printers' Committee acknowledged the difficulties facing boxmakers, carton makers and bagmakers, all 'kindred trades', and Miss McDowell was asked to open negotiations, under specific terms, with the IPF on the question of interchangeability in printing and kindred trades. The Printers' Committee was prepared to sanction such moves if it were agreed that 'all members be protected in cases of redundancy in respective sections'.[29] By January, however, the dispute at Cherry and Smalldridge had been settled, and, reporting to the Printers' Committee on this, Miss McDowell added that 'she was letting the matter regarding interchangeability rest just at present'. The Committee 'fully agreed'.[30] By this stage, however, the IPF were clearly interested in flexibility between the sections, and in

1966 they claimed that they intended ending the demarcation line between women in printing and women in carton making on the basis that 'our members feel that it is quite illogical to dismiss experienced carton girls . . . when they have vacancies for printing girls'.[31]

The move had considerable implications for all journeywomen in this industry, where one-third of the workforce was female. Women in printing and women in boxmaking each completed four years' training. Between 1951 and 1961, however, women in the area of paper and paper products, including journeywomen in boxmaking and bag making, had lost considerable ground. They formed 51% of the workforce in this area in 1951, but ten years later the percentage had declined to 38%, and all the indications were that women rather than men would continue to lose ground.[32] In printing and publishing over the same period women maintained their position as 33% of the workforce, and if decline was evident it was neither rapid nor dramatic.[33]

In 1968 the IPF made an offer to the IWWU which would fundamentally change the position of women in printing and kindred trades in IPF houses. The objective of the proposal was to 'raise the productive capacity of men [*sic*] and equipment by encouraging the extensive use of method study'. The change in the work process, however, was to be complemented by a change in the form of labour.

> To utilise the full skills of all workers by encouraging interchange within and between sections and (subject to retraining) between crafts. . . . This will not be implemented to the detriment of the labour force.[34]

At the Printers' Committee on 21 June, members 'after careful consideration' agreed to recommend the proposals, and a General Meeting of Printers, Carton Makers and Box Makers, in firms affiliated to the IPF, was called at Liberty Hall on 26 June to vote on a package linking 'flexibility' to wages and conditions of labour.

The initial agreement covered printers and carton makers, but extended eventually to cover women in all the kindred trades. By February 1969 negotiations were complete and the agreement 'confirms that the existing carton journeywomen will receive printers' rates of pay'. Under the terms of the Registered Agreement women were guaranteed 'an all round training' in 'all processes in the house', as opposed to earlier agreements covering 'all processes in the Department'. What was not added, however, was that no flexibility was to be introduced in another key area: despite the fact that the Registered Agreement covered the entire industry, the traditional demarcation lines between men and women, and between men in their varied trades, were to be left untouched.[35]

The flexibility clause, seen as an integral part of the Printers' Registered Agreement, marked the end of the last major negotiation conducted under the leadership of Kay McDowell. In accepting the clause quoted she ensured that her members in boxmaking, journeywomen of a trade in decline, had moved to a position of relative job security with full recognition of their value as experienced workers, where higher rates of remuneration prevailed. For carton makers the move was seen as a triumph. The IPF was, however, fully aware that it was potentially contentious. Shortly after finalising the agreement, the IPF wrote to employers about the proposed change, suggesting that their intent was to change demarcation patterns, long-term, throughout the industry.

> Members implementing this Agreement are earnestly requested to bear in mind that these changes (in view of ingrained practices) are somewhat revolutionary. It will be appreciated that traditional practices cannot be abolished by the stroke of a pen and members are requested to use all possible tact in the early days of implementing this Agreement.[36]

However interpreted, the limited application of this Agreement — to cover only areas where women were employed — changed the nature of two areas of women's labour. Women in carton-making and in printing, while continuing to serve a four-year apprenticeship, became, in effect, general workers in this industry. If such change in status was viewed as a loss, the confidence of the Printing Section in their negotiator was undiminished. They asked Miss McDowell, prior to her retirement, to continue for as long as she felt able to negotiate future settlements on their behalf.

Prior to Convention in 1968 Kay McDowell recommended that the Executive, with the endorsement of the membership, should appoint an Assistant General Secretary to ensure continuity of personnel, pending her own retirement, and in May, Maura Breslin accepted the position on the basis that it would be permanent. A working woman totally dependent on her own earnings, she was reluctant to relinquish a lifetime commitment to her profession under any other terms. These conditions were agreed, and Nurse Breslin resigned from St Brendan's Hospital shortly before her appointment as Assistant General Secretary to the IWWU in January 1969.

At the end of her period of office Miss McDowell left a legacy of potential for growth, but an acknowledgment that a small union, however efficient, was by definition subject to external pressures. The finances of the Union were, however, sound — income exceeded expenditure by £2,139 — and the mood was militant. At Annual Convention, the President, Mrs O'Brien, assessed the government's call for wage restraint. 'He meant the lower paid workers — there could be only one answer to that — no! The Ministers themselves are taking home £110 a week'.[37] Such militancy would be necessary to defend gains, by working women, which were consistently threatened by employers eager to return to conditions of labour which had earlier prompted historic resistance from the working class.

In her Annual Report Kay McDowell referred to nineteen young factory workers who had, with considerable trepidation, offered in 1968 to join the IWWU. The manager, on hearing of their folly, had given notice to all nineteen. In response, the Executive instructed the Union solicitor to sue on behalf of the girls on the basis of wrongful dismissal — an ambitious tactic, given the absence of any legislation providing such protection. The case was, however, won on the basis of the girls' constitutional right to free association. Such employer tactics, Miss McDowell argued, had to be resisted at all levels in the future, as they had been in the past.

> If the Trade Union Movement allows such a practice to grow up, the standard of living will gradually deteriorate

and we will be back in 1913 when women and girls were working for peanuts.[38]

The militancy now advocated for the IWWU reflected a period of expansion of trade union membership throughout the Republic, with a growth of 25% recorded between 1960 and 1970.[39] Towards the close of the decade the increased participation of women in the workforce and in trade unions was reflected in the request from the 1969 Congress to the government to 'set up a permanent consultative body to consider the problems of women at work'.[40]

The final months of Miss McDowell's period of office echoed with the cries of hard times all round, yet in the tenth wage round, women achieved a significant victory in negotiations when a higher percentage increase was granted for women than for men. While this was welcome, the smaller wage base from which women operated meant that the financial gains for women were, in fact, less than those for men. While employers across the negotiating tables resisted such developments by advancing pleas of straitened circumstances, Kay McDowell suggested that their reticence in matters financial was not universal, and that when 'the same gentlemen meet their shareholders at the AGM — profits are up, dividends are up and bonus shares thrown in for good measure'.[41]

While employers had continued to lament the shortage of women workers, they had refused to consider rates of pay commensurate with a working woman's needs. In September, the General Secretary wrote to the newspapers to challenge employers to justify their own rhetoric, so often employed to facilitate the erosion of women's hard-won gains.

> There is a lovely phrase (coined by I don't know whom) used in industry employing a large proportion of female labour, and it is 'natural wastage'. From experience I have found that this mainly covers girls leaving on marriage, so that the phrase used raises a rather debatable point.[42]

Throughout the year Kay McDowell had been listening to

two equally loud, but dissonant, choruses. One of them sang about 'natural wastage' and the absence of any employer responsibility in cases where redundancy notices were served on married women workers. The other, however, bewailed labour shortages when these and other women no longer brought their labour to the market place. The Union had been approached in the 1960s by a number of employers, including Gallaher's and Maguire and Paterson's, on 'the question of continuing to employ your members after marriage'.[43] Such a proposal was not unrelated to the increasing use of short-time shifts. By December 1969, for example, final negotiations had been completed with Maguire and Paterson on the introduction of two shifts: 9.45 a.m.–2.15 p.m., and 11.30 a.m.–4.30 p.m. The Executive minutes record 'a majority in favour of these hours'.

Although the marital status of the women who worked such shifts is not recorded, the recruitment policy of another company, Chez Nous Chocolates, was. In a circular to all women on their personnel records, Chez Nous offered a range of options to facilitate the employment of women with domestic constraints.

> On a full-time basis, or on a part-time basis, for those who are married with young children or with other domestic responsibility, we would be very pleased to interview you to discuss the possibilities of fitting you into one of our vacancies.[44]

For a Union previously dominated by women workers who retreated from the workforce upon marriage, the growth in participation of married women workers would later challenge the Union to develop a policy more attuned to their needs.

The predictable intricacies of such negotiations would no longer, however, engage the talents of Kay McDowell. Her retirement from active service in the labour movement in 1969 prompted a measure of speculation on the future terrain upon which negotiations would inevitably take place.

> Machines are taking over more and more gradually elim-

inating the human element. Just what can't a computer do, except move itself from place to place. Still, this machine is merely in its infancy. Terrifying to think what it will do in another 20 years.[45]

CHAPTER 18

Labouring women

Miss McDowell's perception of a computerised future reflected her close association with the printing section of the IWWU. The Thomson proposal in 1962 had served as a prelude to further employer endeavours to avail of the benefits of new technologies on terms most favourable to themselves and in 1970 Folens sought special cooperation from the IWWU in regard to the unionisation of its workforce. They intended henceforth to adopt two methods of production in publishing: one would employ male compositors on hot metal, who would be paid craftsmen's rates; the other would use 'girl typists on golfball machines', who would be paid 'women's rates'.

By 1971 the use of these different levels of technology, in tandem, demonstrated a clear pathway to a parity of sorts for skilled women workers. Folens offered to pay women working on electric typewriters the same rates as men on hot metal, where such women 'could set in four languages'. With a disarming, if disquieting, lack of guile, Folens conceded that 'male lack of languages', and women's acknowledged superiority in this area, presented them with two options. To seek highly qualified men, adept in such languages, and pay them 30% more than the rate currently enjoyed by other male craftsmen, was one alternative. The other involved securing the services of highly qualified women, adept at typing and multi-lingual to boot, and to offer such women 'parity' with male compositors. A trend had undoubtedly begun.

While such industries moved headlong into a different era, others languished in the nineteenth century. In February 1970 Maura Breslin, Assistant General Secretary, reported to the Executive that she was having difficulty in organising the workers at Orrwear, in Kells, Co. Meath.[1] The case of these workers had prompted Miss Breslin to write to the Minister for Labour proposing the introduction of specific protective legislation to provide minimum standards of hours and conditions for unorganised labour.[2] The move to organise clothing workers at Kells had been initiated after a request to the Union from the parents of young girls employed at Orrwear. The firm, which received considerable financial assistance from the State through adaptation grants, was accused by its workers and their families of treating girls 'in the most tyrannical manner'. Girls claimed that they had been 'threatened to be slapped' for speaking while working.[3] Excessive overtime at rates well below the standard was the norm, and the factory, by order of the management, 'is "policed" by men standing beside the girls to see that they do not speak to each other. That these men accompany each girl to the door of the toilet and time her while she is inside'.[4] The company employed the girls 'on the line.' For forty hours a week the girls thus employed were required to insert zips in forty dozen pairs of jeans every eight-hour day.

Following a campaign by the IWWU, twenty-two of the workforce of thirty-eight girls joined the Union. The management, however, refused recognition and the shop steward nominated to voice the girls' grievances was dismissed for 'interfering with management'.[5] Eight others were dismissed for supporting the shop steward, and an official picket was mounted on the premises the following day. After 'long and difficult' negotiations, and the direct intervention of James Tully, Labour TD for Meath, all were reinstated under a 'no victimisation' provision. Although resolved, this incident served notice on the Women's Union that while concessions to equality provision were welcomed, the march of women workers would be measured in relation to the lives of its most exploited members.

An awareness of such conditions among unorganised workers, together with a wary eye to falling Union contributions, prompted an Executive decision to authorise an organisation drive for membership. The financial position of the Union was, they suggested, 'something to be concerned about but not alarmed about'.[6] The move to organise further afield coincided also with the election of a new General Secretary. Five nominations were received. Three withdrew and one was deemed 'not acceptable', and, at Annual Convention in May, Maura Breslin was elected sixth General Secretary of the IWWU.

Eighty-five delegates from Dublin, Drogheda and Waterford attended the Annual Convention at Fleet Street. A number of voices drew attention to the effects of automation and to 'whole time work study' in every factory, mill, printing house and hospital. The concern of most delegates, however, focused on the twelfth round wage negotiations then under way. Since the seventh round in 1959 the allocation of 'half for the women' had been challenged and defeated. The eighth round had introduced shorter working hours and a move towards the five-day week in all industries. The eleventh round in 1967/68 had been notable for a significant improvement for women: overall, an increase of 75% of the men's claim had been awarded. The twelfth round was now in progress and negotiators had 'achieved awards in some cases of £4 per week for men and women', paid over eighteen months. This equality of increase in financial terms marked a departure — a precedent in a context where women continued to be awarded 75% or 80% of the male award and 'a great step forward in the campaign for equal pay'.[7]

The boost to the campaign for equal pay reflected the continued shortage of women workers, a changing work context, and the increasing activism of women trade unionists. In direct negotiations with Greenmount and Boyne in the course of the twelfth round claim, Maura Breslin advanced the case for her members, articulating the confidence of a workforce which perceived itself as much in demand.

> They are not satisfied with the difference in their wages to those of their male fellow-workers and they are greatly dissatisfied at the wide gap between their wages and the wages and salaries taken home by management at every level.[8]

Taking advantage where it presented itself, Maura Breslin assured management that the current shortage of women workers indicated the existence of a range of opportunities for women which had not been evident hitherto, and hence greatly increased the value of the woman worker's labour.

> As a union we would have no trouble whatever in finding better paid employment in more up to date conditions for as many women as we have working here.[9]

Throughout that industry, however, the conditions of labour left much to be desired. Weavers complained that their wages, based on piece-work rather than on time, had dropped significantly due to the incidence of bad yarn, inadequate supply of weft, and an increased number of looms to attend. This increase had been considerable — from ten to fourteen — with no new rate being set, and a weaver on the Jacquard looms complained that she was losing wages 'because she herself had to fill the shuttles'. When the women weavers voiced their discontent at the absence of parity between themselves and their male colleagues, the Manager, Mr Hall, conceded 'that the term weaver could be a man or a woman. Shouldn't be a major difference in rates'.[10]

The early moves for equal pay in textiles were a measure both of the dominance of women in this industry and of the masssive upheaval in a sector which had resulted in the modernisation of some plants and the closure of redundant mills. Such factors contributed to a challenge to traditional demarcation lines, some of which simply disappeared with the advent of changed processes and new machinery, and formed the context in which the battle for new territory and equal pay for women would reach the top of the IWWU agenda.

Conditions of labour for all workers, although differing across industry in terms of detail, remained uniformly poor. At Gilbey's bottling plant, women expressed their dissatisfaction at working on the line, and at 'uncivil' supervisors pressuring workers to increase productivity on a line 'which is now speeded up from sixty dozen to 110 dozen an hour'. Working in close cooperation with the WUI, Maura Breslin reported that women operatives found the line 'too fast and the bottles too heavy'. Mr Tyrell, the supervisor, was accused of applying unnecessary pressure by 'clapping his hands to come back after meals and breaks'.[11]

Employees of the state fared little better than did those in the private sector. Although unestablished female workers in government service had secured pension rights by 1970, the thirty-six IWWU members at the Post Office Factory continued to complain of 'lack of heating, severe cold from draughts,' and work done in overcrowded conditions with 'a complete lack of ventilation in the entire shop'.[12] The renewed zeal in the area of working conditions reflected an unexpected development in an old relationship. Kay McDowell had been nominated to the Factories' Advisory Council, and until her death in 1975 continued indirectly to serve both the Union and the wider cause of working women.

By 1970, an estimated 40% of such women were in trade unions: a figure calculated by Mary Daly[13] as representing 100,000 women. This growth begun in the 1930s, had suffered in the overall decline heralded by the depression of the 1950s, and had been revived in the 1960s. The increased proportion of women in the workforce, and their membership in a range of trade unions, inevitably impinged upon the agendas of the movement overall. Individual women, notably all previous General Secretaries of the IWWU, had achieved positions of power within trade union structures. Louie Bennett, Helena Molony and Helen Chenevix had served as Presidents of the Congress, and Kay McDowell had served on the Administrative Council of the Labour Party. Collectively, however, the exercise of women's power in the movement had no formal avenue or structure until the establishment of the Women's Advisory Committee in 1959. Initially, this body received only nominal support from the IWWU and from other women trade unionists. Its role was advisory, and the sporadic attendance by IWWU members, such as Lizzie Caffrey, reflected their own assessment of its potential impact.

In October 1970, however, Maura Breslin signalled a change in the Union attitude. Writing to Ruaidhrí Roberts, General Secretary of the ICTU, she suggested that while attendance by IWWU members had been infrequent, this was in part a reflection on the Committee itself, and 'when we previously nominated a member to that Committee, she was never summoned to attend any of its meetings'.[14] Mai Clifford and Mary Byrne, a printer from De La Rue and chair of the Printers' Committee, who were elected to act on the Committee on behalf of the Republic's trade unionists, now became vigilant in their attendance and, in time, formidable critics of any tendency towards elitism which would effectively exclude ordinary women workers. In 1971 they registered their view that 'the actual workers were not wanted on this Committee and that it was more for professional workers'. The Committee acknowledged such criticism, but refuted any suggestion that women of any category were being excluded.

While professional women were increasingly active in the movement, Mrs Clifford represented other women who had received their formal education in the workplace, who had graced picket lines when women's trade unionism was in its infancy, and who, by 1970, had begun to reassert their claims in the decision-making processes of the labour movement. Such claims, however, were inevitably constrained by the context in which women workers now found themselves.

While some progress in the direction of equal pay was evident, the effects of competition from Northern Ireland and the UK and the prospect of Irish entry into the European Economic Community [EEC], made gains uneasily dependent upon the survival of specific industries. By 1971 Greenmount and Boyne justified the persistent loss of earnings for pieceworkers by reference to a lack of orders and the subsequent reduction in output from machinery. The firm was losing money, and 'there will definitely be redundancies'. A quarter of the staff in the weaving shed were under threat, with management conceding, almost without a battle, that 'they could not beat the Six Counties for weaving'.[15] The threat was echoed in other sectors. When the laundry industry had agreed to a 40-hour week, despite the reluctance of the employers, the Union accepted a productivity deal aimed at reducing the possibility of closures by improving efficiency in the industry. Breaks not required by the terms of the Conditions of Employment Act were abandoned, and agreement was reached that all steps would be taken 'to make full use of the hours available to ensure full utilisation of plant'. A further agreement conceded management's right, in the face of labour shortages, to employ part-time workers where necessary.[16]

The maximum wage for women in this industry remained low — £8. 13s. a week — while women in other employment earned up to £12 per week, and the lack of pensions and sickness benefit and the advanced age of many laundresses led to cases of severe hardship. In 1971 Maggie O'Connor of Terenure Laundry retired because of ill-health. The Executive were informed that when her doctor had advised Miss O'Connor not to work again, 'her landlady would not let her remain at home all day'. As a result, and owing to the good grace of Mr Simpson of Terenure Laundry, Maggie O'Connor presented at the laundry 'for a few hours each day'. Although too ill to work, she was required to absent herself daily from her home in order to satisfy the demands of the owner of property.

To ensure a less arduous old age for its younger members, the Union confronted the employers with the implications of their low level of remuneration for work that was not only difficult but a direct threat to workers' health. Submitting a claim for service pay and sick pay, the Union argued that there was a direct relationship between the need for such provision and the incidence of work-induced illnesses.[17] The complaints by members in this regard were graphic in their detail. From the Adelaide Hospital Laundry members complained 'that the incontinent linen is kept over the weekend in the laundry, causing what they describe as a most inhuman odour and atmosphere'. Writing to the House Governor, Maura Breslin embellished the point.

> We were horrified to learn that it is under these circumstances and in that atmosphere that laundresses are compelled to eat their lunch because no canteen facilities are provided.[18]

In response, the House Governor cited the impact on weekend staffing levels of the introduction of the 40-hour week, a battle that had been won despite considerable resistance by such employers.[19] At Sir Patrick Dun's Hospital, the Matron was accused of presiding over 'extremely unsanitary and unhealthy conditions' in her laundry.

A visit had left Union officials 'appalled at the filthy linen these women are expected to handle' and the erstwhile Nurse Breslin delivered a severe and informed reprimand. 'It should not be necessary for us to point out to a Hospital Authority the grave danger to health which this constitutes'.[20] In other laundries working women downed tools. At Court Laundry girls stopped work over the conditions of labour — a combination of excessive heat from the machinery at which they worked in overcrowded conditions, and the absence of ventilation. At White Heather Laundry members refused to pay union contributions unless some changes in conditions were forthcoming. Management argued that the uncertainty that the plant would remain on the existing site in the future made improvements impractical, but the threat by the women — should the union fail to deliver — added zeal to the negotiations. When they concluded, promises were extracted, and the Union emerged with its reputation among its members enhanced.

While arrears from members were settled, others at this laundry remained outside any trade union. When Mrs Davis, Laundry Official, and Mr McManus of the ITGWU, held a card check, many who were not in the union agreed to join the IWWU on condition that it challenged the more visible and clearly offensive manifestations of their working relationship with their employer — in effect, if the Union would 'see that they were paid their wages in pay packets, and not in a tin box'.[21]

By 1971 the Union was advocating, in its discussions with employers, the wisdom of improved working conditions as a means of presenting a more attractive prospect to women workers who were increasingly unwilling to embark on the acknowledged drudgery of the laundress's life. While calling for sick pay and pension schemes, the Union now confronted the precise terms on which employers sought the services of the married women workers they had earlier courted so assiduously. Miss Breslin confirmed that her members 'would not accept the preclusion of married women' from any pension or sickness benefit award. From the employers there came, in return, a litany of complaints: married women were 'more likely to abuse' a pension scheme; they had 'domestic problems that would keep them out of work'; and, in addition, 'their husbands would be in good employment'. In response Miss Breslin claimed that, contrary to such expectations, the experience of the Union was that 'married women were very conscientious on their work and were reluctant to stay out'. It was agreed, however, that no demand would be made for pregnancy to come under any provision for sick pay, and a beginning was made when the FUE agreed to consider the cases in regard to pensions for 'deserted women and unmarried mothers'. Quite clearly such negotiations would be both difficult and protracted. Already, employers had blamed the improved position of women workers in the aftermath of the eleventh round pay settlement for the closures of Phoenix, Harold's Cross and Dunlop laundries. In the face of the undoubted impact of washing machines and launderettes the employers now made their terms abundantly clear — no drudgery, no jobs.

In 1971 Clery & Co. closed their laundry without notice to either their employees or to the Union. In the same year, Court Laundry claimed that it was unable to continue to trade profitably. Swastika, however, was negotiating to take over their service, and women rather than men would be assured of permanent employment. This closure of Court gave rise to a conundrum for the Union which was never effectively resolved. Redundancy claims were effective only from the sixteenth birthday of employees onwards. Many members, however, had worked in the laundries since they were fourteen, and two years of their labour was now, by statute, outside the reckoning. While some women were offered places at White Heather, over seventy were made redundant by the final closure at Court. When offered placement on terms which resulted in a reduction of £5 in their monthly income, laundresses from Court were told by management that they were clearly not obliged to accept the terms if they were not satisfied. The general level of disquiet among workers, and within the Union, arose from the mechanism of closure. Court Laundry was, both in terms of its site and of its name, finished, yet as far as its clientèle and many of its experienced workers were concerned the 'company' had been absorbed by Swastika. On the other hand, no worker was to enjoy continuity of service or any other entitlements. Mrs Pat Davis, laundry official, argued that the owners of Court Laundry would benefit from considerable profits from the sale of their site, and that IWWU members had given their loyalty to the company long after it had ceased to be viable. If they had left the service of Court at an earlier date, Mr Robb of the Laundry 'would only have got a fraction of the price he is now getting for the premises. They could have been establishing themselves elsewhere, where now they are losing career and service pay'.[22] Her protests fell on indifferent ears, and the closure of Court was followed by that of Metropolitan, Bloomfield and White Heather. Although redundancy settlements and relocation varied, the steady loss of such membership did little to enhance the overall figures of the IWWU.

Such losses now served, in effect, to undermine a major aspect of the IWWU's claim for equal pay for women in industry. The widespread shortage of women's labour — commonplace in the mid-sixties and at the beginning of the seventies — had by 1972 become less acute as redundancies in some industries left a surplus of women available for work. Battles on the shopfloor would subsequently be less readily resolved — a prospect implicitly acknowledged by the Union in 1971 with the re-introduction of courses for shop stewards organised by Fleet Street.

The effect of redundancies and the increasing cost of services resulted in an excess of expenditure over income in 1971. Such financial pressure was not, however, confined to the IWWU: in 1971 the Executive had reported that 'all the small unions are finding the financial position very difficult'.[23] At that time, without making any definite commmitment, the Union had agreed to 'explore the possibilities with regard to further cooperation between the unions'. Such cooperation would need to be clearly defined. The continuing talks on one union for all workers in the printing industry, at which the IWWU held a watching brief, could, if it led to a decision that all the workers involved would withdraw from the general unions, make the survival of the IWWU itself highly problematic. While these talks were ongoing the Union agreed, in response to overtures from Denis Larkin, Secretary of the WUI, 'to discuss the situation' pertaining to members in all sections of the Union, and a formal delegation consisting of the President, General Secretary, Trustees, an official, and two members of the Executive prepared to meet for discussions with the WUI and the Printing Group of Unions.

While such talks were most decidedly of a preliminary nature, the position of the IWWU was unenviable. The difficulty it faced in claiming new areas for organisation was exacerbated by the form of organisation in the trade union movement that the IWWU had itself fostered. In May a member of the Executive asked why the Union had refused to accept 200 women from Arnott's who had sought membership. Miss Murray pointed to a fundamental difficulty: the ITGWU had an agreement in the hosiery trade for 100% membership. For its part, the IWWU would seek a similar accommodation in its favour at the new Hospitals Joint Services' Board [HJSB] Laundry which opened at the end of 1971, and where the ITGWU were 'doing their utmost' to recruit the women in addition to the men. In January 1972 a victory for the IWWU in this area was underlined by the comment, 'we had fought hard for this'.

Such developments, however, did not change the situation in any fundamental sense. By the 1970s the IWWU represented women workers employed in no real growth area, and their most secure members, the printers, were not indifferent to the negotiations for an all-print union. In the face of potential stagnation, the dogged pursuit of new members was a testament to the undoubted courage of the IWWU officials, and a measure also of the impact on such women of the changing social and political climate for women in Ireland.

By 1972 the IWWU membership stood at 3,410. In industrial terms it was constrained by the vulnerability of the industries where its members were employed, and by the limitations of what it could offer, both in terms of service and of 'clout', as a small union. In political and social terms, however, it used its position as a union of women workers to take advantage of a changing ideological climate. In a paper resplendent with biblical references, Maura Breslin delivered her considered views to the Commission on the Status of Women. She accused Irish society of 'placing strictures around the rightful status of women' in an endeavour to 'perpetuate the historical limbo in which women are relegated from birth'.

On behalf of the Irish Congress of Trade Unions' Women's Advisory Committee, Miss Breslin attended the Commission on 24 March 1972 to discuss recruitment, training, and the promotion of opportunities for women. In common with other speakers she argued for training for women 'in all the processes of their present jobs and further to establish apprenticeship training in all fields of industry'.[24] As a woman and as General Secretary of a women's union Miss Breslin's views were, on this important occasion, made abundantly clear.

> It must not be thought that women should try to abandon their femininity and assume an amazonian matriarchal role . . . they must demand and be prepared to work for equal opportunities of education and training.[25]

Unlike the Commission, the IWWU served a function beyond that of reporting on the status of women. In negotiations with government and private employers it had, for more than sixty years, demanded a change in the status of women who had ventured into the workplace. At precisely the same moment that the Commission was gathering its resources to present a report to government, however, the Employer Labour Conference Working Party was throwing down the gauntlet to working women of Ireland.

The employers in this forum referred to equal pay as 'being very much a leap in the dark', and expressed the profound hope that 'Congress will not ask for any change in this clause'. An equal increase for women, if suggested, would be rejected by employers on a number of counts:

'Women are doing very well, better than men;
Industry cannot afford it;
Male counterparts would not approve'.[26]

If Congress sought a change to accommodate equal pay in the first phase of the National Wage Agreement, the FUE would, it warned, seek further changes in the second phase to ensure compensation for the costs incurred. Two weeks later the IWWU gave the FUE and Congress notice of its own intentions. The fourteenth round National Wage Agreement would be rejected by the IWWU on the basis of its lack of provision for low-paid workers, which ensured that 60% of IWWU members would not benefit from the Agreement until mid-1973. The membership had expected an equal increase for women and men, and 'they are utterly disappointed that this was not secured'. In short, neither members nor the Executive of the IWWU were 'satisfied that negotiations had made any significant progress towards the objective of equal pay'.[27]

Following concessions by both sides, the NWA was accepted, but its usefulness as a mechanism for achieving parity was, under severe question by the IWWU. The capacity, on the part of both employers and Congress, for postponing equality claims, and the manifestly long-term recommendations of the Commission on the Status of Women, did not augur well for working women. The Union rejected the Commission's timetable out of hand and declared that in future it would look to legislation rather than to the agreements as a mechanism for change .

> We do not accept that we should wait until 1977 for the introduction of equal pay. If we go into the EEC our Government will be committed to implementing equal pay for work of equal value and it should not take five years to determine work of equal value.[28]

The question of establishing the concept of equal value was given a high priority, and at the Annual Convention delegates urged Congress to 'set up a study group to include ICTU work study officers to determine work of equal value'. Claims for equal pay were served on the Irish Printing Federation, Maguire and Paterson Ltd, and C.A. Parsons Ltd. Work studies began before the 1972 NWA was completed, and one work study, at Gallaher's, had already been finalised. In both 1973 and 1974 some advance was made, but the major difficulties remained in the area of establishing work of equal value. The ICTU work study department advised the Union, in the light of the considerable expenditure of time and resources involved, to serve equal pay claims in one sector of employment first, and to use this as a headline for other employments.

The experience of women in the printing industry between 1972 and 1975, however, demonstrated how very difficult it would prove in practice to set such precedents. In 1973 Mai Clifford, now President of the IWWU and, since 1971 an Executive member of the Dublin Council of Trade Unions [DCTU], addressed Annual Convention. On the question of equal pay, she drew the attention of delegates to the efforts made on their behalf by the IWWU representatives on the Equal Pay Committee of Congress. Such representation was, by definition, limited. Mrs Clifford advanced a claim that women had to assert themselves within all areas of industry.

> We ourselves as individuals must be prepared to accept all the opportunities open to us to perform a greater role in the industries in which we work and to adapt ourselves to greater flexibility and interchangeability . . . in order to establish that our work and our ability is equal to that of men.[29]

Women, undoubtedly, would now be required to protect their own areas. Yet the support by any trade union for an adaptable and accommodating workforce in the absence of statutory safeguards would, undoubtedly, leave women workers with little defence against exploitation by employers.

At the beginning of 1974 Bailey and Gibson served notice that the complaints by women workers about the increased use of part-time, untrained staff would be given short shrift.

> If they gave any real thought to the problems of running the business they would realise that we cannot do without part-time staff and as far as their being untrained is concerned the company must be the judge of whether what they do is satisfactory or unsatisfactory.[30]

This company had earlier reported considerable difficulty in recruiting female labour, a state of affairs that had conferred a sense of security on women in printing and kindred trades, and had left the question of potential recruits from outside the industry problematic. In tandem with this development, women at Bailey Gibson suggested to management that an area of work traditionally that of women was now considered by them to be 'too heavy'.

At a meeting in the Carton Department in regard to 'breaking out', the girls agreed that two men could be put on breaking out 'provided the girls who do the same work are paid at the same rate as men'.[31] The company pointed out that men were already engaged on this work at night, and that pursuit of an equal pay claim at this time would serve 'only to confuse'. Precisely who would be confused was not clear.

> As far as your members are concerned there is a national commitment to equal pay. To crucify individual companies at this juncture without being able to supply simultaneously adequate labour, for certain types of work . . . can only harm the long term employment opportunities for women in this industry.[32]

What had previously been of advantage to women — the shortage of their labour and hence the drive to make recruitment a more attractive proposition — had become, in the era of equal pay, a veiled threat to the traditional demarcation lines between men and women workers.

The assumption by women in this company that work could be discarded when options were plentiful, and reclaimed when they were not, demonstrated a somewhat underdeveloped trade union consciousness among working women. The logic of the management position at Bailey Gibson was compelling — men already worked in 'breaking out' at night and the shortage of women's labour resulted in serious logistical problems in maintaining supply. Bailey Gibson now proposed that male staff from the ITGWU work alongside women during the day, and that these men would handle 'the heavier elements of breaking out using power tools most of the time and allowing the female staff to concentrate on lighter breaking out and table work'.[33] Management assured the Union that such a procedure, involving the splitting of an operation, had already been established by precedent in the city and beyond, and had the virtue of 'neither precipitating equal pay nor obstructing the ultimate aspiration.' That aspiration was now pursued by the IWWU. In reporting to the Printers' Comittee Miss Breslin advised that a claim had been served for equal pay in Bailey Gibson, and each member was asked to 'pinpoint any case of which she is aware where women and men do the same work'. Should the Committee accept the proposal to move men into the area of breaking out, in the short term women's work would undoubtedly be under threat. In the long term, however, men and women working alongside each other would be an extremely useful context within which to establish work of equal value.[34] The Committee agreed, and the proposal was accepted. From the shop floor, however, such tactics were considered misplaced.

In September, contrary to the advice of officials of the Union, the women at Bailey Gibson 'refused point blank to work alongside men doing breaking out'. As a result, the equal pay claim 'fell through in this case'.[35] What had become clear to members was that claims for equal pay that countenanced the incursion by men into areas of women's work threatened, long-term, to undermine their claim to such work.

In the absence of such accommodation from women in regard to the use of male labour, the managements of Bailey Gibson, of Smurfits, of Associated Printers and others considered another option. Since 1973 all three companies had employed part-time workers. By 1974 the numbers involved were considerable, and were employed both on day and on evening shifts, much to the disquiet of the Union, and in December Maura Breslin reminded Bailey Gibson that the IPF agreement to a 40-hour week for the industry implicitly included a guarantee of forty hours' work. The employers reiterated their complaints about a shortage of female workers, yet persisted in their refusal to take on learners to the trade.[36] While extremely chary about issuing cards to untrained and part-time women workers, the Printers' Committee were left with little option but 'reluctantly agreed on condition that the learners' rate be reviewed and that the employment of part-time untrained women be seen as a temporary expedient only'.

Smurfits, which by 1975 had 'the bulk of print in Ireland',[37] had since 1975 engaged part-time shift workers on both day and evening work. In addition, in 1973, 'our members in this firm discovered that work was being sent out to be done in private homes of people not working in the firm'.[38] Almost 100% of such outworkers were women. When the IWWU members, on Union instructions, refused to handle the work coming from outworkers, they were locked out. In their own defence, Smurfits stated that the practice was under way 'everywhere' and that the IWWU had been the only union to voice an objection. The question of the use of outworkers was despatched to the Labour Court, but in the face of the oil crisis and an economically bleak prognosis, no clear answer was forthcoming. The practice continued, at least until 1976.

Meanwhile, at Bailey Gibson, there was an influx of untrained women who, unlike learners, were not entitled to training in 'all the processes of the house'. These were now reported by members to be 'working in the machine bag department and getting almost as much money as journeywomen'.[39] By stealth, and over a period of years, the profile of women in printing and kindred trades had clearly been changed. While the bulk of such workers remained full time, an increasing number were part-time on day and evening shifts, and others, totally unquantifiable, were outworkers. Many of these untrained shiftworkers were married women, and accounted in part for the increasing participation by such women in the workforce during this period.[40]

At the beginning of 1974 the oil crisis seriously threatened production in printing. The evening shift, predominantly of married women, at Smurfit Polypak were given notice to the 'annoyance' of members both full- and part-time. To forestall further dispute the management offered full-time employment to women whose evening shifts had clearly been designed with an eye to accommodating their domestic constraints. Predictably, for such women, forty hours' regular employment was not an option, and these women, entitled to 'no redundancy', became 'natural wastage'. While the day shift between 8 a.m. and 1 p.m., similarly accommodating for women with school-age children, continued, part-time workers on this and similar shifts were clearly vulnerable and eminently disposable. By 1975, with the economic crisis spreading throughout Ireland and the western world, at least ten employers in printing and paper pleaded inability to pay the 6% NWA. Members in Exchequer Printers, Wax Carton, and Massey Bros. were put on a three-day week, Powell Press 'say they are in a bad way', and Smurfit Carton let all part-timers go.[41]

In February, three married women who had been employed on an evening shift for five days each week between 6 p.m. and 10 p.m. sought a meeting with the Printers' Committee. In common with all the other shift workers employed on a part-time basis — the flexible, adaptable workforce seen as a prerequisite for the survival of women in printing — these women had discovered the extreme vulnerability of their position as industrial workers. The women were journeywomen, 'but could not work a full 40-hour week due to family commitments'. In the context of a shortage of female labour, such women had been courted through the arrangement of special shifts to accommodate their needs. In February, however, they had received notice and, as in the case of the women at Smurfit Polypak, had been offered a 40-hour week. Again, the terms were — predictably — rejected.

The IWWU was now placed in an invidious position. The agreement with Maguire and Paterson in 1965 conceded the right of management to take on part-time workers in a temporary relief capacity. Such a concession, however, was made in the context of gains for full-time women workers. By 1975 full-time women workers were numbered among the casualties of the oil crisis and deepening recession: redundancies were widespread and the impact on the IWWU was considerable. In these circumstances, the Union could offer no recompense to part-time workers, and in common with all other trade unions, retained their major commitment to the full-time workers, employed generally on the basis of a 40-hour week.

From 1975 onward the numbers of part-time workers in

the Irish labour force increased, and for the next decade, despite fluctuations, they maintained their position as 6% of the workforce.[42] This was in the context of a deepening recession and suggests that, while individual employers 'shed' part-time workers, overall they continued to be employed on a consistent basis throughout industry. This workforce was predominantly composed of married women, and for these and others — notably the outworkers, for so long a concern of the IWWU — the profile of the full-time industrial worker was acknowledged by the Union to be simply not appropriate. In the short term, however, no resolution of the problem which could take account of the needs of different categories of workers was forthcoming.

Acknowledgment of a changing profile for the woman workers was made more difficult by the increased momentum for equality at the place of work. Any conceding of a structural difference between the working week for women and that for men — a difference amplified by the increased numbers of women in part-time work — would render the case for equality of treatment as industrial workers less compelling.

In 1974 the Anti-Discrimination [Pay] Act had become law, although the IWWU, in common with other trade unions, had sought and secured equal pay since the late 1960s. By 1975, however, when International Women's Year was declared, the position of women in printing, in textiles and in laundries had, ironically, rarely appeared more bleak. Membership of the IWWU had declined through redundancies and the fiction of 'natural wastage'.[43] Its affiliation to the ICTU was now on the basis of a membership of 3,000. Yet, despite an increasingly hostile economic climate, and the clear reluctance of employers to concede equality for women workers, the IWWU served claims for equal pay on every employer. The social context was favourable, and the undoubted mixture of enthusiasm and political expediency which had sponsored Equal Pay and Anti-Discrimination legislation served to sustain officers of the Union confronting the daily round of redundancies and summary dismissals. The terrain upon which such claims would be fought out on behalf of members of the IWWU, however, was amply demonstrated by reference to the extremes. While the anticipated impact of EEC legislation on equality, and the Report of the Commission on the Status of Women, had been welcomed by the IWWU, within its own ranks an internal disparity in relation to working conditions and rights prevailed. One member at Morco reported that their employer 'has two 12½ year-old girls working at the bottom of the room. They work a 40 hour week for £4. . . . Needless to say they have not joined the union.'[44]

While those who had joined trade unions fared better, many women workers, despite the vigilance of their unions and of their officials, were employed by owners of industry who dispensed rights with a most reluctant hand. One woman, retiring from Usher's after fifty-two years of work, was offered '£3 pension, no more'. Another, after persistent illness, and twenty-three years of service, was given one day's notice of dismissal, and no redundancy.[45]

CHAPTER 19

Parity begins at home

While clearly aware of a lack of parity in conditions among its own membership, the IWWU nonetheless concentrated its energy, in the wake of the passage of the Anti-Discrimination (Pay) Act 1974, in the pursuit of a measure of equality for its members in their workplaces. Claims for equal pay were served in Gallaher's and Maguire and Paterson's, and the IPF conceded in principle that where there was equal work they would discuss equal pay. On the home front also, negotiations were under way: Miss Breslin, acting on behalf of her colleagues at Fleet Street, recommended that the Executive accept that officials of the Union were doing work equal to that of officials of other unions. Her point was well received; those who had any level of contact with Fleet Street were by now acutely aware of the pressure under which the officials of the Union worked. Depleted resources, and officials who were clearly over-extended, left the IWWU vulnerable as an institution, and its officers were subject to often distressing and frequently misplaced levels of criticism from the membership.

At Annual Convention in 1975 delegates were urged by their President, Mai Clifford, to convey a particular message to their fellow workers in this, 'the most severe economic crisis since the early 1930s' Working people, she suggested, would have to 'give their best productivity ever and maximum flexibility for Ireland and their jobs'.[1] The oil crisis of the mid-1970s had erupted in the context of profound change in Irish society. Ireland had witnessed a population growth of more than 3% in the first half of the decade; it was increasingly urbanised, with migration from many rural communities creating pressures to provide work and reasonable standards of living for those gravitating towards the capital and other centres of population. Both rural and urban Ireland had been affected by entry into the EEC. The new prosperity, however, had been unevenly distributed, and this had exacerbated already latent divisions in Irish society. Some enjoyed an often ostentatious wealth, while others lived below the poverty line in conditions acknowledged by few and conceded only in retrospect by researchers and public commentators.[2] Inflation massively eroded the purchasing power of wages — in one year the figure reached 23% — and the debate on the value of National Agreements, particularly as far as the lower paid workers were concerned, continued to simmer throughout the trade union movement.

By 1975 the Auditor's Report on Union finances confirmed what was already feared: expenditure for the year exceeded income by £2,000, and for the first time in its history, the IWWU looked to the sale of its capital assets to finance current expenditure. The balance of the lease on the now vacant ground floor and basement of Fleet Street were put on the market. All unnecessary expenditure was curtailed. While affiliation to the Irish Labour History Society was maintained, that to the People's College was allowed to lapse, 'as our members did not seem interested in attending'. Hospital Benefit would be discontinued, subject to the agreement of Convention, and the suggestion was raised that Convention itself should be held only every second year. Despite such straitened circumstances, however, the Union maintained an essentially even hand in the giving of alms: the Executive sanctioned 'a donation of £2 to the Sacred Heart Home and to the Distressed Protestants' Association'.

At the level of the Executive the strain associated with the constant need to juggle finance and general resources took its toll. When Pat Davis, Laundry Official, left the service of the Union in the mid-seventies, a decision was made not to replace her. All officials and staff agreed to take on additional tasks, at no extra pay. While members, such as Mai Clifford, achieved considerable standing within both the Union and the Dublin Council of Trade Unions, less publicly-known officials, such as Jenny Murray, were now required to extend an already long working-day to ensure continuity of service for members.

For a period, business proceeded with little evidence of either dispute or dissent. Scant explanation for a variety of proposals was given in the Executive minutes other than that 'Miss Breslin has given the matter much thought and is recommending very strongly.' Such differences of opinion as existed on the conduct of Union business, as could have been anticipated in any such organisation, were no longer recorded; by 1975 minute-taking in the IWWU had, as in all organisations, lost much of the literary flourish of earlier years, and the pursuit of efficiency had stayed the revealing hand. Since the era of Miss McDowell an increased professionalism had been reflected in more precise, but ultimately less informative, records of the business of the Union. The membership, however, gave some indication of a lack of trust in the judgement of their leadership.

In January 1975 twelve members of the IWWU were dismissed by Morco in Drogheda for refusing to work for the piece rate offered by management. While relations between management and workers were consistently poor, it was the relationship between the members and their leaders that showed the strain. The dispute that led to the dismissals was evidence of the former — the picket that workers subsequently placed on the premises of their own Union at Fleet Street was testimony to the latter.

Morco, a family business involved in production 'on the line'[3] of 'ladies' dresses', employed 150 workers in Drogheda, 100 in Nenagh and 150 outworkers. Basic wage rates for all except the outworkers were laid down by the Joint Labour Committee [JLC], the statutory wage-fixing machinery. The Union, however, had long complained of 'a complete absence of normal industrial relations', with the setting of a rate for piece-work, of its nature, provoking considerable 'discord' on the shop floor. Stewards and Union officials sought to ensure that minimum rates were applied, but despite their diligence in this area, when the dispute erupted, Morco was paying £4 a week below that rate.

Machinists, at Morco and elsewhere, worked on piece rates,[4] and thus the timing and pricing of each new garment style was crucial to overall earnings. Jenny Murray, senior official for this area, recalls negotiations with the Morgan brothers, who had collectively inherited the firm from an uncle and aunt, as verging on 'pantomime', replete with high drama and, given the level of expenditure involved, quite inappropriately spiced language. Discussions, Jenny recalled, often continued far into the night on the wisdom or logic of conceding the additional halfpenny for a frock.[5]

By 1974 members at Morco had become 'increasingly dissatisfied . . . with the method of timing their work'. The Union called on the services of the Work Study Department of the ICTU, while the women themselves pointed to the management practice of requiring women in the factory to 'put right' faulty work from outworkers. Such practices led inevitably to a diminution in the take-home pay of women paid by the piece. When the members refused to handle such work, management made its own position abundantly clear: if the Union insisted on stopping the outwork, the Morco factory in Drogheda would be closed.[6]

Such threats, while hardly conducive to good working relations, were undoubtedly effective. Outwork continued, pay remained below statutory minimum levels, and attempts by the Union to forestall further problems by the establishment of a Works' Committee failed. Discontent, predictably, remained, and in early 1975 erupted when the machinists failed to reach an agreement with management on the price to be paid for a dress, and refused to continue to work. At the urging of the managing director, the majority of the women returned to their machines. Twelve, however, refused to do so unless their claims for an increased rate were conceded. They were dismissed.

In a quite unprecedented move, the twelve took their grievance to Fleet Street, claiming Union negligence in serving their needs. On the evening of 26 March 1975, members of the Executive, arriving at the IWWU premises for a meeting, were greeted by a picket. While short-lived, such tactics did not lack dramatic impact. The Union, demonstrating a clear preference for adherence to established procedures at every level, sought to have the members reinstated. When management at Morco refused, the Union pursued the case through the machinery available under the 1967 Industrial Relations Act.

The Rights Commissioners' hearing on 21 April found both sides at fault and recommended three months' suspension and then reinstatement. General relations between management and members, and between members and their Union were, however, damaged, with personal disputes taking their inevitable toll. Relations between Nuala Early, the shop steward, and Maura Breslin, deteriorated, as the dissatisfaction with working procedures continued.[7]

The extent to which such disputes owe their intensity to personal differences is a moot point. While Mrs Early was considered by some members to be a 'strong character', Maura Breslin was considered by others to be a conservative leader. Other factors, however, bear consideration. Drogheda had originally been organised by Louie Bennett and had involved the recruitment of members from Usher's, Greenmount and Boyne, and Morco. Morco was in fact the first clothing manufacturer to be organised by the IWWU. Miss Bennett, using the most effective persuasive powers to hand, offered reduced contributions and extensive services as the spoils of membership of the IWWU. Such reduced contributions continued for many years but, when discovered by the Printers' Section, became the subject of considerable discord. Such discord was not lessened by the nature of disputes peculiar to 'working on the line', which occupied an inordinate amount of Union energy. By the mid-1970s the impact of passionate arguments about the virtues of halfpennies and pennies, which had considerable implications for the wage levels of piece workers, had nonetheless done little to promote feelings of kinship between Fleet Street and its country cousins.

While relations between individual officials and workers remained cordial, those between members and the Union leadership did not. Maura Breslin had become an official of the IWWU, and then its General Secretary, in the era of National Wage Agreements and Employer Labour Conferences. Much negotiation which would previously have been carried out in a more public domain was now carried on away from the daily theatre of the working lives of women. It was also conducted primarily between head office Union officials and management, a feature of procedure that was not peculiar to the IWWU but, in a context marked by a dimunution of confidence, did little to reassure a membership increasingly ready to believe that the details of such agreements affected many but were disclosed only to a few.

Between June and December, in a climate of some disquiet, negotiations continued. A new system was phased in by early 1976 and the negotiated trial period ended in May. Further discussions considered unmeasured work, waiting time, machine breakdowns and a litany of difficulties intrinsic to piece-work. The whole issue was referred to the conciliation service of the Labour Court, and a ten-point proposal on the new pay structure was put to both sides for acceptance. The members rejected the proposal.

On 3 September 1976, and with scant warning, Morco closed its doors. Further Labour Court talks ensued, the Union having advised that acceptance might result in a resumption of business. At the urging of both the General Secretary and the shop stewards, members agreed to accept the new pay structure. Morco, however, stayed closed. A receiver was appointed at the end of September.

The Union, having represented its members in Drogheda since the 1940s, now spared no efforts in its attempt to find alternative finance to ensure that production could resume. Through the good offices of James Tully, the Labour TD, an application sponsored by the Union was made on behalf of the company to Foir Teoranta, the Industrial Development Authority [IDA] and to private banks. The members on their own initiative offered to work overtime 'for nothing for six months to get the company on its feet'. Although the entire workforce supported the sale of the factory as a going concern, serious consideration was given by IWWU members to the question of a worker co-op, to be financed by the anticipated redundancy settlements for the women in the industry. In October 1976 *The Drogheda Independent* sported a front page headline: 'A Worker Co-op is Mooted for Morco Factory'.[8] While enthusiasm for such a venture was undiminished, reality — in financial terms — was rapidly conceded by all involved. In early 1977 Morco was purchased by Dutch industrialists,[9] and became 'Confexin Fashion Ltd'. Many were promised re-employment but all jobs were lost in the short term, and members were paid their entitlement under the Minimum Notice and Terms of Employment Act.

The closure allowed time for reflection on all sides. In January 1977 Miss Breslin spoke to the Executive of the difficulties of continuing the Union service to all members, particularly those outside Dublin.

> Miss Breslin feels that we cannot continue to give the degree or extent of attention which is demanded from us in Drogheda, and intends to seek the advice of Congress and our solicitor on the subject.[10]

She received the unanimous backing of the Executive. Meanwhile, however, members from Morco had reached their own conclusions. Although a considerable proportion of the original Morco workforce was eventually placed with Confexin, the effects of perpetual uncertainty of employment with the firm did little to endear the Union to its members. At Easter 1977, Miss Breslin was accompanied by Jenny Murray to a meeting of IWWU members from Confexin. Feelings ran high, and Miss Breslin's leadership and her commitment to her members were called into question. By the end of a memorable evening, 137 members served notice that they would leave the IWWU. Before the end of the year the members had transferred to the Tailors and Garment Workers' Union. Despite the preliminary steps it had itself taken in regard to withdrawing its service the IWWU did not officially cease organisation in Drogheda, but no further recruitment was evident, and the Union witnessed a period of gradual decline in the region.

The IWWU was caught in the unenviable position with which many small unions were now familiar. Failure to organise further would result in increasingly depleted resources as membership dwindled. At the same time, the inevitable consequence, both in terms of finance and of personnel, of any such further organisation carried out in an attempt to recruit more members, would be a reduction in the services extended to the current membership — a membership which was already critical of the range and quality of services now offered by Fleet Street.

Away from Dublin, complaints about the lack of service offered by the Union echoed those of Morco. Members at Usher's in Drogheda and Ormac in Kells complained of a lack of attendance at meetings and a lack of Union presence in their place of work, but depleted resources and reductions in staff numbers left little possibility of redressing such grievances. Officials, interpreting their own roles, were not untouched by such criticism, and were also affected, by changing work contexts and by the development of new management strategies.

The IWWU officials, although experienced negotiators, were — as were most of their colleagues — left with little room for manoeuvre when confronted by the strategy and wiles of aspiring Irish industrialists, such as Michael Smurfit. In 1977 Maura Breslin had reported that Mr Smurfit had expressed concern that 'if . . . costs continue to increase at the present rate the printing industry in Ireland will not be viable within two to three years'.[11] The company proceeded to employ a heightened level of management expertise that was applied both to its own personnel and, over lunch and with considerable panache, to the management of trade union officials. In quite a new departure the representatives of labour became 'over informed' of the minutiae of the pressures of industry, at least one effect of which was a preoccupation with 'unit costs' becoming a familiar aspect of Executive vocabulary within the walls of Fleet Street. Such a practice, while useful for management in the short term, was not consistently effective. By 1981, when Smurfit Cartons were suffering recurrent redundancies, Maura Breslin challenged the company on the basis of published reports of its £80 million empire, of Michael Smurfit's own salary of £1.5 million, and Jefferson Smurfit's salary of £450,000.[12]

While such trends in management strategy affected all trade unions at differing levels, the IWWU was, in addition, confronting further difficulties. By 1977 an illness which had reduced Miss Breslin's capacity to work at her customary pace became acute, and in 1977 and 1978 she was hospitalised for a considerable period of time. In her absence, and of necessity, Jenny Murray and the staff in Fleet Street reassessed both procedures and service. In a number of areas Jenny Murray moved to heal breaches between headquarters and the factory floor. The price, however, was high, and difficult to sustain.

In 1977 members at De La Rue threatened to leave the Union. Their disquiet stemmed from apparently infrequent meetings and the by now familiar complaint from members on the shop floor, that negotiation took place only between management and officials, and that working women felt excluded from the conduct of their own affairs. Increasingly aware of the need to reassure members by a readiness to appear at their place of work, Miss Murray secured the use of a small room at De La Rue's. Here, on a regular basis, she met shop stewards and members, and developed relations with the lower ranks of management. This procedure had the desired effect. Members no longer talked of leaving the Union, but it became evident that such servicing would demand a far greater expenditure of time and resources in this arena than had, imperceptibly, become the norm.

The need to focus increased attention in such areas was accompanied by greater demands on the professional expertise of Union officials. Although the IPF had conceded equal pay in principle, it remained the responsibility of the Union to establish specific cases to give foundation to their claims. Following talks with the Work Study Department of the ICTU on the most effective way of securing evidence of inequality, the Union considered a number of options. While the IPF had suggested that it could be done on a group basis, the Act stipulated that studies had to be done on location. The IWWU therefore proposed pilot studies in a number of firms chosen specifically on the basis of the number of operations in process. Three firms — Bailey Gibson, Cahill's and Iona Print — were nominated by the Printers' Committee. Miss Breslin, now back on the strength at Fleet Street, instructed members to form a committee drawn from the shop floor in each individual house.[13] While such studies were under way, a parallel development in the pursuit of equal pay was embarked upon.

While the Union had long championed the training of

women in all processes of the printing and paper industry, the continued practice of the interchangeability and flexibility of women workers was now seen as fundamental to the achievement by them of pay equal to that of their male colleagues. In early 1977 a member complained of her continual movement by management from one machine to another. The complaint suggested a lack of awareness of Union policy in this regard, but served to make the long-term strategy of the Union in this industry abundantly clear. Responding directly to the complaint from her member, Miss Breslin explained both the history and the ambitions of the IWWU for women in printing and kindred trades.

> The position both in the Printing and Paper industry going back over a period of approximately ten years is that there is complete interchangeability and flexibility between the women employed in that industry, and furthermore this union has been pursuing a policy of equal opportunity for women and equal pay which we hope will bring about a position of complete flexibility and interchangeability between men and women.[14]

Clearly, the agreement to sponsor the formation of a women's workforce familiar with all aspects of the trade, and hence offering the flexibility long desired by management in this industry, was given in anticipation of a changing work context overall. If women were to surrender the protection of demarcation lines, their position as workers could be safeguarded only if all labour, male and female, was employed on the same basis.

The terms of this proposed equality, as negotiated between the IWWU and the IPF, were based not only on historical understanding, but on signed agreements and a Production Bonus Payment of £2.05 a week which was incorporated into the basic pay of all IWWU members in the industry in May 1975. These terms, as Miss Breslin pointed out, had been accepted by both sides, by IWWU and management, and hence — even if in the short term the consequences proved unpalatable to members at their place of work — it was reaffirmed in 1977 that there is absolutely no reason why our members, within the Printing and paper industry, should not be moved from one machine to another as the requirements of the work demand.[15]

When first discussed, the concept of 'unisex', or the promotion of complete interchange between men and women, had not been acceptable to members,[16] and Miss Breslin had resumed negotiations with the IPF, stressing that no loss of jobs would be accepted by women workers. In April she read a letter from the IPF, offering a 30-month phasing-in period for equal pay in return for acceptance in principle of interchangeability in all work processes between men and women. Miss Breslin cautioned her members to consider the seriousness of the move and the implications of the pursuit of equality on such terms, feeling it 'her duty to convey as seriously as she can the possible results of equal pay in the printing and paper industry'. The Printers' Committee duly considered the position, and, having suggested a concession in terms of a reduction in the phasing-in period, accepted the terms on offer.

The provision of this flexible workforce underlined all IWWU negotiations for equal pay in this industry. In June the Printers' Committee accepted the implementation of proposals leading to equal pay. In all its negotiations, and with the offer of its final proposal, the IPF suggested that they had been greatly persuaded by the points raised by the Irish Women Workers' Union officials 'in our many discussions', and that the proposal had been made

> in the context of our agreement to broaden the scope of jobs currently being undertaken by journeywomen so as to bring them up to the same value as jobs in the general worker category currently performed by men.[17]

Given that the initial moves to agree such interchangeability were taken in the context of widespread redundancies in box and carton-making, and the need to secure a future in the industry for these journeywomen, the potential risk in becoming a flexible workforce was a necessary consequence of the protection of women's jobs. The reaching of such an agreement, however, undoubtedly begged many questions, not least that relating to the anomaly whereby women who had completed four years' learnership to achieve the status of journeywomen would become 'equal' to men in the trade, general workers who, by definition, were operatives who received no training.

The movement of women from one machine to another continued at management's discretion. From the IPF, however, came a further proposal to extend, in effect, the period of learnership for women in the trade. The IPF suggested a new starting age of sixteen years, rather than fifteen years, and an apprenticeship which would conclude at the age of twenty-one years, when the top rate as journeywomen would be achieved. These women would, at that stage, achieve equality with the operatives. The move would abolish the over-eighteen learner rates, and delay the award of equal pay until women had completed all five years of their learnership. In doing so it would increase the period of apprenticeship from four to five years. From the factory floor, and from already cautious women, came a decided 'No', accompanied by resistance to the idea of a five-year learnership, more especially 'as the rest of the trade seem to be reducing theirs'. The IPF was informed that, in this regard at least, the status quo would be maintained.

The question of extending the training facilities available to women and the agreement to train them in all aspects of the trade was also tested. In June 1979 Rose Thompson, Member of the Executive, placed the case of four girls in Bindery at Wiggins Teape before the Printers' Committee. The members 'were anxious to study printing in the College of Technology, Bolton Street'. A meeting between the Union, Bolton Street, and the IPF followed, and the limits of interchangeability, and of 'all round training in the house', were carefully defined. The IPF considered, with regret, that it would be 'too expensive' to release journeywomen for such training, but would consider releasing learners. In the short-term, members had already rejected the evening classes currently available, arguing that after a day's work such classes were in effect a lengthening of their working day. In the long-term, the Union agreed to pursue the question of 'all round training for members on the floor' at the level of the company.[18] Predictably, the employers over the years demonstrated little fidelity to the idea of such training for women. Working women, in common with their male counterparts, however, gauged success quite reasonably by the size of their pay packets. By 1980, these had improved dramatically in this industry. In her Annual Report, Maura Breslin made a quite justified boast.

> When we began our negotiations for equal pay in this section the adult rate for a journeywomen was £32 per week. Today that rate is £74.11 per week.[19]

In voicing its misgivings in relation to national pay agreements the IWWU had served notice both on the trade union movement and the State that it would, during the 1970s, seek legislative protection for women and for other low-paid workers. Such a move was seen as preferable, both politically and in terms of union resources, to an agenda increasingly dominated by the necessity to negotiate on the basis of individual members in a wide range of industries.

The provision of statutory rights in the pursuit of equality, which was to become the hallmark of the 1970s, did not, however, ensure the unfettered progress of equality of pay or opportunity for women workers. Predictably, the process of establishing the basis for claims proved both cumbersome and often inadequate to the task, as was evident from the early incursions by the IWWU into the domain of Equality Officers, Job Evaluations, and Determinations from the Labour Court. In the latter part of the 1970s the legislative machinery established to redress the balance of pay and opportunity was used extensively by the Union. In a number of cases where claims had been established through the agreed procedures, the IWWU threatened the ultimate sanction of the strike weapon, should employers fail to implement Equal Pay Agreements. In 1977 Playprint had so refused, but after strike notice had been served proved willing to reassess their position. Before notice expired the company had conceded the claim in full.[20]

At Smurfit Carton Ltd in 1978 a rationalisation programme

drawn up by the company proposed the redundancy of half of the IWWU members employed. The company claimed that the rigid box-making department was no longer viable, but, ultimately, pointed to equal pay as bearing direct responsibility for this latest threat to women's jobs. 'They blame equal pay for all this. They want us to agree to a cut in wages to £37 a week, or rotation or total closure'.[21] A meeting of members decided unanimously to 'put up a stiff fight', and having called for retraining of the women involved, the Union entered negotiations. By December the Executive reported that the threat of redundancy had been 'staved off for the present', and the resistance by the women to the rhetoric and the threats of their employers ensured that when redundancies did occur in 1980 they were far fewer than had earlier been anticipated.

The combined effect of established trade union practice — resistance, negotiation, and ultimately the threat to withdraw labour — and the legislative provision for equal pay could clearly be seen to be effective. Union officials, however, became increasingly aware that the procedure involved in establishing claims and winning determinations in their favour would demand a whole range of skills and expertise at this stage largely undeveloped in traditional negotiating practice.

In 1977 the Union had served its first claim for equal pay on the Hospital Joint Services' Board [HJSB]. The HJSB had been established in 1971 as a corporate body set up by the Minister for Health. In the Laundry Division, 105 operatives were employed — eighty-nine women and sixteen men — in addition to nine supervisory staff, seven of whom were women. While preliminary discussions took place between the IWWU and the HJSB, a claim was also served on the commercial laundries, based 'on the conviction that the work of our members in the laundries is equal to a general operative and they should be paid at an equal rate.'[22]

In 1979 the Union proceeded to serve a claim on St James' Hospital, but the early discussions with the job evaluation unit of the ICTU indicated that if the procedure available under the Anti-Discrimination (Pay) Act 1974 were to be invoked, the Equality Officer could recommend a claim for equal pay that would apply only to a limited number of members. The WUI and the ITGWU had to an extent both anticipated and resolved this problem by the successful serving of a claim in 1979 which secured a uniform rate of pay for all their members in the laundries. The IWWU considered following a similar procedure, but in 1979 the results of the Equality Officer's deliberations in the HJSB claim forced a more immediate response.

The procedure applied in the IWWU claim for equal pay in the HJSB had been the outcome of a job evaluation conducted at the behest of the Union by the ICTU, and a further evaluation carried out on behalf of the HJSB by a firm of business consultants. Agreement could not be reached on the two evaluations, and the question was referred to the Equality Officer for investigation and recommendation under the Act. In July the Equality Officer recommended that the work done by women in the separating of long sheets and stacking sheets was not equal in value to either of the male jobs; nor were either the pressing of uniforms or the sorting of sheets found to be equal in value to the male cleaner's job. The work done by these women, however, was deemed to be equal to that done by the van helper.

The Union appealed the decision, advancing a total of twenty-three principal reasons why the Equality Officer had, in their view, made an inappropriate recommendation. The Union argued that evaluation had been 'largely determined by management objectives', and that no account had been taken of the features peculiar to women's work in the laundry. These workers 'are flexible to a degree that is far higher than that practised by male workers', and such flexibility meant that 'experienced female laundry operatives are normally competent to perform most operations'.[23] The Labour Court, however, upheld the recommendation of the Equality Officer and equal pay was conceded only to those members covered by the original recommendation. Although by 1981 equal pay was conceded in the HJSB, with retrospection, the rejection of this claim served notice on the Union that the machinery provided under the Act was more complex and less satisfactory than had been anticipated. It also gave warning that the status of a flexible workforce would not, by definition, be interpreted positively.

The need to ensure familiarity with the appropriate machinery of equal pay claims was, however, only one aspect of claims procedure. Employers could delay implementation of equal pay, even after it had been established, by recourse to a variety of points of clarification. It was also the case that, even before implementation, the granting of equal pay and status to a range of women workers would inevitably be perceived as a threat by male workers whose ascendancy in the workplace would subsequently be eroded.

In 1977 a group of psychiatric nurses invoked the terms of the Employment Equality Act. Although affected by the impact of the marriage bar until 1973, qualified psychiatric nurses who married had been consistently employed by the Eastern Health Board [EHB] 'to fill staff vacancies on a temporary basis'. For many such nurses, in the years up to 1973, service had been broken on a regular basis either by the Board or by the nurses themselves, for personal reasons. A considerable number, however, had been employed since 1960 without any break in service, but had remained classified as 'temporary' because of the marriage bar. As the Union pointed out in its claim for equal pay, these nurses had returned to duty as the result of a direct appeal from the Board, due to a shortage of psychiatric nurses willing to accept appointment even on a permanent basis.[24] In 1973 these women applied for permanent status. They were refused, and in the negotiations that followed an agreement was reached whereby 'temporary' married females were given permanent appointment with effect from 1 October 1977. The agreement gave formal recognition to the entitlement to pension rights based on the earlier years of employment of these nurses. An anomaly, however, arose in the area of seniority, and the seventy-nine nurses, members of a number of unions, including the IWWU, the ITGWU and the WUI, and representing many hundreds of women in the same position, pressed their claim of discrimination.

Promotion within the EHB structure had been the subject of intense negotiations between the unions and the Board and had resulted in the decision, always accepted reluctantly by the Board, that promotion must be based on seniority rather than on what were perceived as more contentious subjective judgments, such as personality, fitness for the post, etc. The seventy-nine nurses now claimed that, despite the unbroken service by many of them since 1960, the existence of a marriage bar had in fact discriminated against them. Following the Equality Officer's Recommendation No. 2 of 1979 in favour of the nurses, the EHB offered to restore seniority to the nurses with effect from 23 August 1973, the approximate date of the lifting of the bar. For many women, this proposal ignored more than ten years of continuous service. It was rejected.

Although only ten of the total number of nurses involved were members of the IWWU, the case represented the first occasion that Maura Breslin — a qualified psychiatric nurse — had been in a position to mount a campaign on behalf of her former colleagues. It also became the focus of a major bone of contention related to the implications for other workers of the winning of equality for women in the workforce. In 1979, at a meeting of all unions involved — the IWWU, the WUI and the ITGWU — Maura Breslin had submitted her Union's case, arguing that the retrospective application of the Anti-Discrimination (Pay) Act should be examined. The WUI agreed that 'there is a great deal of sympathy with married nurses' and that it would agree to service being recognised from the date of the original appointment of the nurses involved.[25] The ITGWU, while supporting the claim for purposes of pension entitlements and the achievement of permanent status, was less forthcoming in relation to seniority claims which would, if implemented, adversely affect their members.

Miss Breslin sought legal advice, both from the Equality Officer and from the Union solicitor, on the feasibility of mounting a case for the retrospective application of the Act. She was advised that

> the Act permits an Equality Officer to recommend the removal of 'inherited' discrimination, that is, continuing disadvantages to a person's career which occur as a result of conditions existing and applying before the terms of the Employment Equality Act came into force.[26]

The claim for implementation of the Equality Officer's recommendation No. 2/1979 now entered the labyrinth of the Labour Court machinery. This claim included a submission that nurses should be placed on seniority panels 'giving each individual credit for her aggregated service in the hospital'.

On 2 January 1980 the ITGWU, in a letter to the Labour Court, registered its dissent. It had already acknowledged the justice of the claim made by the seventy-nine nurses to establish their right to a permanent appointment and to all rights based on continuous permanent service. In the context of the Labour Court's examination of the EHB's appeal against the Equality Officer's recommendation, however, the ITGWU had voiced grave misgivings about the validity of this particular claim by the nurses involved.

> The nurses concerned in this case cannot expect, in all reasonableness, to leapfrog over others on the established promotional panels through the operation of long established agreement and norms.[27]

The anomaly which was detailed in the submission on behalf of the nurses involved the recognition of the seniority of married nurses in the original claim, for promotional purposes, from October 1977. All trainees appointed to the EHB were appointed on a temporary classification, and on completion of their training, were credited with seniority from the date their training had commenced, although they were not made permanent until they had qualified. This procedure created a situation in which trainees who had been recruited in 1975 and who had qualified in 1978 were regarded as senior, for promotional purposes, to the married women in question, many of whom had qualified before 1970, and some of whom had given unbroken service as trained personnel since 1960.

Many of the younger more recently-qualified nurses and attendants, and those in training, were members of the ITGWU, which was vigilant in defending the interests of its membership. It claimed, with considerable justice, a leading role in advancing the original claim for recognition of the rights of married nurses. The IWWU's judgement on the

ITGWU's challenge to the claim of these women for promotional rights was, however, unequivocal.

> We would describe this as an exercise in semantics and we regard the failure to perceive the nature of the discrimination as an example of selective blindness.[28]

The Labour Court Determination DEE-4-80 found in favour of the nurses. The implications of the finding were directed immediately to the EHB, and notice was served that the Union would now seek 'the various benefits which would have accrued had equality existed'. Such benefits would extend to the existing posts of Ward Sister, Deputy Ward Sister, choice of leave dates, and all other entitlements related to their seniority. In addition, the Union notified the Board that 'members' claims for financial recompense will be forthcoming'.[29]

Although the recommendation of the Court was abundantly clear the IWWU, between 1980 and 1982, would accuse the ITGWU of 'sharp practice' in relation to moves by that union to have junior nurses who were in positions of seniority in an 'acting capacity' appointed to these posts on a permanent basis before the full implementation of the Labour Court determination. The EHB was similarly accused of procrastination in its own favour. In applying again to the Labour Court in 1981 for implementation of the terms of the determination, the IWWU claimed that the seventy-nine nurses

> are entitled to exactly the same 'status and benefits' which are applied to all their colleagues . . . with great respect to the Court we feel sure we will be forgiven for wondering how deliberate is the EHB's inability to understand.[30]

While the case of the '79' continued, seemingly on an indefinite basis, the experience served as the impetus for the mounting of a major offensive both from Fleet Street and from the shop floor to secure equal opportunity for women workers.

At Annual Convention in 1980 a resolution urged the Executive to campaign 'to secure full equality of opportunity for all our members within the meaning of the Act'. The printers at the debate at Annual Convention led the field: they were the most powerful section in the Union, and their industry was one in which changes of technology had been introduced on such a wide scale that women had become acutely aware of the need to stake their claim if they were not to lose their territory.

A resolution came from the members in Cahill's urging an advance in the cause of women by ensuring the acquisition of skills appropriate to the new methods, including photo-setting, and requests for training on a wider range of machines. Throughout 1980 the Union pursued both that company and the IBATU on this question, but their efforts were effectively limited by the reluctance of the women to extend what was presented as an opportunity in kind to the men. In early 1980, in response to overtures from the IWWU, the Executive Comittee of the IBATU gave their considered view of the proposed incursion. 'They had no objection to girls being instructed in the setting up of folding machines, but they insist that the status quo be maintained'.[31] Precisely how such acrobatic feats were to be achieved was unclear, and when prompted by a request for a more precise definition of the 'status quo', the IBATU replied that they had nothing further to add. Miss Breslin recommended that the IWWU's ambitions should be pursued at the level of the company.

Following a wide-ranging discussion with management on the projected programme for machines already in use, members detailed their requests for training. Rosaleen Bracken, shop steward, presented the case of a member seeking training on the Brehmer folding machine. By November, the men delivered their well-considered verdict — they 'would be agreeable provided the girls let them do the sewing machines'. Neither the company nor the women, in the short term, considered such a prospect inviting. Negotiations ceased, and the erstwhile challengers withdrew to consider the wisdom of their case.

At Fleet Street, a further implication of the equality legislation was considered: a change in the name, and hence the composition, of the IWWU. Although the Union was under no immediate pressure to make any such changes, these matters were undoubtedly on the agenda. There had been a specific request from Ormac in Kells that men should be allowed to join the IWWU and, under the terms of the Act, indefinite exclusion would constitute discrimination. The admission of men into the Union would mark another transformation — from an all-woman union into a general union. As such, both the negotiating power and the most distinctive feature of the IWWU would change, and unless membership were to increase dramatically with the opening of the doors the capacity of the Union to compete for members would undoubtedly diminish.

By 1980 membership stood at 2,654. Miss Breslin's own position on questions of amalgamation or any other arrangements now under consideration had not changed over many years of discussions with other unions. She, in common with Louie Bennett, had always favoured a Confederation of General Unions which would ensure that each constituent body would maintain its own identity. Talks on the possibility of reaching agreement on such matters were ongoing with both the FWUI and the ITGWU.[32] Other possibilities were also placed tentatively on the agenda.

Discussions over a number of years between all print unions had involved the IWWU in an observer status, and by 1980 the possibility of an all Irish Print Union was being seriously considered. The women in printing had established themselves as perhaps the most effective section in the Union in terms of their strong sense of identity with their trade — and, despite differences, with their male colleagues — and in terms of their capacity to wield considerable influence within the Union. If the question of some form of a merger or amalgamation for the IWWU was to be considered, the attraction to the IWWU printers of joining forces with others in their trade would have to be articulated, inevitably and as a matter of some urgency. With a view to encouraging debate on such matters Kathleen Monaghan, shop steward at Newman's and later to be elected President of the IWWU, proposed that a discussion of all aspects of such a merger, and its implications for other sections of the Union, should be considered. At Annual Convention 1980-81, she proposed

> That this Union have meaningful talks with all interested parties with a view to our joining (as equal partners) the new Irish Print Union.[33]

Debate centred on questions of status and unity. The General Secretary informed the Convention that the proposed rules of the new Union would be structured for different classes of members, but that there would be no provision for non-printing members. Following a general discussion the resolution was not pursued but the question of general talks with other unions was left open.

While such discussions, both at Fleet Street and among the membership at their places of work, would continue sporadically, an awareness of the complexities revealed by the debate undoubtedly served to reinforce the IWWU's celebration of its continuing autonomy. Such developments did not indicate any sense of an early relinquishing of the independence of the IWWU. It was, in fact, quite the contrary: as finances became more precarious, and discussions of affiliations and mergers more commonplace, such independence as remained was flaunted defiantly. In 1980 the ICTU proposed the holding of Annual Congress in Belfast. A measure of disquiet was evident in Fleet Street, and when the Executive were notified that the venue could not be changed, they 'agreed that no delegation would attend'. The decision provoked considerable discussion in the daily papers, and in a letter from Cooperation North the by-now besieged Executive were urged to reconsider. In an undoubtedly defensive posture, but exercising to the full the prerogatives of independence, 'the Executive decided to ignore it as we are under no obligation to anyone to explain our decision and it is a confidential matter'.[34]

By the end of the year deliberations of a different order occupied the agenda. On 19 November 1980, under 'Any Other Business', Maura Breslin informed the Executive that she had been advised by her doctors to consider retiring from the position of General Secretary. She suggested that within the ranks no one person presented as the obvious

Parity begins at home 335

candidate for succession, although among both officials and staff women of undoubted competence and ambition continued to serve the Union. They included Mai Clifford, first woman President of the Dublin Council of Trade Unions [DCTU], and who was at this stage buoyant with the success of the huge tax demonstrations of 1979. Her own brand of optimism had been forever enshrined in Irish labour history when she headed the tax marches and, on one such occasion, took to the platform with a passionate defence of the PAYE worker and a memorable rendition of 'One Day At A Time'. Her enthusiasms and commitment were echoed in others; the two Roses — Mrs Thompson and Miss Bracken, printers active in the Union for more than twenty years, both of whom served alternately as President and Vice President of the Union in the 1970s and who represented the IWWU both at ICTU and DCTU over many years; Jenny Murray, daughter of Theresa Behan, first laundry official of the IWWU, and the only second generation official in the Union; and June Winders, office administrator, the first married employee of the IWWU explicitly requested to return to the ranks in time of need, and one of the earliest of the 'new women' who had continued in full-time employment while raising a family of four children.

Miss Breslin, clearly anxious to relinquish her responsibilities, urged members of the Executive also to consider a candidate from outside the IWWU. Over a number of years she had observed 'a very able young woman', and now proposed that the Executive consider approaching Padraigín Ní Mhurchú, 'a trade union official in the FWUI . . . who particularly addresses herself to women's issues' as nominee for the position of Assistant Secretary. The question of the financial implications of the appointment of a new official provoked some concern, but by the end of the evening, members of the staff, having indicated that they would not seek a nomination, agreement was sought in principal for the appointment of an Assistant to Miss Breslin. Miss Frances Byrne proposed, and Mrs Pat Davis seconded, a resolution to this effect. When put to the vote the resolution was carried: six votes for, two against. Between meetings, further soundings were taken, and at the final meeting of the year, it was proposed by Mai Clifford that Padraigín Ní Mhurchú would be invited to accept the position of Assistant Secretary of the IWWU. The proposal was carried unanimously.

CHAPTER 20

The future of work

Since the early 1970s Padraigín Ní Mhurchú had been known to the officers of the IWWU, particularly in relation to her work on the Womens' Advisory Committee of Congress. As a member of this Committee she, with her colleagues, had addressed the complexities involved in encouraging women's participation in the decision-making process of the trade union movement. in 1980 she was informally approached by Mai Clifford to establish her willingness to make an institutional commitment to the Irish Women Workers' Union, and the following year Maura Breslin moved to formalise procedures. She approached Ms Ní Mhurchú and the General Secretary of the FWUI, Mr Paddy Cardiff, with a view to inviting Padraigín Ní Mhurchú to become Assistant General Secretary of the IWWU.

In February Paddy Cardiff wrote to confirm that Officers and Trustees of the FWUI had considered and agreed to

> the secondment of Padraigín Ní Mhurchú . . . for an unspecified period and setting out wages and conditions of employment in that union and indicating that such a transfer could not be effective until the end of March, as she had to be replaced in the FWUI.[1]

Under the terms agreed between the two unions, Padraigín Ní Mhurchú initially remained on the payroll of the FWUI and went on secondment to the IWWU. The IWWU in turn re-imbursed the FWUI an agreed amount for her services.

The new Assistant General Secretary assumed office in May 1981. At Annual Convention that year she addressed the question of women and power — in particular their lack of representation at the decision-making level of the trade union movement, and in general the social, industrial and political effect of their absence from the power structures of the wider society. To the women workers, in her encouragement for training programmes and her endorsement of reserved seats on executive bodies, if that were necessary, she now signalled her advocacy of significant structural change in the trade union movement.

Ms Ní Mhurchú, while known to the officers of the IWWU, was a largely unknown quantity to its members. A native of rural Co. Monaghan, she had been educated at St Louis National School there and at the Convent of Mercy Secondary School in Castleblaney. In 1967 she was appointed as Executive Officer in the Office of the Revenue Commissioners. In 1970 she had been elected local representative for the Civil Service Executive Union and, in 1972 to its Executive Committee. In that year she became involved with the Common Market Defence Campaign working in opposition to Ireland's entry into the EEC, and was increasingly active both in trade unionism and in the wider political sphere. The following year she applied to the Federated Workers' Union of Ireland for a position as Assistant Branch Secretary and held that position until 1977, representing clerks, general workers and hostesses at Dublin Airport. By 1977 she had been appointed Branch Secretary, representing clerical and managerial workers in the private sector — a position she held at the time of her secondment to the IWWU.[2]

With an Assistant General Secretary now prepared to review the entire structure and policy of the IWWU, Maura Breslin prepared to ease herself out of the Union. Acknowledging the necessity to take account of the financial implications of the new appointment, she served notice that, after Annual Convention, she would continue her work for the Union on the basis of a two-day week. She intended, on the other days, to continue her work on the Employment Appeals Tribunal, to which she had been appointed by Congress and, although retiring from the Union, Miss Breslin clearly intended to continue her involvement in the labour movement.

In 1981, nominated by the Executive Council of the ICTU, she canvassed for a place on the Labour panel in the Seanad election. Letters of support, solicited by herself and her supporters, indicated that her commitment to working people was not unacknowledged. As a member of the Labour Party her support from rural deputies, Jimmy Tully and Joe Bermingham, was indicative of her own political disposition; from other quarters, however, support was also forthcoming. Both Charles Haughey and Brian Lenihan recommended her 'as someone well worthy of support' (but after Fianna Fáil candidates), and from the Workers' Party Tomás Mac Giolla promised his vote. Although unsuccessful in her political ambitions, Maura Breslin quite clearly intended no quiet retirement to tend the roses.

Within the Union itself, the changed personnel had little time to pause for reflection. The threats of redundancies from Smurfit Carton and Bailey Gibson became unpalatable reality. To the disquiet of officials, who had strongly advised them of the necessity to protect existing jobs, members at Bailey Gibson had submitted their own names for redundancy, with no reference to the Union and despite many years of official resistance to such a move. At Dakota, demarcation lines were breached and Jenny Murray took up arms on behalf of members who claimed that 'men were creeping in on the machines formerly run by women'. In a valiant bid for the rights of future members she secured a promise from Dakota that a female learner would be recruited to ensure some continuity in the supply of skilled women workers.

Widespread unemployment threatened to create divisions between workers in the battle for jobs. At Frederick Press the shop steward reported that the new automatic Camco folding machine had arrived, and that both IBATU and ITGWU members were contesting the women's right to setting up. Elsewhere, the steady loss of members continued to sap morale. At Dublin County Council twenty IWWU members sought transfer to the Local Government and Public Services' Union. They were refused and, in a new departure, were personally approached by P. Ní Mhurchú and J. Murray and asked to remain loyal to the IWWU. To copper-fasten such loyalty, claims were successfully served on the County Council for 'service pay and two extra days under the National Understanding, and privilege days'.[3] At De La Rue, an important source of secure employment for the IWWU, members spoke of small attendance at meetings and 'the apathy among workers' in relation to trade union matters.[4]

This combined assault by redundancies, applications for transfers and lack of interest resulted in a decline in membership, but the tone of the Annual Convention in 1981 conveyed the sense of an even greater threat — one which extended beyond the IWWU and threatened the trade union movement itself. An emergency resolution was sent from Convention to the Taoiseach, Charles Haughey.

> This Convention . . . gravely concerned at the disastrous level of unemployment which is growing daily, calls upon you and your Government to declare a State of Emergency in relation to unemployment and to take whatever emergency measures may be necessary to halt the increasing redundancies and to provide jobs for all our people.[5]

While Maura Breslin remained General Secretary of the Union until 1982, the evidence of change in the leadership was everywhere felt. Ideas about selling Fleet Street were abandoned in favour of improving the premises and seeking tenants for all available space.

As further space was available in the building, an agreement was reached with the fledgling feminist publishing company — Irish Feminist Information — to take one floor and to organise training courses for Women in Publishing [WiP]. This agreement served two purposes: it utilised the building in the interest of the Union and it made facilities available to a small group of women seeking to establish themselves as a feminist publishing concern. From this group both Attic Press and the Women's Community Press evolved, as did a further disparate group of women equipped, through the original publishing course, with an impressive range of non-traditional skills.

In a structural sense, putting the house in order involved elimination of dry rot and installation of new wiring; putting the Union in order involved a more complex re-appraisal, not only of finance but of structure and organisation. New areas were to be considered for recruitment. Although the IWWU was widely perceived as a union for non-white-collar women workers, Ms Ní Mhurchú signalled quite clearly that her intention was to broaden the ambitions of the Union's officials and members in regard to potential recruits. Throughout the late 1960s and early 1970s women had entered the trade union movement in greater numbers than ever before. That same period, however, had witnessed the erosion of membership of the IWWU. Although the reasons for such an erosion were varied, new areas had been largely unexplored, due to lack of resources and the undoubted need for greater vitality in the organisation drive of the IWWU.

Finances from 1980 onwards were often in deficit on a month by month basis. A report from the auditors in 1982 suggested, however, that the Union was also losing money because of the way in which it invested its funds. In the short term, surplus in current accounts was now moved to deposit accounts; in the long term a review of all finance and investment was undertaken by the Assistant General Secretary with a view to consolidating assets and to ensuring the basic right of all union employees to a pension.

In recalling her first twelve months in the Union, Padraigín Ní Mhurchú equated the experience to that of 'running a fire brigade — a series of little crises, meeting after meeting, dealing with a very badly serviced membership'. The logistical difficulties inherent in the organisation and day-to-day servicing of members in a small union had, over the years, militated against the IWWU's ability to adapt itself to a changed terrain. While membership in redundant areas of industry inevitably declined, recruitment had not been actively pursued in new areas to offset such losses. In the confidence that financial difficulties could be overcome, either by selling capital assets or by relying on the reassurance from sister unions, a major reassessment of the direction of the Union was begun.

Courses for shop stewards were organised with the assistance of the ICTU and the FWUI. Although the ICTU Education and Training Section organised such courses on behalf of all trade unions affiliated to Congress, the increasing distance of many members of the IWWU from the organisation to which they paid contributions and from which they sought service, prompted other considerations. In-house training served a number of functions and was facilitated both by ICTU and FWUI professional help. The courses were seen as introductory — a preliminary to other courses at Congress level.

Reporting on the response to the first courses for shop stewards and for women in trade unions, Ms Ní Mhurchú pointed to the undoubted advantage in terms of arresting the decline in members' interest.

> The advantage of doing our own course initially is that we get considerable opportunity to explain the structure of the Union, how people are elected and what goes on at the different levels within the Union.[6]

Although the 'major problem' of enlisting the enthusiasms of younger members in the service of the Union remained, the sessions at Fleet Street were seen to 'certainly produce positive results'. Their major intent, however, was to equip shop stewards with the means to deal with the increasingly complex local problems arising in every industry.

By 1981 a number of companies had introduced short time — Ormac, Moore Paragon and Newman's worked a three-day week. At Bailey Gibson the women reported 'major pressure on our members to let Transport men do their work'.[7] The women workers were united in their opposition to such pressure, and in other areas of industry made ready to stake a claim in the future of work.

At Richview Browne and Nolan the introduction of a new Muller Martini Perfect Binding Machine was imminent.[8] The final installation would result in a staff reduction of twenty — all women — based on the assumption by both the management and the IBATU that ten men would operate the new machine. This assumption was challenged, and the IWWU claimed that women could, and would, operate the new machine. Prior to the installation of the new plant at Botanic Road, representatives of all unions involved were to be sent by the company to view the Muller machine in operation in

Oslo. From the IWWU Padraigín Ní Mhurchú and Brigid Fagan, shop steward, joined the contingent.

In Oslo two factories were placed on the itinerary, both of which employed men on the Muller. Undaunted, and armed with the knowledge that women in other companies, including Sandyford Printers, had operated Mullers since 1980, the women returned to Richview Browne and Nolan and persuaded management that women would undertake the work. Despite doubts on the part of management, and disquiet on the part of the men, a trial period of six months was agreed, involving a team of five women and five men. Redundancies were reduced from twenty to nine, and no learners were let go. Those who volunteered to take redundancy were despatched, to the annoyance of management, with the negotiated agreement, plus two and a half times their statutory entitlement under the Act.

In January the trial period began. Two weeks later, IBATU lodged a claim for all jobs. While the women complained that the job was 'too hard', they were urged to take the necessary time to adapt to the new methods. At the Joint Industrial Council for the Printing Industry in March, the IBATU claim was discussed, and IWWU members were reminded that if they refused to do the work, five more jobs would have to go.[9] Despite teething problems, the women persisted, and secured both the right to work the Muller Martini Perfect Binding Machine and a wage increase of £15 per week.

A re-assertion of women's claims to existing jobs and to new areas was reflected in a major recruitment campaign begun in 1982. The intention, as articulated by the Executive and by officials, was to take membership from any quarter as long as this did not breach Congress rules. Major emphases would be put on areas of growth, including part-time and contract workers, with an early focus on contract cleaners and on specific sectors such as solicitors' clerks. The former would prove to be a major success; the latter failed to materialise.

By 1982, despite overall redundancies affecting the entire movement, the Union had gained a new momentum and, having remained until now only to ensure the effective transition of power in the IWWU, Maura Breslin retired as

General Secretary. While Padraigín Ní Mhurchú had served as her Assistant, and had been the instigator of the major drive for new recruits and a new agenda for women workers, the retirement of the General Secretary inevitably forced a number of changes.

For health reasons, Jenny Murray was unwilling to lay a claim to higher office, but assured the Executive and the membership of her continuing service as an official. Padraigín Ní Mhurchú, optimistic despite a hectic twelve months, was nominated for the position of General Secretary of the IWWU. In 1982 at Annual Convention Maura Breslin retired from the Union and Padraigín Ní Mhurchú was elected General Secretary.

Having severed her connections with the FWUI, she took office in uncertain times. At Newman's, one IWWU member had been affected in the latest batch of redundancies, and others were under protective notice; at the Dublin Laundry Co., members were owed money dating back to the beginning of the 1980 National Understanding; De La Rue were on a 3-day week. In the midst of uncertainty, however, new members had been recruited: cleaners at Holy Trinity School in Donaghmede, operatives at Plastic Fabricators, and enquiries had come from 'a company at Sandyford'. Most wage negotiations now included commitments to pursue pension talks, and at Maguire and Paterson's an equality clause had been written into an agreement on pay grading. The new General Secretary called for solidarity and for a commitment from members to the cause of the Irish woman worker.

> It is essential that we all work together to strengthen the union both in terms of our existing performance and in bringing in new members. We believe that there is room for improvement.[10]

In charting new territories, few avenues were left unexplored.

Towards the end of 1982, RTÉ radio and the Gay Byrne radio programme had played host to a chorus of traditional handknitters. All had described massive exploitation of their labour by middlemen, capitalising on their skill, and on their isolation from other workers owing to the nature of their home-based employment. In October 1982, in a quite unprecedented response, handknitters and machine knitters from all over Ireland flocked to the Gresham Hotel for a seminar organised by the producer of the programme, John Cadden, to seek some solutions to the problems of supply, markets, and the organisation of a potentially vast, but widespread, workforce. Amongst contributions from NIHE's Business Faculty in Dublin, the Irish Productivity Centre, and the Irish Cooperative Society, Padraigín Ní Mhurchú represented the trade union movement and concerned herself with the basics. She saluted the skills of the women, but warned that such recognition and the securing of rights would not be automatic: 'No one will give you recognition merely on the grounds of the justice of your cause'. She pointed out that the reticence of the women in regard to taking organisational responsibility was largely related to their isolation. All had voiced their individual concern over tax liabilities, working hours, differing rates of pay: but the negotiation of separate arrangements for them, as for other contract workers, was advantageous only in the short-term. In the long-term, as the women testified, such arrangements led to the undercutting of prices, loss of quality control and exploitation of their skills. She concluded by calling for one rate for the job, a co-operative spirit in any further organisation, stressing the logic for such workers of combining with the trade union movement.[11]

Ms Ní Mhurchú's own enthusiasms were prompted by the potential for organisation represented by 3,000 Irish women workers — women outside the traditional workplace — but nevertheless receptive to the call to combine. In responding some time later, one handknitter acknowledged the relevance of the trade union movement to workers such as herself.

> I feel that it is through your organisation that our hope lies. I approached the idea of unions with the same scepticism as the other people present, but your generosity and the openness of your contribution and that

of your colleagues to our problem has given me restored faith in our community and I feel we can really make this project work.[12]

The IWWU offered information and accommodation; members of the Traditional Handknitters Association used Fleet Street as a meeting place for the period of their existence as an association. Predictably, difficulties arose, but although the prospect of placing further resources in this direction was not promising at this time, the potential for the development of less orthodox organisation projects remained. It marked one of the few areas of optimism when the persistence of the shorter working-week at De La Rue increasingly threatened large-scale redundancies amongst IWWU members.

In the course of a lengthy controversy which ran from 1982 into 1983 the IWWU also adopted a policy on part-time workers, an area not only long considered to have potential for recruitment but also contentious in relation to full-time workers. In effect, the development of this policy arose through force of circumstances when the vulnerability of part-time casual workers could no longer be ignored.

At Sandyford Printers members of the IWWU were employed in tablework and Mullering, producing *The Sunday Tribune*. They were classed as temporary, casual workers and employed on a week to week basis and on Saturday nights. On 11 October 1982 members due in on the evening shift were told they were 'no longer required' as the Mullers were not operating. Management argued that as the machines were no longer being used, the temporary workforce was, in effect, no longer employed. The work involved, however, which was previously done by machine, was now being done by male workers — some casual, most on overtime.

The Union argued that this work belonged to the women and an official picket was placed on the premises. This picket, maintained from seven in the evening until seven in the morning, was passed by the majority of full-time workers, and it was pointed out by the other unions involved that the women were eligible to apply for full-time work where it was available and if they were 'members of the appropriate unions'. In this instance, the limited jobs available were non-casual ITGWU jobs. In short, the women, even to be considered eligible to apply for such work, would have to abandon the IWWU. If they remained casuals, and members of the IWWU, they were unemployed. If they left and joined the ITGWU, they would be preceded by all the men already on the list in the Union Office seeking work and would therefore remain unemployed. Agreement was reached after a strike of three days and three nights and the women were re-instated and paid for the period of the strike.

The victory, however, was brief. Sandyford Printers produced the *The Sunday Tribune* and the short-lived *Daily News*. On 27 October 1982 both titles, owned by Hugh McLoughlin, suspended publication and Sandyford Printers gave protective notice to all employees.

In 1983 the Union resumed the battle for the establishment of their rights. In April *The Sunday Tribune*, now owned by Vincent Browne with various financial backers, was re-launched but was printed outside Dublin. The Union argued that women who had been let go by Sandyford were entitled to employment on the work of printing *The Sunday Tribune*. On its return to a Dublin printer, however, a number of IWWU members who were employed full-time at the new printers, Richview Browne and Nolan, disagreed, as the Saturday evening and night work involved would be lucrative overtime for them.

The members argued that women, who were let go by Sandyford, were entitled to apply for such work in addition to their existing employment: a move which prompted the formulation of policy by the Union in relation to double jobbing and the rights of part-time workers to employment. The IWWU Executive exerted its full authority in defence of part-time, casual employees in relation to full-time workers. Eventually, and despite opposition from within the Union's own ranks, the *Tribune* printing was staffed by the original fifteen IWWU members. The settlement formula provided for fifteen jobs for the ex-Sandyford women and a sixteenth to be rotated between the Richview Browne and Nolan women on an overtime basis.

While the battle to establish the rights of the part-time

workforce was under way, the full-time workforce came under increasing attack. In 1982 the Printers' Section was devastated by a series of redundancies and threatened closures. In February De La Rue had begun a two-day week. Newman's proposed further redundancies, and S.A. Roantree served notice of redundancy, but with some hope of recall. While shop steward Kathleen Monaghan negotiated for worksharing for her members at Newman's, those at Design Print in Waterford and Rutland Ltd and Stephen D in Dublin were closed without notice. All three firms claimed that no money was available for extra redundancy payments beyond the statutory entitlement.

Other sectors were not unaffected by what was now a crisis in the economy. On 28 May the Dublin Laundry Co. closed. In March the Labour Court had recommended that members in this company be paid retrospectively for pay increases and arrears detailed in IWWU claims,[13] and the company cited increased labour costs as being among the factors serving to undermine its business.

Beyond such predictable rhetoric, however, the changing nature of domestic technology had, inevitably, taken its toll. Claiming that 'the increased sophistication of washing machines in domestic use' and 'in house washing facilities in hotels and hospitals' had undermined the established laundries, the financial advisor of the company pointed out to the *Irish Times* that, at the beginning of the 1960s, sixteen general laundries had operated in Dublin, but that by the 1980s, only three were left.[14] The peremptory nature of the closure, however, left members and the Union with no position from which to negotiate. The 30-day notice prescribed by the Protection of Employment Act was covered by members being let go without any notice but paid by post for the required number of weeks stipulated by the Act. In effect the company closed its doors on 28 May while, technically, it ceased operations at the end of June.

The Union protested that such a practice was 'contrary to the spirit and intent of the Act',[15] and began what became a campaign of sorts to have the legislative procedures, so abundantly prepared throughout the 1970s, re-assessed. While charging the Dublin Laundry Company thus, the Union notified Peter Cassells, Chief Legislative Officer of the ICTU. Detailing the nature of the dispute, the Union informed the ICTU that staff had been notified on a Friday evening. By the time the Union had been informed, courtesy of An Post, the closure was a *fait accompli*. Complaints to the Minister had been to no avail as, in effect, the Minister had countenanced such an interpretation. Ms Ní Mhurchú pointed to the implications of such a move:

> I have written back to the Minister contesting this interpretation and in the meanwhile would request that Congress would look into the matter as such an interpretation, if accepted, would render the Act meaningless.[16]

The limitations of such legislation were, over a period, made patently clear.

On Friday 13 August members at Rutland Ltd were similarily served: closure would be effective as of that evening. Again the mandatory 30-day notice requirement was ignored. Other legislative provisions aimed at protecting working people were being similarly flouted. The Minimum Notice and Terms of Employment Act, 1973, in respect of payments due in the event of closure of a company, was ignored. Rutland Ltd claimed insolvency, and all cash reserves had been distributed to 'various competing claims' — all predictably more compelling than those of the workforce.

As members reeled from the distress of closures and redundancies and of finding protective legislation so wanting, the pressures of unemployment throughout the labour movement prompted the abandonment of much solidarity and a tendency towards competitiveness in the depleted market. While many women workers received no compensation for the loss of their employment, others found their jobs under threat from a similarly besieged male workforce. At Bailey and Gibson a dispute raged over breaking out, as management sought a sharing of the process with the ITGWU. The IWWU opposed such threats to traditional demarcation lines, but similar problems of encroachment into the traditional areas of female employment by male workers (without any reciprocity) were apparent in Smurfit Carton, Capital Spicer and Dakota.

With members everywhere rendered permanently insecure through lack of knowledge of the state of their companies, the Union moved to re-assess the lines of communication at the various places of work. At the end of 1981 the General Secretary formalised the procedure instigated by Jenny Murray at De La Rue. A workers' committee was established, comprising four shop stewards and four members from different areas of the factory.[17]

De La Rue was a major employer of women workers. In 1982 the IWWU had 320 members there, or 52% of the total workforce. The work involved was of a high quality: De La Rue supplied banknotes to eighty developing nations which had no State currency presses. Between 1980 and 1981, however, orders fell, and at the end of the year the company wrote to the Dublin Printing Trades' Group suggesting a suspension of talks then in progress on productivity proposals.

> As you are aware we have for the past 6 weeks or so suffered a severe shortage of work in some production areas. . . . I am sure you will agree with me that, with the present shortage of work, and the problems that have arisen from that shortage, a fresh start in the New Year . . . would be more appropriate.[18]

By January the company reported that there had been 'no change in our order book situation' and that the 3-day week would take effect from '06.00 hours, Monday 8 February 1982' ostensibly for six to eight weeks. In March, at a meeting at the FUE, the Unions were notified that short-time would continue until 30 May but that the 'jobs were secure'.[19]

If such reassurance had been effective, it was to be shattered within weeks. On 7 April a notice was posted in the factory in Clonskeagh. All workers were informed that:

> interruption in order input will be of longer duration than was anticipated. . . . Therefore, as required by law, a submission is being served today with the Department of Labour to the effect that we shall reduce the workforce by 242 people, these coming from all areas of the operation.

Although the manner of informing both workforce and

unions was condemned, De La Rue reiterated its statement before the end of the month: the redundancies were not negotiable, 'the market is not available'.

The Union, together with the Dublin Printing Trades' Group, extracted as high a price as they could for the redundant workers. The 160 women who lost their jobs were cushioned temporarily by redundancy payments of five weeks wages for every year of service. Included in these redundancies was Mary Byrne, Honorary Treasurer of the IWWU, a former Chairwoman of the Printers' Committee and a member of the ICTU Womens' Advisory Committee.

In an effort to protect those remaining, the Union moved on two fronts. Notice was served on management that while some disruption, pending rationalisation, was predictable,

> we do not now, and will not accept in the future, that our members can be moved about at will — we expect management to behave in a professional manner in dealing with trade union members.[20]

On behalf of those made redundant, negotiations to update qualifications began. Members were informed that

> AnCO, in conjunction with Bolton Street Tech, are prepared to run a training course, and there is also the possibility of some temporary jobs on a training basis in other houses.

Members were urged to take advantage of the Union facility for unemployed members and to ensure that their names were listed in the Union in the event of employment becoming available.[21]

In the wake of De La Rue and the additional printing women now unemployed, the General Secretary raised serious questions about the position of women in printing. Now a representative of the Union on the AnCO Apprenticeship Working Party, Padraigín Ní Mhurchú staked a claim for sixty IWWU members, whose apprenticeships would be terminated by redundancy, to further training via AnCO. In doing so, she gave voice to her members' concern at the disappearance of women from print. They were now consistently more affected by the slump than were men, and over a twenty-year period women's jobs had shown a steady decline in the industry. The loss of jobs, through the effects of recession and of new technology, had not, however, prompted retraining, and women in the carton industry had been particularly affected.

In 1960 Alex Thom's had employed 200 members of the IWWU. Their jobs no longer existed, and neither did Alex Thom.

> So how many of these 200 workers are still in the industry? Precious few, by all accounts. Presumably, most have returned to housework, a role recommended by the craft traditionalists in the industry.[22]

The temptation to dispose of workers with such a depressingly predictable response to the deepening recession was confined neither to employers nor to the bastions of male labour. Dissent from within the ranks of the IWWU was made disconcertingly public at the first ICTU Women's Conference in February 1983.

In the course of a debate on a resolution seeking protection for the right of married women to work, the President of the IWWU, Rosaleen Bracken, rose to speak. Miss Bracken expressed her support 'with reservations'. She went on to suggest

> that some women do not want to work outside their homes, and they also should have the right to choose and they should not have to work for financial reasons.

While proposing family income supplements as a way of resolving the problem for these women she went on to say

> that most married women <u>do</u> work for financial reasons, but there are an awful lot of women who work, not for financial reasons but for social reasons, for they're bored in their homes and they want to meet people and so on and so forth, and I would think that these ladies, with respect, should be able to find or they should be helped to express themselves otherwise.

A ferocious discussion followed at the Conference with women from north and south coming to the microphone to repudiate such a philosophy.

The General Secretary, at the conclusion, spoke on behalf of the IWWU and assured Conference that the views expressed by Miss Bracken did not represent union policy. At the following IWWU Executive meeting on 2 March, Ms Ní Mhurchú asked the Executive to take action on the matter which was, in effect, 'against the civil rights of 50% of our members'.

In her own defence, Rosaleen Bracken claimed that since the Conference had no policy-making function, as such, she had felt entitled to voice the misgivings of 'a considerable number of members of our Union'. Around the table, competing claims debated the point. Jenny Murray reminded the Executive of the long tradition of married women in the laundries — her own mother, Theresa Behan, a founder member in the Laundries Section of the Union, included. At present, she estimated, two-thirds of this industrial workforce was composed of married women.

A motion asking Miss Bracken to resign her position was passed unanimously. The matter, however, did not rest. At the following meeting in April Miss Bracken continued to defend her position and sought leave to appeal to the judgement of Annual Convention. Such an appeal could not democratically be denied, and, pending a final decision, Rosaleen Bracken remained in office.

In May, Annual Convention opened with the Presidential Address. With the political acuity of the long-time activist, Miss Bracken spoke of the ICTU Women's Conference 'as a great step forward for women in the trade union movement'. She added that discrimination against women by craft unions persisted, and declared her unequivocal support for 'women's right to work and equal opportunities'.

The political wisdom of such an address reaped immediate dividends, but produced a harvest of undoubted bitterness. Lillis Adams, of Newman's, proposed a vote of no confidence in the President in connection with her statement made at the Conference on the rights of married women workers. The Convention discussed the issues for some time, but while criticism was rife, no seconder was forthcoming, and the motion fell. Rosaleen Bracken was replaced as President by Kathleen Monaghan, and defeated in the Vice-Presidential election by Beth Tunney, a De La Rue shop steward in her twenties and the youngest member ever to hold a position of executive authority in the Union. Of the same generation and also elected at the 1983 Convention was Kay Marron, a new shop steward from Smurfit Carton.

The face of the Executive was changing. Kathleen Monaghan, the new President, was a long-serving member of the Union and had been shop steward in Newman's Bindery for some time. A married woman, she had worked most of her married life serving as bread winner for herself and four children. She had wide experience in the printing trade and now approached the task of serving as President during recessionary times with considerable energy and enthusiasm. At its first meeting the new Executive co-opted Clare Bullman, a graduate of the *Sunday Tribune* dispute, to represent unemployed members and Mai Clifford took office as Honorary Treasurer — a position of considerable status within the Union hierarchy and regarded as an honour by the older members.

In the year that followed, Padraigín Ní Mhurchú ensured that members were left in little doubt about Union policy on the seeking of scapegoats for the problems of widespread unemployment. Addressing Convention, she reminded members of the IWWU tradition of protecting 'the right of everyone to a decent job'. She served notice that the former President's sentiments, wherever publicly expressed, would be tolerated from no other quarter.

> Any attempt to suggest that married women should not seek or remain in full time employment must be fought, not just within the Union but within the trade union movement and society generally.[23]

Ms Ní Mhurchú had long championed the rights of women to paid work, regardless of their marital status. She was also of a generation that had seen an increased participation by such women in paid employment and as such had a clear appreciation of the competing claims of the workplace and of the domestic arena, and of the potential for recruitment from their numbers.

Over a period of twenty years the proportion of all women in the Irish workforce had remained relatively stable at 28%. A number of factors, however, had come to alter the composition of that workforce. Since World War II both the marriage rate and the fertility rate of Irish women had been falling. These factors undoubtedly contributed to the largely unexamined increase in the proportion of married women workers from approximately 5% in 1961 to 15% in 1981. Predictions from the National Economic and Social Council [NESC], the Allied Irish Banks' Review, and other sources, suggested that this proportion could grow to 40% in the next twenty years.[25] The changing composition of the female labour force had also been reflected in a rise in the incidence of part-time work and an unquantified increase in the use of contract workers.

The implications of such a trend, if it persisted, had been debated both by the women's movement and by the trade union movement, the combined energies of which were evident in the Women's Committee of Congress. In 1983 this committee issued a document on job and work sharing — a method proposed, from a number of quarters, to meet the needs of women with childcare and domestic responsibilities who favoured a changed structure of their working day. While the document was welcomed by Padraigín Ní Mhurchú, herself a member of the Women's Committee, particularly in relation to its dealing with the political and economic realities of such a formula for change, she sounded a note of caution:

> Unless job sharing/part time work options were availed of equally by male and female workers it is likely to lead to further disadvantage to women in the workforce, in that they are still the workers who readjust their working lives to suit family responsibilities.[26]

The concern to mount a vanguard both in defence of married women at work and of the part-time workforce in general arose from an awareness of the growing numbers of both in the Irish economy. It was prompted in a more immediate sense, however, by the demands of some of the latest recruits to the ranks of the IWWU. The predominantly female, married workforces of Contract Cleaners Ltd, Noonan Building Cleaning Ltd, Professional Contract Cleaners Ltd, Home Counties Contract Cleaners Ltd and Grosvenor Cleaning Ltd — the 'big five' — had been recruited by the Union between 1982 and 1983. Such workers constituted a part-time, 'off-site' workforce. As such, in common with homeworkers, they enjoyed none of the legislative protection, however flawed, which now extended to workers employed at their employers' place of work.

In 1978, when Maura Breslin and Jenny Murray had first encountered cleaners on contract work at the ESB, their wages had been, at most, 86p an hour. For those in other areas, employed at the lower end of the scale, Miss Breslin reported that the rate of pay in many cases was 21p an hour.[27] The use of contract workers at such low rates of pay had clearly served to undermine the position of women employed as cleaners both in the ESB and elsewhere.

In November 1982 the IWWU brought the case of twenty such workers, all members of the IWWU and employed by Contract Cleaners Ltd, to the Labour Court. The company held the contract for cleaning the Bank of Ireland Computer Centre in Cabinteely. Members worked a $17\frac{1}{2}$-hour week, below the 18-hour threshold required for protection under the Unfair Dismissals' Act, the Redundancy Payments' Act, the Minimum Notice Act and the Holidays Employees' Act. They were paid £1.70 an hour. On their behalf the IWWU claimed £2.50 an hour. The Court recommended £1.84 an hour from 1 May, and £2 an hour from 1 October.[28]

The company refused to implement the recommendation, claiming that to do so would immediately render it unable to compete. Members decided unanimously on strike action, and strike notice was served before Christmas. Before the strike came into effect, however, Contract Cleaners Ltd, the employer, withdrew from the contract, leaving the union in somewhat of a dilemma. The Bank, while eschewing all responsibility, sought tenders, and while encouraging the women to tender themselves as a group, which they did, awarded the contract to Noonan Building Cleaners.

The Union responded by placing pickets on the Bank to secure their jobs. The Bank, however, retaliated, arguing that it was not the employer of the women, and secured a court injunction againt the strikers. The injunction was served and the women, all new to trade union membership and activity, were supported by the Union and led by a courageous shop steward, Ann Daly. With considerable spirit they declared themselves willing to eat Christmas dinner in Mountjoy Jail rather than accept defeat. The Bank and Noonans, under the weight of potentially very public pressure, negotiated. Jobs were offered to all women, and accepted, at £1.90 an hour.

With business thus despatched, a new generation of 'obstreperous lassies' returned home for Christmas dinner.

By 1983 the IWWU conceded that the use of normal collective bargaining procedure on behalf of these members was insufficient. The problems inherent in this new workforce ensured that if wage increases threatened to undermine profitability, employers could withdraw from a contract and thus effectively, and legally, end their obligation to their workforce. Alternatively, companies willing to pay increases could be undercut by those paying lower wages. In association with the ICTU, the Union moved to challenge the threshold on working hours and to seek to extend the protection of a wide range of legislation to part-time contract workers.[29] In addition they called on the Minister for Labour, Liam Kavanagh, to consider the establishment of a Joint Labour Committee to secure basic rates and conditions in the industry.[30] In the short-term the Union joined forces with the ITGWU and the FWUI to negate, in relation to the contract cleaning companies, a long familiar employer tactic — that of divide and rule. Negotiations began with the 'Big Five' to settle an agreed rate.

In the face of strike notice from the three Unions for all their members in Dublin a rate of £2.20 an hour for members who received transport to their place of work, and £2.30 for those who did not, was agreed and in return the Unions agreed to use their industrial muscle, wherever possible, to discourage the use of non-union contract labour. The proposal from the unions to move towards the establishment of a JLC, was opposed by the FUE, who continued their opposition until the JLC, despite their objections, was established by the Labour Court. A tacit agreement obtained from the 'Big Five' however, involved their distancing themselves from the FUE position by effectively absenting themselves from the relevant discussions.[31] When the JLC was eventually established in 1985 the then Minister for Labour, Ruairí Quinn, gave full acknowledgement to the IWWU for its major contribution in securing this protective machinery for the contract cleaning industry.[32]

The case of the contract cleaners demonstrated the growing IWWU support for contract, part-time low-paid women workers. By 1984, however, the IWWU had noted the development of contracts of a different kind in the laundry industry. In a newsletter to all members the General Secretary gave an account of the developments in this industry throughout the year. Major problems were involved in negotiations in the HJSB laundry 'where management intended cutting the workforce, displacing the evening shift and introducing a "rationalised structure"'. The problems of serving the needs of IWWU members were particularly evident where depletion of orders was related to the practice now evident in a number of hospitals.

> Many hospitals are contracting out work to non-union laundries which are run on the basis of exploiting labour, mostly female labour.[33]

The wheel had come full circle.

CHAPTER 21

Postscript

The 1980s promised, or threatened, profound change in the position of working women. In 1982 the twenty-second round wage negotiations saw developments within the Irish Printing Federation and the beginnings of moves by employers to implement the interchangeability clause of the equal pay agreement. In the same year the ban on nightwork for women was lifted. The Executive Council of Congress made a number of recommendations to affiliated unions, including a request that

> the arrangements for nightwork should take into account the family responsibilities of workers — in particular arrangements for childcare services.[1]

The Congress had taken care to note that family responsibilities impinged on the lives of all workers.

At the ICTU Women's Conference in February 1983, however, the continuing reality of women bearing the major responsibility for childcare and matters domestic had injected a note of caution into the debate about rights for part-time workers. The Association of Scientific, Technical and Managerial Staffs [ASTMS] had sought the adoption of a positive policy on part-time work. From the IWWU delegation, which included married women workers and a part-time worker as an observer, came a reference to the 'undoubted pressure' now exerted on married women to take part-time work to facilitate domestic responsibilities. While supportive of positive moves to establish rights for such workers, the Irish Women Workers' Union mounted a convincing argument that pressure had to be brought on employers to provide childcare facilities at the place of work.

Amongst employers the disposition towards equality for women workers was somewhat jaundiced. From many came the promotion of 'extras' and the bonus system — accessible in reality to few women — ensuring that equal pay would retain its status as a mythical concept. The legislation had been found wanting, and at the Women's Conference also a resolution from the IWWU called on Congress to contest the 'traditional opinion of job value', to review cumbersome procedures and to debunk the reliance on the 'hypothetical man' in facilitating equal pay claims. From both the IWWU and the Conference as a whole came a reaffirmation of the conviction that full employment equality would be won only when 'the segregation of jobs on the basis of sex is fought and won by the unions'.

In 1982 the IWWU had lodged a claim for equal pay under the Anti-Discrimination (Pay) Act for twenty-nine women workers employed in the Post Office Factory. The women were engaged in 'dismantling, cleaning and reassembling telephones and related apparatus, cutting and sewing materials for mailbags, toolbags, flags, etc, and in engraving objects, such as medals and switchboard facings'. They claimed equal pay with a male worker graded as a labourer, who was involved in 'cleaning, collecting and delivering various items, lending general assistance'. The subsequent investigation and conclusions of the Equality Officer resulted in a recommendation that the women's work was 'higher in value' than the male's work and, hence, not 'equal.' It was thus ineligible for equal pay in accordance with the legislation.

This recommendation, and the subsequent unsuccessful appeal to the Labour Court, demonstrated very clearly and publicly the distinct gap between the reality for women workers seeking equal pay with men and the intricate and technical machinery that had evolved to cope with an essentially simple, though costly, issue.

This case was to become a landmark case as it was later appealed to the High Court unsuccessfully and then, as the Bord Telecom case, with success, to the European Court of Justice in Luxembourg. The Court of Justice ruled the Equality Officers' decision to be contrary to the terms of

Article 119 of the Treaty of Rome. However, the basic claim for equal pay was in 1988 unresolved and awaited a Labour Court Determination following the clarification from the European Court.

The increasingly Byzantine world of the equality legislation provided a somewhat inappropriate backdrop to the largely cost-benefit analysis which was by 1983 forced upon the officers of the IWWU. If cost cutting exercises were in vogue, the IWWU was immune neither to the necessity for, nor the unpalatable results of, their implementation. By 1982 Mrs Dignan, the 'Finance Department' of the IWWU, had retired on reaching sixty-five. Brenda Doyle, initially employed as a clerical assistant and several years on the Union staff carrying out many and varied office duties, was introduced to the art of keeping and, when possible, balancing the Union books.

It is difficult for participants in the final chapter in the life of the Union as an independent entity to identify precisely when it became clear that the continuation of the IWWU as such was no longer in the interests of its members. Padraigín Ní Mhurchú felt that such a moment came in late 1982 or early 1983.

> My feeling was, we weren't delivering a service. We were, in the sense that if somebody rang up and said, we have a problem, somebody would go out . . . but we were reacting, we were not standing back, we weren't developing policy. We didn't have the resources to do so.[2]

The members also felt the lack of a sound base from which to mount their claims in an increasingly hostile working climate. The state of the Union was discussed at the Executive, but, more pertinently at this stage, between and after meetings, and wherever members of the IWWU came together. It was conceded with regret, but in recognition of the necessity to provide women workers with the institutional backing they now required in order to retain and expand their rights in the workplace, that there was no longer a basis for the continuation of the IWWU.

At Annual Convention in 1983 members were informed that the finances of the IWWU over the past year had shown 'an alarming increase in expenditure'. Income had continued to decline. On a resolution from the Executive, and with a reluctant concession to reality, the delegates agreed to 'hold talks with interested unions with a view to rationalising our own position in the trade union movement.'[3]

The moment for amalgamation was considered to be opportune.

> At present we could do an honourable deal with another union without dismissing the history of the IWWU and with our heads held high.[4]

The Executive, in considering the decision, set up an amalgamation sub-committee of officers and trustees to meet the relevant 'interested' unions and to report back.

Specific criteria were given to the sub-committee as a basis for further negotiation. These involved the stipulations of:
- Staying together as a separate unit.
- Executive representation in the new Union.
- As good a service, or better, to members.
- Staff security.

Four unions, The Federated Workers' Union of Ireland, Irish Printers' Union, Irish Transport and General Workers' Union and Irish Union of Distributive Workers and Clerks were all approached and meetings sought. All responded positively. Between May and October 1983, meetings took place with the four Unions and the amalgamated sub-committee while normal business and wage negotiations, rationalisation programmes and recruitment, mostly of contract cleaners, continued.

At the 1983 ICTU Conference in Cork a move forward for women within the trade union structures was made. A resolution calling for reserved seats for women tabled by the National Union of Public Employees [NUPE] and supported by the IWWU was carried by a small number of votes. This was the result of a four-year campaign for greater representation of women in the trade union movement initiated in 1980 by NUPE at the Belfast Conference and tabled in alternate years since then by either IWWU or NUPE. The Women's Conference had been established in 1983 as a result of this campaign and now the ICTU Executive Council itself would have two extra seats reserved for women members to be elected separately from the general panel but with full executive status. Such a move was controversial, with allegations of 'discrimination' in favour of women being made. It was, however, considered essential by the women who campaigned for it in the face of evidence that on only two occasions since 1959 had a woman been elected to the ICTU Executive — Maura Breslin in 1973 and Inez McCormack of NUPE in 1980.

While such victories were important to women and to the trade union movement itself, at Fleet St the day-to-day reality of survival in the climate of the 1980s was more pressing. By mid-1983 Jenny Murray had signalled her intention of resigning by the end of the year. As the last of the old school of IWWU officials, her quiet and conscientious diplomacy had averted numerous disputes. Jenny Murray's commitment to the cause of labour had also found her, when necessary, at the forefront of many of its battles, and her absence was immediately felt. The continuing widespread threat of redundancies, however, ensured that a replacement could not, in financial terms, be sustained. Padraigín Ní Mhurchú had the unenviable distinction of becoming, in the seventy-second year of the IWWU's existence, its sole official.

Since the redundancies in 1982 an uneasy peace had prevailed at De La Rue. A new managing director had been installed by the British head office to effect the 1982 redundancy package. Efforts were renewed by the Union in early 1983 to establish clear written procedures on general conditions of employment. The productivity claim of the IWWU, postponed in early 1982 was also re-activated — a claim which sought to re-establish pay parity with ITGWU members, referred to as 'the men', whose basic wage had been increased by 14%. Throughout the months of 1983 discussions took place and correspondence exchanged on the standard minute values used to calculate bonuses and the Union's view of the value of the resultant increased productivity in the different departments — the Union claiming 14%

and the Company arguing the merits and demerits of the method of arriving at these figures.

> The Company responded to the union's claim by putting forward much tightened work study values, in effect offering parity in basic rates, by transferring the money from bonus.[5]

While no tangible progress was made on the claim, normal relations appeared to be restored.

The insecurity felt by the workforce was, however, evident in mid-1983 when a small group of maintenance staff took unofficial action. Shop stewards from all the unions sought the immediate intervention of the Dublin Printing Trades' Group [DPTG], to resolve the problem, rather than risk a lengthy dispute.

However, such efforts were lost on the management of Thomas De La Rue Ltd. On 6 October, without prior discussion, notice of closure was issued to the Unions. During the bitter talks which followed, management in Britain complained of absenteeism, a depressed level of demand, and 'poor labour relations'. The latter claim, appearing in a report in *The Guardian,* provoked angry recrimination, and a demand from the DPTG for a withdrawal.

The DPTG publicly condemned the manner in which Thomas De La Rue management had handled this whole matter both from an industrial relations and legal perspective. A claim was made that the company had sufficient accumulated wealth, having a group profit of £31.6 million the previous year, to survive the recession and that staff at the Dublin plant should be maintained. The call was echoed by Ruairí Quinn, Minister of State at the Department of the Environment. While acknowledging that all western democracies, and many companies, were experiencing difficulties, he suggested that

> these difficulties should not be the basis to excuse a company for arbitrarily deciding to close a major printing plant without having regard to the welfare of all the workforce or indeed recognising the proper process of communication and consultation.[6]

Protest was unheeded, despite representations to Government, the Industrial Development Authority [IDA], who had grant-aided the company, and direct talks with British head office.

The ICTU were again approached to record both their own and the Group of Unions' concern at the flaunting of the Protection of Employment Act, which required that prior notice of intention to close be given together with the right of consultation before proceeding. By 25 October, having sought through all the normal consultative and legislative procedures open to them to stop, or at least delay, the proposed closure, the Unions met 'to hear the company's offer'.

The process of negotiation on redundancy payments began. The IWWU lost a total of 320 members and was devastated. Before Christmas the General Secretary sent a circular to all women at De La Rue, urging them to continue their association with Fleet Street.

> The Union wishes you to retain your membership of the Union as an unemployed member. The costs are one penny (Yes, 1p!) per week.[7]

At Thomas De La Rue, meanwhile, matters global proceeded apace. Should redundant members consider expanding their horizons, in September *The Straits Times* of Singapore had advertised vacancies. The Far Eastern branch of De La Rue sought the service of printers, and an Effluent Treatment Operator.

On 1 October 1983 the IWWU Executive met to consider a comprehensive report from the amalgamation's sub-committee. All four unions had been met and the requirements of the IWWU put to them. While the loyalties of the various members of the Executive and, indeed, the officers, differed even within the IWWU itself, a consensus emerged after a day-long discussion. The FWUI and the IUDWC were perceived as being the most willing to meet the IWWU agenda of a separate unit, executive representation, service to members and security of staff'.

The IUDWC, while an attractive proposition in terms of

autonomy and image, had no involvement in the traditional IWWU spheres of influence and, in the course of deliberations, did not present as a rational first choice. Given the extent of a common history, and closer working relationships in the more recent past, it was decided at a formal Executive meeting on 26 October 'to negotiate to finality for a mutually acceptable agreement with the FWUI'.

The history of the IWWU was inextricably linked with that of the FWUI and the ITGWU. All three unions, despite the political battles intrinsic to any combining of interests, shared the legacy of Larkin and of Connolly. In its infancy, the IWWU had survived the years of the Lock-Out under the guidance of Delia Larkin, Helena Molony and James Connolly. In its later years it had engaged in serious disputes, both with craft and with general unions, and had survived skirmishes with each of the unions eventually considered in relation to a possible merger and combining of interests.

The IWWU in recent years, however, had moved closer to the FWUI and had received considerable moral support from that union during Padraigín Ní Mhurchú's period of office. Soundings had in fact taken place, formally and otherwise for over fifteen years, on the possibility and desirability of uniting part of the legacy of the Larkin tradition by an amalgamation of the IWWU with the FWUI.

On a mandate from the Executive, the General Secretary, the President, the Honorary Treasurer, and a representative of the Trustees, began to negotiate an agreement. The preliminary talks earlier in the year had been led for the FWUI by Paddy Cardiff whose mother, Catherine Maguire, had been a member of the IWWU in Dunlop's Laundry. Mr Cardiff, when General Secretary, had made the FWUI's position very clear: they were interested in an honourable merger, sought no profit out of same and proposed that any surplus funds be used to benefit the IWWU members in a manner to be agreed.[8] The FWUI delegation was now led by Billy Attley who had replaced Paddy Cardiff as General Secretary.

Between December 1983 and March 1984 the talks continued and letters were exchanged on such issues as executive representation, branch organisation staff pensions and security and the disposal or otherwise of the IWWU premises at 48 Fleet St. Many meetings, formal and informal, were held between the two unions on the broad principles of the merger proposal. When this stage was completed, details concerning staff and premises, and precise arrangement for executive representation were the subject of further discussion between the general Secretaries, before either Executive could agree formal proposals.

In February 1984 Maura Breslin, the former General Secretary of the IWWU, died. The trade union movement paid its respect to her and Paddy Cardiff, President of the ICTU, in a graveside oration, spoke of her long and loyal service to the IWWU as General Secretary for twelve years and as President for many years before, serving with such, by now, legendary names as Bennett, Chenevix and Molony.

In one of her last public contributions to the debate on the position of women in trade unions, Maura signalled her support for the need for internal change:

> All unions affiliated to Congress should be prepared, if they are sincere about according equality to men and women, to set up study groups of women and men, from within their own membership to determine the policies to be pursued with a view to convincing all male members — and indeed, some women members too – to review and revise their opposition to their women members' equal right, from the shopfloor level up to the Union, Executive Committee and Congress levels, and to translate these policies into active reality.[9]

As one era drew to its close, another began for women workers as a clearer package of proposals emerged from the FWUI. These included provisions that the IWWU would be a branch of the FWUI; that one Executive member and one Trustee from the IWWU would secure a position on the Executive of the FWUI for a fixed period to be negotiated; and that the General Secretary of the IWWU would become the Branch Secretary of the Women Workers' Branch of the FWUI. Provision would be made for other staff, and for the honouring of pension arrangements, ensuring in particular that 'Ms Murray's service to the Union would be fully recognised'. The IWWU would dispose of its major asset — 48 Fleet Street — but with the clear assurance that the FWUI

> do not wish to make a financial gain resulting from this merger, rather to restore a historical link between our respective unions.

The IWWU responded positively, endorsing the proposals and reaffirming the desire to formally re-establish the historical link between the two unions.

Padraigín Ní Mhurchú acknowledged the 'courtesy and assistance' of Billy Attley, General Secretary of the FWUI, in 'these sometimes delicate talks', and reported that

> I am, and our Executive are, confident that the Larkinite tradition of democratic trade unionism upon which both trade unions were founded will ensure the successful outcome of these talks.[10]

Delia Larkin, in the misty past of the IWWU's chequered history, no doubt would have permitted herself a wry smile.

In March 1984 all IWWU members received a newsletter from the General Secretary giving details of the proposed amalgamation. The letter had been prompted by inaccurate newspaper reports relating to the discussions between the two unions. Such disquiet at the degree of change was further reinforced by a request from the FWUI that Padraigín Ní Mhurchú accept their nomination to fill a vacancy arising at the Labour Court as a workers' representative. Between settling disputes on overtime at the Sunday Tribune and opposing lay-offs at the HJSB, the members of the Executive 'expressed concern at the difficulties this might create'.

By the following meeting, the ICTU having added its weight to the FWUI nomination, Padraigín Ní Mhurchú's appointment to the Labour Court became assured. The popularity of the choice outside the Union was self-evident. While the Irish Federation of University Teachers wished Ms Ní Mhurchú 'every success', they entered 'just one plea: be merciful'. From the NUTGW came the assurance that 'the workers will have a "friend at Court"', and, in a letter from Donal Nevin, a historical note was sounded

> Apart from my personal pleasure at your being nominated, I am especially pleased that at last, after almost 40 years, there is a woman member of the Labour Court.[11]

At Fleet Street, members of the Executive were reassured that the nomination of their General Secretary to the Labour Court would not adversely affect the procedure of amalgamation.

On 26 April the General Secretary had written to the FWUI detailing new provisions to cover the effect of her appointment to the Labour Court. The provisions called for the secondment of Janet Hughes, Assistant Branch Official of the FWUI, prominent member of the Women's Committee of Congress, and feminist, to the IWWU, 'to become Branch Secretary on transfer'. In addition to the existing agreement, a Benevolent Fund named in honour of Maura Breslin was to be set up, drawing on surplus funds on closing the IWWU books and disposing of the premises 'to help retired members and to fund research into the history of the Union'.

On 30 April the Executive unanimously recommended the acceptance by members of the Transfer of Engagements. At the AGM on 2 May the last President of the Irish Women Workers' Union, Kathleen Monaghan, welcomed delegates to the Convention at Fleet Street. Following the introduction by Padraigín Ní Mhurchú, Mr Billy Attley, General Secretary of the Federated Workers' Union of Ireland, was invited to address Convention.

In his first address to members of the IWWU Mr Attley reminded them of the historical links between the two unions — a link which not only focused on the Larkins but which had also endured over the years in a spirit of comradeship and solidarity. He welcomed the amalgamation as both desirable in itself and a necessary rationalisation of resources and potential for the trade union movement overall, now facing the most serious threat in its history. He called for solidarity, reassuring women workers that a merger with the larger union need not diminish their contribution and would undoubtedly be mutually productive. Officials of both unions had negotiated on their behalf, the focus of their concerns being the servicing and advancing of the women workers of Ireland.

Padraigín Ní Mhurchú gave a detailed report on the series of meetings which had culminated in the document which was now before members. The minutes of the final AGM of the IWWU record that '. . . members seemed pleased about the merger'. Delegates were asked to take ballot papers to their members, to encourage voting, and to await, with others, the decision of the rank and file of the IWWU. On 21 May, under 'Legal Notices', readers of *The Irish Independent* were informed that voting by tally would proceed, and on 15 June the results were publicly announced.

Out of a valid poll of 1,268, the response of members was unequivocal: 1,086 had voted in favour of the Transfer of Engagements of the Irish Women Workers' Union [IWWU] to the Federated Workers' Union of Ireland [FWWU] and 182 had voted against it.

In August plans were laid for a celebration of the merger. The FWUI offered to cover the cost of the nuptials. The IWWU, long a champion of the economic independence of women workers, proposed, however, that the cost be divided equally. It was a celebration but had the intimations of a wake: the first and only all-women's union in Ireland was laid, in its own fashion, to rest.

A number of formalities remained. In September 1984 notice was 'hereby given' by the Registrar of Friendly Societies that registration of the Irish Women Workers' Union would be cancelled 'unless cause can be shown to the contrary in the meantime'. No protest was forthcoming, and this being so,

> The grounds of our proposed cancelling is that the Trade Union has transferred its engagements to the Federated Workers Union of Ireland . . . and has thus ceased to exist.[12]

On 1 September 1984 the amalgamation came into effect.

After seventy-three years of honourable struggle, the Irish Women Workers' Union, changing its banner, proclaimed its allegiance to the movement, and continued its march.

Notes

CHAPTER 1 (pp. 1-20)

1. L.M. Cullen, *Life in Ireland*, London 1968, especially chapter 7, Post-Famine Ireland.
2. Charles McCarthy, *Trade Unions in Ireland 1894-1960*, Dublin 1977.
3. *The Employment of Women*. Report by Miss Orme and Miss Abraham (Assistant Commissioners) on The Conditions of Women's Work in Ireland, Royal Commission on Labour 1893-94, National Library of Ireland. See also Factories and Workshops Annual Report (1907): Truck and Gombeening in Donegal by Miss Martindale.
4. Cullen, *Life*, 168.
5. Dermot Keogh, *The Rise of the Irish Working Class*, Belfast 1982, 180.
6. *Trade Unions in Ireland, History 1790s-1970s*, Local Government and Public Services' Union Handbook, Dublin 1985.
7. Letter, William O'Brien to *The Irish Times*, 1 May 1955. This letter refuted the claim that two women were directed by the Trades Union Congress in Sligo in 1917 to organise women. In 1918 William O'Brien became a member of the Executive of the Transport Union, and succeeded in securing a re-interpretation of Rule 5, so that 'person' would be read as 'man or woman'.
8. See n. 6 above, 30-33.
9. See IWWU Executive Minutes 23 October 1919, in reference to a meeting with the Executive of the Typographical Society: 'They said they did not wish to take the girls into this Society at all. They got 80 signed applications asking the Typographical Society to take members over. Mrs Kelly said 'the Typographical Society should not have encouraged our members by giving them a room for their meetings', IWWU Archives, 48 Fleet Street.
10. Many women entered the workforce under specific terms: apprentices were often, by the terms of their indenture, forbidden to join trade unions without the express consent of their employer. Such restrictions were in force as late as 1959. In that year the proposed indenture between Mrs R.T. O'Neill, dressmaker of 4 St John's Square, in the City of Limerick, of the first part, and Margaret Sheehan of Nolan's Cottages, Limerick (hereinafter called the apprentice) of the second part, was explicit. In return for Mrs O'Neill's agreeing to 'during the said term to the best of her power, knowledge and ability instruct or cause to be instructed the said apprentice in the trade or business of dressmaker', Margaret Sheehan 'shall in all things conduct, acquit herself as an honest and faithful Apprentice ought to do and shall not join or become a member of any Trade Union, Society, or Combination during the existence of this Indenture without the consent in writing of the said Rose T. O'Neill'.
11. *The Irish Worker*, Women Workers' Column, 'M.L.U.', Saturday 14 October 1911.
12. *Ibid*. Letterbox, ref. 'Women Brought in to Take Men's Places', Saturday 24 June 1911.
13. *Ibid*. Women Workers' Column, 30 September 1911.

14. *Ibid.* Women Workers' Column, 9 September 1911.
15. The IWWU became an autonomous body in 1917. See p.24.
16. *The Irish Worker*, Women Workers' Column, see nn. 13 and 14 above.
17. Reported in *The Irish Worker*, 17 February 1912. The Act came into force in England on 11 March 1912.
18. *The Irish Worker*, Women Workers' Column, 9 March 1912.
19. The first practice for the Irish Workers' Choir was held in the Antient Concert Rooms on Thursday 1 February 1912.
20. 'Years of Tension', unpublished manuscript by Helena Molony in the Hugh O'Connor Private Collection. These memoirs were probably begun in response to a letter from the Bureau of Military History to Helena Molony on 21 May 1948. It noted, 'in view of your close association with the Rising and with the developments which led to it, the Director is anxious to get from you, for historic record, your story of the events of that period'. See also R.M. Fox on dismissals in *History of the Irish Citizen Army*, Dublin 1946, and the Women Workers' Column, 24 May 1913.
21. *The Irish Worker*, Women Workers' Column, report from the UK, May 1914.
22. See S. Cody, J. O'Dowd, and P. Rigney, *The Parliament of Labour: 100 Years of the Dublin Council of Trade Unions,* Dublin 1986, 95-106; also Keogh, *The Rise*, chapter 8.
23. ITGWU minute-book, 1914-1916, MS 7298, National Library of Ireland.
24. See R.M. Fox, *The History of the Irish Citizen Army,* Dublin 1946.
25. A revolutionary women's organisation founded in 1900 by Maud Gonne McBride with Countess Markievicz and Francis Sheehy Skeffington; was instrumental in preventing a Loyal Address to Queen Victoria on her visit to Dublin in 1900; produced a magazine in 1908, *Bean na hÉireann,* with Helena Molony as editor; was absorbed by Cumann na mBan in 1913.
26. A monthly magazine. See n. 25 above.
27. Undated and untitled newspaper clipping, Hugh O'Connor Collection.
28. O'Connor Collection, typescript by Helena Molony recalling the influence of Connolly following the collapse of the IWWU after 1913.
29. *Ibid.*
30. *Manifesto: Linen Slaves of Belfast 1913,* Irish Textile Workers' Union (Textile Section IWWU) 1913, Ulster Museum.
31. *The Irish Citizen,* 20 November 1915.
32. *Ibid.*, 172.
33. *Ibid.*, 171.
34. Section 5 of the first Constitution of the Irish Citizen Army stated that members of the Army had to be members of the relevant union. See Fox, *History*, 64.
35. 'Years of Tension'. This episode is also referred to by R.M. Fox in *History* but Fox refers to the publication being *The Gael*, rather than *The Irish Worker*.
36. Founded in Dublin in November 1913 it became the women's division

of the Irish Volunteers founded at the same time. It succeeded Inghinidhe na hÉireann. See n. 25 above.
37. Résumé by General Sir John Maxwell ICCB, General Officer Commanding the Forces in Ireland, of books and documents seized by the military at 2 Dawson Street and Liberty Hall on 11 May 1916.
38. In a draft copy of 'Years of Tension', Helena Molony gives some account of the disappearance of James Connolly when he was apparently held by the Volunteers in January 1916. Although Connolly remained silent on detail he referred to his belief that 'I converted my captors'.
39. Chief Secretary's Office, Dublin Castle. This refers to documents seized from both Liberty Hall and 2 Dawson Street (headquarters of the Irish Volunteers and Cumann na mBan). The documents from Dawson Street were apparently destroyed, but no reference is made to the fate of the documents from Liberty Hall, which undoubtedly included papers relating to these years of the IWWU.

CHAPTER 2 (pp. 21-31)

1. Sheila Greene, second instalment of the life story of Louie Bennett, General Secretary of the IWWU, *Reynold's News*, undated, but probably the 1950s.
2. Notably an unsigned article in *The Irish Times*, 29 April 1955, in reference to the events of August 1916, and an article in *The Irish Press*, 'Profile of Louie Bennett' by Ann Daly, 2 May 1955.
3. Report of the 22nd Annual Irish Trades Union Congress and Labour Party, Sligo, 1916, 51.
4. *Ibid.*, 63.
5. William O'Brien, letter to *The Irish Times*, 1 May 1955.
6. *Ibid.*
7. Registrar of Friendly Societies. Although the Union was not registered until 1918 the registrar's information on membership for the previous year indicates that membership was 2,300.
8. Report of the International Congress of Women, Zurich, 1919, ILO publication, Geneva, 1920, IWWU Archives.
9. Committee on Reconstruction of the Viceroy's Executive Council, Memorandum by Sir Thomas Stafford and Mr Frank Brook, 20 November 1918, French Papers, Imperial War Museum, London.
10. Memorandum on Reconstruction and Development, Mr MacCartney Filgate, 1918, for the Committee on Reconstruction of the Viceroy's Executive Council, French Papers, Imperial War Museum, London.
11. IWWU to Wm. & M. Taylor, Tobacco, Cigarette and Snuff Manufacturers, 2 April 1918.
12. Leinster Laundries Association to IWWU, 18 September 1918.
13. Hotel workers' dispute, minutes, Dublin Trades' Council, 23 September 1918, recorded in *The Saturday Post*.
14. Delia Larkin File, IWWU Archives.
15. Letter, Helena Molony to IWWU Executive, Executive Minutes, 9 July 1936.

16. Delia Larkin File, IWWU Archives.
17. Minutes of Dublin Trades' Council recorded in *The Saturday Evening Post*, 23 September 1918. See MS 12780, National Library of Ireland.

CHAPTER 3 (pp. 32-43)

1. See S. Cody, J. O'Dowd, and P. Rigney, *The Parliament of Labour: 100 Years of the Dublin Council of Trade Unions*, Dublin 1986.
2. *Ibid.*, 130. In 1921 the IWWU affiliated to the rival grouping.
3. IWWU Excecutive Minutes 19 June 1919
4. See Charles McCarthy, *Trade Unions in Ireland 1894-1960*, Dublin 1977.
5. Miscellaneous documentation 1919, IWWU Archives.
6. IWWU Executive Minutes 9 October 1919.
7. Registrar of Friendly Societies. Record of Union membership 1918: 5,300; 1919: 3,425.
8. On 7 February 1919, the ITGWU wrote to the IWWU with reference to a number of women who had carried on a branch or section of the IWWU 'in this Hall'. 'They say that no money has been sent to your office during 1918 and the women are not favourable to joining up with the Irish Women Workers' Union but wish to continue in our premises and link up with this union.' About 115 women were involved.
9. IWWU Executive Minutes 30 October 1919.
10. See McCarthy, *Trade Unions*, the Annual Meeting of the Irish Labour Party and Trades Union Congress in Drogheda, August 1919, and reference to 'the drive for a specifically Irish OBU', 46.
11. Rules of the IWWU 1920: 'The Irish Nurses' Union, the Domestic Workers' Union, and similar sections of the IWWU which cannot be classified as industrial, shall be independent organisations as to the administration of all their affairs, except finance. Their financial relations with the IWWU shall be decided by agreement with the Executive according to circumstances.'
12. IWWU Executive Minutes 10 December 1919
13. Reported in *The Waterford Evening Star*, Saturday 11 September 1919.
14. *Ibid.*
15. Undated cutting from *Reynold's News* Profile: 'The Grand Old Lady of Irish Trade Unions'. Series of articles on the life story of Louie Bennett by Sheila Green, Manning Collection.
16. IWWU Executive Minutes 18 December 1919.

CHAPTER 4 (pp. 44-53)

1. Miss Kelly, Lismore, Co. Down, letter to the IWWU 27 May 1919.
2. Rules of the IWWU, Dublin 1920.
3. Oral history: May Bannon, boxmaker, born 1902, worked from the age of 14 and retired in 1985 aged 83.
4. The Truck Act Amendment Act of 1887 forbade the practice, particularly common where outwork was distributed by middlemen, of deal-

ings based on 'payment in kind', either groceries from a store also owned by the middleman or some other non-cash payment. See, for instance, Factories and Workshops: Annual Report for 1907, Appendix IV; also Patrick MacGill, *The Rat Pit,* London 1915.
5. See for example the series of letters between the Union and Alex Thom & Co., August 1920.
6. Handwritten reference certifying that Helena Molony was available for special service as a member of the Irish Citizen Army from 1916 to 1923, reference by P. Ní Dhroim, old ICA, South Co. Dublin, 4 April 1937 (O'Connor Collection).
7. *Reynold's News,* series of articles on Miss Bennett by Sheila Greene, undated but probably 1950s (Manning Collection).
8. IWWU Executive Minutes April 1920.
9. Reported in *The Irish Citizen* 20 February 1920, 69-70.
10. *Ibid.,* February 1917.
11. *Ibid.,* June-July 1920.
12. *Ibid.*
13. Self-description in *The Irish Citizen.*
14. *Ibid.,* May-June 1920, 93.
15. *Ibid.,* January 1920, 58.
16. *Ibid.* The series in question began in November 1919 and ended in January 1920.
17. Letter, Louie Bennett to Town Clerk, City Hall, Dublin, 6 May 1924.
18. As reported in *The Saturday Post;* see minutes of Dublin Corporation, 19-20 May 1924.
19. Letter, Louie Bennett to Mr Robertson, Alex Thom & Co., 18 December 1922.
20. Letter, Messrs Alex Thom to IWWU, 15 March 1923.

CHAPTER 5 (pp. 54-69)

1. *The Irish Citizen,* April-May 1920, 85.
2. *Ibid.*
3. The General Strike was urged by the Congress for the day before the re-convening of the Dáil as a protest against increasing militarism.
4. IWWU Executive Minutes 23 November 1922; also special meeting December 1922.
5. *Ibid.,* 15 June 1922.
6. *Ibid.,* 8 December 1921.
7. Letter, Louie Bennett to Minister for Industry and Commerce, Provisional Government, 1 December 1922.
8. Memorandum: Employment for Women, from the IWWU to the Minister for Industry and Commerce, November 1922.
9. *Ibid.*
10. Letter, Minister of Industry and Commerce to Minister of Finance, 6 January 1923.
11. Inter-Departmental Minutes referring to above letter and proposal, Ministry of Finance to Ministry of Industry and Commerce, 9 January 1923.

12. Letter, Minister of Finance to Minister of Industry and Commerce, 10 January 1923.
13. IWWU Executive Minutes 14 December 1922.
14. The Irish Women's Labour Council was based at Fleet Street. Its President was Louie Bennett, Treasurer M. Burke-Dowling, and Joint Secretaries Helena Molony and Sighle Bowen. Although the activities of the new committee were indicative of a formal move beyond the industrial arena, the Irish Women's Labour Council worked with the Labour Party. The IWWU, until politically affiliated, could not, constitutionally, work with a politically aligned group such as this.
15. The IWWU suggested the formation of this Guild, based initially on the prayer-book and rosary bead industries. 'The Guild would be formed of all concerned in the industries, managers, technicians, artists, crasftsmen, clerical and industrial workers. The idea of profit for individuals would be eliminated: all would work for salaries or wages based on a fair standard of living, and graduated according to the education or skill demanded for each branch of the work'.
16. Annual Report of the IWWU 1924.
17. Roneo letter to all affiliated unions of Congress, July 1924.
18. Statement prepared by the IWWU Executive to be read to the Thirteenth Annual Meeting of the Irish Labour Party and Trades Union Congress. 1924.
19. *Ibid*.
20. Report of the Proceedings of the Thirteenth Annual Congress of the Irish Labour Party and Trades Union Congress 1924,197.
21. St Brigid's Club, located in a field behind Miss Bennett's and Miss Chenevix's homes, became both an attractive summer club and the focus of some confusion in the Union. Throughout 1922 and 1924 the precise ownership of the Clubhouse and land was unclear. Miss Bennett, on 18 May 1924, requested the Executive Committee to authorise the investment of £200 at 5% interest in a scheme to develop the Clubhouse, indicating that 'if the Union were in any financial difficulty Miss Chenevix and I can guarantee to raise up to £300 from the bank on the securities they now hold from us . . . our idea will be to pay off the £100 the Union has already lent us by degrees. We propose to start a Quarter Million Penny Fund to pay off the whole debt'. Although precise plans for the holiday centre for working women were unclear, Miss Bennett's letter had been prompted by enquiries at the Executive meeting on 8 May when Miss B. Kelly raised a question as to 'who was erecting and financing the building of a house for the Irish Women Workers in Killiney. Miss Cannon and Miss Kennedy, members of the Finance Committee, thought it strange they had not heard of it until now'. IWWU Executive Minutes 8 May 1924, and statement from Miss Bennett, 18 May (approximately) 1924.
22. IWWU Executive Minutes, special meeting, 11 December 1924.
23. Executive Minutes 17 July 1924.
24. *Ibid*. 29 October 1925.
25. The rules had been negotiated in two series of conferences between

the printing group of trade unions and the Dublin Master Printers' Association. In 1924 the proposed rules had been accepted by the IWWU. In December 1923 the DMPA repudiated the agreed proposals unless they were accompanied by the use of time dockets.
26. Letter from the IWWU to the Secretary, Ministry of Industry and Commerce, Lord Edward Street, Dublin, 5 March 1924.
27. *Ibid.*
28. Messrs Armstrong, IWWU Executive Minutes 27 January 1926.
29. IWWU Annual Report 1926.
30. *Ibid.*, 4.
31. IWWU Executive Minutes 24 March 1926.

CHAPTER 6 (pp. 70-87)

1. Minutes of the IWWU Annual Convention 1 February 1926.
2. The Executive Minutes suggest that Miss Bennett in particular considered that officials of the IWWU should take part in public action only on behalf of the Labour Party — a view not shared by all her colleagues. See Executive Minutes 6 April 1927.
3. In 1927 the IWWU urged the Trades Union Congress to campaign for a shorter working day 'as a means of counteracting the unemployment due to the introduction of machinery'.
4. *An Bhean Oibre* December 1926.
5. *Ibid.*, 4.
6. *Ibid.*
7. *Ibid.* August 1928.
8. *Ibid.* September 1926.
9. *Ibid.* December 1926
10. Over a period of at least two years the paper was published on a monthly basis. Only three copies are available, although others may be found in time. It served as a useful tool for the Union and within its pages the priorities of the IWWU were voiced with some style: 'This paper has resolved itself into a plea for vocational continuation schools for girls in order that as women they may be intelligent and useful citizens, not mere bits of machinery in a factory or drudges in a household among their own workers'.
11. Report of the proceedings of the Special Congress to deal with the Shannon Electrification Scheme, Irish Labour Party and Trades Union Congress 30 November 1925.
12. IWWU to members involved in 'poaching' episode at Browne and Nolan, 19 February 1926.
13. Letter, Mr Harroway to Mr Burke, Dublin Secretary, Amalgamated Society of Binders, 25 February 1926.
14. Letter, member at Browne and Nolan to Louie Bennett, 21 April 1926.
15. Response to Mr Harroway re IWWU right to organise women in Printing and Kindred Trades, Louie Bennett to General President, Amalgamated Binders' Union, 22 March 1926.
16. Louie Bennett to Mr Harroway, 9 April 1926.

17. IWWU to Congress 18 April 1926.
18. Louie Bennett to shop steward at Messrs Kelly, 11 May 1926.
19. Both the IWWU and the commercial laundries where women were organised were continuously undermined by institution laundries, most notoriously the Magdalen Homes, which utilised the labour of inmates and persistently offered services which undercut those laundries where women were paid a negotiated price for their labour.
20. Letter, IWWU to LLA, 10 March 1926.
21. *Ibid.* 21April 1927
22. IWWU Executive Minutes 11 May 1927.
23. Letter, IWWU to Contracts Officer, Office of National Education, 1928.
24. *An Bhean Oibre* August 1928, 4.
25. *Ibid.*
26. Statement issued by the IWWU clarifying the 'various misapprehensions' in regard to dispute within the industry, 1928.
27. Letter, IWWU to Secretary, Minister of Industry and Commerce, 3 September 1928.
28. Letter, Louie Bennett to members, 4 June 1928.
29. Meeting, Burgh Quay 1927.
30. Letter, IWWU to Irish Engineering Union, 30 August 1927.
31. The Executive of this Society had no power to prevent scabbing. The Irish section of the Society was not covered by the JIC which governed the procedure in Britain.
32. *An Bhean Oibre* August 1928.
33. Letter, IWWU to Minister of Justice, 28 August 1928.
34. IWWU Executive Minutes 10 September 1928.
35. The agreement would cover only Boxmakers. In September 1928, under strong protest, the IWWU had withdrawn its claim that paper boxmakers be included under the 'Kindred Trades' in agreements between the Alliance of Printing and Kindred Trades and the DMPA.
36. IWWU Executive Minutes, 24 October 1928.
37. *Ibid.* 5 December 1928; Miss Bennett refuses to act as a worker representative on the Sugar Confectionery Trade Board.
38. *Ibid.* 29 February 1928.

CHAPTER 7 (pp. 88-99)

1. IWWU Executive Minutes 1 August 1928.
2. *Ibid.* 23 January 1929.
3. *An Bhean Oibre* August 1928. *An Bhean Oibre* ceased publication in November 1928.
4. IWWU Executive Minutes 27 February 1929.
5. *Ibid.* 5 February 1929.
6. IWWU Annual Convention 1 May 1929, Motion 1.
7. *Ibid.* 1 May 1929.
8. IWWU Executive Minutes 28 May 1929.
9. *Ibid.* 27 June 1929.
10. *Ibid.* 19 September 1929.

Notes 379

11. The appeal against the High Court Decision in the Union's favour was not heard until 1930, when it was eventually lost.
12. IWWU Executive Minutes 16 January 1930.
13. *Ibid.* 15 May 1930.
14. IWWU Annual Report 1930.
15. *Ibid.*
16. IWWU Executive Minutes 3 July 1930.
17. *Ibid.* 18 September 1930.

CHAPTER 8 (pp. 100-112)

1. Letter, Helen Chenevix to Eamonn Lynch, Secretary ITUC, 20 May 1931.
2. Letter, Mr Lynch to IWWU, 1 June 1931.
3. IWWU Executive Minutes 11 September 1930.
4. *The Irish Worker* 22 August 1932.
5. Louie Bennett, Presidential Address to Trades Union Congress, published in *The Watchword of Labour,* 30 July 1932.
6. Letter, Horn and Metal Industries to IWWU, 28 October1933.
7. Letter, Sighle Dowling to Louie Bennett, 16 March 1932.
8. Letter of resignation, Sighle Dowling to Miss Bennett, 16 March1932.
9. Letter to the Editor of *The Irish Independent* from Helena Molony, 19 July 1932.
10. 'Miss Molony and the Pope', *The Irish Independent,* 20 July 1932.
11. Louie Bennett, Presidential Address, Trades Union Congress 1932; see n. 5 above.
12. Report on Organisation, IWWU Annual Convention 1932.
13. Report on meeting with Mr Lemass, Department of Industry and Commerce, 5 December 1933.
14. IWWU Executive Minutes 17 August 1933.
15. *Ibid.* 14 September 1933.

CHAPTER 9 (pp. 113-133)

1. IWWU Executive Minutes 17 May 1934.
2. Charles McCarthy, *Trade Unions in Ireland, 1894-1960,* Dublin 1977.
3. Most of the women at Bailey Gibson joined the Union in 1934. It was acknowledged that this firm had grown 'enormously' since a tariff was imposed on imports.
4. IWWU Annual Report 1934.
5. IWWU Executive Minutes January 1934.
6. *Ibid.* 15 February1934.
7. In 1932 Miss Molony had represented the women workers on a delegation from the Dublin Trades' Council to the ESB. Following that meeting, the Union had been asked to submit proposals which would secure a day's wage for cleaners.
8. Annual Convention 1934.
9. IWWU Executive Minutes 17 May 1934.
10. *Ibid.* 7 June1934.

380 *These Obstreperous Lassies*

11. No Union records of this early correspondence or the ensuing campaign were found in the Union Archives. A request to the relevant government departments yielded no further information.
12. Letter, Louie Bennett to the Editor, *The Irish Press* 14 May 1935.
13. IWWU Executive Minutes 28 February 1935.
14. *Ibid*. 27 June 1935.
15. Resolution: Women's Right to Work, IWWU Annual Convention 1935.
16. Forty-First Annual Report, ITUC, and Proceedings of the Forty-First Annual Meeting, Guild Hall, Derry, 1935.
17. *Ibid.*, 145
18. *Ibid.*
19. *Ibid.*, 146.
20. *Ibid.*
21. *Ibid.*
22. *Ibid.*, 147.
23. *Ibid.*, 149.
24. *Ibid.*, 151.
25. IWWU Executive Minutes 30 October 1935.
26. Letter from John Flanagan, Canon of the Pro-Cathedral, to the IWWU, November 1935.
27. IWWU Executive Minutes 12 December 1935.
28. Resolution 3, Annual Convention of the IWWU 1936.

CHAPTER 10 (pp. 134-149)

1. Exclusion regulations permitting the employment of women outside the normal hours prescribed by the Act included Order No. 160 of 1936 (women cleaners in industrial premises); No. 168 of 1936 (bakeries); No. 156 of 1955 (rayon); No. 120 of 1959 (nylon, rayon and terylene yarn winding); No. 63 of 1962 (instant potato flake industry); No. 86 of 1963 (veneer industry), etc.
2. Letter, IWWU to ITUC, 5 February 1937.
3. Letter, IWWU to Minister for Industry and Commerce, 3 February 1937.
4. IWWU Executive Minutes 4 February 1937.
5. IWWU Annual Report 1936, 4.
6. *Ibid*. 1936-37.
7. IWWU Executive Minutes 27 February 1936.
8. Letter, Miss Doyle, Wexford, to Louie Bennett, 7 December 1936.
9. Memoranda from the Commission of Enquiry into the Irish trade union movement. Confidential document on terms of reference, IWWU Archives.
10. IWWU Executive Minutes 28 May 1936.
11. *Ibid*. 10 December 1936.
12. *Ibid*. 21 October 1937.
13. *Ibid*. 1935.
14. Draft Constitution, 1937, Article 40, 6, (iii), IWWU Archives.
15. Louie Bennett, handwritten notes on specific articles of the draft Constitution considered repugnant to the rights of women, IWWU Archives.

16. Dorothy McArdle, 'The Constitution: A Woman's Point of View', handwritten letter 'Dear Sir' ref. Articles in the draft Constitution considered prejudicial to women, IWWU Archives.
17. IWWU Executive Minutes 27 May1937.
18. Letter, Louie Bennett to the Editor, *The Irish Press* 18 May 1937
19. 'Women Workers and the Draft Constitution', statement from IWWU, 7 June 1937.
20. *Ibid.*
21. Meeting of the IWWU Political Wing, 8 July 1937.
22. IWWU Executive Minutes 8 June 1937.
23. IWWU Annual Report 1937-38.
24. *Ibid.* 1936-37, 9.
25. IWWU Finance Committee 11 November 1937.
26. IWWU Annual Report 1937-38.
27. IWWU Executive Minutes 9 September 1937.
28. IWWU Annual Report 1937-38.
29. Letter, IWWU to DMPA, 3 September 1937.
30. Time Docket Dispute: handwritten note from M. Mackey, Shop Steward, Dollards, to Miss Bennett, IWWU Archives.
31. IWWU Executive Minutes 7 October 1937.
32. H. Vick, 'Costing in the Bindery Industry' (article), Manchester. One of a series of articles in the file on this dispute, suggesting resistance by the binders in England.
33. Letter, Dublin Master Printers' Association to IWWU, 4 April 1938.
34. IWWU Annual Report 1938.
35. IWWU Executive Minutes 14 July 1938.
36. *Ibid.*
37. Letter to the Editor, *The Evening Mail*, Dublin, Thursday 4 August 1938.
38. IWWU Executive Minutes 18 August 1938.
39. Statement from the Executive to members of the Printers' Section of the IWWU, drafted by the Executive and passed unanimously at the Printers' Committee, 17 August 1938.
40. Extract from instructions issued to members of the Dublin Master Printers' Association, 8 September 1938.
41. Statement from the Printing Trades' Group, 6 December 1938.
42. IWWU Executive Minutes 1 December 1938
43. *Ibid.* 12 January 1939.

CHAPTER 11 (pp. 150-165)

1. IWWU Annual Report 1937-38.
2. *Ibid.* 1938.
3. *Ibid.*
4. IWWU Executive Minutes 1 September 1938.
5. Labour Court records: wage rates for women: comparative scale, 1939 and 1955, IWWU Archives.
6. IWWU Executive Minutes 1 December 1938.
7. Social and Political Report, IWWU Annual Convention 1939.

8. IWWU Annual Report 1938.
9. Proceedings of the 43rd annual meeting of the Irish Trades Union Congress, 1936-37, 24. Letter read to Congress on 4 August 1937.
10. IWWU Executive Minutes 23 February 1939.
11. *Ibid.* 20 January 1938.
12. For a full account of the terms of reference see the Preliminary Report of the Commission on Vocational Organisation, Dublin, Stationery Office 1943, 1.
13. IWWU Annual Report 1938.
14. Article by Louie Bennett in reference to her education in economic affairs in 'Farming Today', a supplement to *The Irish Times*, 23 February 1954.
15. Undated brief on IWWU officials' duties, 1930s, IWWU Archives.
16. IWWU Executive Minutes 11 April 1940.
17. *Ibid.* 3 February 1938.
18. Sheila Greene, series of articles on Louie Bennett in *Reynold's News*, undated, but probably 1950s (Manning Collection).
19. IWWU Executive Minutes 25 April 1940.
20. *Ibid.*
21. *Ibid.*
22. *Ibid.* 23 January 1941. Membership in 1934 was 4,510. By 1940 it was 5,614. It had, however, apparently 'peaked' in 1937 and the drop between 1938 and 1939 was quite dramatic.
23. Letter, IWWU to ITUC, 14 September 1939.
24. *Ibid.* 22 September 1939.
25. IWWU Executive Minutes 4 September 1941.
26. IWWU to ITUC, 6 March 1941.
27. IWWU Annual Report 1940.
28. *Ibid.*
29. Rosary Bead Enquiry: this had been convened, through the intervention of Fr Coyne, in response to a 10-week strike by rosary bead assemblers at Mitchells. The strike was provoked by a proposal from Mr Mitchell that certain sections of the workforce accept a reduction in wages. In a notable display of solidarity at a time when there were hard times everywhere, the women came out *en masse*.
30. Helen Chenevix, 'Notes on Being a Christian', one of a series of handwritten missives, largely undated, and included in a collection of press clippings, photographs and miscellaneous documents donated to IWWU Archives by Betty Taylor, daughter of a lifelong friend of Miss Chenevix.
31. The name was derived from the emblem of the IWWU, which featured in both the banner and badge of the Union, authorised by the Executive in 1922. The earlier banner was presumably destroyed or lost between 1912 and 1916.
32. This Fund had been organised for many years by Helena Molony. The method of fund-raising had not always been universally praised. Miss Chenevix, indeed, had strongly protested when, with great success, Miss Molony organised the then illegal lotteries to provide funds for the

Notes 383

unemployed.
33. The Union had been associated with this Club for some time. It had, at one stage, been seen by trade unions as representing a threat to the interests of their members. In 1938 the Boot and Shoe Operatives' Union had complained that the training of members of the Club to mend their own shoes might, if extended beyond their own immediate needs, affect the industry itself.
34. IWWU Annual Report 1940.
35. Letter, IWWU Executive to Helena Molony. See Annual Report, 1941-42.

CHAPTER 12 (pp. 166-187)

1. Letter, Louie Bennett to Mr Ferguson, Department of Industry and Commerce, 5 December 1940.
2. Letter, IWWU to Mr Ferguson, Department of Industry and Commerce, 5 December 1940.
3. Dublin Trades Union Council to all affiliated unions, 23 May 1941.
4. Leaflet issued by IWWU May 1941, IWWU Archives.
5. Resolution sent to An Taoiseach by the IWWU, 23 May 1941.
6. See file on Trade Union Bill, IWWU Archives, for details of these amendments.
7. Letter, IWWU to ITUC, 26 August 1941.
8. And, although Mr MacBride did not mention company or 'house' unions, to discriminate in their favour and against traditional working class organisations.
9. Opinion upon matters raised at consultation in reference to the Trade Union Bill 1941, Seán MacBride, 11 June 1941, IWWU Archives.
10. Letter, M. McDunphy, Secretary to the President, to Wm. McDowell & Co., Solrs., 23 September 1941.
11. IWWU Executive Minutes 18 December 1941.
12. Letter, Miss Bennett to Miss Dunbar, Textile Operatives' Society of Ireland, 20 February 1942.
13. Report of the Proceedings of the 48th Annual Meeting of the Irish Trades Union Congress, Bundoran, July 1942.
14. *Ibid.*, 101.
15. *Ibid.*, 103.
16. *Ibid.*
17. Parliamentary Debates, Dáil Éireann, Vol. 83, No. 3, 14-16, October 1942. List of applications for negotiating licences in response to Dáil Question by J.P. Pattison, TD (Labour). Ironically, in view of the subsequent history of both unions, the Workers' Union of Ireland claimed a membership of only 5,000, for which a deposit of £1,000 was taken from its coffers!
18. See, for example, Charles McCarthy, *Trade Unions in Ireland 1894-1960*, Dublin 1977, 181-221
19. *Ibid.*, 204, and reference to the William O'Brien papers, MS 139 74, National Library of Ireland.

384   *These Obstreperous Lassies*

20. IWWU Annual Report 1943-44.
21. *Ibid*. 1944-45.
22. *Ibid*.
23. Letter, IWWU to ITUC, 20 November 1940.
24. Memorandum on Factory Inspection sent to Dublin Trades Union Council in response to their request to the IWWU, 20 January 1945.
25. Women Workers' Charter, IWWU Annual Convention 1940.
26. Previously Leinster Laundries' [LLA] Association.
27. Women Workers' Programme for Industrial Workers, IWWU Archives 1943.
28. IWWU Annual Report 1936-37.
29. Laundry Section Committee meeting 28 March 1939.
30. Laundry Section, statement to the Press 1945.
31. Letter, Helen Chenevix to Dr C.P. Clancy-Gore, 16 January 1945.
32. Laundry Section Committee meeting 18 February 1941.
33. IWWU Executive Minutes 3 April 1941.
34. In the Annual Report 1943-44, the Union referred to the formation of an employers' trade union which 'has considerably altered the character of negotiations. Behind every industrial dispute stands a united front of employers. . . . We realise that the forces arrayed for defence against the workers' claims are immensely strengthened by unity and cooperation. It is important that the trade unions should give serious study to this new development of trade unionism, which has arisen through the Trade Union Act of 1942.'
35. In 1944, for example, Mr Neill-Watson of the Court Laundry, following an appeal by the Union to all laundries, responded 'by giving each of his workers a summer bonus of £2 which enabled them to take a second week's holidays without financial loss'. See *The Irish Catholic*, 20 September 1945.
36. IWWU Annual Report 1944-45.
37. IWWU statement to the press, March 1945.
38. Letter, Helen Chenevix to Mrs Waters, *The Irish People*, 19 January 1945.
39. FUE to Louie Bennett, 23 March 1945.
40. IWWU to FUE, 28 March 1945.
41. *The Fortnight's Holiday as a Symbol*, printed sheet, IWWU July 1945.
42. *Ibid*.
43. Letter, IWWU to FUE, 9 July 1945.
44. IWWU to members of the medical profession, 15 July 1945.
45. Letter, IWWU to P. Burke TD, 2 August 1945.
46. *Ibid*.
47. *Ibid*.
48. The movement split into two sections and two Congresses, the division being primarily based on the issue of the movement being wholly Irish based and Irish controlled. The Irish Trades Union Congress was composed of unions with headquarters both in England and Ireland. The Congress of Irish Unions was composed of unions with headquarters

in Ireland. The IWWU affiliated to the former. The split lasted until 1959.
49. Letter to IWWU, 21 July 1945.
50. Letter, Dundalk Trades' and Workers' Council to IWWU, 28 August 1945.
51. Letter, Arthur H. Smith, Merchant and Broker, to the IWWU, 21 August 1945.
52. *Ibid.*
53. Undated letter, 1945, Marjorie Wilkinson to Helen Chenevix, Laundry Strike File, IWWU Archives.
54. Letter to the Editor, *The Irish Times* 1 September 1945.
55. IWWU Annual Report 1945-46.
56. Letter, Capt. Robert W. Lefroy, Gardenton House, Athy, Co. Kildare, 5 September 1945.
57. Response of Union to letter from Department of Industry and Commerce, 5 September 1945.
58. Letter, ITUC to all affiliated unions, 20 September 1945.
59. *An Open Letter to the Public*, Louie Bennett and Helen Chenevix, 15 September 1945. Roneo copy in IWWU Archives.
60. Letter, IWWU to ITUC, 20 September 1945.
61. Resolution to An Taoiseach, 23 September 1945.
62. Letter, Thomas McQuaid to the Editor, *The Evening Mail*, Dublin, 24 September 1945.
63. Open letter to all members of the Oireachtas, 9 October 1945.
64. Press Release, IWWU 11 October 1945.
65. IWWU newspaper advertisement placed in response to that of the Dublin District Laundries' Association, 17 October 1945.
66. Dublin Trades' Council, 12 October 1945.
67. Letter, IWWU to Manager, National City Bank, 10 October 1945.
68. Letter, C.D.D. Kingsmill Moore to Manageress, Kelso Laundry, 19 October 1945.
69. Letter, 'A Worker', to Miss Bennett in appreciation of 'your Miss Brennan, Miss McGrath and Miss McDowell', 26 October 1945.
70. Letter in Laundry Strike File, IWWU Archives.
71. *Ibid.*
72. Letter from *Quidnunc* to Miss Bennett and Miss Chenevix, 9 November 1945.

CHAPTER 13 (pp. 188-207)

1. IWWU Annual Report 1947-48.
2. *Ibid.*
3. JIC for the Laundry Industry 8 April 1948. The JIC, established in 1946, included two IWWU members on the workers side: Miss Bennett, Miss O'Brien and Miss Chenevix.
4. *Ibid.*
5. *Ibid.*
6. Louie Bennett to Manager, Swastika Laundry, 23 May 1947.

7. Laundry Committee Minutes 13 May 1948.
8. IWWU to Harold's Cross Laundry, 19 March 1948.
9. IWWU to Bloomfield Laundry, 29 October 1948.
10. IWWU to Matron, St Mary's Chest Hospital, 29 April 1949.
11. Laundry Committee 13 May 1948.
12. *Ibid.* 8 May 1948
13. *Ibid.* 19 October 1948.
14. Letter, Swastika to IWWU, 19 October 1948.
15. Letter, IWWU to Secretary, Department of Industry and Commerce, 21 April 1948.
16. Letter, IWWU to Chief Factory Inspector, 3 December 1947.
17. Letter, IWWU to Minister for Health, 26 November 1948.
18. Letter, IWWU to Matron, St Laurence's Hospital, 9 June 1948.
19. Letter, member in Dargle and Bray Laundry to IWWU, 21 July 1949.
20. Emigration, IWWU Annual Report 1941-42; also Union Memorandum to Commission on Emigration 1948.
21. Letter, IWWU to Manager, Grangegorman Mental Hospital, 20 June 1947.
22. IWWU Executive Minutes 19 August 1948.
23. Factory Premises: a memorandum from the IWWU 1948, IWWU Archives.
24. *Ibid.*
25. IWWU Annual Report 1949.
26. *Ibid.*
27. *Ibid.* 1948-49.
28. Series of letters, Maguire and Paterson and the IWWU, December 1947, and a meeting with Maguire and Paterson, 11 July 1949.
29. IWWU Annual Report 1949-50.
30. *Ibid.*
31. Letter, IWWU to Maguire and Paterson, 25 May 1949.
32. Letter, IWWU to Labour Court, 14 July 1949.
33. Minutes, Laundry Council, 1950.
34. Minutes, Laundry Section Committee, 7 December 1949.
35. IWWU Annual Report 1951-52.
36. Notably the WUI dispute with General Textiles Ltd in 1961, with reference to the use of work studies to ascertain rates for pieceworkers. Contributions to the JIC for the Linen and Cotton Industry indicate some resistance on the part of female core winders following the initial study report.
37. Urney Chocolates File 1952-1959, contains an interesting series of letters referring to seven women resisting management in the operation of the bonus scheme, IWWU Archives.
38. Paul Thompson, *The Nature of Work, An Introduction to Debates on the Labour Process,* London 1983, 60.
39. See nn. 20-34 above.
40. Letter, IWWU to Typographical Association, 13 April 1949.
41. Letter, Monument Press to IWWU, 17 August 1949.
42. Letter, Bray Urban District Council to IWWU, September 1945.

Notes 387

43. Letter, Mr. Flynn to IWWU, undated but following IWWU withdrawal of overtime ban prior to strike.
44. File on dispute with the IBATU 1945-48, IWWU Archives.
45. IWWU Annual Report 1947-48.
46. Letter, IWWU to the Typographical Association, 25 August 1949.
47. Letter, IWWU to Dublin Trades Union Council, 20 October 1949.
48. *The Irish Independent,* 20 October 1949, Louie Bennett on Women's Wages in the Printing Trade.
49. Monument Press File, IWWU Archives.
50. IWWU Executive Minutes 15 December 1949.
51. *Peace and Fraternity,* issued by the IWWU, June 1952.
52. IWWU Executive Minutes 15 August 1950.
53. *Ibid.*
54. Letter, ITUC to all affiliated unions, May 1950.
55. Letter, IWWU to ITUC, 13 February 1948.
56. Notes on ILO Questionnaire on equal remuneration for Men and Women workers for work of equal value, ILO, Geneva, 1949, published in IWWU Annual Report 1949-50.
57. *Ibid.*
58. IWWU Annual Report, 1948-49.
59. Dublin Trades Union Council File, Lower Prices Campaign 1947-48.
60. Oral account, June Winders, Office Administrator of the IWWU.

CHAPTER 14 (pp. 208-230)

1. IWWU Executive Minutes 19 April 1951.
2. Letter, K. O'Brien to Miss Chenevix, undated but probably early 1950s.
3. A printers' pension scheme proposed in 1950 was particularly appropriate. Provision existed for married women returning to the trade to be credited with time previous to marriage; married women in the trade at the commencement of the scheme would, for pension purposes, be credited with work experience prior to marriage. It was rejected by members.
4. Notably, for the Union, in the area of psychiatric nursing.
5. IWWU Executive Minutes 27 March 1952.
6. Letter, Nellie O'Brien at Annual Convention 1951. Read to Convention in Miss O'Brien's absence through ill-health.
7. IWWU Executive Minutes 11 May 1950.
8. *Ibid.* 20 March 1951.
9. *Ibid.* 15 August 1950.
10. Letter, Kathleen Coyle to Mrs Buckley, 6 January 1950.
11. Letter, WUI to IWWU, 4 April 1950.
12. Letter, WUI to Chief Clerk, Grangegorman, 15 February 1950.
13. *Ibid.*
14. IWWU Notes, Observation Room, Grangegorman 1950.
15. In 1945 the Irish trade union movement had divided into two sections and two Congresses. The division was primarily related to the issue of the trade union movement in Ireland being Irish based and Irish con-

trolled. The Irish Trades Union Congress was comprised both of unions with headquarters in Ireland and those with headquarters in Britain. The Congress of Irish Unions was comprised solely of unions with headquarters in Ireland. Although the IWWU had no affiliations outside Ireland, it was not in principle against British based unions and it was affiliated to the Irish Trades Union Congress for the duration of the split.

16. Letter, IWWU to WUI, 19 December 1951.
17. Letter, IWWU to Mr McDowell, 31 October 1951.
18. Letter, IWWU to WUI, 12 November 1951.
19. Helen Chenevix, President, Annual Conference of the ITUC, Kilkenny 1951.
20. General Statement from IWWU on status and working conditions of the Mental Nurse, 21 May 1951.
21. Meeting, Fleet Street 23 October 1951.
22. Letter re special duty, IWWU nurse to Matron, Grangegorman, early 1950s.
23. Letter, IWWU to Nurses' Shop Stewards, 19 June 1952.
24. Letter, IWWU to WUI and ITGWU, 3 June 1952.
25. Newspaper clippings, 29 January 1952, seeking women aged 18-35 for Hellingley Mental Hospital, Hailsham, Sussex, IWWU Archives.
26. Roneo sheet, IWWU Nurses' Section 1954.
27. Letter from all unions to Grangegorman and Portrane authorities, 22 February 1954.
28. IWWU dossier, staff/patient ratios at Grangegorman and Portrane 1954, IWWU Archives.
29. Letter, IWWU to Chief Clerk, Portrane 27 June 1953.
30. Joint Staffs Committee, Grangegorman and Portrane Mental Hospitals, draft of Submission to the Minister's Expert Committee 1956.
31. Report on Printing Trades Dispute 1952, Executive Minutes 13 August 1952.
32. Printers' Committee 8 September 1852.
33. Statement by Louie Bennett to Printers' Committee and Executive 11 September 1952.
34. IWWU Executive Minutes 27 November 1952. The Annual Convention file for 1953 contains a confidential document on finance, suggesting that it had been a difficult year, in part because of the cost of lock-out pay for the printers. The total cost was £8,434.
35. Letter, Louie Bennett and Helen Chenevix, to *The Evening Mail,* undated, but referring to 1952 dispute and demonstration.
36. Roneo letter, Louie Bennett to women workers, 10 March 1953, IWWU Archives.
37. IWWU Annual Report 1950-51.
38. IWWU Executive Resolution, adopted 8 June 1951.
39. Letter, IWWU to Minister for Health, 23 April 1951.
40. IWWU Annual Report 1950-51.
41. Letter, Louie Bennett to Mr Waldron, Secretary Dublin Trades' Council,

11 December 1952.
42. IWWU Executive Minutes 27 November 1952.
43. Letter, Miss McDowell to Miss Bennett, 31 December 1951.
44. IWWU Executive Minutes 28 April 1953.
45. *Ibid.*
46. IWWU Executive Minutes 4 February 1954.
47. Louie Bennett, notes for special meeting of Executive, 17 February 1954.
48. IWWU Executive Minutes 17 February 1954.
49. IWWU Annual Report 1944-45.
50. See, for example, the file for Castle Forbes Works Ltd 1952-59, in regard to management strategy adopted by Lever's.
51. IWWU Executive Minutes 25 November 1954.
52. Meeting 13 October 1954, Fleet Street, convened to 'arrange plans for education social activities'.
53. *Ibid.*
54. See Rules of the IWWU 1951, IWWU Archives.
55. Oral history, Lottie Waldron, member of the Printers' Committee, 1950s.
56. Helen Chenevix, The Pacifist Message in a World at War, 1940s, IWWU Archives.
57. Letter, IWWU to Minister for Local Government, 5 October 1955.
58. Obituary of Helen Chenevix, *The Irish Times* 5 March 1963.
59. *Ibid.*
60. Linen and Cotton JIC Minutes 18 August 1954.
61. IWWU documentation, presentation of case of women workers, taken in association with the WUI and ITGWU to the Labour Court 1955. See Labour Court recommendation No. 738.
62. *Ibid.*
63. IWWU documentation on reassessment of the position of women in printing, IWWU Archives.

CHAPTER 15 (pp. 231-251)

1. IWWU Annual Report 1951-52.
2. Figures as reported to the Registrar of Friendly Societies suggest a different total: 5,437.
3. Maura Breslin, Presidential Address to Annual Convention 1956.
4. *Ibid.*
5. Letter from Louie Bennett, Killiney, to 'Dear Fellow Workers', Fleet Street, 30 April 1956.
6. Annual Convention 2 May 1956.
7. IWWU Annual Report 1955-56.
8. Lottie Waldron, oral history.
9. Letter, IWWU to Dublin Artisans Dwellings Co., 30 September 1955.
10. One of a collection of similar letters on file, IWWU Archives.
11. Letter to Miss Chenevix from 'Farmer', Co. Limerick, requesting reply in 'closed plain brown envelope'. Personal letters file, IWWU Archives. The situation revealed by the Report of the Commission on Emigration,

on the low marriage rate of Irish males in the period covered by the Report must have made the Union seem an unusually attractive option for someone in these circumstances.
12. IWWU Executive Minutes 24 April 1957.
13. Letter, Helen Chenevix to Kay McDowell, 6 July 1960.
14. IWWU Annual Convention 1957.
15. Letter, IWWU to Chief Executive Officer, St Kevin's Institution, 9 June 1955.
16. *Ibid.*, resolution 21.
17. IWWU Executive Minutes 23 May 1957.
18. *Ibid.* 21 November 1957.
19. *Ibid.* 23 January 1958.
20. Under the terms of Statutory Instrument No. 265 of 1953, Part III (Rules regulating the minimum rate of wages per week during apprenticeship) details are given for all rates over a six-year period for males and a four-year period for females. In 1955 these rules were amended to ensure that minimum rates would be no different 'as between male and female'.
21. Letter, Kay McDowell, Assistant Secretary IWWU, to IPF 1955.
22. Resolution passed at Extraordinary General Meeting of the IPF, 19 September 1957.
23. Evidence of the marital status of the De La Rue and the Jacob's workers may provide a starting point for an analysis of why women responded in different ways to moves to change the pattern of the working week. No strictly accurate records were kept by the IWWU in this regard, but they may have been kept by the firms concerned.
24. Printers' Committee Minutes 10 September 1958.
25. IWWU Annual Report 1957-58.
26. IWWU Executive Minutes 30 April 1958.
27. Minutes, IWWU Annual Convention 1958.
28. Letter of complaint to IWWU re Mrs Drew, Management, Morco Ltd, Drogheda, from Mrs C. Farrell, 23 April 1938.
29. IWWU Annual Report 1959-60.
30. Maura Breslin, Presidential Address, IWWU Annual Convention 1958.
31. IWWU Annual Convention 1958.
32. Printers' Committee Minutes 15 May 1978.
33. IWWU Annual Report 1958-59.
34. *Ibid.*
35. *Ibid.*, 1959-60.
36. IWWU Executive Minutes 10 December 1959.
37. Kay McDowell, letter to Ruairí Roberts, ICTU, undated copy, but approximately 1960.
38. It is unclear from the Union records under whose auspices the conference was held.
39. IWWU Executive Minutes 24 November 1960. In 1950 the Union had urged Congress to develop a Research Department. In reference to the need to meet the employers equipped with the necessary information, the Annual Report for that year noted: 'We owe much to Mr Nevin of

the TUC for his generous and valuable assistance but it is time for all Trade Unions to agree to establish and to pay for a more ambitious plan of research than a one man show'.

CHAPTER 16 (pp. 252-272)

1. Quoted in S. Cody, J. O'Dowd and P. Rigney, *The Parliament of Labour: 100 years of the Dublin Council of Trade Unions*, Dublin 1986, 212.
2. Terence Brown, *Ireland, a Social and Cultural History 1922-1979*, London 1981, 246.
3. IWWU Executive Minutes 16 March 1961.
4. Kay McDowell, delivery of Annual Report 1961-62.
5. IWWU Annual Report 1962-63.
6. Printers' Committee, 30 November 1960.
7. *Ibid*. 13 September 1961.
8. *Ibid*. 5 February 1962.
9. Temple Press File, IWWU Archives.
10. Meeting, Harold's Cross Laundry 14 September 1960.
11. Discussed at Laundry Committee 6 March 1962. In the 1960s a number of firms had started a variety of shifts for women: Bailey and Gibson, Cherry and Smalldridge, Irish carton printers, to name a few.
12. *Ibid*.
13. In 1962 the IWWU was upbraided for being allegedly sanctioning such habits because it informed piece-workers that their lateness would not affect the firms involved, as all workers were paid by the piece, not by time. The Union denied the suggestion.
14. Resolution from members at Cherry and Smalldridge, Annual Convention 1961.
15. IWWU Executive Minutes 17 May 1962.
16. Letter, Shop Steward, The Meath Chronicle, to IWWU, 27 February 1962.
17. Letter, Shop Steward, Greenmount and Boyne, to IWWU, 1962.
18. Letters from Robert Usher and Co., Drogheda, to IWWU, with reference to redundancy of women weavers, 1962.
19. Notes by Miss McDowell, Robert Usher and Co. File, 1963, IWWU Archives.
20. Department of Industry and Commerce to Greenmount and Boyne, 29 June 1961.
21. IWWU Executive Minutes 22 February 1962.
22. Handwritten notes, Kay McDowell, Court Laundry, 1960-61.
23. Report on laundries, *The Irish Times*, 16 November 1963.
24. Meeting, JIC for Dublin Laundries, 7 May 1968.
25. See Court Laundry File 1960-70.
26. The Mayo News File, 1960-1970, IWWU Archives.
27. Proposal from Thomson International Ltd to JIC for the printing industry, October 1962.
28. *Ibid*.

29. Printing Industry JIC to Major McDowell, 2 November 1962.
30. See Cynthia Cockburn, *Brothers: Male Dominance and Technological Change*, London 1983.
31. Letter, T.B. McDowell to B. Ó Cearbhaill, Side Secretary, Printing Industry, JIC, October 1962.
32. IWWU Annual Report 1963-63. The reference is to the 1913 Lock-Out.
33. IWWU Executive Minutes 13 February 1964, and Annual Convention 1964, Resolution 1.
34. IWWU Annual Report 1962-63.
35. IWWU Executive Minutes 17 October 1963.
36. *Ibid.*
37. *Ibid.*
38. *Ibid.*

CHAPTER 17 (pp. 273-292)

1. IWWU Executive Minutes 18 February 1965.
2. Printers' Committee February 1965.
3. *Ibid.* 10 March 1965.
4. IWWU Annual Convention May 1965.
5. IWWU Annual Report 1965
6. IWWU Executive Minutes 27 August 1965.
7. *Ibid.* 13 January 1966.
8. See Maguire and Paterson Files 1964-1973, IWWU Archives.
9. Kay McDowell to IPF, May 1965
10. Letter, IWWU to IPF, May 1965.
11. Letter, IPF to Mr Ó Cearbhaill, Side Secretary, JIC workers' side. Copy to each affiliated union, 16 August 1965.
12. IWWU Annual Report 1965-66.
13. IWWU Executive Meeting 9 December 1965.
14. IWWU Annual Report 1965-66.
15. Report by Miss McDowell to IWWU Executive 3 March 1966.
16. IWWU Annual Report 1965-66.
17. *Ibid.*
18. IWWU Annual Convention 1966.
19. IWWU Special Executive Meeting 12 April 1968.
20. In a party sense, within the Labour Party, and also in the sense that negotiations with employers and with government were viewed in the wider sense as being political activities.
21. IWWU Annual Report 1966-67.
22. IWWU Laundry Ledger.
23. IWWU Unemployment Register 1967-68.
24. Oral history, June Winders, (*née* Aust).
25. IWWU Special Executive Meeting 16 December 1966.
26. Printers' Committee 17 October 1962.
27. Gibson, Guy and Smalldridge Ltd., Rationalisation Programme, sent to IWWU 22 September 1965.
28. Kay McDowell informing IPF of this move, by letter, 25 January 1966

29. Printers' Committee 5 October 1966.
30. *Ibid.* 25 January 1967.
31. IPF to IWWU 1966.
32. Census of Industrial Production 1951, 1961.
33. *Ibid.*
34. IPF Proposals on Productivity sent to IWWU June 1968.
35. Presumably the protective clause mentioning 'not to the detriment of the labour force involved' was employed to ensure the maintenance of the status quo.
36. Letter, IPF to all members, 14 February 1969.
37. Presidential Address, IWWU Annual Convention 1969.
38. Annual Report 1968-69.
39. S. Cody, J. O'Dowd, and P. Rigney, *The Parliament of Labour: 100 Years of the Dublin Council of Trade Unions,* Dublin 1986, 222.
40. Mary E. Daly, 'Women, Work and Trade Unionism' in *Women in Irish Society: The Historical Dimension,* Dublin 1978.
41. *Ibid.*
42. Kay McDowell, letter to the editors of five daily papers, 24 September 1969.
43. Letter from Director, Gallaher (Dublin) to Miss McDowell, 10 January 1969.
44. Circular letter (copy in IWWU Files) to all women on personnel records, 4 June 1970.
45. Annual Report 1968-69.

CHAPTER 18 (pp. 293-312)

1. IWWU Executive Minutes 26 February 1970.
2. Maura Breslin to Minister for Labour, February 1970.
3. Letter, Maura Breslin to Mr Andrew Orr, Orrwear, 13 February 1970.
4. Letter, Maura Breslin to Minister of Labour. See n. 2 above.
5. Report in *The Meath Chronicle* on picket at Orrwear, 21 February 1970.
6. IWWU Executive Minutes 19 March 1970.
7. IWWU Annual Convention 1970.
8. Twelfth round negotiations, IWWU and Greenmount and Boyne 1970.
9. *Ibid.*
10. Problems aired at meeting at Greenmount and Boyne 20 March 1970.
11. Minutes of WUI Committee, Gilbey's section, 14 October 1970.
12. Letter, Maura Breslin to Controller of Stores, 27 June 1973.
13. Mary E. Daly, 'Women, Work and Trade Unionism' in *Women: The Historical Dimension,* Dublin 1978.
14. Letter, Maura Breslin to Ruaidhrí Roberts, 29 October 1970.
15. Meeting, IWWU, ITGWU, and management, Greenmount and Boyne, 25 May 1971.
16. JIC for the Laundry Industry 3 June 1970.
17. Minutes, JIC for Dublin laundries 14 May 1970.

18. Letter, IWWU to House Governor, Adelaide Hospital Laundry, 30 April 1970.
19. Agreement signed on 20 December 1971 at the Joint Industrial Council for the Laundry Industry. The original claim from the IWWU was lodged in 1961, and the files from this JIC indicate that the battle was won only through the persistence of employees.
20. Letter, Maura Breslin to Matron, Sir Patrick Dun's Hospital, 30 September 1970.
21. Laundry Report Book 22 April 1970.
22. Meeting at Court laundry 15 March 1971.
23. IWWU Executive Minutes, 1 October 1970.
24. Miss Breslin's notes are extensive in relation to this meeting. They are, however, somewhat scattered and difficult to interpret beyond this general claim.
25. Maura Breslin, paper to Commission on Status of Women 1972.
26. Employer-Labour Conference Working Party 10 July 1972.
27. Wage conference, fourteenth round National Wage Agreement, 24 June 1972.
28. IWWU Annual Report 1972.
29. Presidential Address, IWWU Annual Convention, 1973.
30. Letter, Bailey Gibson to IWWU, 7 January 1974.
31. Letter, Maura Breslin to Manager, Bailey Gibson, Carton Department, 19 March 1974.
32. Works Manager, Bailey Gibson, to Maura Breslin, 9 April 1974.
33. Letter, Works Manager to Maura Breslin, 12 April 1974.
34. Printers' Committee 24 April 1974.
35. *Ibid.* 18 September 1974.
36. The reference to Bailey Gibson's preference for untrained workers is in the IWWU Executive Minutes 25 July 1973.
37. Meeting, Smurfit Group and Dublin Typographical Provident Society, 18 February 1975.
38. IWWU Executive Minutes 12 December 1973.
39. Handwritten note, Maura Breslin, 10 June 1974.
40. Between 1971 and 1975 the participation rate of married women in the workforce doubled. The increase continued steadily throughout the decade. See Labour Force Surveys 1971-1981. Also Donal Garvey, *A Profile of Demographic and Labour Force Characteristics of the Population,* sample analysis of the 1981 Census of Population, CSO, Dublin, April 1983, read before the Statistical and Social Enquiry Society of Ireland. See also *Population and Labour Force Projections by County and Region 1979-81* in NESC Report No. 63, July 1982.
41. IWWU Executive Minutes 26 February 1975.
42. CSO Labour Force Surveys, unpublished figures, 1975, 1977, 1979, 1981.
43. IWWU Executive Minutes 22 January 1975.
44. Letter, member at Morco's to IWWU, 15 July 1973.
45. Letter from Shop Steward at Usher's to IWWU 1976.

CHAPTER 19 (pp. 313-336)

1. Presidential Address, Annual Convention 1975.
2. See Frank Litton (ed.), *Unequal Achievement: The Irish Experience 1957-1982*, Dublin 1982. In his contribution to this volume Blackwell argues that the data available from official and other sources for this period show that inequality remained undisturbed by the apparent prosperity of the1960s and early 1970s and, quoting Stark (1977), suggests that 'If anything, this distribution of income became more unequal' in 1965-1975.
3. A process whereby production of a garment was reduced to its constituent parts. At Ormac Ltd in Kells, Co. Meath, twenty pairs of hands were responsible for the production of a pair of jeans. The cut-out jeans are sent 'on the line' to girls at machines who each completes one or more aspects of the total operation. Women who have worked 'on the line' for the duration of their working lives become proficient at sewing on pockets, fixing zips etc. – but few could complete the entire process.
4. See n. 3 above.
5. Meeting 24 October 1975, Jenny Murray and management, Morco Manufacturing Co.
6. Miss Breslin to meeting of IWWU members in Drogheda, 29 July 1976.
7. Correspondence between Nuala Early, Shop Steward, and Maura Breslin, January 1976.
8. *The Drogheda Independent* 1 October 1976.
9. Members dispute both the nationality of the purchaser and the accuracy of the description, particularly in the light of the subsequent closure of Confexin Fashions. The Executive Minutes, however, state that the purchase was as described.
10. IWWU Executive Minutes 19 January 1977.
11. Meeting at Santry, Jefferson Smurfit Group, 7 January 1977.
12. Meeting of Dublin Printing Trades' Group 26 February 1981.
13. Printers' Committee 30 June 1976.
14. Maura Breslin, letter to members, 13 January 1977.
15. *Ibid.*
16. Printers' Committee 26 June 1977.
17. *Ibid.* 22 June 1977.
18. *Ibid.* 20 July 1979.
19. IWWU Annual Report 1979-80.
20. IWWU Executive Minutes 21 September 1977.
21. *Ibid.* 18 October 1978.
22. *Ibid.* 12 July 1978.
23. IWWU appeal to Labour Court against Equality Officer's recommendations 36/1979.
24. Submission to the Equality Officer by 79 psychiatric nurses, 1979.
25. Meeting of IWWU, WUI and ITGWU 3 April 1979.
26. Letter, M. Uí Chlochasaigh to Maura Breslin, 24 May 1979.
27. ITGWU to Labour Court, 2 January 1980.

396   *These Obstreperous Lassies*

28. IWWU to ITGWU, 13 March 1980.
29. IWWU to Eastern Health Board, 5 August 1980.
30. Submission to the Labour Court by the IWWU, 23 March 1981, on foot of persistent delaying tactics employed by the EHB in regard to the implementation of DEE-4-80.
31. IWWU Executive Minutes 27 February 1980.
32. In 1979 the Federation of Rural Workers had merged with the Workers' Union of Ireland, and the name was changed to the Federated Workers' Union of Ireland.
33. IWWU Annual Convention 1980-81.
34. IWWU Executive Minutes 25 June 1980.

CHAPTER 20 (pp. 337-358)

1. IWWU Executive Minutes 25 February 1981.
2. This and other quotations in this section are from an interview with Ms Ní Mhurchú by the author in May 1987.
3. IWWU Executive Minutes 17 June 1981.
4. *Ibid.* 28 February 1981.
5. Annual General Meeting 20 May 1981.
6. Letter, Padraigín Ní Mhurchú to Patricia O'Donovan, ICTU, re IWWU shop steward courses, 26 April 1983.
7. IWWU Executive Minutes 23 September 1981.
8. *Ibid.* 21 October 1981.
9. JIC meeting 27 March 1982.
10. IWWU Annual Report, 1982.
11. See Mary Jones, 'Homeworking Research Project', Dublin: AnCO 1982, 88.
12. Letter, member of Traditional Handknitters Association to Padraigín Ní Mhurchú, November 1982.
13. Labour Court Recommendation No. 7003, 5 March 1982
14. Report on company liquidation, quoting Mr Norris, accountant/advisor to group, *The Irish Times* 1 June 1983.
15. Letter, IWWU to Dublin Laundry Co., 5 August 1982.
16. Letter, IWWU to ICTU, 18 August 1982.
17. Roneo letter, Padraigín Ní Mhurchú to members, 8 September 1981.
18. Letter, De La Rue to Secretary, Dublin Printing Trades' Group of Unions, 26 November 1981.
19. Handwritten notes, Padraigín Ní Mhurchú at meeting at FUE, 31 March 1982.
20. Letter, Padraigín Ní Mhurchú to Manager, De La Rue, 30 June 1982.
21. Letter, IWWU to members at De La Rue, 12 July 1982.
22. *The Irish Printer*, February 1983, 16-17.
23. IWWU Annual Convention 1982-83.
24. Report from Personnel Department, ESB, spring 1982. See also Labour Force Surveys 1960-1980.
25. *Allied Irish Banks' Review* October 1981. See also Donal Garvey, *A Profile of Demographic and Labour Force Characteristics of the*

Population, Dublin 1983 and NESC Report No. 63 1982.
26. Letter, Padraigín Ní Mhurchú to Donal Nevin, ICTU, 27 June 1983.
27. Contract Cleaners meeting, IWWU and FWUI, 14 September 1978.
28. Labour Court Recommendation No. 7541.
29. IWWU meeting with An Tánaiste, Dick Spring, July 1983.
30. Letter, Padraigín Ní Mhurchú to Minister for Labour, 25 July 1983.
31. *Ibid.*
32. Ruairí Quinn, Minister for Labour, announcing the establishment of a JLC for the contract cleaning industry, Equality Employment Agency launch of research project *The Hidden Workers,* Dublin 1983.
33. Newsletter, Padraigín Ní Mhurchú to members, 1984.

CHAPTER 21 (pp. 359-370)

1. ICTU Executive Council report to Women's Conference 1983.
2. Interview, Padraigín Ní Mhurchú, June 1987.
3. IWWU Annual Convention 1983.
4. Padraigín Ní Mhurchú to Executive at Special Executive Meeting, 1 October 1983.
5. Letters from ICTU Advisory Service, De La Rue File.
6. Statement from Ruairí Quinn, Minister of State, 13 October 1983.
7. *The Straits Times,* Singapore, 24 September 1983.
8. Notes in Amalgamation File, IWWU Archives.
9. ICTU Annual Report Cork 1981.
10. Letter to W. Attley.
11. Letter, Donal Nevin ICTU, to Padraigín Ní Mhurchú, 25 April 1984.
12. Registrar of Friendly Societies, 26 September 1984.

Abbreviations

ABA	An Bord Altranais [the Nursing Board]	FUE	Federated Union of Employers
ABU	Amalgamated Binders' Union	FWUI	Federated Workers' Union of Ireland (merger of FRW and WUI)
APKT	Alliance of Printing and Kindred Trades		
ASB	Amalgamated Society of Bookbinders	FWW	Federation of Women Workers
ASLP	Amalgamated Society of Lithographic Printers	HJSB	Hospital Joint Services' Board (established in 1974)
ASTMS	Association of Scientific, Technical and Management Staffs	IBATU	Irish Bookbinders' and Allied Trades' Union
		IBOA	Irish Bank Officials' Association
ASW	Amalgamated Society of Woodworkers	IBU	Irish Binders' Union
ATGWU	Amalgamated Transport and General Workers' Union	ICA	Irish Citizen Army
		* ICTU	Irish Congress of Trade Unions (1959)
BMRS	Bookbinders' and Machine Rulers' Society	ICW	International Congress of Women
BRA	Boxmakers' Registered Agreement	ICWU	Irish Clerical Workers' Union
BSOU	Boot and Shoe Operatives' Union	IDA	Industrial Development Authority
CBTB	Cardboard Boxmakers' Trade Board	IGS	Irish Graphical Society
		ILO	International Labour Organisation (based in Geneva)
* CIU	Congress of Irish Unions		
CSO	Central Statistics Office	IMPA	Irish Master Printers' Association
CTG	Clothing Trades' Group		
DCTU	Dublin Council of Trade Unions	INO	Irish Nurses' Organisation
		INTO	Irish National Teachers' Organisation
DDLA	Dublin District Laundries' Association (previously LLA)		
		INU	Irish Nurses' Union
DMPA	Dublin Master Printers' Association	IPF	Irish Printing Federation
		IPU	Irish Printers' Union
DPTG	Dublin Printing Trades' Group	ITB	Irish Trades' Board
		ITGWU	Irish Transport and General Workers' Union
DTC	Dublin Trades' Council		
DTLC	District Trades' and Labour Council	* ITUC	Irish Trades Union Congress
		ITWU	Irish Textile Workers' Union
DTPS	Dublin Typographical Provident Society	IUDWC	Irish Union of Distributive Workers and Clerks
DTUC	Dublin Trades Union Council	IWIL	Irish Women's International League
DWC	Dublin Workers' Council		
DWU	Domestic Workers' Union	IWLC	Irish Women's Labou Council
EEA	Employment Equality Agency	IWPDL	Irish Women Prisoners' Defence League
EEC	European Economic Community		
		IWRL	Irish Women's Reform League
EHB	Eastern Health Board	IWSF	Irish Women's Suffrage Federation
EPCC	Equal Pay Committee of Congress		
		IWTU	Irish Women's Trade Union
ESB	Electricity Supply Board	IWWCS	Irish Women Workers' Co-operative Society
FRW	Federation of Rural Workers (merged with WUI to become FWUI)		
		IWWF	Irish Women Workers' Federation
FTG	Furnishing Trade Group		

398

Abbreviations

IWWU	Irish Women Workers' Union (merged with FWUI in 1984)
JIC	Joint Industrial Council
JLC	Joint Labour Committee
LCTMA	Linen and Cotton Textile Manufacturers' Association
LLA	Leinster Laundries' Association (later DDLA)
LWS	Learners' Wage Schedule
NESC	National Economic and Social Council
NIHE	National Institute for Higher Education
NSB	National Society of Brushmakers
NUFTO	National Union of Furniture Trade Organisations
NUPBPW	National Union of Printing, Bookbinding and Paper Workers
NUPE	National Union of Public Employers
NUTGW	National Union of Tailors and Garment Workers
NUWW	National Union of Women Workers
NWA	National Wage Agreement
OBU	'ONE BIG UNION'
PKT	Printing and Kindred Trades
POWU	Post Office Workers' Union
PWS	Piece-Work Schedule
RBU	Rulers' and Bookbinders' Union
RUC	Relief of Unemployment Committee
SCTB	Sugar Confectionery Trade Board
SITB	Shirtmaking Industry Trade Board
SLADE	Society of Lithographic Artists, Designers, Engravers
TA	Typographical Association
TS	Typographical Society
TOSI	Textile Operatives' Society of Ireland
VEC	Vocational Education Committee
WF	Women's Federation (British)
WIL	Women's International League
WIKPF	Women's International League of Peace and Freedom
WIP	Women in Publishing
WUI	Workers' Union of Ireland (merged with FRW to become FWUI)

*A split in the Irish trade union movement in 1945 resulted in two congresses: The Irish Trades Union Congress, comprising unions with headquarters in Britain and those with headquarters in Ireland, and the Congress of Irish Unions, comprising only unions with headquarters in Ireland. The IWWU was affiliated to the Irish Trades Union Congress until 1959 when the Irish Congress of Trade Unions was established which resolved the division.

Select Bibliography

PRIMARY SOURCES
Irish Women Workers' Union
Executive Minutes 1919-1984, Vols. 1-12. IWWU Archives, Dublin.
Annual Reports 1924-1983. IWWU Archives, Dublin.
IWWU Annual Convention general documentation 1940-1983.
Printers' Committee. Minutes of the Printers' Section of the IWWU.
Laundresses' Committee. IWWU Minutes. Laundry ledger, Laundry Report Books. IWWU Archives.
Boxmakers' Committee. IWWU Minutes.
General Workers' Committee. IWWU Minutes.
IWWU Unemployment Register. IWWU Archives.
Files relating to the activities of all sections of the IWWU at their places of work, including correspondence between individual firms and Fleet Street. IWWU Archives, Dublin, 1918-1984.
Files relating to the involvement of the IWWU in a range of social and political activities. IWWU Archives, Dublin, 1918-1984.
Roneo open letter to The Public. Louie Bennett and Helen Files comprising miscellaneous documentation on all General Secretaries and a number of officers of the IWWU. IWWU Archives, Dublin, 1918-1984.Chenevix. 15 September 1945. IWWU Archives.
Roneo letter from Louie Bennett to Women Workers. 10 March 1953. IWWU Archives.

Dublin Trades' Council
Minutes 1918. MS 12780, National Library of Ireland.
DTUC File: Lower Prices Campaign 1947-48.

Joint Industrial Councils
Minutes of the JIC for the laundry industry, April 1948, December 1971.
Minutes of the JIC for the linen and cotton industry, August 1954.
Minutes of JIC for Dublin laundries, May 1968.
Minutes of JIC for printing industry, October/November 1962.

O'Brien, William
Diaries, MS 16273, National Library of Ireland.

PRIVATE COLLECTIONS
Hugh O'Connor Collection, Dublin
This collection relates primarily to the activities of Helena Molony.

Select Bibliography 401

John Manning Collection, Dublin
This collection contains a number of newspaper clippings on the retirement of Louie Bennett in 1956, miscellaneous articles by Louie Bennett, and a small photographic collection.

PRINTED MATERIAL

Bunreacht na hÉireann
The Constitution of Ireland 1937, Dublin. Also Draft Constitution 1937, and file on the Union response to particular Articles by Louie Bennett and Dorothy McArdle. IWWU Archives.

Central Statistics Office
Census of Industrial Production 1951-1961.
Labour Force Surveys, 1971-1981.

Commission on the Status of Women
Report. Dublin 1972.
Commission on Vocational Organisation
Preliminary Report. Dublin 1943.
Evidence of IWWU to Commission. MS 938. National Library of Ireland.
Daly, Mary
'*The Hidden Workers*'. Research Project, Dublin 1983.
Daly, Mary
'Women, Work and Trade Unionism' in *Women in Irish Society, the* Daly, Mary*Historical Dimention*. Dublin: Arlen House, Women's Press 1978.

International Labour Organisation
Report of the International Congress of Women. Zurich 1919. ILO Publication, Geneva 1920.

Irish Trades Union Congress
Memoranda from the Commission of Enquiry into the Irish Trade Union Movement 1936. Confidential document on terms of reference. IWWU Archives, Dublin.
Report of the Proceedings of the 43rd Annual Meeting of the ITUC, 1936-37.
Report of the Annual Conference of the ITUC, Kilkenny, 1951.

Irish Labour Party and Trades Union Congress
Report of the 22nd Annual Irish Trades Union Congress and Labour Party, Sligo, 1916.
Report of the Proceedings, 13th Annual Congress of the Irish

Labour Party and Trade Union Congress, 1924.
Report of the Proceedings of the Special Congress to deal with the Shannon Electrification Scheme, 30 November 1925.
Annual Report and proceedings of the 41st Annual Meeting, Guildhall, Derry 1935.

Irish Textile Workers' Union
Manifesto: The Linen Slaves of Belfast, 1913. Ulster Museum.

Jones, Mary
Homework Research Project. AnCO Report. Dublin 1982.

Martindale, Miss
Truck and Gombeening in Donegal. Appendix IV, Factories and Workshops Annual Report 1907.

Orme & Abraham, Misses, (Assistant Commissioners)
The Conditions of Women's Work in Ireland. Royal Commission on Labour, 1893-1894. National Library of Ireland.

NEWSPAPERS AND PERIODICALS

*National and Economic and Social Council [NESC] R*eport no. 63, July 1982. *Population and Labour Force Projection by Country and Region 1979-1981*. Established 1926 and ceased in November 1928.

An Bhean Oibre
Vol. 1, No. 5, September 1926; Vol 1, No. 8, December 1926 (IWWU Archives); and also August 1928 (National Library of Ireland).

Bean na hÉireann,
Magazine of Inghinidhe na hÉireann. Established 1908.

Evening Mail, The
Dublin daily paper established in 1823.

Evening Star, The
Waterford daily paper established 1917.

Independent, The
Drogheda weekly paper established 1884.

Irish Catholic, The
Weekly paper established 1888.

Irish Citizen, The,
Weekly paper of Irish Women's Suffrage Movement from 1912 - 1920.

Irish Independent , The

Daily paper established 1891. Letters to the Editor in reference to 'Miss Molony and the Pope', July 1932.
Irish People, The
Weekly paper established 1899.
Irish Times, The
Daily paper established 1859.
Irish Worker, The,
Weekly paper founded by James Larkin in 1911. 'Women Workers Column', ed. Delia Larkin.
Meath Chronicle, The,
Weekly paper established 1891.
Saturday Post, The,
Dublin weekly newspaper established 1910.
Straits Times, The
Contemporary paper published in Penang, Malaysia.
Torch, The,
Established 1919. Published by Catholic Truth Society.
Trade Union Information
'Women at Work'. November 1970
Voice of Labour, The
Labour Party and Trade Union Movement Paper, 1922-1927. Succeeded by *The Irishman* 1927-30.
Watchword of Labour, The
Succeeded *The Irishman* 1930-1932. Presidential Address to Congress by Louie Bennett published 30 July 1932.
Wicklow People, The
County newspaper.
Workers' Republic, The
Socialist weekly newspaper founded by James Connolly, 1898.

SECONDARY SOURCES

Boyd, Andrew. *The Rise of the Irish Trade Unions, 1729-1970.* Tralee 1972.

Brown, Terence. *Ireland, a Social and Cultural History 1922-1979.* London 1981.

Cockburn, Cynthia. *Brothers: Male Dominance and Technological Change.* London: Pluto Press 1983.

Cody, Seamus, O'Dowd, John and Rigney, Peter.
The Parliament of Labour: 100 Years of the Dublin Council of Trade Unions. Dublin 1986.

Connolly, James. *Socialism and Nationalism.* Dublin 1948.

Cullen, L.M. *Life in Ireland*. London 1968.
Cullen Owens, Rosemary. *Smashing Times, A History of the Irish Womens' Suffrage Movement 1889-1922*. Dublin 1984.
Fox, R.M. *History of the Irish Citizen Army*. Dublin 1946
Louie Bennett: Her Life and Times. Dublin 1958.
Glandon, Virginia E. *Arthur Griffith and the Advanced-Nationalist Press, Ireland 1900-1922*. New York: Long Island 1985.
Greaves, Desmond. *The Irish Transport and General Workers' Union: The Formative Years 1909-1923*. Dublin: Gill and Macmillan 1982.
Hareven, Tamara K. *Family Time and Industrial Time*. Cambridge 1982.
Keogh, Dermot. *The Rise of the Irish Working Class*. Belfast 1982.
Kelly, Joan. *Women, History and Theory*. Chicago 1984.
Kessler-Harris Alice. *Out to Work, A History of Wage-Earning Women in the United States* Oxford. 1982.
Larkin, Emmet J. *James Larkin, Irish Labour Leader, 1876-1947*. London 1965.
Lee, Joseph. *The Modernisation of Irish Society*. Dublin 1973.
Litton, Frank. *Unequal Achievement: The Irish Experience 1957-1982*. Dublin 1982.
Lyons, F.S.L. *Ireland Since the Famine*. London 1971.
McCarthy Charles. *Trade Unions in Ireland 1894-1960* Dublin: Institute of Public Administration 1977.
MacCurtain, Margaret and Ó Corráin, Donncha (eds.), *Women in Irish Society*. Dublin 1978
McGill, Patrick. *The Rat Pit*. London 1915.
Thompson, Paul. *The Nature of Work, An Introduction to Debates on the Labour Process*. London 1983.
Ward, Margaret. *Unmanageable Revolutionaries, Women and Irish Nationalism*. Kerry 1983.

PAMPHLETS

IWWU *Peace and Fraternity*. Issued by the IWWU, June 1952.
The Fortnight's Holiday as a Symbol. July 1945.
A Guide for the IWWU. The application of the Conditions of Employment Act.
Do Employers Want Strikes? 1945.

Index

Abbey Theatre, 14, 15, 19
Abraham, Miss, 3
Adams, Lillis, 353
Adelaide Hospital, 299
Allied Irish Banks' Review, 355
Amalgamated Binders' Union, 75
Amalgamated Society of Bookbinders, 73-7
Amalgamated Society of Lithographic Printers, 26
Amalgamated Society of Woodworkers, 14
Amalgamated Transport and General Workers' Union, 171, 172, 228, 281
AnCo, 351
Annual Conventions, 37, 60, 63, 67, 90-93, 95, 97, 100, 105, 123-4, 153, 173, 209-10, 231, 234, 269, 282, 289, 295, 313, 337
   admission of men, 117-18
   on automation, 246-7, 254, 331-2
   Conditions of Employment Act, 133
   on equal pay, 305
   on hours of work, 195
   letter from Miss Bennett, 222
   on married women, 353-4, 359
   merger discussions, 271-4, 362, 369
   Miss Bennett retires, 225-6
   Miss Breslin retires, 344
   Miss Chenevix resigns, 235-6, 238
   on part-time work, 243-4
   role of, 112, 225, 232, 245
Anthony, R.S.,171
Anti-Conscription Campaign, 19, 26
Anti-Discrimination (Pay) Act 1974, 311, 313, 326-7, 329, 360
Anti-Imperialist League, 99
Apprentices' League, 63
Apprenticeship Act, 101-2, 115
Apprenticeship Committee for Furniture Trade, 242
Apprenticeship Working Party, AnCo, 351
apprenticeships, 4, 51
   bookbinding, 36
   lowered age limit, 256
   need for, 241-3
   printing industry, 124, 323-4
   retraining, 351-2
   wage rates, 241
   for women, 241
   working conditions, 2
Armstrong's, 88, 95, 112, 121, 196
Arnott, Lady, 17

Arnott's, 303
Associated Printers, 308
Associated Properties Ltd, 143
Association of Scientific, Technical and Managerial Staffs, 359
Attic Press, 340
Attley, Billy, 366, 368
Aust, June, 238
Automac, 110
automation
   cause of unemployment, 66, 77, 120-22
   demarcation disputes, 257-8, 339, 342-3
   increased stress, 193-5
   in laundries, 78-9, 94-5, 108, 176, 177
   in printing industry, 73, 332
   and productivity, 245-7
   spread of, 71
   textile industry, 261-3
   and wage rates, 101, 230
   and working hours, 238, 253, 264-5

bagmaking, 52-3, 60, 73
Bailey and Gibson, 161, 285, 306-9, 339, 342, 349
Balbriggan, Co. Dublin, 136, 137
Bank of Ireland Computer Centre, 356-7
Bannon, May, 45
Batchelor's, 275
Bean na hÉireann, 14-15
Bedaux system, 135
Behan, Theresa, 32, 48, 207, 335, 353
Belfast, Co. Antrim, 7-8, 39
   ICTU visit, 334
   linen industry, 316
Bennett, James Cavendish, 21
Bennett, Louie, 32, 41, 49, 107, 114, 239, 251, 367
   on apprenticeship, 51
   automation campaigns, 116
   clothing industry campaigns, 317
   on Commission for Vocational Organisation, 155-6
   Conditions of Employment Act campaign, 126, 127, 131
   Constitution campaign, 140-41
   death, 233
   defends employment of women, 124-5
   and DTC, 34
   early career, 21-2
   and Emergency, 164

on government and unions, 43, 111-12
holidays campaign, 176, 179, 180, 183-4, 186
housing scheme, 143, 152
international interests, 232
and ITGWU split, 63
IWWU Executive member, 21-3, 25, 227
　on admission of men, 117
　General Secretary, 33
　Honorary Secretary, 26
　influence of, 29
　internal disputes, 33
　joint secretary, 91
　leave of absence, 154-5, 161
　on marriage benefit, 106
　opposition to, 217-18
　recruitment campaigns, 39-40, 42
　resignations, 89-90, 98-9, 202-5, 221-2
　retirement, 224-6
　revival of IWWU, 23-4
　role of, 164-5, 197, 202-5, 207, 216-21, 240
　salary, 48, 62
　and staff appointments, 61, 157-9
laundry industry campaigns, 78-9, 200-202
minimum wage campaign, 82, 85, 86
on outworking, 52
political involvement, 46-7, 59, 97-8, 173
　President TUC, 102
　Senate nomination, 154-5
　Vice-President of ITUC, 98, 99
printing industry campaigns, 36, 56, 73, 215-18
and strikes, 37-8, 217
time dockets campaign, 145, 197
tobacco industry campaigns, 109
and Trade Union Bill, 170
on trade union movement, 166, 333
visits ILO, 102-3
on woman's place, 153
working conditions campaign, 190
Bermingham, Joe, 339
Bhean Oibre, An, 70-72, 80, 84, 88
Binders' Union, 257
Birch, Mr, 128
Bird, Miss, 24
Black and Tans, 43, 46-7
Blackrock Hosiery Co., 39, 58
Bloomfield Laundry, 176, 189, 282, 302
Bolton Street Technical School, 101
bonus systems, 246, 360
　laundries, 194, 195-7
Bookbinders' and Machine Rulers' Society, 35-6
bookbinding, 35-6
Bord Altranais, An, 237
Bord Telecom, 360-61
Boxmakers' Registered Agreement, 286
boxmaking industry, 24, 45, 57, 58
　decline, 233
　lockout, 277
　redundancies, 326
　renegotiation, 247-8
　threat to employees, 285-8
　wage rates, 7-8, 81-6, 89, 215
　wartime shortages, 159, 160
Bracken, Rosaleen, 332, 335, 352-4
Bray and District Trades' Council, 226
Bray Council of Action, 201-2
Bray Printing Company, 201
Bray Trades and Labour Council, 200
Bray Urban District Council, 198
Brennan, Miss, 63, 186, 239
Brenner, Mr, 180
Breslin, Maura, 207, 210, 220, 356, 369
　automation campaign, 246-7
　clothing industry campaigns, 293-4, 317-19
　deaths, 367
　and ICTU, 297-8, 363
　ill-health, 320-21
　IWWU Executive member, 283, 315
　　Assistant General Secretary, 289
　　General Secretary, 224-5, 295
　　and merger, 333
　　on policy, 274
　　President, 231, 233
　　retirement, 334-5, 337, 338, 343-4
　　salary, 240
　　support for staff, 313
　laundry industry campaigns, 300
　on married women, 300-301
　nursing campaigns, 329
　on part-time work, 308
　political involvement, 338-9
　printing industry campaigns, 321-3, 325, 332
　on status of women, 304
　trustee IWWU, 217
　on work measurement, 250
　working conditions campaigns, 296-7
Brook, Frank, 27
Brown, Frances, 45
Brown, Terence, 253
Browne, Dr Noel, 192, 219
Browne, Senator, 132
Browne, Vincent, 347

Index

Browne and Nolan, 67, 73-7, 147, 257
Brunswick Press, 161
Bryan, Brigid, 25, 32, 48, 204, 207
   on woman's place, 153
Buckley, Miss, 60, 238
Buckley, Mrs, 54, 94, 111, 154, 204, 210
   in Balbriggan, 136-7
   and FWW, 40-41, 47
   retirement, 232
   on staff appointment, 158
Bulb Factory, Bray, 137
Bullman, Clare, 354
Burke, Miss, 189
Burke, Mr, 74
Butler, Eleanor, 184
Byrne, Frances, 335
Byrne, Gay, 344-5
Byrne, Mary, 298, 351
Byrne, Miss, 47, 96, 97

C.E. Litho Printing and Co., 45
Cadden, John, 345
Caffrey, Lizzie, 24, 171-2, 197, 216, 297
   General Secretary election, 224-5, and ICTU, 250
Cahill's, 60, 94-5, 145, 147, 270-71, 273
   applications for IGS, 278
   automation, 332
Caldwell's, 36
Callender, Mrs, 54
Camco folding machine, 339
Campbell, Patrick (Quidnunc), 182-3, 187
Campbell, Senator Seán, 83
canteen facilities, 189, 190, 299
Capital Spicer, 349
Cardboard Boxmakers' Trade Board, 81-3, 85, 86
Cardiff, Paddy, 337, 366, 367
Carney, Winifred, 16, 21
Carpenter, Walter, 14, 15
Carroll, Miss, 162
Carrolls, Messrs, 93
Casey's, 118
Cassells, Peter, 349
Cauldwell's, 112
chemical industry, 113
Chenevix, Helen, 32, 49, 138, 239, 251, 367
   Conditions of Employment Act campaign, 126-7, 131
   early career, 226-7
   health service campaigns, 212
   holidays campaign, 176, 177, 183-4
   hours of work campaigns, 28

   housing scheme, 143
   IWWU Executive member, 22, 161-2
   and admission of men, 111, 115
   General Secretary, 98, 224-8
   Honorary Secretary, 26
   influence of, 29
   reorganisation, 89-90
   resignation, 232
   retirement, 236, 238
   revival of IWWU, 24
   role of, 197, 204-5, 240
   on salaries, 48
   salary, 91
   services to members, 234
   laundry industry campaigns, 47, 188-9, 230
   minimum wage campaign, 86
   night work campaign, 100-101
   on poaching, 118
   political involvement, 97-8, 173, 222, 227-8
   President ITUC, 212, 297
   school leaving age campaign, 102
   on strikes, 37
   textile industry campaigns, 55
   wardsmaids campaign, 218
   on woman's place, 153
Cherry and Smalldridge, 81, 85-6, 259
   interchangeability dispute, 285-6
Chez Nous Chocolates, 291
child care facilities, 359
City and County Managers' Association, 207
Civic Commissioners, 68
civil service, 218-19, 297
Civil Service Arbitration Awards, 218
Civil War, 55, 57, 59
Clancy-Gore, P.C., 176
Clarke, Mr, 146
Clarke, Mrs Tom, 132
Clarke's Tobacco Factory, 62
cleaners, 57, 119-20, 143, 188-9; *see also* contract cleaners
Clerical Workers' Union, 56
clerks, 57, 92
Clery and Co., 301
Clifford, Mai, 233, 280, 298, 313, 314, 335, 336
   on equal pay, 306
   President IWWU, 306
   Treasurer, 354
clothing industry, 112, 113, 138, 230
   conditions of work, 294
   demarcation disputes, 117
   reserved for men, 138, 139
   unionisation, 115
   wage rates, 2, 312

working conditions, 2
co-operative movement, 44; *see also* Irish Women Workers' Co-operative Society
Coady, Miss, 91
College of Technology, Bolton St, 324, 351
Command Laundry, 93-4
Commission of Enquiry into Trade Union Movement, 137-8
Commission on Emigration, 191-2
Commission on the Status of Women, 304, 305, 312
Commission on Vocational Organisation, 155-6
Committee on Reconstruction, 27
Committees
    Boxmakers' Committee, 247
    Civic Committee, 62-3, 66, 102
    Finance Committee, 32, 143, 157, 202-3
        strike pay, 181, 185-6, 277
    Industrial Organisation Committee, 269-70
    Laundry Committee, 187
    Old People's Committee, 283-4
    Organising Committee, 92
    Printers' Committee, 216, 217, 225, 278, 317, 321-2, 351
        apprenticeship age limit, 256
        and boxmaking, 247-8
        guaranteed week dispute, 243-4
        interchangeability campaign, 286-8, 322-3
        and merger talks, 273
        part-time work, 308-9, 310
    Social Committee, 223-4
    Vocational Education Committee, 102
    Waterproof Workers' Committee, 117-18
Common Market Defence Campaign, 338
Communism, 97, 107, 227
Conditions of Employment Act, 123, 139, 150, 177, 298, 348, 365
    amendments suggested, 193
    controversy among unions, 125-33
    effects of, 134
    exclusion orders, 262-3, 275
    holidays, 136
    IWWU Guide to, 135
    IWWU representations on, 125
    and laundries, 175
    restrictive of women, 261-2
    Section 16 (earlier Section 12), 125-33, 139, 143, 154
Conditions of Women's Work in Ireland, 3
conditions of work, 2-3, 23, 28, 45-6, 66, 188-93, 197

bad work, 228
campaigns, 174-87, 300-301
clothing industry, 294
injurious to health, 299-300
inspections, 259
laundries, 188-90, 195-6
nurses, 71, 192, 211-15
still poor, 296-7
see also automation
Confexin Fashion Ltd, 319
Congested Districts Board, 3
Congress of Irish Unions, 224, 231
Connolly, James, 13, 14, 18, 22, 200, 366
    Easter Rising, 19-20
    in USA, 15
    and women workers, 15-16, 17
Connolly, Miss, 91
Connolly, R.J., 200
Constitution, *see* Irish Constitution
contract cleaners, 343, 356-8
Contract Cleaners Ltd, 356
Co-operation North, 334
co-operatives, 156-7, 318-19
Cork, 60, 62
Cosgrave, W.T., 87
cost of living, 220
Council of the Unemployed, 68
County and City Managers' Association, 237
Court Laundry, 194, 263-5
    bonus system, 195-6
    closure, 301-2
    working conditions, 300
Coyle, Kathleen, 210
craft unions, 4-5, 65
Cross, Miss, 48
Cullen, Miss, 32, 48
Cumann na mBan, 19, 20

Dáil Éireann, 32, 43, 63
Daily News, 347
Dakota, 339, 349
Daly, Ann, 357
Daly, Mark, 185
Daly, Mary, 297
Daly, P.T., 1, 29, 169, 170
Dargle and Bray Laundry, 115, 191
Davis, Messrs, 174
Davis Miss, 24
Davis, Mrs Pat, 300, 302, 314, 335
De La Rue, Thomas, Ltd, 256, 298, 344, 346, 348, 354
    closure, 363-5
    IWWU members in, 321, 340

part-time work, 243-4
redundancies, 350-1,
de Valera, Eamon, 103, 106, 123, 131, 203, 252
  Constitution, 139-42
Defence, Department of, 163
Defence of the Realm Act, 13
demarcation, 35, 112
  clothing industry, 117
  and Conditions of Employment Act, 261-2
  effects of automation, 116, 275-8
  interchangeability campaign, 285-8
  printing industry, 76, 94-5, 117, 247-8, 257-8, 265-8, 306-9, 307, 339, 349
  sex-based, 4, 206
  textile industry, 296
Denmark, 254
Derry, 47
Design Print, 348
Dignan, Mrs, 361
Distressed Protestants' Association, 314
Do Employers Want Strikes?, 178
Dolan, Mr, 93
Dollard, Messrs, 67, 145, 146
  time dockets, 196-7
Dolphin Hotel, 179
domestic servants, 29, 41, 93-4, 109, 143, 165
  difficulties of organisation, 8
  emigration, 191
  IWWU campaign, 143-4
Domestic Workers' Union, 54
Donegal, 56
Donegal Trades Council, 126
Donnybrook Convent Laundry, 176
Doran, Alice, 234
double jobbing, 347
Douglas, Co.Cork, 55
Douglas, Senator, 132
Dowling, Sighle, 96, 97, 105-6
Doyle, Brenda, 361
Doyle, Miss, 137
Drew, Mrs, 246
Drogheda, Co. Louth, 56, 60
Drogheda Independent, 318
Dublin and District Laundries' Association, 185
Dublin Box Company, 45, 81-4, 86
Dublin Commercial Public Utility Society, 143
Dublin Corporation, 40, 143, 152, 173, 197, 226, 234
Dublin Council of Trade Unions (DCTU), 306, 314, 335
Dublin County Council, 339-40

Dublin District Laundries' Association, 175, 229
Dublin Laundry Co., 344, 348
Dublin Master Printers' Association, 25, 50, 62, 76, 81
  employment of women, 88
  hours of work, 132-3, 136
  ITGWU dispute, 118-19
  printers' strike, 215
  time dockets, 67, 95, 144-6, 149
Dublin Port Milling Company, 210
Dublin Printers' Protection Campaign, 78
Dublin Printing Trades' Group, 350, 351, 364
Dublin Trades' Council, 1, 19, 25, 96, 139
  and Delia Larkin, 29, 30-31
  financial assistance from, 37
  holidays dispute, 184
  and IWWU, 29, 33-4, 92, 152-3, 197, 233
  Monument dispute, 200-201
  Trade Union Bill, 166, 167, 169, 170
Dublin Typographical Provident Society, 24, 84, 267, 276
Dublin Union, 143, 165
Dublin Workers' Council, 69
Duffy, Luke, 169
Dun Laoghaire Borough Council, 227
Dun Laoghaire Corporation, 173
Dunbar, Mrs, 170
Dundalk, Co.Louth, 115, 117
Dundalk Trades' and Workers' Council, 180
Dunlop's Laundry, 78, 301, 366

Early, Nuala, 317
Eason, Messrs, 56
Easter Rising, 1916, 19-20
Eastern Health Board, 328-31
Economic Development, 252
Economic War, 107, 113
economy
  depression, 107, 113
  development, 113-14, 279-80
  oil crisis, 313-14
Eden, Maud, 24
Edenderry and District Trades and Labour Council, 39-40
education, 34, 57, 92, 210
  job training, 101-2
  school leaving age, 60, 102
  school meals, 227
  shop steward courses, 302, 341-2
egg-packing, 191
electrical appliance industry, 112, 113
Emergency *see* World World 2

Emergency Power Order, 170
emigration, 13-14, 51, 73, 191-2, 197, 236, 241, 255, 257, 258
of nurses, 213
Employer Labour Conferences, 304-5, 317
Employment Appeals Tribunal, 338
Employment Benefit Scheme, 144
Employment Equality Act, 328-32
Engineering Union, 83
England, 1, 11, 17, 56
emigration to, 51, 191-2, 213
minimum wage, 81
temporary work in, 277
working conditions, 211
equal pay, 101, 117, 129, 139, 197, 311
attitude of employers to, 304-5
and demarcation, 321-5, 328
growing campaign for, 295-6,
ILO questionnaire, 206
IWWU claims, 306, 311, 313, 326-8
printing industry, 306-10
slow progress, 298-9, 328, 360
Equal Pay Agreements, 325
Eucharistic Congress, 107
European Court of Justice, 360-61
European Economic Community, 298, 305, 312, 314, 338
Europrint, 266-7
Evening Mail, 147-8, 184, 218
Ever Ready, 136
Exchequer Printers, 310
Executive, 24-5, 37-8, 49, 72, 259, 270-71, 289
and admission of men, 111
changes in, 224-6, 354
commitment of, 138
criticisms of, 39, 47, 300, 313, 317-21, 361-2
dependence on, 209-10
and efficiency systems, 193, 194-5
Golden Jubilee, 283-4
holidays campaign, 186
housing scheme, 143
and ICTU, 334
lack of policy, 34-5,
minutes, 32, 315
need for assistance, 157-9
need for reorganisation, 89-90, 92
need to reduce expenditure, 91-2
nurses' campaign, 89
political involvement, 29-30, 59-60, 96-8, 173-4, 197
pressure of work, 120
printing industry campaigns, 215-17
on productivity, 247
profile, 154-5, 204-5, 239
on protective legislation, 100-101
recruitment, 294-5
relations with members, 46-7, 96, 102, 317-18
resignations, 89-90, 98-9, 164-5, 202-5, 278-9
retirements, 232
salaries, 48, 61, 90
time dockets campaign, 145-9
vote of confidence, 274

Factories' Advisory Council, 297
Factory Act, 177
Factory Inspection, 52, 62
Fagan, Brigid, 343
Falconer's, Kilmainham, 91
Farming Today, 156-7
Farrell, Mrs, 246
Farrell, Nellie, 112
Fascism, 113-14, 156, 168
Faulat Shirt Factory, 121-2
Federated Union of Employers, 205, 229, 358
on equal pay, 305
holidays dispute, 177, 179, 182-7
National Wage Agreement, 269
pensions, 301
Federated Workers' Union of Ireland, 335, 337, 338, 344
and contract cleaners, 357
IWWU merges with, 368-70
merger talks, 333, 362, 365-8
shop steward training, 341-2
Federation of Women Workers, 47
Fegan, Miss, 99
Fellowship of Reconciliation, 226
feminism, 48, 150, 153
Ferguson, Mr, 85, 166
ffrench-Mullen, Madeline, 24, 26, 46
Fianna Fáil, 132, 339
Finance, Department of, 58
Fine Gael, 114
fines, 46
Fingall, Lady, 17
fishing industry, 56
Fitzsimons, Mrs, 115
Flanagan, Fr John, 24, 132
Flynn, Mr, 198, 201-2
Foir Teoranta, 318
Folens, 293
Foran, Thomas, 12, 23, 29, 30-31
Forrestal, J.P., 200
Fortnight's Holiday as a Symbol, The, 178

Index 411

fowl pluckers, 39
Fox, R.M., 83
Frederick Press, 339
Freeman's Journal, 61
fruit pickers, 190-91
Furnishing Trade Group, 101
furniture manufacture, 121, 242

Gallaher's, 108-9, 122, 291, 305, 313
Galway, 55
Gannon, Miss, 111
Garment Workers' Union, Sweden, 255
General Nursing Certificate, 120
General Textiles, 134, 196
George, David Lloyd, 46-7
George V, King, 14
Geraghty, Jennie, 235
Geraghty, M., 24
Gibson, Guy and Smalldridge, 285
Gilbey's, 296-7
Ginnell, Mrs, 24
Gloucester, Miss, 63
Gonne, Maud *see* MacBride, Maud Gonne
Goodbody's, Messrs, 35, 68, 92-3
Government Order, 120
Grangegorman Joint Committee, 173
Grangegorman Mental Hospital, 120, 192, 207, 210, 236-7
   married women employed, 242
   working conditions, 211-15
Graphic Films Ltd, 266-7
Greenmount and Boyne Linen Co., 160, 261, 262-3, 275, 295, 317
   loss of earnings, 298
Grosvenor Cleaning Ltd, 356
Guardian, The, 364
Guild of Church Industries, 62
Guild of Youth, 161
Guy and Co. Ltd, 285
Gwynn, Dr R.M., 161-2

Hackett, Rosie, 18, 20, 24, 26
Hall, Mr, 262, 263, 296
handknitting, 57, 344-6
Hanley, Rita, 104
Hanraty, Bridgit, 84
Harold's Cross Laundry, 188, 189, 258, 301
Harrison, Miss, 24
Harroway, Mr, 74-6
Harvey's, Waterford, 210, 233, 259
Haslan, Mrs, 17
Haughey, Charles, 339, 340
Hayes, Father, 157

Hayes, Miss, 239
health
   work-induced illnesses, 299-300
   health services, 219; *see also* nurses
Hearne, Mr, 131
Hely, Edward and Co., 28
Hely Thom, 275
Hely's, 37
Hibernian Hotel, 179
High Park Convent Laundry, 176
Hill and Sons, Messrs, 25
Hilton, Messrs, 116, 241
holidays, 28, 94, 98, 133, 155, 174
   under Conditions of Employment Act, 136
   laundries, 174-87, 196
   mandatory, 123
Holidays Employees' Act, 356
Holmpatrick, Lady, 17
Holy Trinity School, 344
Home Counties Contract Cleaners Ltd, 356
Horn and Metal Industries, 104
hosiery trade, 303
Hospital Joint Services' Board, 303, 326-7, 358, 368
Hospital Sweeps, 162
hospitals, 191, 192, 260; *see also* nurses
   employment in, 80
   equal pay claim, 326-7
   laundries, 179, 189, 299-300, 358
hotel workers, 29
hours of work, 132-3, 162, 253
   and automation, 122, 238, 253
   changing patterns, 275
   forty-four-hour week, 37
   forty-hour week, 136, 195, 238, 265, 298
   IWWU campaigns, 248, 260
   laundries, 28, 79, 135-6
   and married women, 309-10
   part-time work, 243-4, 306-7, 310--11
   short-time shifts, 291, 342
   textile industry, 228-9
   and wartime shortages, 160
housing, 227, 234
   IWWU scheme, 66, 70, 143, 152-3
Hughes, Janet, 369
Hunt-Hackett, Miss, 24

Ideal Trading Co., 143
Imco Laundry, 189
Incorporated Orthopaedic Hospitals of Ireland, 179
Industrial Development Authority, 318, 365
Industrial Relations Act 1967, 317

Industry and Commerce, Department of, 58, 85, 103, 131, 179
  exclusion orders, 262, 275
  holidays dispute, 183
  IWWU representations to, 73, 82, 93, 115-16, 139
  and strikes, 148
  and Trade Union Bill, 166, 203
  wartime shortages, 160
Inghinidhe na hÉireann, 14
injury compensation, 8
ink industry, 115
International Congress of Women, 26
International Industrial Relations Institute, 154
International Labour Organisation, 56, 100, 102-3, 206
International Women's Year, 311
Ireland, John and Co., Tailors, 116
Irish Bank Officials' Association, 172-3
Irish Binders' Union, 56
Irish Bookbinders' and Allied Trades' Union, 116, 332
  organising rights dispute, 198-202
  rivalry over machines, 339, 342-3
Irish Carton Printers, 256
Irish Citizen, 16, 17, 22, 48, 51, 54
  offficial IWWU paper, 49-50
Irish Citizen Army, 13, 14, 19, 26, 46
  and IWWU, 17-18
Irish Clerical Workers' Union, 30
Irish Congress of Trade Unions, 270, 286, 334; *see also* Women's Advisory Committee
  Conferences, 251
  and equal pay, 305-6, 306, 326-7
  Executive Council, 359, 363
  IWWU involvement, 154, 249-50, 274, 335, 338-9
  National Wage Agreement, 269
  and protective legislation, 349
  reserved seats for women, 362-3
  shop steward training, 341-2
  textile industry study, 255
  Women's Conferences, 352-3, 359-60, 363
  and work measurement, 250-1
  Work Study Department, 316, 321
Irish Constitution, 1937,103, 147, 151, 199
  and Trade Union Bill, 169-70
  and working women, 139-42
Irish Co-operative Society, 345
Irish Federation of University Teachers, 368
Irish Feminist Information, 340
Irish Graphical Society, 276, 277-8,

Irish Independent, 5, 107, 132, 201, 370
Irish Labour History Society, 314
Irish Master Printers' Association, 198, 200-201
Irish Medical Association, 219
Irish Nurses' Co-operative Hostel, 44
Irish Nurses' Organisation, 237
Irish Nurses' Union, 40, 41, 62
Irish Pacifist Movement, 226
Irish People, 176, 177
Irish Press, 124, 132, 141
Irish Printing Federation, 243, 247, 276
  equal pay, 305, 313, 321-4
  interchangeability, 285-8, 359
Irish Productivity Centre, 345
Irish Seamen and Port Workers' Union, 171
Irish Sweeps, 236
Irish Times, 73, 132, 182-3, 187, 201, 264, 348
Irish Trades' Board, 7-8
Irish Trades' Union Congress, 3, 42, 113-14, 226
  appeals to, 76, 134, 224
  Conditions of Employment Act campaign, 125-31
  Constitution campaign, 139
  holidays campaign, 183, 184, 185
  on hours of work, 195, 238
  IWWU involvement, 22-3, 98, 99, 102, 122, 159, 161, 297
  IWWU wins decision against, 284
  mental health service, 212
  Monument dispute, 201
  night work, 100-101
  pacifist resolution, 227-8
  and PAYE, 233
  Provisional Congress, 231
  split, 1924, 63-6
  trade unions enquiry, 137-8
  on unemployment, 224
  and wage rates, 103-4
  Women's Advisory Committee, 205
  and WUI, 30
Irish Transport and General Workers' Union, 1, 12-13, 33, 180, 347, 366
  boxmakers' campaign, 81, 83, 86
  Conditions of Employment Act campaign, 128
  and contract cleaners, 357
  EHB dispute, 328-31
  equal pay claims, 327
  Lockout, 1913, 10, 12-13
  male membership only, 4
  mental health service, 211

Index 413

merger talks, 333, 362
negotiating licence fee, 172
nurses' pay claim, 207
poaching, 118
printers' strike, 215-17
relations with IWWU, 6, 9, 62, 118-19, 237, 273, 280-81, 282, 300, 363
   demarcation disputes, 303, 307-8, 339, 342, 349
Irish Union of Distributive Workers and Clerks, 128, 129, 362, 365-6
Irish Volunteers, 19
Irish Women Prisoners' Defence League, 107
Irish Women Workers' Co-operative Society, 11-12, 15-18, 20
Irish Women Workers' Federation
   suggested, 40-41
Irish Women Workers' Union, 41-2, 256-8
   affiliations, 29, 38, 249, 314
   and automation, 193-5
   branches, 49, 54-5, 60, 110
   Conditions of Employment Act campaign, 125-33, 135
   conservatism, 204-5
   Constitution campaign, 139-42
   control of, 112
   controversies within, 278-9
   demonstrations, 10, 73
   early campaigns, 7-8
   and Easter Rising, 19-20
   election campaigns, 59, 67, 151
   during Emergency, 163-4
   on emigration, 191-2
   as employment agency, 234-5
   finances, 91-2, 143
      contributions increased, 282
      cost-benefit analysis, 361-2
      good, 62, 155, 208, 249, 289
      organisation of, 32
      problems, 37, 61, 245, 302, 314
      review of, 341
   foundation of, 1-2, 5-7
   Golden Jubilee, 283-4
   and government interference, 43, 45
   holidays campaign, 175-87
   housing scheme *see under* housing
   independence celebrated, 334
   inter-union rivalry, 35-6, 73-7, 118-19, 198-202, 241, 266-7, 276, 280-81, 282, 319, 339-40
   and JICs, 61
   and Labour Party, 59-60, 67, 69, 70, 87, 96, 122-4, 131, 150-51
   lockouts, 60-61, 119, 276-8
      1913, 10-13
   and married women, 244, 291, 300, 301, 352-3, 354-5, 359
   membership
      admission of men, 110-11, 115-18, 333
      apathy, 96, 209, 245-6, 255
      arrears, 237, 255, 283
      benefits, 44, 50, 282
      contributions, 317
      criticism from, 39, 47, 300, 313, 317-18, 319-20, 321, 361-2
      declines in, 38-9, 104, 120-21, 155, 158-9, 231-2, 235, 236-8, 240, 248-9, 282, 311, 319, 339-40
      fluctuating, 44
      increases, 28, 32, 135, 282
      intimidation of, 80
      inward-looking, 232
      militancy, 259-60, 289-90, 295, 332
      numbers, 29, 108, 114, 150, 172, 197, 208, 249, 274, 282, 303, 333
      picket placed on IWWU, 315-17
      profile, 153-4
      support for automation, 246-7
      unemployed members, 162-3
   merger discussions, 302-3, 333-4, 365-70
   negotiating licence fee, 172-3
   newspaper, 49-50, 70-72, 88
   opposed to industrial unions, 270
   organisation, 315
      difficulties, 209-10, 270
      modernisation, 340-42
      outside Dublin, 49, 115, 136-7, 249, 317, 319
      reform, 240-41
   policy, 34, 37, 44, 45, 143, 151
   political fund, 67, 70, 122, 232
   political involvement, 63-6, 67, 69, 106-7, 122-4, 150-51, 173-4
   political tensions, 13, 26, 29-30, 47-8, 57, 59, 87, 96-8
   premises
      Denmark House, 28
      Eden Quay, 57, 99
      Fleet St, 111, 314, 340, 368
      Gardiner St, 24
      Great Brunswick St, 8-9
      Liberty Hall, 6, 24
   Provident Fund, 167
   recruitment, 39-40, 55-7, 107-8, 115, 135, 137, 274, 294-5, 341, 343
   registered trade union, 26

revival, 21-6
role of, 234-5, 304
on shift work, 134-5
shop steward courses, 302
social activities, 7, 9, 11, 55, 57, 66, 92, 95-6, 223-4, 284
staff, 238-9, 335
  pressure of work, 284, 313
  problems, 157-9
  salaries, 61-2, 90, 208, 240
  working week of, 32
status of, 137-8
strikes
  cost of, 25, 37, 181-2, 185-6, 280-81
study groups, 92
successes of, 8
support from other unions, 28-9
Trade Union Bill campaign, 166-73
Unemployment Fund, 123, 162
wartime shortages, 159-61
and WUI, 237-8
see also Annual Conventions; Committees; Executive; Sections
Irish Women's International League, 21-2
Irish Women's Reform League, 21, 22
Irish Women's Suffrage Federation, 21, 22
Irish Worker, 8, 10, 13, 102
  letters to, 3, 5
  report on 1911 meeting, 1-2
  scabs in, 8, 9
  suppressed, 13, 17
  on victimisation, 15
  Women Workers' Column, 6-7, 8, 9, 11
Irish Workers' Choir, 9
Irishman, The, 94
Irwin's, 37-8

Jacob's Factory, 2, 3, 10, 217, 244
Jewellery and Metal Manufacturing Co., 235
John XXIII, Pope, 252
Johnson, Thomas, 63, 64, 83, 187
Joint Industrial Councils, 61, 81, 237
  Laundry Industry, 178, 185, 188, 230
  Linen and Cotton, 228
  Printing Industry, 119, 216, 217, 266-7, 277, 343
  Women's Clothing, 230
Joint Labour Councils
  Contract Cleaners, 357-8
  Women's Clothing, 260, 315
Joint Staffs' Committee of Grangegorman and Portrane, 214-15
Journeywomen, 256-7

boxmakers, 81, 248
further training, 323-5
loss of status, 45
printing industry, 67, 145-6, 248, 287, 310
  Monument dispute, 197-202
ratio to apprentices, 67-8, 102
shortages of, 241
unemployment among, 73
wage rates, 119, 325

Kavanagh, Liam, 357
Kavanagh, Margaret, 104
Kavanagh, Miss, 149
Keegan, Miss, 145
Kellett's, 162
Kelly, Anne, 263
Kelly, Miss, 63
Kelso Laundry, 94, 186, 189
Kennedy, Mrs, 96, 99, 123-4, 141, 157
Keogh, 4
Keogh, Mr and Mrs, 8
Kilkenny, 54-5
Kilkenny Corporation, 55
Kilkenny Woollen Mills, 55
knitters, 57, 344-6
Knowles, Messrs, 163

Labour, Department of 294
Labour Court, 195, 215, 217, 254, 277, 368-9
  and contract cleaners, 356-8
  decision against ICTU, 284
  EHB dispute, 330-31
  equal pay claims, 360-61
  interchangeability, 286
  mechanism of, 284-5
  and Morco dispute, 318
  outworkers complaint, 309
Labour News, 137
Labour Party, 13, 83
  apprenticeship bill, 102
  attitude to women, 60, 103-4
  Conditions of Employment Act campaign, 125, 126, 129-31
  and ITUC, 23, 42
  and IWWU, 59-60, 67, 69, 70, 87, 96, 122, 123-4, 131, 150-51
    IWWU involvement, 173, 197, 221, 225, 226, 250, 297
  Trade Union Bill Campaign, 169, 170-71
  and TUC, 63-5
  Women's Council, 60
Labour Research Department, 56
Lamb Bros, 28

Index 415

Lambe, Molly, 190
Larch Hill, 66
Larkin, Delia, 11, 15, 41, 368, 369
   conflict with ITGWU, 12-13
   foundation of IWWU, 1, 2
   General Secretary IWWU, 5-6
   and ITB, 7-8
   and ITGWU, 9
   rebuffed by IWWU, 29-31
Larkin, Denis, 303
Larkin, James, 10, 29-30, 200, 366, 369
   and ICA, 13
   Irish Worker, 2
   and ITGWU, 12
   and IWWU, 1-2, 3-4
   TUC split, 63-4
Larkin, James, TD, 187, 200
Larkin, Luke, 41-2
Larkin, Mr, 152
laundry industry, 24, 38, 42, 47, 143, 165
   automation, 71, 108, 114, 121, 176, 177, 248
      Bedaux system, 135
      pace of work, 194
      pressing machines, 67, 78-9, 94-5, 124
   bonus systems, 195-7
   casual labour, 108
   changing social context, 229-30, 264
   charitable institutions, 80, 176
   closures, 282, 301-2
   dismissals, 55
   equal pay claims, 327
   health problems, 299
   holidays, 79, 94
   hours of work, 28, 79, 135-6
   juniors, 79
   legal status of workers, 93-4
   negotiating problems, 358
   overtime ban, 177-8, 284
   part-time work, 158, 264-5
   productivity, 263-5, 298-9
   redundancies, 348-9
   short time, 78
   strikes, 9, 176-87, 280
   time dockets, 135
   wage rates, 55-6, 229-30, 248, 301
   wartime shortages, 159-60
   working conditions, 174-87, 188-90, 195-6
Laundry Conference, 161
Lawlor, Tommy, 33
League of Nations, 123, 126, 131
Learners' Wage Schedule, 104
Lee, Joseph, 253
Lefroy, Capt. Robert W., 183

legislation, protective, 114-16, 122-3, 125-33, 325
   and contract cleaners, 356-8
   reassessment needed, 348-9
Legitimacy Bill, 1929, 98
Leinster Laundries' Association, 28, 94, 121, 175
   conflict with IWWU, 78-9
   wage rates, 55-6
Lemass, Seán, 109, 110, 203
   and Conditions of Employment Bill, 126
   economic development, 252-3
   and emergency provisions, 164
   holidays dispute, 179, 182, 185
   Joint Industrial Councils, 119
   labour legislation, 114
   protective legislation, 123
   representations to, 134, 139
   and Trade Union Bill, 167
   and trade unions, 272, 279
   on woman's place, 115
Lenihan, Brian, 339
Lenin, V.I., 197
Lennon, Miss, 126-7, 131
Leo XIII, Pope, 156, 168
Letterkenny, Co. Donegal, 136
Lever's, 160, 195, 223, 248-9, 254
Liberty Hall, 6, 9, 11, 23-4
   workers' co-op, 16
Limerick, 8, 49, 62
Limerick Trades' Council, 60
Linen and Cotton Textile Manufacturers' Association, 228-9
linen industry, 3, 16, 136
Lloyd, Mr, 129
Local Government, Department of, 120
Local Government and Public Services' Union, 339
local government elections, 59, 67
lockouts
   1913, 10-13, 22, 34
   Jacob's, 10
   payment for, 44, 60-61
   printing industry, 37, 118-19, 215-17, 276-8, 286
   Savoy Cafe, 9
   tobacco industry, 37
Lucan Woollen Mills, 25, 60, 98
Luke, Miss, 10
Lynch, Eamonn, 100-101, 125, 129-30, 131
Lynch, Mr, 171, 228
Lynn, Dr Kathleen, 24, 26, 46

Mac Giolla, Tomás, 339
McArdle, Dorothy, 131, 140
McArdle, Mr, 14
McBirney's, 162
MacBride, Maud Gonne, 14, 59, 106-7, 169
MacBride, Seán, 169-70
McCarthy, Charles, 114, 172, 173
McCarthy, Miss, 39, 55, 60
McCormack, Bridie, 246-7, 270
 President, 273-4
 resignation, 278-9
McCormack, Inez, 363
McCoy, Miss, 263-4
McDonnell, Miss, 207
McDowell, Kay, 90, 136, 210, 257, 269, 315
 on changing industry, 271-2
 clothing industry campaigns, 230
 on demarcation, 268
 early career, 61
 and Factories' Advisory Council, 297
 holidays campaign, 181, 186
 and ICTU, 250-51
 IWWU Executive member, 197, 204-5, 220-21, 222, 233, 271
  criticism of, 259, 271-2, 273
  General Secretary, 224-6, 235, 236, 238-40, 281-2
  relations with membership, 234, 245, 254-5, 283
  retirement, 288-92
  salary, 240
  vote of confidence in, 280
 joint committee candidate, 173
 laundry industry campaigns, 264
 political involvement, 297
 and Prices Advisory Committee, 207
 printing industry campaigns, 276-7, 278, 286
 on productivity, 246
 staff salaries, 91
 textile industry campaigns, 262-3
 Trade Union Bill campaign, 167
 on trade union movement, 279-80
 on wage rates, 229
 on woman's place, 153
McDowell, Major T.B., 266-7
MacEntee, Seán, 167, 173, 203
Macey's, 162
McGrane, Mrs, 264
McGrath, Margaret, 185, 186
machinery *see* automation
Mackey, M., 145
McKnight, Miss, 86

McLaughlin's Clothing Factory, 191
McLoughlin, Hugh, 347
McManus, Mr, 300
McMaster Hodgins, Messrs, 28
McQuaid, J. C., Archbishop of Dublin, 163
McQuaid, Thomas, 184
Magdalen Asylum, Donnybrook, 176
Magee, Miss, 32
Maguire, Catherine, 366
Maguire and Paterson's, 9, 159, 265, 275, 291
 automation, 193-4
 dispute, 195
 equal pay, 305, 313, 344
 part-time workers, 310
 shorter week, 253
Malone, Miss, 40
Management Directors Ltd, 266
Manchester, 146
Mandleberg, 110
Manor Mill, 160
marches, 10, 73, 218-19
Marine Port and General Workers' Union, 249
market gardening, 58
Markievicz, Countess, 1, 14, 18, 20, 22, 24
 arrested, 26
 Minister of Labour, 43
 portrait of, 231
Marks, Messrs, 56
marriage bar, 209, 242, 282, 328
marriage benefit, 105-6, 209, 282
married women, 73, 140, 209, 355-6
 attitude of IWWU to, 72, 91, 105-6, 352-5
 benefits for, 208-9, 291, 300-301
 casual labour, 261
 employers' complaints of, 301
 as mental nurses, 242
 part-time work, 243-4, 258, 265, 309-10, 311
 permanent status claim, 328-31
 pressure to work, 359
 sacked on childbirth, 119-20
 shift work, 275
 twilight shift, 229
Marron, Kay, 354
Massey Bros, 310
matches industry, 152, 159
Mattress Makers' Union, 101
mattress manufacture, 112, 116, 152, 241
Mayo News, 265
Meath Chronicle, 259
Melia, Sarah, 84
Memorandum on Communal Dining-rooms,

163
Memorandum on Factory Premises, 192
Merchandise Marks Act, 109
mergers, 38, 270, 271-2, 274
  IWWU discussions, 302-3, 333, 365-70
metal polishing industry, 112
Metropolitan Laundry, 79, 189, 302
Milltown Laundry, 94, 108, 189
Minimum Notice and Terms of Employment Act 1973, 319, 349, 356
Mirror Laundry, 160
Mitchell's Bead Factory, 35, 36, 77-8, 104, 109-10, 223
modernisation, 252-3, 268
Molony, Helena, 33, 41, 197, 206, 231, 366, 367
  Conditions of Employment Act campaign, 126, 127, 129
  domestic servants campaign, 29
  and DTC, 34
  early career, 14-15
  and Easter Rising, 19-20
  and ICA, 26, 46
  ill-health, 154
  IWWU Executive member, 21-3, 52, 98
    leave of absence, 161
    opposed to re-organisation, 89
    recruitment, 15-17
    resignation, 164-5
    retirement, 204
    salary, 62
    Secretary, 24
  laundry industry campaigns, 108
  motion on unionisation, 118
  Organising Committee, 92, 107-8
  political involvement, 57, 96-8, 106-7, 113-14, 156
  President ITUC, 30, 297
  on status of IWWU, 137-8
  and TUC, 63-5
  at unaffiliated unions conference, 69
  unemployment benefit campaign, 68
  Unemployment Fund, 123
  Vice-President ITUC, 127
  Vocational Education Committee, 102
  on woman's place, 153
  and Workers' Republic, 17-18
Monaghan, Kathleen, 333-4, 348, 369
  President IWWU, 354
Monument Press, 197-202
Moore Paragon, 342
Moran, Miss, 244
Morco's Clothing Factory, 246, 259, 312
  piece-work dispute, 315-18
Morgan brothers, 316
Morning News, 61
Mortished, Mrs, 40
Mortished, Ronald, 131, 233
Mother and Child Scheme, 219
Mount Street Club, 162-3
Mount Temple Press, 257-8
Mountjoy Jail, 14
Muller Martini Perfect Binding Machine, 342-3, 346
Mullingar Trades Council, 181
munitions industry, 27, 59
Murphy, Mr (DTC), 1
Murphy, William Martin, 10
Murray, Jenny, 207, 270, 281, 303, 335, 339
  clothing industry campaigns, 316, 319
  contract cleaners campaign, 356
  IWWU Executive member
    resignation, 363
    role of, 314-15, 321, 339, 344
  on married women, 353
  printing industry campaigns, 350
Murtagh, Miss, 24

National City Bank, 163
National Economic and Social Council, 355
National Economic Council, 114
National Health Insurance, 210
National Institute of Higher Education, Dublin, 345
National Labour Programme, 23
National Society of Brushmakers, 128
National Understanding, 1980, 344
National Union of Furniture Trade Operatives, 241
National Union of Public Employees, 362-3
National Union of Railwaymen, 172
National Union of Tailors and Garment Workers, 128, 368
National Union of Women Workers, 17
National Wage Agreements, 269, 271, 280, 295, 301, 317
  debate on, 314
  employers' inability to pay, 310
  equal pay negotiations, 305
nationalism
  in IWWU, 6, 13, 17-18, 22, 26, 33
'natural wastage', 261, 290-91, 309, 311
Nevin, Donal, 251, 368-9
Newman's Bindery, 333, 342, 344, 348, 353, 354
Ní Mhurchú, Padraigín, 339, 343

early career, 337-8
on future of printing, 351-2
IWWU Executive member
  Assistant Secretary, 335-6, 341
  General Secretary, 344-5, 363, 365
  joins Labour Court, 368-9
  laundry industry campaigns, 358
  on married women, 353, 354-5
  merger discussions, 361-2, 366
  on protective legislation, 349
  and Women Workers' Branch of FWUI, 367-70
night work, 98, 103, 112, 134, 229
  ban lifted, 359
  exclusion order sought, 262
  legislation on, 100-101
Nolan, James, 1
Nolan, Tess, 239, 254
Noonan Building Cleaning Ltd, 356-7
Norton, William, 103, 109, 122, 185, 207
  and Conditions of Employment Act, 125-6
nurses, 40, 110, 120, 136, 165
  emigration of, 192
  IWWU members threatened, 80
  leave IWWU, 236-8, 245
  permanent status claim, 328-31
  status claim, 253
  wage rates, 88-9, 93, 207
  working conditions, 71, 192, 211-15
Nursing Board, The, 237

O'Brien, Mrs, 289
O'Brien, Mrs K., 208
O'Brien, Nellie, 209-10
O'Brien, William, 4, 23, 127-8
O'Connor, Elizabeth, 151
O'Connor, Maggie, 299
O'Connor, Miss K., 11, 63, 84-5, 86, 164
  and Constitution, 141
  unemployment benefit campaign, 68
Office of National Education, 80
O'Gorman, Mr, 128
oil crisis, 309-10, 313-14
O'Kelly, Miss, 91
O'Loughlin Murphy's, 36
O'Moore, Seán, 171
O'Reilly, Molly, 20
O'Reilly's, Poolbeg St, 81, 83, 85-6
Ormac, 342
Orme, Miss, 3
Ormond Press, 247
Orrwear, Co. Meath, 294
O'Sullivan, Miss, 101

Our Lady's Hospital, 260
outworkers, 52-3, 109, 309, 311, 316
overtime, 79, 258, 277
  ban lifted, 284
  IWWU opposition to, 248
packaging industry, 121
pamphlets, 35
Paper Bag Manufacturers' and Printers' Association, 52
paper mills, 2, 160
Parnell, Anna, 15
Parnell Square Technical School, 101
Parsons, C.A., Ltd, 305
part-time work, 275
  laundries, 264-5
  in laundries, 299
  printing industry, 306-10
  vulnerability of workers, 346-7
pay see equal pay; wage rates
PAYE system, 233
Peace and Fraternity, 203
Pembroke Laundry, 9
pensions, 62, 208, 312
  civil service, 297
  married women, 328, 329
  nurses, 212
  printing industry, 243
  schemes, 155, 247, 300
People's College, 224, 240, 250, 314
periodicals, 159
Perolz, Marie, 23, 24, 26
Phelan's, 101, 243
Phoenix Laundry, 78, 301
piece rates, 53, 68
piece-work, 191, 253-4, 259, 296
  laundries, 78
  Morco dispute, 315-18
Piece-Work Schedule, 78
Pius XI, Pope, 114
Plastic Fabricators, 344
playgrounds, 62, 227
Playprint, 325
Plunkett, Miss, 35
poaching, 62, 118, 199, 249, 270
polish industry, 115
Poor Law Commission, 68-9
Poor Law Guardians, 59
Poor Law Union, 33
Portrane Mental Hospital, 120, 236-7, 242
  wage rates, 88-9, 93
  working conditions, 211, 213-15
Post Office Factory, 136, 218-19, 284, 297
  pay claim, 360-61

Post Office Workers' Union, 129
posters, 35, 68, 98, 125
Powell Press, 36, 310
Prices Advisory Board, 220, 221
Prices Advisory Committee, 207
Printers' Registered Agreement, 288
Printing Group of Unions, 303
printing industry, 24, 36, 73, 108, 137, 143, 235, 351-2
   apprenticeship, 62
   automation, 66, 114, 121, 124, 276, 293
   and boxmaking, 247-8
   calls for one union, 302-3
   demarcation disputes, 94-5, 116-17, 266-8, 342-3, 349
   employment of women, 246
   equal pay, 321-5
   hours of work, 136, 306-10
      short-time working, 243-4, 342
   interchangeability, 285-8, 306, 321-5, 359
   layoffs, 309-10
   lockouts, 37, 276-8
   non-union shops, 92
   oil crisis, 309-10
   organising rights dispute, 197-202
   pension scheme, 243
   printing union discussed, 333-4
   rationalisation, 285-8
   redundancies, 350-51
   rotation of work, 160-61
   shortage of skilled workers, 256
   strikes, 25, 215-17
   time dockets, 66-8, 88, 95, 135, crisis, 144-9
   vulnerability of women, 346-8
   wage rates, 50, 56, 152, 201, 230, 253
   wartime shortages, 159
production line methods, 121-2
productivity, 66, 193-7, 223, 245-6, 250-51, 296-7
   laundry industry deal, 298-9
Productivity Conference, 251
Professional Contract Cleaners Ltd, 356
protectionism, 71, 73, 93, 103, 108-9, 113, 115, 121
Public Health Committee, 52
Purtell, Mrs, 128

Quadragesimo Anno, 114
Quidnunc (Patrick Campbell), 182-3, 187
Quill, Mr, 36
Quinn, Ruairi, 358, 364

Redmond, Bridget, 141
redundancies, 279, 286, 298, 312, 365
   and IWWU, 301-2
   laundries, 301-2, 348-9
   oil crisis, 310
   printing industry, 320, 339-40, 344, 348, 350-51
Redundancy Payments' Act, 356
Registrar of Friendly Societies, 232, 274, 282, 370
Relief of Unemployment Committee, 87
Rerum Novarum, 156, 168
Reynold's News, 46, 158
Rialto Mental Hospital, 237
Richview Browne and Nolan, 342, 343, 347
Roantree, S.A., 348
Robb, Mr, 302
Roberts, Ruaidhrí, 250, 297
Rosary Bead Enquiry, 161
rosary bead manufacture, 35, 53, 77-8, 103, 104, 109-10, 165
Royal Commission on Labour, 3
Royal Hibernian Hotel, 208
Ruddell's, 174
Rulers' and Bookbinders' Union, 54
Russia, 197
   DTC visit, 96-7
Rutland Ltd, 348, 349
Ryan, Miss, 24, 157

sackmakers, 8
Sacred Heart Home, 314
St Brendan's Hospital, 289
St Brigid's Housing Society, 152
St James' Hospital, 326-7
St Joseph's Laundry, 176, 180
St Kevin's Institution, 218, 236-7
St Laurence's Hospital, 191
St Mary's Chest Hospital, 189
St Ultan's Hospital, 46
Sandyford Printers, 343, 346-7
Saturday Post, 24
Savage, Rev. R. Burke, 277
Savoy Cafe, 9
scab labour, 8, 83, 84, 86, 200
   laundries, 180
school leaving age, 60, 102
Scotland, 51, 56, 108
Scott's, 190-91
Sections
   Bookbinders' and Kindred Trades, 44
   Clothing Trades' Group, 138
   Domestic Servants Section, 41

General Section, 32, 108-9, 174, 207, 239-40
Laundries Section, 32, 94, 160, 353
Printers' Section, 25, 36, 80, 115, 215
  ABU poaching, 74-6
  automation and demarcation, 56
  call for full equality, 332
  and married women, 91, 105
  redundancies, 348
  time dockets, 88, 144-5, 147, 149
Printing Trades' Group, 160-61
Textiles Section, 16
Senate, 132, 154-5
  Breslin campaign, 338-9
Shanagan, Miss, 33
Shanahan, Jennie, 18, 20, 24, 26
Shannon, Mary, 20
Shannon Electrification Scheme, 72
Sharkey, Miss, 212
Shaw bequest, 224
Sheehy-Skeffington, Hannah, 1, 22
Shelbourne Hotel, 179
Shepherd, Essie, 104
shift work, 229, 264-5, 291
  exclusion orders, 262-3
  increase in, 134-5, 275
  twilight shift, 229
shirtmaking industry, 88, 121-2
shop assistants, 2-3, 54-5, 143
Shortt, E., 124
sick pay, 300, 301
Simpson, Mr, 299
Sir Patrick Dun's Hospital, 80, 299-300
Sisters of Mercy, 180
Sligo, 56
Smalldridge, Mr, 85
Smurfit, Jefferson, 320
Smurfit, Michael, 320
Smurfit Carton, 310, 320, 339, 349, 354
  redundancies, 325-6
Smurfit Polypak, 309, 310
Smurfits, 308-9
soap industry, 152, 160
Society of Lithographic Artists, Designers, Engravers, 83, 267
solicitors' clerks, 343
Somerville Large, Mr, 162
spoiled work, 67
Stafford, Miss, 52, 103
Stafford, Sir Thomas, 27
Standstill Wages Order, 156, 172
Stanhope Street Convent Laundry, 176
stationery industry, 28
Stephen D, 348

strikes, 4, 44
  boxmakers, 83-6
  contract cleaners, 356-8
  Jacob's, 2
  Keogh's, 8
  laundries, 176-87
  Monument Press, 200-202
  Pembroke Laundry, 9
  printing industry, 25, 147-8
  Sunday Tribune, 347
  tramworkers, 10, 123
  waterproof industry, 110
suffragists, 21, 22, 48
sugar confectionery industry, 16-17, 58, 280-81
Sugrue, Mary, 237, 238
Sunday Tribune, 346-7, 354
supervisors, 191, 194, 263-4, 294, 296-7
Swastika Laundry, 125, 180, 189-90, 301-2
Sweden, 254-5
Swift, John, 187

tailoring trade, 139, 147
Tailors' and Garment Workers' Union, 110, 319
tax reform, 233, 335
Taylor, Frederick Winslow, 193
Taylor, Wm and M., 27-8
Taylor's, Dundalk, 115, 117
Taylor's Tobacco Co., 33
Telefís Éireann, 252
Temple Press, 174
Terenure Laundry, 94, 189, 299
testimonials, 33-4
textile industry, 2, 24, 126
  outworking, 53
  piece-work, 253-4, 259
  shortage of skilled workers, 261-3
  unionisation efforts, 25-6
  work study, 255
  working conditions, 296
Textile Operatives' Society of Ireland, 170
Thackaberry, Helen, 191
Thom, Alex and Co., Messrs, 35, 45, 149, 352
  machinery, 53, 68, 104
Thompson, Rose, 324, 335
Thompson T. and Son, 27
Thomson, Roy, 266
Thomson International Ltd, 266, 267
Thomson's Shirt Factory, 98
Tierney, Louis A., 107
time and motion system, 193-4, 196, 197, 223,

Index 421

246
time dockets, 196-7
  opposition to, 95
  printing industry, 66-8, 88, 95
    crisis, 144-9
  spread of, 135
tobacco industry, 33, 93, 108-9
  automation, 121
  lockout, 37
  wage rates, 27-8
  working conditions, 71
Torch, The, 152
Torch and Distaff Guild, 162-3
Trade Board Acts, 7, 42, 104
  amendments, 23
Trade Boards, 86, 119
  minimum wages, 81-6
  opposition to, 34-5, 42-3
  Shirtmaking, 88
Trade Union Act 1941, 156, 199, 203
  negotiating licences, 170, 172
  opposition to, 166-73
trade union movement, 100, 103, 107-8, 117
  attitude to working women, 4-5, 35-6, 54, 65, 103-4, 137, 228-9, 281-2
  Back to the Unions Campaign, 92
  Commission of Enquiry, 137-8
  debate on NWAs, 314
  employer attitudes towards, 9, 10-11, 15, 17, 25
  and government control, 111-12, 113-14, 279
  growth of, 290
  holidays campaign, 179-80
  industrial unions, 270, 302-3, 333-4
  inter-union rivalry, 33-4, 237, 241, 303
  merger moves, 273-4
  minimum wage campaign, 86
  poaching, 38, 62, 73-7, 248
  position of women in, 136, 137-9, 297-8
  priorities of, 51-2
  protective legislation, 123, 348-9
  Trade Union Bill, 166-73
  unaffiliated unions, 69
Trades' Councils, 63
Trades Union Organisation meeting, 273, 274
Traditional Handknitters' Association, 346
tramworkers, 10, 123
Transport Union, 14, 15, 23, 75
  and ICA, 19
  and IWWU, 16, 28-9, 35, 41
  poaching, 38, 54, 76
  suggests merger, 38-9

Trotsky, Leon, 197
Truck Act, 46
Tully, James, 294, 318, 339
Tunney, Beth, 354
Turney, Mrs, 38
Turnover Tax, 269
twilight shift, 229
Typographical Association, 128-9, 139, 171, 200, 201
Tyrell, Mr, 296-7

unemployment, 61, 87, 104, 113, 159, 236
  and automation, 66, 77, 120-22
  benefit, 60, 68, 93-4
  changes in working week, 122, 248
  contributory causes, 77-8
  growth of, 57-8, 73
  IWWU campaign, 68-9, 70, 224, 234-5, 340
  rotation of work, 160-61
Unemployment Acts, 93
Unemployment Insurance Act, 68
Unfair Dismissals' Act, 356
United States of America, 13, 15, 46
United Stationary Engine Drivers, 179-80
University College, Cork, 210
Urney Chocolates, 196, 250, 275, 280-81
Usher, Robert, and Co., 229, 261
Usher's, 275, 312, 317, 320

victimisation, 11, 15-16, 44
Voice of Labour, 48

wage rates, 2-3, 8, 16-17, 53, 101, 143, 152, 223
  apprentices, 241
  and automation, 121, 230
  based on age, 104
  changing social context, 229-30
  clothing industry, 312
  contract cleaners, 356
  and cost of living, 153, 161
  cuts threatened, 55-6, 60, 72-3
  IWWU rejects proposals, 205-6
  journeywomen printers, 201
  justification for low rates, 290-91
  laundries, 135-6, 182, 229-30, 248, 299, 301
  minimum wage, 37, 81-6, 206-7
  tobacco industry, 27-8
  wage rounds, 269, 271, 290, 295
Wage Standstill Emergency Order, 168
Waldron, Lottie, 236
Waller, Major, 152
war bonus, 175

wardsmaids, 143, 191, 218, 260
Waterford, 39, 73, 201, 233
  bacon factories close, 60-61
  branch of IWWU, 54
  munitions conflict, 27
  unionisation, 42
  woollen mills, 50
Waterford Trades' Council, 41-2, 92, 136-7
waterproof industry, 110, 115, 117-18, 139
Waters, Mrs, 177
Watson and Warnock, Shirtmakers, 88
Watson's, 62
Wax Carton, 310
Wexford, 58
Wexford Trades' Council, 136-7
Whitaker, T.K., 252
White, Capt. Jack, 13
White, Miss, 17, 210
White Heather Laundry, 260, 300, 301-2
White Swan Laundry, 108, 135, 258
Wicklow People, 201
Wiggins Teape, 324
Wilkinson, Marjorie, 181
Wilkinson, Mr, 247
Williams and Woods, 35, 135
Wilson, Sir Henry, 59
Winders, June, 283, 335
Woakes, Mr, 86
women in employment, 2-5, 26-7, 102-3, 112, 113, 302
  apprenticeships, 51
  and automation, 261-3
  benefits, 144
  cheap labour, 5, 117, 127, 139
  commitment of, 255-6
  effects of interchangeability, 285-8
  exploitation of, 306-7
  government attitude to, 57-9, 87, 115-16
  ILO committee on, 102-3
  industry-by-industry negotiation, 260-61
  insecurity of, 45, 263, 311-12, 346-52
  junior displacement, 79
  and male employment, 4-5, 35, 136, 137-9, 228-9, 257-8
  night work, 98, 100-101, 103
  part-time workers, 306-10
  place seen as home, 5, 103, 124-5, 153-4
  printing industry, 294
  proportion of, 355
  protective legislation, 114, 115-16, 122, 123, 125-33, 294
  separate economic class, 138
  short-time working, 243-4
  shortage of skilled workers, 256-8
  unionisation of, 50-51, 92, 295, 296
  value of woman's work, 223, 230, 234, 276-7, 281-2, 360
  wage rounds, 290
  work measurement, 253-4, 268
  see also married women
Women in Publishing, 340
Women Workers' Charter, 174
Women Workers' Federation, 51
Women Workers' Programme for Industrial Workers, 174-5
Women Workers' Union Club, 223-4
Women's Advisory Committee (ICTU), 279, 297-8, 304, 337, 351, 355
Women's Community Press, 340
Women's Council of Action (DTUC), 166-7, 197
Women's Emergency Committee, 163
Women's Federation, 40-41
Women's Industrial Conference, 1915, 16-17
Women's International League of Peace and Freedom, 59, 226
Wooden Horse, A, 114
woodworkers, 101
woollen mills, 55
work measurement schemes, 66, 223, 245-6, 250-51
Workers' Party, 339
Workers' Republic, 16-17, 19
Workers' Union of Ireland, 30, 75, 102, 196, 207, 250, 273
  EHB dispute, 328-9
  equal pay claims, 327
  and IWWU, 237-8, 296
  mental health service, 211-12
  merger talks with IWWU, 303
  negotiating licence fee, 172
  TUC affiliation row, 63-5
Working Conditions in Industry (conference), 193
worksharing, 348
World War 1, 19, 26-7, 38
World War 2, 155, 191, 205
  effects of, 159-61, 175
Wright, Lady, 17
Wyse-Power, Mrs, 132